Tall, dark
extraordi

Her Personal Protector

no matter what the cost...

*Dixie Browning and Sheri WhiteFeather
show us just how honourable these men are
especially when love and hearts are at risk!*

Dear Reader,

A very hot summer welcome to Desire!

We aim to send your temperature soaring this month starting with the wonderfully exotic **Seduced by the Sheikh** featuring *Sleeping with the Sultan*—the last instalment of Alexandra Sellers's THE SULTANS—and *Hide-and-Sheikh* by Gail Dayton.

The Millionaire's First Love brings together *The Millionaire Comes Home* by Mary Lynn Baxter and the final THE BARONS OF TEXAS novel with the last of the Baron sisters to be hit by love—*The Barons of Texas: Kit* by Fayrene Preston.

Protecting the innocent is the theme of our final volume this month, **Her Personal Protector**, where you'll find Dixie Browning's *Rocky and the Senator's Daughter* and *Night Wind's Woman* from Sheri WhiteFeather.

They're great summer reading!

The Editors

Her Personal Protector

DIXIE BROWNING
SHERI WHITEFEATHER

DID YOU PURCHASE THIS BOOK WITHOUT A COVER?
If you did, you should be aware it is **stolen property** as it was reported *unsold and destroyed* by a retailer. Neither the author nor the publisher has received any payment for this book.

All the characters in this book have no existence outside the imagination of the author, and have no relation whatsoever to anyone bearing the same name or names. They are not even distantly inspired by any individual known or unknown to the author, and all the incidents are pure invention.

All Rights Reserved including the right of reproduction in whole or in part in any form. This edition is published by arrangement with Harlequin Enterprises II B.V. The text of this publication or any part thereof may not be reproduced or transmitted in any form or by any means, electronic or mechanical, including photocopying, recording, storage in an information retrieval system, or otherwise, without the written permission of the publisher.

This book is sold subject to the condition that it shall not, by way of trade or otherwise, be lent, resold, hired out or otherwise circulated without the prior consent of the publisher in any form of binding or cover other than that in which it is published and without a similar condition including this condition being imposed on the subsequent purchaser.

Silhouette, Silhouette Desire and Colophon are registered trademarks of Harlequin Books S.A., used under licence.

First published in Great Britain 2002 Silhouette Books, Eton House, 18-24 Paradise Road, Richmond, Surrey TW9 1SR

HER PERSONAL PROTECTOR © Harlequin Books S.A. 2002

The publisher acknowledges the copyright holders of the individual works as follows:

Rocky and the Senator's Daughter © Dixie Browning 2001
Night Wind's Woman © Sheree Henry-WhiteFeather 2000

ISBN 0 373 04759 2

51-0802

Printed and bound in Spain by Litografia Rosés S.A., Barcelona

ROCKY AND THE SENATOR'S DAUGHTER

by
Dixie Browning

DIXIE BROWNING

is an award-winning painter and writer, mother and grandmother. Her father was a big-league baseball player, her grandfather a sea captain. In addition to her nearly 80 contemporary romances, Dixie and her sister, Mary Williams, have written more than a dozen historical romances under the name Bronwyn Williams. Contact Dixie at www.dixiebrowning.com or at PO Box 1389, Buxton, NC 27920, USA.

One

The suite was small, the acoustics brutal. The guests were a mixture of media types, politicians, wives and significant others. All were talking at once; few, if any, were listening. At least there was no band to overcome. The noise level had hit him when he'd first stepped off the elevator. Considering that until recently, as an accredited journalist, Rocky had covered nearly every noisy, crowded hotspot on the globe, it shouldn't have been a problem.

It was. He wanted out.

From across the room he watched as the honoree edged past two network anchors, who appeared to be comparing pinky rings, and absently handed his glass to a well-known syndicated sportswriter.

Rocky waited. He had come to help honor his old bureau chief. So far he hadn't managed to get close enough to pay his respects.

"Not leaving yet, are you?"

Dan Sturdivant, retiring bureau chief at Graves Worldwide, had trained a surprising number of the reporters in the business today, including Rocky. Now pushing seventy-five, he had a heart condition, ulcers and essential tremors. Which was the sole reason Rocky, even though he hadn't worked with the man in years, had given up his quiet Sunday evening for this bash at the Shoreham. He'd been a hungry young idealist fresh out of college when Dan had taken him in, sifted through his headful of useless garbage, refilling his brain with a few basic tenets, and set him to work covering court news.

Welcome to the real world. Everything he had gone on to achieve, Rocky owed to this man.

"Heard you'd quit the business," the old man said by way of greeting.

"News travels fast." It was a standing joke between them. "Call it a sabbatical."

"Skip the euphemisms. You're too young to quit."

"I'm tired, Dan."

"You and me both, son, but tired won't cut it. You gotta have a better excuse than that."

He had one. And, yeah, tired would do it when a man had been carrying a load of heartbreak for eight years. Dan knew the story, but it wasn't something either man had ever discussed.

"Stick around, this bash can't last forever. God, what did I ever do to deserve this kind of punishment?" He shook his shiny bald head and tried to look as if he weren't loving every minute of it.

"Braves game. If I leave now I can probably make it home by the third."

"Mets'll take 'em, you don't want to watch the slaughter."

"In your dreams."

"You know where I live if you want to talk."

Rocky nodded. Dan nodded. Message sent and received.

He wasn't ready to talk about what he was going to do with the rest of his life. Financially he had to do something, but he didn't have to decide yet—not for a few more weeks. Or months. Maybe if he got hungry enough, he could find the motivation to try a weekly column. Two different syndicates had put out feelers.

But first he had to get over Julie. His marriage had ended in the summer of ninety-four, when a drunk driver had rammed head-on into the car his wife had been driving home from the library, breaking her back and causing irreparable damage to her head. He had buried her six months ago. He hadn't cried then. More than seven years of watching her lying there, alive and yet not alive—Julie and yet not Julie—had used up his lifetime quota of tears.

For seven years he'd taken her bouquets of her favorite flower. Flowers she couldn't see, couldn't smell, but he told himself that deep down, she sensed they were there. And that he loved her—would always love her, no matter what. Finally in early February, on a cold, rainy morning, he had buried her beside her parents, after a private memorial service. Then he'd gone home alone and deliberately drunk himself insensible.

A week later he had handed in his resignation, poured three bottles of double-malt whisky down the sink and stocked up on colas. He'd spent the summer brooding, watching baseball and rereading *War and*

Peace. Once the baseball season ended, he'd promised himself, he would start thinking about what he was going to do with the rest of his life.

It had taken Dan's retirement party to pry him out of his apartment and back into circulation. About time, he acknowledged with bitter amusement. His social skills, never particularly impressive, had grown dull with lack of use.

"Mac, glad to see you." Quietly, he greeted a guy who had once covered the White House for one of the major networks, then edged past him.

"Hey, Rock—where you been? Haven't seen you around lately."

"Rocko, good to see you, man," someone else called out.

He made it about halfway to the door, weaving his way through clusters of people he knew vaguely. Got held up between one of the massive sofas and a cluster of women picking over the bones of some poor devil obviously known to them all.

"Did you see him at that last press conference? I swear, if I looked like that, I'd slit my—"

A redhead wearing a black suit about two sizes too small leaned forward, sloshing her drink dangerously close to the rim of her glass, and said in a whisky-thickened voice, "Honey, I peeked into his underwear drawer, and believe you me, those rumors are the gospel truth!"

Gossip was the order of the day. Snide comments, catty remarks. Rocky glanced at his watch. He'd planned on being in and out within twenty minutes, tops. It had taken him that long just to work his way across the room. Anyone who had been around pols and media types as long as he had should have known what to expect. With scandal in D.C. as plentiful as cherry blossoms in spring, it didn't take much effort to pick up a thread here and another one there and weave them into a story that could ruin a few lives and leapfrog a career.

Thank God he hadn't chosen that route. He didn't have the stomach for it. Once he'd realized that his objectivity as a reporter was beginning to give way to advocacy, he had asked for reassignment. It had meant not seeing as much of Julie, but then, the hours spent by her bedside had been more for his sake than for hers. The doctor had told him right from the first that, while she might appear to be responding, critical portions of her brain had been injured. That it was only a matter of time before her vital functions began to shut down.

Despite the prognosis, he had gone on hoping. Reading to her, taking her flowers, relating news about people they both knew. Resignation had set in slowly, over a matter of years. He wasn't even aware of when he'd stopped hoping.

Someone bumped into him, spilling a drink on his sleeve.

"Oops, sorry."

"No problem." He had to get out of here. This time he almost made it to the door. "Excuse me—pardon me."

The woman blocking his exit turned. Her eyes widened as she gave him a slow once-over. "Well, hello, honey. Not leaving so soon, are you?"

"Another appointment." *No thanks. It's been a long, dry spell, but I'm not that hard up.*

Three women emerged from one of the suite's two bathrooms and paused, still talking, blocking the door to the hallway. A brunette with a spectacular superstructure was saying, "Well, anyhow, like I said, the first two publishers turned it down flat. They as good as told us to take it to the tabloids, but the very next day my agent showed it to another publisher and he offered us a six-figure advance, and my agent said—"

"Forget what your agent said, Binky, check with a lawyer. He's the one you want beside you the first time you're sued for libel."

"No chance. Who's going to step forward and claim credit for something like that? Besides, my agent says I'm safe because this is a first-person account and I'm not actually naming names."

"Aw, come on, Binky, you're not claiming to be Sully's first, are you?"

All three women laughed. "Are you kidding?"

Amused in spite of himself Rocky squeezed past and waited for the elevator. The woman called Binky was still holding forth. If he wasn't mistaken, she did a social column for one of the weeklies. He'd once heard her chest referred to as the Grand Tetons.

"Listen, I'm talking group stuff here," she said, her heavily made-up eyes sparkling avidly. "Kinky like you wouldn't believe! Poor Sully said his wife was about as exciting as wet bread. He had a taste for fancier fare, if you know what I mean."

"I met her once at a fund-raiser. His wife, I mean. She struck me as real uptight. All the same, I'd watch my back if I were you. You know what they say about those quiet types."

Rocky would take his chances with a quiet type

anyday over these pampered piranhas. He felt sorry for the wife of whatever poor jerk they were discussing. Evidently she'd been victimized first by her husband and now was about to be pilloried all over again by the public's insatiable appetite for dirt.

"Yeah, well who's interested in her?" Binky unbuttoned her black jacket to reveal the scrap of ecru lace she wore instead of a blouse. "Did I tell you they're rushing production? They've got three editors working on it, and marketing has booked me on all the talk shows. I mean, with a title like *The Senator's Daughter's Husband's Other Women,* it's gonna make all the lists, probably the top slot, because my agent says—"

The elevator stopped. The doors opened. Rocky stood there, frowning in thought until the doors silently closed again. He had once known a senator's daughter who had later married a congressman. Was she talking about *that* particular senator's daughter? The one who had married *that* particular congressman? Even by Washington standards, that had been rough. The press had been all over it.

Not that he'd really known her, Rocky amended as another elevator stopped to let off a couple of late arrivals. Still frowning, he stepped onboard. Actually, he'd only spoken to her one time, years before her father's misdeeds had begun to surface. Years before she had married the senator's trained seal in the House—a man who had gone down in flames in a separate scandal shortly after the senator had been figuratively tarred and feathered and ridden out of town on a rail.

Rocky had been covering the Middle East Summit

when the wedding had taken place. He remembered watching some of the coverage. The Sullivans and Joneses, while hardly in the Kennedy class, had still made a pretty big splash. Even the veep had attended the festivities. She'd made a beautiful bride. Not pretty in the usual sense, but with an innate poise that could easily be called regal. He'd caught a flash of that funny little half smile he remembered from their one and only meeting years earlier.

It had been a few years after that when the lid had blown off the first scandal. There'd been rumblings before, but nothing that couldn't be blamed on partisan politics. Finally, with its back to the wall, Justice had appointed an independent council to investigate, and Rocky had watched from whatever assignment he happened to be on as one after another, Senator J. Abernathy Jones's sins were laid bare.

The feeding frenzy had eventually brought down half a dozen smaller fry, but if memory served, the young congressman his daughter had married some six years earlier had not been among them. Sullivan's downfall had come a year or so later, following what had started out as a simple drug bust. By then the senator had been history.

Rocky hadn't wanted to watch the second chapter unfold, but with all the networks covering the story, it was unavoidable. And, unfortunately, understandable. Juicy scandals had a way of selling newspapers, hiking ratings, making careers. That had been proven too many times to be in doubt.

So he'd witnessed the handsome young congressman's downfall, watched as the press—his own peers—had hounded the man's wife, his office staff, even his barber. He remembered thinking once, seeing Sullivan's wife trapped by a mob of yelling reporters between the front door of her Arlington house and a car driven by her housekeeper, that Joan of Arc might have worn the same stoic expression.

That had been more than a year ago. Immersed in his own crisis, Rocky hadn't thought of her since then.

Now he did.

Her name had been Sarah Mariah Jones the first time he'd ever seen her. It had been at a fund-raiser sponsored by a couple of Hollywood celebrities. She must have been about fifteen years old at the time. He'd been a green reporter and she'd been a gawky kid trying hard to look as if she weren't dying to be someplace else. *Anyplace* else. He remembered reading somewhere that her mother had died recently. The senator's habit of using her for photo ops, then shoving her into the background had been pretty well established. Rumor had it that years ago he had forgotten and left her at a town hall meeting in a school gymnasium for about six hours before he'd remembered to send someone to pick her up.

It had occurred to him that day at the fund-raiser that she'd been painfully aware of her own role in her father's struggling reelection campaign. She was there to be used the way he used everyone else, then shoved aside until the need arose again. The old pol had played the family card for all it was worth, ever since his opponent, a married man with three children, had been caught in a compromising situation with an aide.

It had been the standard celebrity bash. Only those journalists who shared the senator's ideology had been invited to meet and mingle with the glitterati. Rocky, who had considered himself politically unbiased at that early stage of his budding career, had been on his way out when he'd spotted the girl.

In a dress that was obviously expensive and painfully unflattering, the young Sarah Mariah had watched her father buttonhole another major contributor, clasp his hand, slap him on the arm and then proceed to apply the thumbscrews. Something about her expression had caught his attention. It reminded him too much of children he'd seen with eyes far too old for their tender years.

Which was probably why, from a mixture of boredom and sympathy, he had collected a cup of tea and a finger sandwich—asparagus and cream cheese, he remembered distinctly—and made his way over to the potted palm where she'd gone to earth.

"Hi. My name's Rocky and I'm a truant officer. Do you have your parents' permission to be here?" Silly stuff, but hell—she was just a kid.

"How do you do, Mr. Rocky. My name is Anonymous Jones, and if you blow my cover I'll be deported at the very least, beheaded if the king's having a bad hair day."

"Yeah, I figured as much." They'd both stared at the senator's trademark silver pompadour. "Brought you a last meal just in case. Asparagus sandwiches. They looked like a safer bet than those small brown things."

"The barbecued loin of weasel?"

"Those were all gone. There were a couple of the guppy filets left, but you know what they say about seafood."

"No, what do they say?"

He'd shrugged. "Beats me."

She had smiled then. A quick, spontaneous smile that was gone almost before it appeared. They had talked for a few minutes and then she'd reached for the tea. Her hand had struck the saucer, and in trying to catch the cup before it spilled, she'd managed to dump the sandwich onto his shoes. Cream-cheese side down. Smack on the laces, where it couldn't easily be wiped off.

The poor kid had looked stricken, so he'd forgotten his own irritation and made some crack about asparagus being a known insect repellant. "It's the scent, you know? You ever sniff an asparagus? Whoa. Really bad stuff."

She'd looked so grateful he'd been afraid she was going to do something gauche, like kissing his hand. Mumbling something about an appointment, he'd left before she could embarrass them both.

Even then it had occurred to him that she had vulnerable eyes. Far too vulnerable, considering the circles she moved in. He remembered thinking that with a crook like J. Abernathy Jones for a father, she'd be in therapy before the year was out, if she wasn't already.

Sarah Mariah Jones Sullivan, he mused now. Daughter of Senator J. Abernathy Jones, who had been reelected by the skin of his teeth shortly after their one and only meeting.

Wife—make that widow—of Junior Congressman Stanley Sullivan, the senator's protégé and hand-picked puppet. Despite his reputation as a latter-day John Kennedy, the jerk had been nothing more than a dirty, womanizing lightweight who had barely managed to escape the tail end of the scandals that had put an end to his father-in-law's career, if not to his ambitions.

As it turned out, Rocky had been back in the States after a stint in Kosovo when Sullivan had gone down in flames. Still immersed in his own private, personal immolation, he had not joined the pack, choosing instead to watch the coverage from the privacy of his barren apartment. Looking calm, pale and emotionless, Sarah Mariah had been there each day beside her husband and his lawyers. Comparing the grown-up woman to the teenage girl he remembered, he couldn't help but wonder how much it was costing her. God knows, she must have already suffered enough when her father's sins had come home to roost.

Under the most trying circumstances imaginable for any sensitive young woman, she had never, to his knowledge, lost her dignity. Rocky watched as day after day she'd be caught outside and surrounded before she could escape. Head held high, she would face down her tormentors with that same disconcertingly direct gaze he remembered.

"Miz Sullivan, did you know at the time...?"

"No comment."

"Mrs. Sullivan, is it true that you've already filed for divorce?"

"No comment."

"Hey, Sarah, is it true that you were at some of those Georgetown parties your husband threw? Is it true that a Hollywood director supplied the talent and the—"

"If you'll excuse me?"

Someone—Rocky learned later it was her father's

housekeeper—usually rescued her by pulling her bodily away when she would have stood there with that startled-doe look in her eyes until she ran out of no-comments.

After a while the two scandals had run together in his mind: the senator's illegal fund-raising, aka influence peddling, arranging for the bypassing of certain sanctions to sell classified materials to terrorist nations, and the offshore bank accounts; followed only a few years later by Sullivan's sordid little sex, drugs and booze peccadilloes. The consensus was that the man was incredibly stupid to have continued his activities right on through his father-in-law's investigation.

But then Rocky had been immersed in his own private hell while it was all going on. About the time the first scandal was making the nightly news, Julie's kidneys had begun to fail. Dialysis had held her for a while, but under the circumstances, she had not been a candidate for transplant. After one last quick overseas assignment, he had handed in his resignation, needing to spend as much time as he could with the woman he'd once loved.

So it was all mixed up in his mind—the end of his shell of a marriage, the Jones-Sullivan affair, and the end of his career. A man could run only so far, so long, before life caught up with him.

He did recall wondering more than once how the shy, intelligent girl with the wry sense of humor, the haunting little half smile and the marked lack of physical coordination, could have married a lightweight like Sullivan in the first place. The guy was smooth. He had the kind of face the cameras loved, but Rocky had once heard him on a radio talk show when a caller had asked if he was worried about the Chi-coms controlling both ends of the Panama Canal.

Judging by his response, the poor jerk had never heard of the Panama Canal, much less any possible political ramifications. He had stumbled around in search of a response and ended up parroting the day's talking points about campaign finance reform. By the end of the program he'd been batting 0 for 4.

Still, the guy must have had something on the ball. Sarah Mariah had married him. And just as she had stood by her father during the Senate hearings, she had stood stoically beside her husband as, one after another, all his tawdry little secrets had been exposed. With a face that revealed none of her emotions, she had quietly shamed all but the hardcore paparazzi before it was over into granting her grudging respect.

But by that time Rocky had stopped watching. Enough was enough.

Enough was too damned much.

The congressman's sleazy affairs had been too commonplace to sustain a media barrage for long, once it was determined that national security was not at stake. The mess had sprung up again briefly a few months later when Sullivan had taken dead aim at a bridge abutment and totaled both himself and his car. Shortly after that, Sarah Mariah dropped out of sight.

That must have been about the same time that Rocky himself had dropped out. One way of putting it. He had watched Julie's final decline. He had cried. He had read until he couldn't face another book. He'd watched an entire season of baseball, his own brand of opiate. When he'd realized he was drinking too much, he had quit cold turkey. All things considered, it hadn't exactly been a banner year.

A few nights after Dan Sturdivant's retirement party, Rocky was watching the news and toying with the idea of doing a series of columns when he caught a thirty-second teaser for a daytime talk show featuring Binky Cudahy, author of the upcoming bestseller, *The Senator's Daughter's Husband's Other Women.*

That's when it hit him. Wherever she'd gone, whatever kind of a life she had managed to salvage for herself, the congressman's widow was probably going to come in for some unwelcome attention once the book hit the stands. Did she even know about it? Did she watch daytime TV?

For all he knew she might be lying on the sand soaking up sun on some tropical island by now. God knows, she deserved a break.

But she also deserved to know what was headed her way, in case she needed to duck. Rocky knew he could find her. He'd put in too many years as a reporter not to have sources. Although why he should feel this proprietary interest in a woman he'd met only one time, and that more than twenty years ago, he couldn't have said. Maybe because there was a big, gaping hole where his life used to be.

Well, hell…the least he could do was give her fair warning that the buzzards would soon be circling again.

Two

Sarah Mariah flexed her sore hands and examined the newest crop of injuries. The mashed thumb had been yesterday. The sprained little finger several days before that. Today's scratches were only a minor irritation, but honestly, she was going to have to do better. Good thing she'd had her tetanus booster.

All she'd been trying to do was untangle the wild grapevines from the shrubs that had been allowed to grow unchecked for decades. It wasn't as if she'd been tackling a jungle with her bare hands. The shrubs were threatening to lift the eaves, but she couldn't even prune the blamed things until she could get rid of the blasted vines.

Still, if stiff hands and a few scratches were the worst she had to show for today's work, she'd consider herself lucky. She was still scratching chiggers, and last week she'd had to go after a tick in an inaccessible place with a mirror and a pair of tweezers. Living alone had its drawbacks, but the upside definitely outweighed the downside.

She poured herself a glass of milk and made a salsa and mozzarella sandwich on whole grain bread, feeling righteous because she would rather have had a bacon-cheeseburger with fries. Taking her tray into the parlor, she kicked off her shoes and sprawled out in a recliner that was half a century newer than the rest of her great-aunt's furniture. It was one of the few really comfortable pieces in the house.

There was a TV on a spool-legged table. It had died a natural death several years ago and had never been replaced. Sarah had no intention of having it repaired, although she might decide to free up the table for a potted plant. She had a weather radio and a subscription to the *Daily Advance*. Those, plus weekly trips to the grocery store and sporadic trips to the post office filled her needs for contact with the outside world. If World War III or a tornado threatened, she trusted one of the neighbors to warn her.

It had come as no great surprise that her late great-aunt's lifestyle suited her far better than life in suburban D.C. Sarah had hated Washington, hated the whole political scene. But then, she hadn't chosen it, she'd been born into it. And then she'd had the poor judgment to marry into the same circles. She would like to think she had played her role competently, if with a distinct lack of enthusiasm, right to the end.

During her father's ordeal, Stan had been worse than useless. He'd practically fallen apart. On the few nights when he stayed in, he was drunk by the time she served dinner. She hadn't understood at the time why he'd seemed almost panicked. He couldn't possibly have been involved, she'd reasoned, because if he'd been a part of anything illegal they would have quickly discovered it. He'd had flawless manners and the face of a sexy choirboy. That guileless grin alone had brought in the women's votes. He'd seemed so open, so honest—such a refreshing change from all the others. She remembered once trying to reassure him by telling him not to feel guilty, that none of her father's crimes was his fault. His only sin was being married to the senator's daughter.

She'd said it with a smile—or as much of a smile as she could manage—but he hadn't said a word, either in his own defense or hers. Not that she'd expected him to defend her father. What the senator had done was indefensible. But he might at least have absolved her of the guilt of being J. Abernathy's daughter.

He hadn't. A year or so after the Senate hearings, when her husband had started behaving oddly, she had tried to be understanding. After all, it had been an ordeal for him, too. She remembered thinking that once his term ended she would try to talk Stan into selling the house they'd just purchased and not running for office again. They could go somewhere—anywhere—and start over.

Then the dam had burst and it had happened all over again. The same nightmare, only this time it was even uglier. For the first few days she had been in denial. When she'd been forced to confront the truth—when her husband, in a rare sober moment, had confessed to everything—she'd been devastated. Addie, the old housekeeper who was the nearest thing to a mother she'd had since Mariah Jones had died, had been ready to retire to South Carolina with her granddaughter when the senator's troubles had begun. She had stayed on for Sarah's sake and then returned when Stan's scandal had broken, knowing how desperately Sarah would need her.

While every dirty little secret in her husband's life—every secret but one, thank God—had been exposed, the senator had chosen to hole up in a beach house in North Carolina belonging to his friend, lawyer-lobbyist Clive Meadows. There'd been no reason to expect him to stand by her—he'd never been there for her at any other time in her life, but she could have done with a bit of moral support.

Looking back, Sarah knew he'd made the right choice. His presence would only have stirred up the past. One scandal at a time was all she could deal with.

Thank God for Great-Aunt Emma's legacy. Sarah had visited her maternal grandmother's sister several times as a small child and fallen in love with the stark old farmhouse. The tiny community of Snowden, North Carolina was only a short distance off the highway they always took driving down from Washington to Duck, on the Outer Banks, where her father had the use of Clive's palatial beach house.

When her mother had still been living and the two of them used to go to the beach without the senator, they had usually stopped to visit her mother's only relative. On rare occasions they stayed overnight. Sarah had been eleven the last time they'd spent an entire weekend. She remembered waking in the night with a terrible ache in the pit of her belly and being certain she was about to die. Hearing her crying, both Aunt Emma and her mother had hurried to her room.

"Mariah Gilbert, didn't you even tell the child what to expect?" Emma had demanded. Her great-aunt had never liked the senator, and preferred to ignore the fact that her niece had married him.

"They teach that sort of thing at school, Aunt Emma. I'm sure she knows all about it, don't you, darling?"

All Sarah had known was that she was dying. It had been Emma who had explained that her body was preparing her to be a mother. And that, she remembered, had terrified her even more than the bellyache.

But between the two women they had made her understand that what she was feeling, while unpleasant, was perfectly normal. Then Aunt Emma had brought her a cup of hot, sugared and watered-down whisky, while her mother had located and filled an old rubber hot-water bottle.

After that they hadn't stopped as often. Her mother was diagnosed with leukemia, and Sarah had all but forgotten her great-aunt over the next few years. When Mariah had died, Emma had gone to the funeral, driven there and back in a single day by a neighbor. Sarah had had only a few minutes alone with her. J. Abernathy, distraught over the loss of the wife he had neglected for years, had insisted on having his daughter constantly at his side.

The two women had corresponded, though. Sarah had kept every one of her great-aunt's letters. When Emma had died at the age of eighty-four, she'd left her entire estate, consisting of a house, a Hudson automobile up on blocks in the shed, and sixty acres of land, partly wooded, partly under cultivation, to her great-niece, Sarah Mariah.

It was almost as if she'd known that one day soon Sarah would need a place of her own. The senator—he was still called that, even after being forced to retire in disgrace—had the place on Wye River, but he'd given up the Watergate apartment where she'd practically grown up. Sarah and Stan had bought a tiny house in Arlington, but they'd had to sell it to pay his lawyers. To Stan's credit, he wouldn't allow her to go into the small trust she'd received from her mother, much less sell Aunt Emma's house.

Her father had been no help at all, either financially or emotionally, but she hadn't expected anything from that source. In the end, Sarah had been left with the one thing she valued more than anything in the world.

Privacy. A place of her own where she could retreat, where the world couldn't follow. And if that included loneliness, so be it. She had cut off her friends early on during the first scandal—those that hadn't already cut her. Here the neighbors were few, the closest being almost a mile away. If any of them had connected Emma Gilbert's great-niece-who-married-that-nice-congressman with the recent Washington scandals, they never mentioned it. But then, they weren't inclined to drop by for coffee and gossip.

She missed her old friends, missed the volunteer work she'd been doing for years—the children she'd worked with. Now she kept to herself, paid her utility bills and made the monthly payment to the grandparents of her late husband's secret illegitimate daughter.

What Stan had been involved in had been depraved by anyone's standards to the extent that his political future had been shattered beyond repair. One of the participants had been a juvenile at the time. Her name had not been released, but shortly before Stan's fatal wreck she had called to tell him she'd just had his baby and now she needed money. Utterly distraught, Stan had promised to send what he could, even though at the time they'd been scraping the bottom of the barrel to pay for his defense. He had hung up the phone, blurted out the whole pathetic story, then buried his head in Sarah's lap and cried.

"She...she named her K-Kitty. Oh, God, Sarah, what have I done?"

"Shh, we'll deal with it. Maybe when this is all over we can adopt her."

But before they could make any arrangements, Stan had been killed. By then, a sixteen-year-old girl from Virginia Beach who claimed Stan had fathered her child had been the last thing on Sarah's mind.

Somehow she had managed to get through the following days and do all that needed doing. Her father's old friend, Clive Meadows, had been a big help. The day after the funeral, when a man named Sam Pough had called, claiming his daughter had run off and left him and his wife stuck with her bastard, it had actually taken her several minutes to sort it all out.

If Clive had been there at the time, she probably would have simply handed him the phone and let him handle it. Later on, when she'd had time to think, she was glad she'd been alone. She remembered taking so many deep breaths she had grown dizzy. Once her head had cleared, she'd heard herself calmly promising to send an initial sum and make monthly payments as long as the grandparents promised to look after the baby. They were decent, God-fearing people, the man had repeated several times, but their trailer was too old, too small, and their social security would stretch only so far.

Sarah had done the best she could. By liquidating her trust fund, she'd been able to send a sizable check to cover the cost of a new mobile home. Since then she'd sent monthly payments with the understanding that those payments would continue only so long as the child was well cared for and her identity remained a secret. No child, she told herself, should have to grow up bearing the stigma of a father's disgrace.

As time passed with no further contact from the Poughs, Sarah had made herself learn to relax. It wasn't that easy, in spite of having left the past behind and moved to the country. Growing up as her father's daughter, she'd been expected to dress a certain way, to behave a certain way—to go to the right schools, the right summer camps—to smile at appropriate moments, and to express herself only on noncontroversial topics.

Once she'd become the congressman's wife there had been a whole new set of expectations. Never once had anyone asked her personal opinion on an important issue. And she most definitely did have opinions, on any number of issues. Nor did they agree very often with those of her father or her husband.

Never once in her entire life could she recall being asked how she would have preferred to spend her vacations. Given a choice, she might have chosen to attend a fiddlers' convention with her college friends, sleeping in tents, wandering from campfire to campfire listening to the music, sharing food and easy companionship. Instead, she had spent every vacation with one or both of her parents, usually at Clive's beach house, surrounded by other adults.

Instead of flying lessons, she had taken piano lessons. Instead of choosing her own friends, she'd had appropriate ones chosen for her, at least until she'd gone off to school.

It wasn't that her childhood had been unhappy, it was just that she'd never been allowed off the leash long enough to discover who she was. And now that she was free to be herself, she didn't know where to begin, other than wearing thrift-shop jeans, going barefoot and drinking water from her own tap instead of what her Aunt Em had called store-bought water. After a lifetime of pleasing others, she had only herself to please, and the most rebellious thing she had done so far was to stay up half the night reading and then sleep until noon the next day.

These days she couldn't even manage that. Since she'd started on the long-overdue yard work, tackling one square foot at a time, she was usually so tired she fell asleep in the recliner.

Dull was a matter of degrees. Her life had always been—well, until a little over two years ago—dull, as in *boring*. Now it was dull as in *restful*. As in taking time to sniff the roses, not to mention the honeysuckle and corn tassels and whatever else grew in the country. As in trying her hand at writing and illustrating a special story for a little girl she would probably never even get to see.

But right now—at least once she'd caught her breath—it was time for another attack on that blasted board on her front porch that she'd tripped on at least a dozen times. Tomorrow would be time enough to free the rest of her shrubbery from the strangling clutches of those voracious vines.

After rubbing aloe lotion onto her hands, she picked up the daily paper published in the nearby riverside town. Sipping her milk, she skimmed articles about people she didn't know, who didn't know her. There wasn't a speck of world news, rarely even a political commentary. She liked it that way. She read the obituaries of people she'd never heard of, wedding announcements for young hopefuls who had no idea of the pitfalls ahead. She read notices of fiftieth wedding anniversaries, wondering if the couples knew how fortunate they were, and tried not to feel sorry for herself. Given a choice, she knew she would never go back to her old life.

She read about club meetings and historical reenactments and the progress being made on the town's museum. She read about an art show and a moth-boat regatta and considered attending. Mingling with real people again.

One of these days she was going to have to return to the real world and find work. Find some way to make her liberal arts degree support her, because Kitty's needs would continue to grow—clothes and schools and health insurance. Her trust fund wouldn't last much longer at the rate she was depleting it, but she refused to accept a penny from her father. Not that he'd offered. Where J. Abernathy Jones was concerned, every penny came with strings attached.

One string, she suspected, led to Clive Meadows. She'd known Clive for years. It was his beach house they always used. She had met only one of his three wives and been shocked that the girl was so young.

Not surprisingly, she rarely liked her father's friends. Clive was no better, no worse than most. Once, before she'd married Stan, when Clive was between wives, he had asked her out to dinner. She had declined. A few nights later he'd invited her to a concert. She had thanked him and pleaded another engagement.

Her father had been in Scotland when Stan had been killed in a one-man accident that had been deemed a suicide. Clive had been there to offer comfort and professional advice, to steer her through the formalities. At the time she had gratefully accepted his help.

But as for anything more, Sarah, at age thirty-seven, was far too old for a man of his tastes—his wives had been barely out of their teens. Of course, she might have imagined his interest. Distraught, she could easily have read too much into a few innocent shoulder pats, a few avuncular hugs and the offer, after Stan's private memorial service, of a quiet month at his beach house at Duck.

At any rate, she was safe now, and as long as she could continue paying for Kitty's needs and stretch what was left to cover the necessities—food, books, utilities and property taxes—she intended to stay put. Loneliness was a small price to pay for peace of mind.

Rocky rounded a sharp curve on the narrow highway, humming along with something or other by Sibelius. Years out of practice, he hit only about every fifth note correctly, but then, that was between him and the composer, and the old guy wasn't complaining.

He felt good about what he was doing. Righteous, in fact, which was a big improvement over feeling nothing. Thank God something had come along to drag him out of his lair.

It had already occurred to him that someone else might have already warned her. But in case they hadn't, she needed to know what was about to hit the fan. It probably wouldn't amount to much more than a few jokes on Leno and Letterman, a few sound bytes and film clips—maybe a rehash in the tabloids. After a week at most, the whole thing would die a natural death, but meanwhile, a heads-up might be appreciated.

Besides which, he'd needed a mission. Lately he'd been aware of a growing sense of restlessness. The trouble with being a retired journalist was that the brain refused to retire.

Okay, so he would warn the widow and while he was in the area he might look around for something to quicken his interest. Frontline reporting from the agricultural scene? He could do an investigative piece on the pork industry, maybe hang it on the hook of environmental pollution versus genetic engineering. Would reshuffling a few pig genes render hog lagoons obsolete?

He whistled along with the familiar theme of "Finlandia" and wondered how long it had been since he'd whistled. Or hummed anything. Once an enthusiastic sing-alonger, it had been years since he'd been enthusiastic about anything.

When his watch beeped at noon, he switched off the CD and turned on the news.

"—at Camp David. The meeting is scheduled to cover—" He changed stations and caught the tail end of a report on the latest airline disaster, waited through a string of commercials and heard the farm report. Nothing about the Cudahy book. Maybe he'd overestimated the threat. It might not show up at all in this particular market. Even so, it was about time for the publisher to start chumming the waters if they hoped to see people lined up outside the bookstores, money in hand, on laydown day.

Meanwhile, he'd do well to work on his tactics. "Mrs. Sullivan, I'm an independent journalist, and I've come to warn you about—"

Yeah, right. Considering what she'd been put through these past few years, that might not be the best approach. Direct was his favored method, but direct in this case would probably get him kicked out on his keester. The lady had no reason to welcome the press.

Of course, it wasn't too late to call it off. He could go back to Chevy Chase, refreshed from spending a day in the country, and either watch a few more ball games or start on his version of the Great American novel. The story of how one cynical journalist, semi-retired, discovered a way to put an end to all turf wars, ethnic vendettas and ideological battles.

But as long as he was in the neighborhood, he might as well pay his respects to Mrs. Sullivan. Maybe she'd offer him a cup of tea.

Or a cream cheese sandwich.

Finding her had been easy enough. He was not, after

all, without investigative skills. According to the ex-senator's yard man, she had not been to the Wye River place in nearly a year. None of her former friends had offered a clue—of course, they might have been in protective mode. Taking the next logical step, he had checked out public records. Wills, taxes, tax maps.

Bingo. If he could do it, it was a sure bet he wouldn't be the only one. Sleazy exposés were a dime a dozen. They seldom changed the course of history, but they could generate a few column inches in the tabloids and make life miserable for the victims before they were bumped off the lists by the next contender.

Discounting their one brief encounter, Rocky really didn't know Sarah Mariah Jones Sullivan at all. By now she might even welcome the attention. But if she was anywhere as vulnerable as she'd looked during the hearings—as she'd struck him that day over twenty years ago when she'd watched her father use her and discard her as casually as he would a soiled tissue—then maybe she could use a friend.

And if he happened to have guessed wrong about which way she'd jumped—if she was kicking up her heels in some fancy resort instead of hibernating in corn country—no problem. He'd needed an excuse to get out. Needed to start getting involved again.

Slowing down, he took the Snowden turnoff, rounded a blind curve on a narrow blacktop, crossed over a railroad track and began looking for a dirt road that led off to the right. The only sign of life was a big buck deer and a flock of gulls following a tractor, reminding him that they were only a mile or so from Currituck Sound.

He spotted the dirt road and turned off, driving

slowly. Tax maps didn't reveal a whole lot of detail, but there was supposed to be another road of some sort.

And there it was. Two leaning posts, one supporting a newspaper box, the other a mailbox. The name on the mailbox said Gilbert, which, if memory served, was the name of the relative whose house Sarah had inherited. Rocky pulled off the road and parked behind a dusty red compact. After a moment's hesitation he set the brake, locked his eight-year-old SUV and set out on foot down the winding, rutted lane. He'd gone barely a dozen yards when he spotted a guy armed with a videocam jogging toward the house.

Evidently his suspicions had been justified. The lady was about to find herself in the crosshairs again. "Yo! You with the camera!"

The guy glanced over his shoulder, but instead of stopping, he picked up speed. It occurred to Rocky that he could be an innocent nature photographer—maybe a stringer for some hunting-fishing rag. He didn't think so, though. There was something a little too furtive about the way he kept checking his six.

One thing he'd learned during a career that spanned more than two decades was that while photos could easily lie—and people often did, intentionally or not—the subconscious mind was the closest thing to a truth detector any man possessed. *If* he knew how to use it.

The other fellow had the advantage of youth and a head start. Halfway down the lane, Rocky planted his feet and used his fingers to issue a shrill whistle. Occasionally the unexpected trumped any advantage.

At the sound, the photographer came to a dead halt. Roland "Rocky" Waters stood in the middle of a country lane and wondered, Okay, what now, Rambo?

Three

Damn blasted board. It should have been replaced years ago, just as the gutters should have been repaired or replaced. Aunt Emma had been in her eighties, for heaven's sake. Sarah should have come down here and seen to all the repairs, herself. At least she could have hired someone.

But she hadn't. Too wrapped up in her own woes. And now everything needed fixing. Whether she sold the house, which would break her heart, and moved back to the city to find work, or turned the place into a bed and breakfast catering to people looking for a place in the slow lane—in this case, the *very* slow lane—things needed doing. She tackled them one after another.

Yesterday it had been the grapevines, which she still hadn't finished. Today it was the board she stubbed her toe on every time she walked down to this end of the porch. Clutching the hammer just behind the head, she glanced up at the sound of a car out on the road. It was so quiet she could hear for miles...not that there was much to hear. Crows. Farm equipment. Now and then a barking dog.

Between cornfields that had been leased out to the same farmer for years, the overgrown shrubbery and the tall, longleaf pines that shed all over the roof, clogging the gutters, she couldn't see as far as the dirt road, much less the blacktop. Later on, during hunting season, she might see half a dozen hunters, even though her land was posted.

The man jogging toward her house didn't look like a hunter. Nor did he look lost. In fact, she thought uneasily as she sat back on her heels, scowling against the sun's glare, with that big camera thing he was carrying, he looked suspiciously like one of the flock of vultures that had once made her life such a living hell.

What on earth could have happened to bring the press down on her head *this* time? Surely the Poughs hadn't gone public, not after all this time. That would be killing the golden goose. She hadn't missed a single payment, and while it wasn't much, it was the best she could do.

It occurred to her that it had been weeks since she'd spoken to her father. If something had happened to him, surely someone would have called her. She didn't like the man, certainly didn't trust him and wouldn't particularly care if she didn't have to see him for the next few years, but she supposed she still loved him. Daughters were supposed to love their fathers, and if nothing else, she'd been trained to be a dutiful daughter.

By now she had a pretty clear view of her visitor. He was no one she'd ever seen before, of that she was certain. He certainly didn't look like anyone her father would have sent after her.

Still on her hands and knees, Sarah tried to make up her mind what to do. She had learned the hard way to avoid confrontation whenever possible, but to stand her ground when escape was not an option. She was still trying to make up her mind when a shrill whistle split the air.

A *whistle?* What in God's name was going on?

And then a second man came into sight around the curve in her rutted, overgrown lane. Clutching the hammer, she almost forgot to breathe. Something must have happened—something awful. Maybe someone was in trouble. Maybe there'd been an accident out on the highway. Maybe someone needed her help—or at least, her telephone.

"Miz Sullivan?" The first man was panting, clearly out of shape. At closer range, he appeared younger than the man following him. The second man, taller, darker, slightly older, sprinted forward, grabbed his arm and swung him around.

Sarah scrambled to her feet. "Just what is going on?" she demanded at the same time the older man began to speak.

"Didn't you see the signs? This is private property," she heard him say. Well built, he was wearing jeans and a khaki shirt—standard wear for the locals. Did she know him? Was he a neighbor she hadn't yet met?

"Both of you, stop right there!" She lifted the hammer as a warning. "My land is posted and you're trespassing."

"You heard what the lady said." The dark-haired stranger was still holding on to the younger man's camera arm. At closer range, he didn't look particularly dangerous. All the same, she'd learned to be wary.

Oddly enough, it was his eyes she noticed most as the two men came closer. They reminded her of the icy fjords she had seen on her one and only trip to Scandinavia.

"Hey, get off my back, man, I was here first! Miz Sullivan, what do you think about the book—"

"The lady has no comment." By that time both men had reached the gate at the foot of her front walk.

The younger man wore a headband and a ponytail. Attempting to elbow his pursuer away, he whined, "Hey, butt out, old man, this is my story."

"There's no story here. The lady says you're trespassing. You want a story? Try the county courthouse. Oldest one in the state. Fascinating history."

By now they were halfway up the walk, almost at her front steps. Sarah Mariah had had enough. "I'm calling the sheriff," she warned, and turned to go inside. That's when her foot caught the board she'd been repairing. She flung out her hands to catch herself, and the hammer flew across the porch and landed at the feet of the man with the ponytail.

"Jeeze, lady, you don't have to get physical, I can take a hint." He backed away, muttering under his breath.

Sarah was hurting too much to care what was being

said. She hadn't actually seen stars, but close enough. Rubbing her forehead where she'd struck the edge of the screen door, she tried to assess the damage. The very last thing she needed when she was in klutz mode was a pair of witnesses.

The younger man was halfway down the lane. He was shaking his head. The older man came up onto the porch. "Are you all right? That was a pretty serious crack you took."

Up close, he was even better looking. She had learned the hard way not to trust men who were too good-looking. This one wore the shadow of a beard, which might or might not be a fashion statement. There was a certain watchful quality about him, as if he weren't quite sure of his welcome.

Smart man. "Who are you? What do you want?"

"You've forgotten already? It's only been, what—twenty years?"

"Have we met?" She tried to ignore the pain, but both her eyes were beginning to water. Even so, if she had ever met this man before, she would have remembered. His was not the kind of face a woman could ever forget.

Although on closer examination, there *was* something about him. Something about his eyes...pale gray, set off by thick black lashes and eyebrows. Where had she seen such eyes before?

He seemed almost to be waiting for her to recognize him, but at the moment her head hurt too much to think. "Twenty years?" she repeated. "I'm sorry, but—"

"More like twenty-two, I guess. Rocky Waters,

Mrs. Sullivan. And you were Miss Anonymous Jones. The king was having a bad hair day, remember?"

Rocky Waters, Rocky Waters, Rocky...

Oh, blast and tarnation. "The tea and cream cheese."

"Managed to salvage my shoes, but you know what? You're going to have a beauty of a shiner. Maybe if you put something on it before the swelling starts?"

"The swelling," she repeated, sounding almost as dazed as she felt. It was partly the crack on her forehead, partly the fault of the man standing before her.

To think of all the hours she'd wasted after that one brief meeting thinking about him. Daydreaming. Creating wild, adolescent fantasies about someone she'd met only once, and then in the most embarrassing circumstances. Seeing him now, years later and out of context, it had taken a few minutes to connect. He looked more than ever like one of those dark, dangerous Black Ops heroes in her favorite romantic suspense novels.

God knows what she must look like after a day of wrestling grapevines—with one eye rapidly swelling shut.

No point in hoping he hadn't noticed. Taking her by the arm, he said, "You took a real whack there. Let's go inside—you'd better sit while I get a towel and some ice. Don't suppose you have an ice bag, do you?"

"An ice bag?"

"Thought not. You don't look like the type."

"What type?" Pain was beginning to radiate from her eye socket all the way down to her jawbone. Momentarily dazed into compliance, she let him lead her inside. "Straight through there," she said, her voice now little more than a strained whisper. He pulled out a kitchen chair, and she lowered herself carefully, then watched as he removed a tray of ice from the avocado-green refrigerator, a relic of the last time her great-aunt had modernized her kitchen.

"Hangovers. Bet you've never had one in your life, have you?"

"No—actually, yes." There were a lot of things she'd never done and now probably never would, but he didn't have to know it. "Clean towels are in there." She pointed at the drawer where she kept kitchen linens. "Why are you doing this? Why are you even here?"

Rocky took the time to crack the ice with a meat tenderizer he found in a drawer along with three emergency candles, a ball of string and a few dozen rubber jar rings.

Why was he here? Good question. He'd set out with honorable intentions—mostly honorable, anyway. Warn the lady of what was in the pipeline. Help her with a preemptive strike, but only if she thought it would help defuse the situation.

As for him, part of the problem was that he'd been unable to motivate himself into getting back to writing after Julie's death. If the senator's daughter needed his help, he would give it his best shot.

If not...no problem. He'd warn her of what to expect because he'd seen too many victims blindsided after a tragedy by having a camera and a mike shoved in their face unexpectedly. Warn her, wish her luck and leave.

At the moment, however, he didn't think she was in any shape to hear what he'd come to say. "Here, hold this against your face."

She took the ice-filled towel and placed it gingerly against her eye. "You were a lot younger then," she said. "I seem to remember that our whole conversation was like something out of *Alice in Wonderland.*"

"Right. We were both younger. So...how's Toto?"

"Still in Kansas. Wrong story."

He grinned, managing to look both raffish and kind. "Just wanted to be sure you didn't have a concussion. Want to count my fingers?" He waggled them in front of her face.

"Not really. Are you here for any particular reason? Nobody just drops in because they happen to be in the neighborhood. There isn't any neighborhood, in case you failed to notice."

Sarah wondered if she'd broken the skin. Along with the throbbing, her eyebrow was starting to sting. "You're hovering," she grumbled. "I hate it when someone hovers. If you have something to say, then say it and leave. Please."

"I came to warn you about the book."

She dropped the towel. It came unfolded, and ice scattered across the linoleum. Ignoring it, she tried to focus on the man with one good eye and one that was rapidly swelling shut.

"The book. Right. Which one are we talking about this time, Oz or Alice? No don't bother—the joke's beginning to wear thin." She wanted him to go so that she could give in to the pain. Curse or cry, or at least wallow in self-pity. All of which were luxuries she could only now afford to indulge.

Instead of leaving, he pulled out a chair and sat, uninvited. Then he proceeded to tell her why he'd gone to the trouble of tracking her down. This time the book wasn't *The Wizard* and it wasn't *Wonderland*. It was...

"The Senator's Daughter's Husband's Other Women? Tell me you're making that up." In stunned disbelief, Sarah heard him out. "She can't do that...can she?"

But of course she could. Having spent practically her entire life in Washington, Sarah well knew how each major scandal was rehashed in books that hit the stands in record time. The only curious thing was that this one had taken so long.

Dear God, what if the Poughs thought she was somehow benefiting from her late husband's notoriety and demanded more money? She was already sending as much as she could afford. Even worse, what if, on seeing the Cudahy woman cash in on a rehash of the whole wretched mess, they decided to go public with Kitty's secret? How much would the tabloids pay for something like that? Pictures of an innocent child under the caption, Disgraced Congressman's Secret Lovechild.

Lifting her battered face, she whispered, "Why is that awful woman doing this? If she was actually there—if she was one of the...the—"

"Sluts," Rocky provided.

"How can she be so brazen?"

He shrugged. "Money. Her fifteen minutes of fame. Who knows?"

Sarah placed the wet towel on the table and rubbed her fingers together. They were cold. She felt cold all over. Felt as if she were trapped inside one of those snowstorm paperweights that someone had just given a good, hard shake.

She studied the man seated across the table. He had changed in some ways—twenty-odd years could do that to anyone. He'd been a brand-new reporter when she'd first met him. Her adolescent crush had eventually faded, but she'd gone on following his career, seeing him occasionally on TV covering some foreign affairs flap, reporting from overseas or doing a segment on one of the Sunday talk shows. Somewhere along the line he seemed to have dropped out of sight, but by that time she had already begun playing ostrich.

She had to wonder now if his intentions were quite as innocent as he wanted her to believe.

Carefully she replaced the towel, now minus most of the ice but still cold and comforting. She'd been a fool, living in her pretty bubble, believing herself insulated from the rest of the world. Just because she had stopped keeping up with the news didn't mean the rest of the world had ceased to exist. It was still out there, like a big, hungry bear waiting to devour the unwary. She'd gone into hibernation, and now the bear had followed her into her cave.

"But why?" she asked again. "Sorry. If it sounds as if I'm whining it's because I am."

"You're entitled. Go ahead, whine if it helps, but maybe you'd better take an aspirin first. That bruise is going to be pretty uncomfortable for a while."

It already hurt like the very devil, but she knew better than to show weakness before the enemy, whoever and whatever the enemy in this case was. If the bear was out there, then this man, for all she knew, could be the bear's emissary. "I'll do that. And thank you—I guess. You've warned me what to expect."

"You might want to take a vacation until things blow over."

"Good idea." It would be a good idea if she could afford it. "Do you mind telling me how you found me?"

Briefly he explained about public records, private sources and the powers of deduction. She sighed, knowing that in these days of instant high-tech intelligence it was almost impossible for anyone to disappear without a trace. "If I'd known this was going to happen I might have tried to get into the witness protection program." Her rueful smile was probably more of a grimace, but it was the best she could do. "Maybe I'll get myself a junkyard dog."

"Unless you're used to handling junkyard dogs, he'd be more of a threat than a benefit."

"Well, what would you do in my place?"

He was leaning against the white-painted counter, looking dark and dangerous against the glass-fronted cabinets. The man was simply too big, too masculine, too…tough wasn't quite the right word, but it would do until a better one occurred. She had a feeling that those deceptively clear eyes of his hid a wealth of secrets. And she didn't want to share his secrets, she really didn't. She had enough of her own.

Once, a long time ago, he had been carelessly kind to a fifteen-year-old girl who'd been bored, discouraged, hurt and sorely in need of a friendly smile.

He wasn't smiling now. And kind or not, she had no real reason to trust him. "Did you come here for an exclusive?"

He appeared to consider his answer. "Would you believe me if I said no?"

Sarah knew to her sorrow that entire careers sometimes hung on a single word spoken at the wrong time, to the wrong ears.

Where was your husband on Labor Day weekend?
Labor Day? He was in Michigan, doing a town hall thing.

He said he was home with you, just the two of you, that you'd dismissed your housekeeper and cooked out and then watched a movie on TV.

She'd never been a good liar. It had never occurred to her that she even needed to lie until it was too late. Far too late. So she said nothing.

Rocky watched a series of subtle expressions pass over the widow's face. He was good at reading faces. She was far better than most when it came to concealing her thoughts, but he'd caught her off guard, in a vulnerable position. "Has it occurred to you that you could get the jump on the Cudahy woman by coming out first with your own version of what happened?"

Four

Rocky shoved away from the counter, the motion bringing him just close enough to her chair that he could smell…insect repellent? Shampoo? Under other circumstances he might have touched her on the shoulder in a wordless gesture of comfort before leaving, but something told him that touching this woman would be a mistake.

While she gingerly fingered the lump on her brow, he studied the changes that had taken place since his one and only up-close and personal look. Considering all she'd gone through since then, she had changed surprisingly little. Same great cheekbones. Same expressive eyes. Same mouth—a bit large, given to quick smiles, as quickly withdrawn. Total package? Hardly spectacular, but…nice.

He remembered the expression in her eyes then—a

certain sadness, a wariness. It had changed very little over the years. Grown warier, if anything. With good cause.

Funny, the way a retentive mind could trap a few insignificant details and file them away for years. A smile—a way of tilting the head that indicated a healthy skepticism. No reason why any of it should have stuck with him all these years, but oddly enough it had.

She fingered her swelling eye gingerly. "I think this is what our old housekeeper would call an ouchie."

"An 'ouchie'? My old man would have called it a shiner." His old man was such a dim and distant memory that he had no idea what he would have called it. It was something to say, that's all. Small talk—something he'd never been particularly good at.

"I've never had a black eye before." Her look was one of pride mingled with dismay. He found it oddly disarming.

She was a mess, all right. No makeup, ragbag clothes—pine straw in her hair, scratches on her hands and a brand-new shiner bursting into full bloom. There was nothing even faintly seductive about the woman, yet he found himself looking at her in a way he hadn't looked at any woman in years.

Which one, he wondered, was the real Sarah Mariah Jones Sullivan? The awkward adolescent who'd been used countless times as a stage prop by her father and then ignored? Or the self-possessed woman who had stood at his side while his empire crumpled, then been forced to do the same thing for her husband a few years later under even more embarrassing circumstances?

Or this fragile creature with the leaves in her hair, perspiration stains on her shirt and a dripping towel covering half her face?

She might look fragile, but there was a surprising degree of strength, not to mention courage, inside that delicate frame. He remembered watching the news coverage both times. She'd always tried to slip away unnoticed, but once the pack had her cornered she would stand her ground and politely answer each question until someone—probably the housekeeper she'd mentioned—managed to rescue her.

The same woman was standing not three feet away, looking no less composed despite baggy jeans, a sweaty, green-stained T-shirt and hair that might have been styled by a wind tunnel. It occurred to him that for a journalist who knew better, he was beginning to take a dangerously personal interest.

"Well, hey, why don't I just leave now? I've warned you what's about to hit the fan. Handle it any way you want to."

"No, wait—please?" She held out her hand. It was red, the thumb badly bruised. There was a beaded line on the back where she'd evidently scratched herself and the blood had dried.

What the devil was she doing here, digging herself a bomb shelter?

In spite of his better judgment, Rocky settled back against the counter and waited. She stood, stepped on a piece of melting ice, recovered her balance and grimaced. "You might not believe this," she said ruefully, "but I've actually been known to walk across a room without either tripping or spilling anything."

"No kidding." Rocky thought he might have underestimated her looks. The lady might not win any beauty contests, but there was something about her that stuck in a man's mind....

Which was why he was here in the first place. "Tell you what," he proposed. "While you take care of damage control, why don't I make us a pot of coffee? If you'll tell me where to find sandwich makings, I can put together something to stave off the wolf, and we'll talk over our options."

Our options? He'd meant to say hers. She didn't jump at the offer, but then, he could hardly blame her for being wary. A journalist who had come to warn her about journalists? Maybe she should skip over Alice and Oz and go directly to *Little Red Riding Hood and the Big Bad Wolf*.

It was getting late. Sarah had had breakfast early. Had she eaten lunch or not? Suddenly—illogically—she was starved. The trouble with her new lifestyle was that there was nothing to mark the days, much less the hours. As often as not, she'd work until she was famished, then gobble down whatever was handiest. Or read half the night away and find herself having breakfast at four in the morning.

"Tomatoes on the windowsill, bread in the breadbox. Look in the refrigerator if you want anything else. If you'll excuse me, I need to go—to go..."

Rocky thought he'd better warn her before she confronted a mirror. "Sarah, don't be discouraged by the way it looks now, because—"

"That bad, hmm?" She laughed, shook her head, grabbed her forehead and winced.

Conquering the second urge in as many minutes to

reach out and touch her, he said, "Because it's going to look a hell of a lot worse before it looks better."

"Then maybe *one* of us had better cover our eyes," she said with that same droll sense of humor he remembered from twenty years earlier. "I like my coffee strong, and I want onions and lots of salt and pepper on my sandwich."

Sarah hurried to the bathroom, closed the door behind her and leaned against it. Had she lost her mind? Why had she even allowed him in the house? She knew who he was—or at least, *what* he was. And, whether or not he'd been one of the pack that had hounded her so mercilessly, by now he had to know every sordid detail about her marriage. And like everyone else, he would have drawn the same conclusion. That she'd been such an abject failure as a woman she hadn't even been able to hold her husband's interest.

By the time she returned to the kitchen, he'd made sandwiches, cut them neatly and placed them on a platter. The table was set with Aunt Emma's moss rose plates, cups and saucers and her old-fashioned silver. Almost everything in the house was just the same as it had been for the past forty-odd years—the same appliances in the same sickly shade of green. The same yellow enameled table and uncomfortable straight chairs painted to match. The same wag-tailed clock that was too big for the wall space and consistently slow.

It all looked the same. Until a few minutes ago it had even felt the same. It was nowhere near as luxurious as the apartment where she'd grown up, or even the far more modest house she had shared with Stan.

But for some reason she'd always felt secure here, even as a child.

Now even that had changed.

They ate first and were on their second cups of coffee before either of them brought up his reason for being there. Sarah took a deep breath and said, "It's probably not that big a deal—the book, I mean. After all, it's been a year since Stan—since he—and even longer since my father resigned." She didn't add "in disgrace." It wasn't necessary. "People will have forgotten by now."

"Don't count on it."

She knew better than to count on anything. Or anyone. "Well, what do you recommend, that I go somewhere off the beaten track and wait it out? Or buy myself a vicious dog? Or maybe I could build an electric fence around the entire yard."

Rocky glanced out the kitchen window at the surrounding cornfields and pine woods. Off the beaten track? Was she kidding? "I mentioned issuing a preemptive strike."

"Meaning?"

"Meaning coming out just ahead of the Grand Teton's book with—"

"*Whose* book?"

"Sorry. The name she goes by is Binky Cudahy, but her nickname is—" he cleared his throat "—well, you get the idea."

"She's well endowed, I take it?" Sarah said dryly.

"Let's just say when the sun's directly overhead, her feet are in the shade." He thought he detected a twitch at the corners of her mouth, but he wasn't about to jeopardize any progress he might have made toward disarming her.

"Suppose you tell me the worst that can happen, and I'll decide whether or not I need to take evasive action."

Point by point, he laid out the facts. The book was compiled from material supplied by one Belinda aka Binky Cudahy. It included explicit firsthand accounts of a number of sordid parties involving the usual array of sex, drugs and booze. The only thing that made it worth the gutter press's attention was that the parties had included several Hollywood names as well as that of a young congressman who had once shown promise of being a rising star.

A star, perhaps, Rocky acknowledged silently, but never a statesman. Since the advent of television, intellect had become less a requisite for getting elected than having a marketable personality and the ability to generate good sound bytes. Sullivan had been glib, plus he possessed the kind of clean-cut good looks that had made him a favorite with women voters. Better yet, he'd had excellent connections. With the right handlers he might have gone far. Might eventually even have overcome the stigma of being J. Abernathy's son-in-law, if he hadn't screwed up. In Rocky's opinion, the jerk had deserved what had happened to him.

His widow didn't.

"How long will it take before it blows over?" she asked thoughtfully. Late-afternoon light cast tantalizing shadows on her elegant throat, triggering an aberrant reaction. Rocky found himself wondering how her skin would feel, smell, taste. Warm and slightly moist? Sweet or slightly salty?

Hauling his brain back in line, he said brusquely, "My guess, you'll have a week before and maybe another week after the book hits the stores. These postmortems never last long unless there's an ongoing investigation."

"Why did you bother to track me down and warn me?"

Toying with the salt shaker, he gave it some thought. When she put it to him that way, he didn't honestly know. Maybe because throughout all the floods and famines, the insurrections, revolutions and shaky peace negotiations he had covered in the years since sharing their single previous meeting, he had never quite forgotten a klutzy, embarrassed kid who had struck him as painfully lonely. She wouldn't want to hear it any more than he cared to admit it, but there it was. Considering the places he'd been, the things he had witnessed in the intervening years—including saying a final goodbye to his wife—it didn't make sense that he still remembered that one brief episode. That one vulnerable adolescent girl.

Raking back his chair, he rose and took his plate and cup to the sink. "Anything I can do before I leave?"

She appeared to consider it. "I don't suppose you'd care for a job as a handyman? No, don't answer, I couldn't afford you, anyway."

"You don't know my rates yet."

"Actually, I enjoy staying busy. I'll just go on tackling things one at a time and eventually everything will get done."

"By then it'll all need doing again." Rocky was aware of another conversation going on at another level. He wondered if she felt it, too.

I'm uneasy. I'm not quite sure why, but I wouldn't mind if you hung around a little longer.

Maybe I should. Maybe you need me but you're too proud to admit it.

Crazy. After six months of self-imposed solitude, now he was hearing voices inside his head. "Guess I'd better hit the road while there's still some daylight left," he said abruptly.

As they stood there sharing the awkward moment, it occurred to Rocky that she was taller than he remembered. She'd been skinny then, but not quite so fragile. Obviously the past few years had taken a heavy toll.

"Well...thank you again for warning me. And for running that reporter away. I truly doubt if any more will show up. Stan's gone, my father's not here and I've never done anything more newsworthy than smear cream cheese and asparagus on the shoes of a world-famous journalist."

"World-famous, huh? Move over Bret, Tony and Sam."

She followed him outside and he leaned down to pick up the hammer she'd dropped and placed it in her hand. "Show me how you use this thing."

"What?" She goggled at him.

Grinning, he turned back to the porch, to the swollen board she'd been trying to force back in place and nail. "Go ahead, hit the nail."

Looking at him as if he might have lost his mind—which was a distinct possibility—she adjusted her grip on the hammer and tapped the nail. It tilted, but didn't go in any deeper.

"Didn't you ever study physics?"

"No, I studied history, literature, art and music. Maybe I should have taken a class in carpentry."

He took the hammer from her hand, holding it an inch from the end of the handle instead of an inch from the business end, as she had. "I'm talking about leverage."

"Leverage I know about," she said, again with the funny little half smile he remembered so well. "As in, vote for my bill or I'll let the press know that you once ran over an endangered species and never bothered to report it."

He laughed and then he took her hand and placed it where his had been on the handle. At the feel of his hard, dry hand on hers, Sarah caught her breath and held it. "Hold it like this," he instructed. "No, don't choke up on it. Now go ahead, swing it and hit the nail. You'll never get the job done if you don't know how to use tools properly."

She tried it. Missed the nail, but hit the board with a resounding, satisfying whack. The smile she gave him hurt her face, but there was no holding back. "Oh, I see what you mean about leverage. Well…thank you again for the warning and the carpentry lesson. And the sandwich."

"My pleasure." He hesitated a moment, then touched her on the shoulder, wished her luck and was halfway down the front walk when a car turned off the state road into the lane.

No need to ask if it was someone she knew. Rocky could tell by the stricken look on her face that whoever it was, her visitor was about as welcome as another black eye. He waited a moment, studying the car and driver. Ten to one, it was another representative of the gutter press. If one of the buzzards had tracked her down, the rest of the flock wouldn't be far behind.

Swearing, he turned in his tracks and jogged back to where Sarah still stood on the porch. "Get inside, I'll handle it."

Without a word of protest, she went inside and watched through the screen door as a second car turned into the lane, slowed down and stopped behind the first. My God, she thought, that makes three. It never occurred to her to include Rocky.

Standing on the front steps, arms crossed over his chest, he was truly an impressive figure. Tall, muscular, but not grotesquely so—those measuring eyes and the juggernaut jaw alone would have stopped most people in their tracks.

With everything at stake—Kitty's future peace of mind, her own cozy cocoon, Sarah was amazed to find herself thinking more about the man himself than about the impending threat. Which said a lot about the effects of eleven months of self-imposed solitude, leavened with a few leftover adolescent fantasies.

To think she had begun to feel safe. She had taken such comfort in knowing that the ugliness couldn't reach her here. What possible connection could there be between a widow living alone in northeastern North Carolina, a baby in Virginia Beach and a couple of stale political scandals in Washington, D.C.?

It wasn't going to happen, not if she had to take on the entire fourth estate. She could handle whatever they wanted to dish out, as long as they kept Kitty out of it.

Halfway down the lane, the men talked—Rocky and a scraggly character she would have recognized anywhere as a reporter. Not the type from one of the major outlets, who knew to within an inch how far they could go without getting into trouble with the law. This was the muckraking type that peered into bedroom windows, pawed through garbage cans—the kind that might even use illegal means to get a hook on which to hang a story.

"Just stand back, you jerk," she muttered, shading her eyes against the lowering sun. "I've got a hammer and I know how to use it."

A beige van blocked the lane at the turnoff. Both front doors opened and two men stepped out and paused, apparently waiting to see how the creep with a scraggly beard and digital camera fared.

Evidently, whatever Rocky told him convinced him there was no story here, because he shrugged, climbed back into his car and began backing out the lane. Twice he nearly backed into the drainage ditch that bordered the cornfield, but eventually he made it to the end. The pair from the van got out and walked to meet him. The three men conferred briefly, then both vehicles backed out onto the dirt road and left in a cloud of dust.

Sarah stepped back outside. Rocky continued to watch from the middle of the lane until the dust settled, then turned back toward the house. Now, she supposed he would leave, too. He'd done his good deed—done several of them, in fact. Warned her, fed her, doctored her eye and showed her how to get better mileage from Aunt Emma's hammer. Not to mention driving off the bad guys.

"Who were they?" she asked as he rejoined her on the porch. As if she couldn't guess.

"Gutter press."

"I thought as much. They must be hard up for news if they thought anyone would be interested in me. Dullest woman in captivity."

"Captivity? Interesting choice of words." A quick smile warmed his ice-gray eyes to a remarkable degree. "Look at it from their point of view. It's not an election year, OPEC's behaving, there hasn't been a sinking, a crash, a protest or a strike lately. There's no hurricane on the charts, not so much as a tropical depression yet, no terrorist threats, no—well, you get the picture." He'd been about to say, no scandals.

"All the same, there must be something going on. Congress is back in session. Surely someone's larding a few bills."

As if he had every right, Rocky took her arm and steered her back inside. "You think these guys care about real news? Serious stories about real issues aren't what catch shoppers' attention when they're standing in line at the supermarket. Now, you take an asteroid with a message from Zeus, or a cross between a chicken and a three-headed snake—or a close-up of the senator's daughter, who happens to be a congressman's widow—who also happens to be sporting a three-ring shiner, and you've got an instant hit on your hands."

Sarah started to touch her swollen eye and thought better of it. "Oh, Lord, I hadn't thought about that."

What if Rocky hadn't been here? What if she'd

gone to the door and flashbulbs had started popping before she could get away?

How'd you get the shiner, Miz Sullivan?

Who's the new guy in your life, Sarah? Is it true you and your husband shared—

"I think we'd better heat up the coffee and have ourselves a conference."

Five

The conference never got off the launching pad. Sarah asked politely about his work. Rocky answered that he was on sabbatical. It sounded better than telling her he'd quit cold when Julie had died and hadn't been able to find the motivation to go back to work.

He asked if she had any plans to move back to Virginia or her father's retirement home on the Wye River. She told him that as soon as she caught up with her repairs and yard work, she intended to visit every place on the map within a day's drive with a name that intrigued her, starting with Waterlily, Swan Quarter, Spot and Mamie, and then branch out to those with names she couldn't pronounce.

Stalemate. Privacy was obviously a big issue with Sarah Mariah Jones Sullivan. Odd, Rocky mused, the way different people reacted to the presence of any representative of the media. It had been his experience that with some, the less they actually knew, the more they felt compelled to talk. With Sarah it was just the opposite. He'd thought he knew her—at least knew more about her than was generally known, far more than she would like for anyone to know. But the more he watched the subtle changes of expression in those calm hazel eyes, the more he realized that he didn't know her at all.

Still waters?

Maybe. What was that old line from a hit song a few decades back? "Deep down, she was shallow."

He'd be willing to bet that deep down, Sarah Mariah was even deeper. What, he wondered, lay under those still waters? Why would an attractive, sophisticated woman be content to live alone in a backwater community? Who—or what—was she hiding from? Or waiting for?

He could ask, but Sarah Mariah Jones Sullivan was not the kind of woman to open up to a stranger. And Roland "Rocky" Waters wasn't the kind of man to walk away from a mystery.

Stalemate number two.

Quickly Rocky scanned his mental file on the Jones family. If she'd been an abused child, some hint of it would have come out during the investigation. It was public knowledge that her father was a self-centered, unscrupulous scoundrel, but that didn't necessarily make him a rotten family man.

It was also a well-known fact, however, that he'd dragged his daughter with him to all kinds of public appearances, played the role of doting papa for the media, then shoved her aside to fend for herself. Usually—but not always—there was an aide whose job it was to look after her. A widower for some quarter of a century now, the senator golfed, played poker and drank, all in moderation and with unexceptional companions, so far as anyone knew. One of his closest friends was Clive Meadows, a lawyer-turned-lobbyist who happened to have a taste for obscenely young wives. At no time, however, had his name been linked to the senator's daughter. Going over the files, Rocky would have caught something like that.

Just the thought gave him an unpleasant feeling. Actually, the thought of Sarah and any man was surprisingly unsettling, possibly because she'd had such a raw deal her first time out of the gate.

And, yeah, he knew it was her first time. He had done his research well. No journalist went into a situation cold if he could help it.

She'd been kept on a leash, allowed to date in moderation during her senior year at a private girls' school. But even in college her male friends had been vetted by the senator or one of his close personal aides. Usually after half a dozen or so outings with any one guy, the boyfriend dropped out and another contender took his place. The senator, it appeared, hadn't taken any chances with what might turn out to be—and had, in fact been—a prime asset. The intelligent, attractive daughter of an influential politician, a young woman whose impeccable reputation had been closely guarded from the cradle on.

Talk about your feudal systems.

Still, his internal radar was bothering him. Could there be something else here? Something that hadn't been uncovered in any of the various investigations? "Sarah Mariah, tell me about—"

"Heavens, would you look at the time. I can't believe so much has happened since I went out to nail down that blasted board on the front porch."

Rocky interpreted the remark as his cue to leave. Now that he'd done what he'd come to do, there was no real reason to stay any longer. Next time he had an urge to do someone a favor, he wouldn't cut it quite so close. As it was, by the time he'd made up his mind to step in, it had almost been too late.

"I know you're busy. Well...you're probably on your way somewhere..." She looked at the clock, at the toaster and then stared out the window. "But if you'd like to, you could spend the night here, there's plenty of room. I'm not sure where the nearest motel is, but this time of year—tourist season, I mean—you might have trouble finding a room."

The beach season. He'd forgotten they were only a short distance from the Outer Banks. The invitation, coming as it had out of the blue, knocked him off balance for a moment.

He hadn't imagined it, then—that silent, subliminal exchange. "If any more reporters show up, don't answer the door and you won't have to answer any questions."

She nibbled on a ragged nail, then tucked her hand behind her, as if ashamed of getting caught in the act. Rocky felt a few defenses he didn't even know he possessed begin to crumble. "If you're sure you wouldn't mind, then I'd appreciate it," he said, and then had to scramble to rationalize hanging around in a place where watching the corn grow was probably the favorite pastime. "That way I could get an early start tomorrow. I, uh…I thought I'd look around while I'm in the area. Lot of history around these parts, I understand."

Wordlessly she nodded.

"Meanwhile, I can place a call or two and find out what's going on with the book so you'll have a heads-up. I doubt if you'll have any more trouble, though."

Rocky could only guess at whether or not he'd reassured her. The more she resorted to that polite little company smile—not the quick half smile he liked so much—the more certain he was that there was something going on here he didn't know about.

Not that it was any of his business. Not that he even had any particular interest, but when a guy went out of his way to do a good deed, the least he could do was hang around long enough to make sure it stuck.

Sarah stood, covered a yawn and murmured an apology. "I'll make up the front room for you. There are fresh towels on the back of the bathroom door. If you need anything else…"

How about some answers?

"No, that sounds great. I'll pull my car in off the road and bring in my bag, if you don't mind."

She made omelets for supper and dusted off a bottle of her great-aunt's homemade wine. Over the simple meal they talked about her situation—at least he did some genteel probing. The lady had learned a lot from her father about the art of obfuscation.

"Are you planning on living here permanently?" he asked after they cleaned up the few dishes and moved into what must once have been called a front parlor.

"I haven't done a lot of long-term planning yet."

"I suppose owning a house helps...financially, I mean."

She nodded and stared out the window at the cornfields that surrounded her house, the tops now gilded by the last gleam of sunset. "Wasn't there a movie a few years back about a baseball diamond in the middle of nowhere, and all these old baseball players coming out of a cornfield?"

"If you're thinking about those reporters, Sarah, it was only four guys. Okay, five, counting me. Don't let it spook you."

"I'm not spooked, I was only...oh, all right. I'll admit that if you hadn't showed up in time to warn me what was happening, I'd have been—well, I wouldn't have panicked, but I might have been—"

"A sitting duck."

"Exactly."

"Delighted to have been of service. Who farms your land?"

"It's been leased to the same farmer for years."

"Provides a pretty good income, huh?"

"Are you prying into my personal finances?"

"Who, me? Would a reporter pry?"

"I thought you said you weren't a reporter any longer."

He shrugged. "I'm not." He held out his hands, palms up. "See? No tape recorder, no notepad—I even left my laptop in the car. I'm not wired, but you could search me if you'd like to." His smile invited her to share the amusement. When she didn't, his own smile faded.

"Could you...write something and send it in if I changed my mind?"

"Do you want me to? There might still be time for a preemptive strike before Cudahy's launch date if we hurry. About all it would do, though, is knock some of the wind out of her sails." The more he thought about it, the more he thought it was a lousy idea.

Seated on a sofa that looked as if it might be padded with concrete, she slipped her hands under her thighs, stared down at the faded floral carpet and rocked from the waist. "No. No, thanks. I'll just ride it out."

"Your choice." He still had contacts. Getting her story out would have been no problem if she'd wanted to go that route. And while it wouldn't have enhanced his own career, or what was left of it—he'd never been that kind of a reporter—he would have done it for her sake, if she'd thought it would help.

There was a story here, all right, only she wasn't ready to open up. He might have lost his edge as a reporter, but that didn't mean all his instincts had shut down.

"I've been thinking of doing some writing, myself," she said after a wheezing old mantel clock struggled through nine asthmatic bongs.

"Is that so?" Oh, hell. She was going to write her own story. Maybe he'd read her wrong.

"I thought maybe a survival guide for aging boomers who want to opt out and live off the land? I mean, now that I know how to use a hammer effectively..." Her smile was the self-deprecating kind, so sweet, so tentative, that he wanted to...touch her. "Pretty silly, isn't it? I majored in English lit, minored in studio art.''

"Oh, I don't know—it sounds like something the back-to-earth types could use. Reading, painting and minor carpentry."

Rocky told himself that if he had half a grain of sense left, he'd be out of here by now, but what the hell—he could spare one more day.

He could spare a year, but he'd stay another day, maybe two, just until she was over her jitters. Then he'd leave, feeling righteous for having done a good deed for a woman who meant nothing to him personally, with no thought of any personal gain. The tricky part was going to be hanging on to his objectivity. That was only one of the puzzling aspects of this whole crazy affair.

You can handle it, dude. This isn't world politics, just one decent woman who was about to get caught in the flak.

Oh, yeah, he was a real Don Quixote.

Trying not to stare at the darkening bruise on her left eye, he was wondering why such a blemish didn't diminish her essential attractiveness, when the phone rang. Sarah made no move to pick it up.

"Sarah?"

"Let it ring."

"You know who it is?"

"Probably a salesman."

Probably not. He had a feeling she knew who was on the other end. He had a feeling she wasn't going to tell him, and that was just fine with him. He was already more involved than he'd planned on being.

After eight rings the phone stopped. A few minutes

later it started up again. This time it fell silent after five rings.

They stared at each other. He knew damned well she was no longer a vulnerable kid. She'd been through enough to have learned how to take care of herself. So why was it he felt this overwhelming compulsion to stay and fight her dragons?

Dragons? A handful of fourth-rate hacks?

Whatever had her so spooked, it was more than a few reporters, more than yesterday's scandals reheated and served up a second time.

Morning in the country was noisy. Crows, seagulls, somebody's rooster and the distant diesel growl of a piece of heavy equipment. Rocky's knowledge of farm life was negligible. He knew the difference between a milking machine and a disc harrow, but that was about as far as it went.

Hearing the sound of the shower, he lay on his back, arms crossed under his head, and absorbed the atmosphere. There was no central air. His room didn't boast a window unit, but with both windows open, it wasn't bad. He'd slept in far worse quarters.

Someone had pinged her window with a BB gun. He wondered if she'd noticed. Wondered if she'd noticed that one of the faded green shutters was barely hanging on by a single rusted hinge. God help her if she was no better on ladders than she was with a hammer. As long as he was here, he might as well check it out.

The shower shut off with a protest of pipes. Unbidden came the vision of a tall, thin woman with hair that could have used a professional cut—with a swollen thumb and a few scratches on the backs of both hands. With small breasts, cheekbones a model would kill for and a mouth that—

Oh, yeah. That mouth was beginning to claim a little too much of his attention. He might have lost some of his objectivity where world politics was concerned, but when it came to women, he was too old, too experienced and far too emotionally insulated to fall for a pair of soft, naked lips.

She was in the kitchen when, freshly shaved, his hair still wet from the shower, he joined her there. For one unguarded moment their eyes met over the yellow enameled table. The quick flair of interest in hers was gone almost before it registered, but Rocky knew he hadn't been mistaken.

Hmm. Interesting...

Not that he intended to explore any further than he had. Not that he thought she'd welcome it. "Smells good."

"Sit down. I didn't ask, but if you have a cholesterol problem, I have dry cereal."

"No problem." The table was set with the same old-fashioned dishes that clashed wildly with the yellow table. There was a toaster at one end, plastic place mats and paper napkins. On a shelf between two tall, narrow windows there was an overgrown vine in a jar and a few toothpicks in a hot-pepper-sauce bottle. He had a feeling both had been there long before Sarah took possession of her great-aunt's house.

Oddly enough, the place seemed to suit her, yet he knew for a fact that she'd been a privileged kid—in some ways. Needy as hell in others.

"If you've got a ladder, I can trade you a few

chores for last night's supper and this.'' He indicated the bacon and scrambled eggs she was dishing up.

"There's one in the shed. I fell off it and sprained my little finger last month trying to nail one of my shutters to the wall."

Sarah looked up in time to see the expression of— well, of something or other, on his face. "I know, I know, Grace is not my middle name."

"Your little finger?" He was grinning openly now. The voltage in a pair of pale-gray eyes set in a tanned, angular face, was potent enough to jumpstart a battleship. Heaven help any woman who got too close.

"I think I must have hit it on something coming down." She had to share his amusement. It was the one thing about her that no amount of ballet lessons and deportment classes had ever been able to remedy. "It's not that I'm uncoordinated so much as that my mind's usually on other things. I forget to watch where I'm going."

"Here's another hint for your survival guide. Whenever you're more than three feet off the ground, make certain your mind's on what you're doing."

"I landed in pine straw."

"Congratulations. We'll make a stunt woman out of you yet."

He dropped two slices of whole wheat into the toaster and opened a jar of Aunt Emma's homemade chunky apple preserves. "You do know your shutter's still dangling, don't you?"

"The hinges are so rusted I couldn't get the screws out."

"So you were going to what—nail it to the wall?"

"At least it would keep it from banging whenever the wind shifts."

"What about the BB hole?"

"In the window, you mean? Clear tape."

"Aha. There speaks a truly resourceful woman." He handed her a slice of toast, buttered and spread with preserves.

Rocky watched as she took a big bite and chewed thoughtfully. "I know," she said calmly after she'd swallowed. "At least, I'm finding out."

"What it is you're finding out?"

"How resourceful I am. Who I am. Who I want to be when I grow up. If I even want to grow up."

"Sounds like we've got us a mutual midlife crisis here. You want to join me in Never-Never Land?"

She laughed, and then he did, too, and when he complimented her on her cooking, she looked delightfully confused. "Well, I haven't had a whole lot to do lately but learn new things. Addie, our housekeeper, always did the cooking when I was growing up. Stan liked to eat out, and he never ate breakfast, anyway, even when he was home."

Back to ground zero. The wreckage of her marriage. Neither of them was ready to go there.

Nothing was said about his getting an early start. By late afternoon, after driving to Elizabeth City for hardware and making a couple of impulse buys while he was there, Rocky had replaced the windowpane and the rusted hinges on the west side of the house. There was a lot more that needed doing, but he reminded himself that her house was not his responsibility. He was merely earning his bed and board.

"I can't thank you enough," she said, standing on the ground and squinting up at the newly repaired blind. She was wearing jeans that looked as if they'd been left over from a sixties protest march. Maybe a protest of her own, he thought, amused.

"And for handling those reporters yesterday," she added earnestly.

"No problem. Small-time stringers. I doubt if they'll bother you again."

"Um...I don't remember seeing you at any of the hearings."

It was the first time they'd been mentioned directly. "I was mostly out of the country," he said, hoping she'd let it drop. He hadn't covered them personally, but he'd seen and heard enough. More than enough. On his frequent trips back to the States he'd been invited to air his opinion on a few Sunday-morning talk shows. He had declined. Media circuses left him cold, this one colder than most.

Except for the woman herself. There was a connection here that didn't make sense, but he'd learned never to dismiss his instincts. "Sarah, why do I get the feeling there's something you're not telling me?"

For a split second he thought he'd struck pay dirt, but she was no novice. "Not telling you? I thought anyone with a computer had instant access to everything about everybody. Let's see, now—age? Thirty-seven. Just last week, in fact. Weight? Somewhere between 110 and 117, depending on whether or not I remember to cut down on my salt intake. This is my real hair color and the only silicon on me is what I bring in on my shoes."

She was playing games. He recognized the ploy, but decided to let her run with it.

"I had an A-minus average through the first three years of college, but then it dropped to a C."

That would have been about the time she started seeing Sullivan.

"I like old-time fiddle music and opera, as long as I don't know the story and can make up my own to fit the music. I can play the harmonica pretty well—used to be able to, at least. I haven't tried in years."

He was grinning openly by now. She was a piece of work, all right. Great at playing defense, even if her only defense was facetiousness. Let's see how good she was at playing offense.

He gave her one she could hit out of the park. "I seem to remember reading that you did a lot of work with underprivileged children. Any ideas of looking for work in that area...when you're ready to move on, that is?"

"Do you want some coffee? There's about one cup left in the pot—I could add milk and ice it for you."

Struck out on an easy pitch. The fact that she hadn't even fanned it had to mean something. So now he knew where to start digging.

The trouble was, Sarah thought late that afternoon, that she enjoyed his company far too much. She had no business enjoying any man's company, much less that of a reporter. Or a journalist or a columnist or whatever you called a former political pundit who wasn't actively pursuing his career.

Of course, she only had his word that he wasn't.

What would he say if she told him about Kitty?

Would his first thought be the story, or the child's well-being? Would he think she was crazy for caring so much about a child she'd never even seen? One that proved beyond a doubt that her husband had been unfaithful?

For the sake of Kitty's future peace of mind, she couldn't take the risk. God knows what the Poughs would tell the child when she was old enough to ask about her father....

He was a kind, handsome man with a brilliant future, but unfortunately, darling, he died when you were too young to remember him.

For one brief moment Sarah wondered what Rocky would say if she told him the whole story—about the payments that were beginning to strain her modest resources. And the calls, always wanting to know if she couldn't send more. She was so afraid that if they kept on demanding more, and she kept insisting she couldn't send any more, they might go public. Not knowing what else to do, she'd taken to not answering her phone.

And on top of that, there was Clive and her father. Lord knows what those two wanted from her; she was afraid even to guess. Until she could come up with a good response, she preferred not to hear anyone's demands.

But, oh, how she wished she could walk into Rocky's arms, close her eyes and let the world disappear for one moment. He was the kind of man any woman would turn to instinctively in times of crisis, not because he had all the answers—or even a single answer—but because there were times when a woman simply needed to be held. No questions asked, no answers required—just the luxury of nonjudgmental physical comfort.

Sooner or later—probably sooner—she would have to leave here and find herself a job. Unless you were a farmer, there was no work to be had in Snowden. According to Aunt Emma, when the postmistress had retired before Sarah had even been born, there'd been no one under sixty-five to take her place, and so Snowden had lost its post office.

So maybe she could become a postmistress.

And go through a civil service exam?

No, thanks. There had to be a better way.

Rocky was on the ladder replacing the hinges on the east side of the house. For a reporter, he was surprisingly practical. It had never even occurred to her to plan her outside work around whichever side of the house the sun happened to be on. All afternoon she'd struggled under a blazing sun to pull down the rest of the grapevines.

"Why not use a weed killer, wait until they turn brown, then get rid of them once and for all?" He'd come up behind her so quietly she hadn't heard him.

Sweat dripping off the tip of her nose, she replied irritably, "Well, I guess it just never occurred to me."

Reaching past her, he grabbed a double handful of vine and pulled. Sarah turned and added her weight to the task, and suddenly, the huge, entangled vine gave way. Sarah staggered back.

Laughing, Rocky caught her before she could fall. "Easy there, we don't want anything else sprained, broken or bruised."

"Believe it or not," she said, hastily removing herself from his arms, "I've never broken a single bone."

"Then don't start by breaking one of mine."

She was still standing so close she could feel the heat of his body—smell the healthy male sweat. *Move, Sarah, move!*

"Don't move," he murmured. They were mere inches apart. With one hand he reached toward her hair. As his face came closer she could see the splinters of gold in eyes she had thought were pure silver. Her own eyes closed. Her lips softened expectantly.

"Gotcha!" He exclaimed triumphantly as he tugged at a handful of her hair.

Sarah slapped at his hand, feeling utterly mortified at what she'd been thinking. Expecting.

Oh, all right, *wanting!*

Glaring at the tiny worm he held dangling from a web between his fingers, she shuddered and started to back away.

Rocky caught her by the shoulders. "Whoa, not yet," he said softly. "There's something else we need to take care of."

And heaven help her, she stood there, dumb as a post, and lifted her face yet again.

Six

If she'd had an analytical mind, Sarah might have wondered how being kissed by one particular man could be so different from any other man in the world. Not that she'd kissed all that many men, but Rocky certainly wasn't the first. She'd been married, for heaven's sake! Why was her belly doing flip-flops, her pulse going haywire, just because she was being kissed for the first time in ages? The romance setting?

Hardly. Here she was, wearing her rattiest yard-working clothes, on the hottest day of the summer, knee-deep in a dusty tangle of wild grapevines—with a full-blown shiner, of all things—thinking thoughts she'd almost forgotten how to think!

Even the feel of his bristly jaw against her sun-flushed skin sent tingles all through her body. The feel of her nipples beading against her bra was almost painful. Wrapping her arms around his neck, she clung, savoring the moment. The thrill of his hard male body against hers. The way he tasted, the clean, fresh scent of his skin, his shirt.

You are so pathetic, *Sarah Mariah! Are you so starved for romance that you're turned on by* laundry soap?

Obviously she was.

When his lips finally left hers and he pressed her face against his shoulder, she breathed in deeply, waiting for the symptoms to fade. Was that his thudding heart or hers? His raspy, uneven breathing or hers? It had been so long....

Bitter memories raced back to haunt her. Stan had wanted to make love to her that last night. For the sake of appearances, they had stayed together during the trial. He'd been so distraught, so fragile, she'd been afraid of what he might do if she left him then. After weeks of coexisting in virtual silence while she'd made arrangements to sell the house and file for separation, he had come to her room one night and begged her to forgive him, to let them be together again. Knowing all she'd known by then, she couldn't bear for him to touch her, much less...*that.*

He'd gone down on his knees beside her bed and, with his arms around her waist, he had lowered his head to her lap and sobbed about how he'd been lured into the wild parties.

It had all started so innocently. First, drinks with a few big supporters. Then dinner with a small group of influential activists. After that, he'd been invited to a private party at the Georgetown home of a big contributor. Strictly stag. Not the sort of party a man invited his wife to attend, someone had joked.

There'd been party girls. It had never occurred to him that a few of them might have been underage. None of it had been his fault—someone must have put something in his drink, he'd claimed tearfully. He had sworn over and over that he was sorry, so very sorry—that he'd learned his lesson and it would never happen again.

It hadn't. He'd been killed the very next night. The unofficial verdict had been suicide. Since then Sarah had borne her own share of guilt, telling herself that if she hadn't been so unforgiving—if she'd somehow been a better wife in the first place, it would never have happened.

Now, lost in an unwanted rush of memories, she must have sighed, because Rocky stepped away, his hands still on her shoulders. "I'm fresh out of apologies. If you want me to leave, just say so."

She should. Not because of what had just happened, because she'd all but begged him to kiss her. But because he was a dangerous stranger, and she obviously wasn't quite as intelligent and independent as she'd hoped.

And because her face was throbbing again, and she was in no condition to deal rationally with any man, much less one who had such a powerful effect on her brain, not to mention her hormones.

"Could we please just not talk about it?" All right, so she was also a coward.

His gaze moved over her, making her painfully aware that not only was her face a mess, but she was wearing a T-shirt that dated from her college days and jeans she'd bought at a thrift shop—that her hair hadn't seen a stylist in more than a year, that it was tangled, decorated with twigs, pine straw and all manner of insects.

Nodding briefly, he said, "Sure. Why don't I finish the blinds while you catch your breath? You might want to put something on those scratches."

"Why don't you let me decide what I'm going to do?" she snapped.

So much for thirty-seven years of decorous behavior. *Will the real Sarah Mariah please stand up?*

Without another word, Rocky turned and headed for the shed. Sarah glared at his backside, the wide shoulders in a sweat-stained shirt, tapering down to a pair of narrow hips that were faithfully delineated by a pair of butt-worn jeans. Why was it that when men dressed in work clothes and got all hot and sweaty they looked perfectly delicious, while women just looked hot and sweaty?

If some self-appointed Sir Galahad insisted on riding to the rescue, why did it have to be the one man in all the world—well, other than Clint Eastwood—that she'd ever fantasized about?

Rocky swore under his breath. What the devil was he doing hanging around so long, anyway? So much for his noble intentions. The damned woman had taken advantage of him. She had no business looking at him that way, like she might wither and die if she didn't get kissed.

What was a guy supposed to do? He didn't want to hurt her feelings. And kissing her—well, black eye or not, it wasn't exactly a chore.

Okay, so he might have thought about it a few

times. Might even have wondered what she'd be like in bed—whether those decorous manners she'd practiced all her life would be in force behind closed doors. If she'd be wild and uninhibited in bed—or funny and sweet and klutzy.

Whatever else she was, she was an attractive woman, and he was a normal guy. The fact that he hadn't been with a woman sexually in a few years had nothing to do with it. He would never use Sarah that way.

Over the years there had been a few brief liaisons of a strictly physical nature. Nothing even faintly meaningful, because in spite of everything, he had never ceased to feel married. Which meant that whatever release he'd managed to find had been mixed up in his mind with guilt.

Hell of a thing, lusting after a woman he was trying to protect. Maybe they were both carrying too much baggage. He had come here with the best intentions in the world, but somewhere along the line he'd managed to misplace his objectivity. It wasn't the first time that had happened, which was one of the reasons he'd decided to hand in his resignation. Years of emotional exhaustion didn't leave a man much to work with.

Propping the ladder against the side of the house, he jabbed the feet into the ground to secure it and was halfway to the top before he remembered that he'd left his tools on the ground.

Oh, yeah, he was losing it, all right.

By the time he finished replacing the hinges and the hooks and eyes that held the shutters back against the wall, Rocky had managed to rationalize the situation to his own satisfaction.

With the old scandals about to be revived, even briefly, Sarah was the logical target of speculation. The basic story—the what, who, where and when—had long since been hashed out in public. With the chief perpetrator gone, the only remaining mystery was what had happened to the victim. In this case, the perp's widow. Where was she? Had she remarried? Taken lovers? Adopted her late husband's lifestyle? Would she turn up gracing the centerfold of some slick men's magazine?

Rocky had a feeling Sarah Mariah wouldn't like being considered a victim any more than she would like being tarred with the same brush as either of the two men in her life. As the self-designated good guy, he was in a position to ensure that that didn't happen. Or at least that she didn't suffer any personal embarrassment. And since he was already on the scene, he might as well hang around a few more days until things settled down. It wasn't as if there were any great demands on his time. He'd been in what was technically known as a deep blue funk for the past six months. This just might be the handle he needed to pull himself out.

The fact that they happened to find each other sexually attractive shouldn't be a problem, now that it had been brought into the open and acknowledged. They were both old enough to handle a mature, platonic relationship. With her quirky mind and his inquiring one, they could surely find ways of passing the time without getting into trouble until the hue and cry wore off and it was safe for him to leave. His stated plan of spending a night, then touring the area, had been mutually disregarded.

The phone was ringing some half hour later when he went back inside. Sarah had dragged the vines over to the side of the yard, left them there and was evidently upstairs showering. Rocky answered on the fourth ring.

"Sullivan residence."

Long pause. "Who the devil are you?"

"Friend of the family."

"Put my daughter on."

Rocky would have recognized the arrogance even if the man hadn't identified himself as Sarah's father. "She can't take a call at the moment, but I'll have her get back to you as soon as she's available." Grinning, he hung up on J. Abernathy Jones's squawk of protest.

And then he headed upstairs and rapped on the bathroom door. Hearing the sound of the shower cut off, he said, "Sarah? Call your dad."

Before he could turn away the door opened a crack. Sarah's face, purple shiner and all, emerged in a cloud of scented steam. "Call *who?*"

"The senator."

She started to shut the door, then opened it again. So far as he could tell—which wasn't far, just a glimpse of wet, gleaming shoulder—she didn't have on a stitch of clothing. "Did he say what he wanted?"

"Now, what do you think he wanted?" Might as well play a little devil's advocate as long as he was enjoying the view. Another day and her shiner would reach the apogee and start to fade. He figured the yellow-green stage might take another week, give or take, depending on how quickly she healed.

She chewed on her lower lip, and he was tempted

to say, If it needs chewing, let a real man tackle the job.

"I'm thirty-seven years old, for heaven's sake. I don't have to report to my father."

She looked wet and worried and funny and sexy, a dangerous combination. Rocky tried to ignore his body's eager response. "Shall I pass on the message when he calls back?"

"No, I—would you mind looking behind my bedroom door and handing me my robe? I was in such a hurry to scrub off any ticks and redbugs I forgot."

Glad of a mission—any mission—he turned away. Her room was at the opposite end of the hall from his, but it was a short hallway. Overcoming a reporter's natural curiosity, he located the cotton robe on a hook behind the door. In one sweeping glance, he took in the plain white cotton curtains, the plain white spread on the painted iron bed—and the desk. A guy could hardly be blamed for possessing finely honed powers of observation. It was an occupational hazard.

Mentally he filed away the details—the portable typewriter, the jar of ballpoints, another jar of paintbrushes and colored pencils. Feeling noble, he resisted the impulse to glance through the untidy stack of papers beside the manual typewriter and headed back to the bathroom, carrying the blue-flowered bathrobe.

He rapped on the door and held it out. "Any message in case he calls before you come downstairs?"

Sarah's hand, displaying a freshly applied assortment of strip bandages, reached through the door and took the robe. "Tell him—tell him I'm fine and I'll talk to him in a few weeks."

"Right."

"No, better yet, how about taking the phone off the hook?"

"Sarah, if you've got a problem with your old man, you can handle it yourself. Protecting ladies from the gutter press is one thing. Refereeing a father-daughter match is something else."

The bathroom door swung wide. She had toweled her hair until it stood out around her face in a wild tangle and tugged the robe on over a still-damp body. Later he told himself it was the look of her, all steamy and untidy, with that glorious purple shiner, that short-circuited his brain, allowing impulse to override intellect. Hands braced on the door frame, he leaned forward and touched her lips with his.

Funny thing—*scary* thing—somewhere in the back of his mind Rocky sensed that the kiss was only partly sexual. There was something more involved....

At the moment, however, he wasn't feeling particularly analytical. He knew only that he could no more resist kissing her than he could resist the laws of gravity.

"Well," she breathed long moments later, backing away to stare at him through the open bathroom door.

"My thoughts exactly," he said, which was an outright lie. If she knew what he was thinking, she'd be out of there like a shot, bare feet, wet hair and all.

Because once again he was wondering what she'd be like in bed. Like interference from a distant radio station, the thought kept intruding on his best intentions. There was a basic honesty about her that was enormously appealing, and that was the scary part. There was just too damn much about the woman that appealed to him.

Before he could make another mistake, he left. He was halfway down the stairs when he heard the bathroom door close. *Get it in gear, Waters. You've got a brain—use it!*

There was only one telephone in the house, an old rotary dial model. He could understand why someone might not want to be all that accessible. There'd been times over the past few years when he'd wanted to shout to the world, "Just leave me the hell alone!"

But for a woman living alone in the middle of a cornfield surrounded by forest, with the roof of the nearest neighbor barely visible, it was a different matter. What if she fell and hurt herself? With Sarah, that was a distinct possibility.

What if she had prowlers?

A cell phone would be the quickest fix, but only if she would remember to keep it close by. On second thought, maybe extensions in the kitchen, bathroom and bedroom would be the way to go. He could see to having the jacks installed before he left. He'd known a few people who were intimidated by cell phones. Sarah didn't strike him as a technophobe, but then, who else would use a manual portable typewriter when everyone else in the civilized world used a computer?

When he pictured the stack of papers on her desk, a sliver of curiosity flashed through his mind. He promptly stamped it out. *Not your business, Waters.*

Maybe she actually was working on the survival guide she'd mentioned. He'd thought she was joking at the time, but the more he thought about it, the more plausible it sounded. The lady had survived some pretty nasty stuff, and evidently she'd done it her way.

Maybe he could add a couple of chapters, himself. How to survive marriage without a wife? He had eventually found closure—peace, of a sort, but it hadn't been easy.

As for how to survive cynicism, the loss of ideals and the gradual disintegration of a career, he was still working on that chapter in his life. At the moment he didn't have a single opinion on politics, issues of national significance or world affairs that couldn't be summed up in a classified ad.

Oh, yeah...they were a pair, all right.

After leaving the hardware store in Elizabeth City that morning he'd located a newsstand and bought a selection of papers. Now he picked up the *Virginian-Pilot* and skimmed the headlines above the fold. Next he turned to the sports section and was about to settle down and catch up on the Braves' series when the phone rang again.

"I'm not in," Sarah called from upstairs.

"You're asking me to lie for you?" Tipping back his chair, he could see her at the head of the stairs. Dressed in more respectable white jeans and a baggy green T-shirt, she was worrying her lower lip again.

"I probably shouldn't ask you to do that. I'm sorry."

"Moot point. Whoever was on the other end just gave up."

Slowly she came down the stairs. She was barefoot. She had elegant feet—long, narrow and shapely, with pale, unpolished nails. It occurred to Rocky, not for the first time, that a brain could atrophy from lack of exercise.

"I guess it was the senator again."

She called him the senator. Not Father, not Dad or Daddy. It was a small thing but telling. He stood, waited for her to sit, and when she wandered over to the front window instead, he picked up the sports page again. Halfway through a piece on National League pitchers, he gave up and went back outside.

Even silent and still as a marble statue, the lady made waves.

It was late that afternoon when a car negotiated the crooked, rutted lane and pulled up in front of the house. Rocky was on the front porch fastening down the swollen board Sarah had been trying without success to repair. He stood and called quietly through the door, "Sarah, looks like you've got more company."

"Can you get rid of whoever it is?" He'd left her defrosting the old refrigerator. Messy job, but at least it was one she could probably handle without coming to too much grief.

"You might want to come outside. I don't think it's more reporters this time."

The driver got out and opened the back door of the black, late-model luxury sedan. Half expecting to see J. Abernathy emerge, it took Rocky several moments to identify the elderly man who stepped out. R. C. Detweiller, top aide and general dogsbody to the senator.

He stood and waited for the man to approach. "Detweiller," he said noncommittally. He'd met the man on several occasions. When there was no response, he introduced himself. "Rocky Waters. Formerly with Graves Worldwide and CCB, currently unaffiliated."

He stuck to the literal truth in case the man had a retentive memory.

"Waters." The desiccated individual wearing a three-piece suit on the hottest day in August looked as if had just smelled something unpleasant. "Is Mrs. Sullivan here?"

"I'm here, R.C." Sarah spoke from behind him, then stepped out onto the porch. She didn't invite him inside, even though Detweiller clearly looked as if he'd expected her to. She waved to the driver and called out, "Hi, Ollie. You're looking fit."

To Detweiller she said, "You might as well go back and tell my father I'm fine, I don't need anything from him, and if I ever do, I'll be sure to call."

Sarah hated having to air her personal affairs in public, but she wasn't about to let her father's right-hand man get a foot inside her door. He'd go back and describe every detail, right down to the puddle of melting ice on the kitchen floor. He was staring now in horror at her black eye. "Sarah Mariah, you haven't forgotten that your father's birthday is coming up, have you?"

Seven

"You're asking for trouble," Rocky said quietly as they stood together on the front porch and watched the dusty black luxury sedan turn off the lane onto the dirt road.

"I don't have to ask, trouble always seems to find me."

"Want to go shopping for a birthday card?"

She offered him a wintry smile.

"Sarah, sooner or later you're going to have to deal with the man. He's your father, whatever else he is."

"Do you know, I used to wonder about that? We're nothing at all alike," she mused. "I didn't notice so much before Mama died, but after that... Well, of course I was too old for the usual fantasies—you know, being left on a doorstep or being the secret child of foreign royalty. But I did think maybe I might've been one of those—you know, donor babies? Um—artificial insemination?" She slapped a hand over her face and groaned. "Why am I telling you all this?"

"Because the man who raised you as his daughter, whether it was technically true or not, is old and having a birthday and you're his only child. You're trying to talk your way out of a few perfectly natural guilt feelings."

"Are all reporters as irritating as you are?"

"We're a pretty shabby bunch, all right." Her elbow was there, right beside him, so he hooked his arm through the crook and tugged her against his side. "Ever look at the senator's eyes?"

She frowned up at him but didn't pull away. So he said, "Same mixture of gold, gray, green and brown."

She made a rude noise. "So? Billions of people have hazel eyes."

"Large, slightly tilted, set under perfectly arched brows. Of course, the senator's eyes are pretty well hidden by now unless he's had plastic surgery since I last saw him."

"Oh, I know he's my real father. I never actually doubted it, not down deep. Mama would have told me if there'd been anything—irregular. About me, I mean. My birth."

"How old is he? He's looked about the same age for as long as I can remember."

"Seventy-seven. I think. It's the hair. I'm not sure, but I think he might have had it bleached white when it started to go gray, and I do know he had at least one face-lift. He was supposed to be on an extended foreign trade thing. He is so vain."

Rocky considered reminding her of her filial obligation again, but it wasn't his place. Besides, in light of what the old pirate had put her through—put his entire constituency through, not to mention his country—he didn't deserve a dutiful daughter.

"We've never been big on birthdays. When I was little, Mama used to take me and my two best friends to the zoo and then out for burgers and cake. The year before she died—the year I turned thirteen—she treated us to makeovers. Professional manicures, hairstyles, makeup—the works. We giggled the whole time, and felt oh, so grown-up. Then we went home and stayed up all night watching videos and pigging out on pizza and milk shakes and birthday cake. Of course, the senator had no part in any of these birthday bashes. Mama used to sign his name to whatever gift she gave me, but he couldn't have cared less. Birthdays never interested him, unless it was someone important."

The implication being that she wasn't. Why wasn't he surprised?

The phone rang before the dust had settled out on the road. Evidently R.C. had lost no time in getting back to his employer. After five rings Sarah muttered something surprisingly profane and stalked inside, slamming the door behind her.

"All right, all right," she practically shouted into the receiver. She knew the routine. First her father would send one of his minions to soften her up, then he'd try another tactic. This time he'd called personally, sent in the troops when she refused to answer, and now that he thought he'd softened her up sufficiently, he was going to try again.

"Sarah Mariah?" When had he begun to sound so old? He'd always used his syrupy baritone voice the way he used his silver hair, his courtly mannerisms—even his family. To create an impression. Now his voice sounded querulous, and he had no family left. Only Sarah.

She tried not to feel guilty, but only partly succeeded. "Yes, Father." Closing her eyes, she took a deep breath. Damn him—damn the whole Washington mess—she hadn't been able to work on Kitty's story in days. She had finished the drawings, but she hadn't had time to finish the story.

"I'm having a small celebration next week and I want you to come home."

"Happy birthday, Father. I am home." She wasn't about to give an inch. She knew him too well. At the first sign of weakness, the battle was over. She had lost too many times ever to surrender without putting up a fight.

"It'll be a quiet celebration, naturally. I'm afraid I'm not up to anything more strenuous. Of course, if your mother were still here, God rest her soul, it might be a different matter. Having family around to brighten the home gives a man strength."

Since when? she wanted to ask. His voice actually quavered. Sarah could picture him wiping away a tear and hardened herself against being swayed. When bullying failed, he played the obligation card. Piety was the last resort, but there wasn't a pious bone in his body, and they both knew it.

"The river house is your home, not mine, Father. Why don't you invite a few friends to come fish and play golf and cards with you? You really don't need me."

She didn't know what his household staff consisted

of now, or if he could even afford to hire anyone. She did know better than to let herself be talked into anything. He was good at it—he was superb—but she knew him too well.

Carefully, she hung up the phone on his arguments. She was still standing there, her back rigid with resentment, when Rocky came inside. At the same moment that she became aware of his presence behind her, she felt his hands close over her shoulders, warm and comforting. Instinctively she tipped her head back against his shoulder. If ever a woman needed a friend—a nonjudgmental friend—it was when guilt and doubts and fears were all mixed up in her mind with lust and curiosity and… "Aah," she whispered.

He began to knead the tense muscles. Neither of them spoke a word. Magic hands manipulated the knots in her shoulders, working their way toward her neck. His thumbs reached up and stroked the sides of her throat until she went limp, and then he pulled her back against him and held her there. Simply held her, his arms around her waist, her head tipped back on his shoulder, his cheek resting on her hair.

"How do you feel about seafood?" His raspy baritone reverberated all the way to the soles of her feet, and her mind raced back to their first meeting.

"Are we talking guppy filets?"

He laughed aloud then, his warm breath stirring through her hair. "Don't you ever forget anything?"

"Only important things. Trivia stays with me forever."

"Half an hour or so and we can be at the beach. Want to gamble on finding a vacant table?"

"Deal!" she crowed instantly.

* * *

Sarah couldn't believe how good it felt to get away. With the vacation crowd at its peak, she would be just one of the hoard. And if there happened to be a reporter around—other than Rocky, that was—he'd be far more interested in the sand-sculpture contests, surfing competitions and the hang gliders on Kill Devil Hills than in an almost-middle-aged widow who happened to be slightly connected to a couple of old scandals.

Say, aren't you congressman whatsisname's widow? What do you think of Ms. Cudahy's book? Have you read it yet? Are you going to sue the publisher?

It probably wouldn't be the first time the paparazzi had tried to stir up the coals of an old scandal when they ran out of fresh material. She hadn't read the damn book, didn't intend to and didn't want to hear another word about it. As for suing, what grounds did she have? There was no libel involved, so far as she knew. The whole mess might have died a natural death if Stan hadn't broken down in the most public place—the house floor, with the cameras rolling, no less—and confessed his part of the whole sordid affair.

Naturally the press had jumped on it like flies on roadkill, but in the end, not even confession and public humiliation had been enough to assuage his guilty conscience.

"How do you feel about raw bars?"

Glad of the diversion, she replied, "In a word? Yuk."

They were listening to one of Rocky's CDs, something smooth and heavy and vaguely familiar as they drove onto the Currituck Sound Bridge. He was humming along with the haunting refrain. Sarah would have figured him for soft rock or jazz. So much for her judgment.

They found a restaurant that looked well patronized without being too crowded. He pulled in, switched off the engine and turned to face her. "Look, if you change your mind at any time, we can just get up and walk out, okay? If you feel the least bit uncomfortable, just say the word."

"Oh, for heaven's sake, it's not like I was a celebrity or anything. I doubt if one out of ten million people even know I exist. We're not in Washington now, or even Virginia or Maryland."

"We're not in Kansas now, Toto," he said with a lopsided grin. "Point taken."

Once inside, he drew the hostess aside and spoke a few quiet words. The stylish middle-aged woman palmed the bill, and after one quick glance at Sarah's glorious shiner, which no amount of makeup would completely disguise, led them over to a candlelit table for two overlooking the ocean.

"Oh, this is wonderful! And we didn't even have reservations, can you believe our luck?" Wearing a sleeveless ankle-length cotton dress in a splashy red-and-white print she managed to look cool, sophisticated, yet very much like a kid on Christmas morning. Watching her face glow with excitement, Rocky reminded himself that this was a woman who'd been holed up alone in the middle of a cornfield for nearly a year. Given another few weeks, she might even have welcomed the press.

"This is great, it's just perfect!" she whispered. Leaning over, she peered out the window, watching a lazy surf lap the flat, sandy shore. "I must say, you do have the most marvelous ideas!"

For the next few minutes Sarah studied the menu while Rocky studied the woman.

Odd, the way different women could affect a man. Feature by feature she was nothing out of the ordinary. Yet, even with a few minor flaws—such as the black eye and half a dozen or so awkwardly placed cowlicks—she struck him as one of the loveliest women he'd ever met.

It had been Julie's looks he'd noticed first. Any man would. She could have made it as a model, easily, if she hadn't been more interested in getting her degree. They'd both wanted kids, Julie because she'd come from a large family, he because he'd come from a long line of foster homes. They'd planned to wait a few years, find an affordable place in the country to raise a family—and then suddenly it was too late.

Too late...

"Do you mind if I order the seafood platter and don't eat everything? I hate waste. My great-aunt— the one who gave me her house? She always used to say, 'Remember the poor starving children,' when I didn't clean off my plate, but I hate to eat too much."

"My wife would have liked your great-aunt."

And there it was. "Your...wife?"

"Her name was Julie. She died this past February after a long illness." It was all he intended to say. Hadn't intended to say that much, but suddenly he'd heard himself bringing Julie into the conversation, as if she'd needed to be there.

Sarah reached across the table and covered his hand with hers. "I'm sorry."

Those expressive eyes of hers said more than her words. He nodded and glanced down at his menu, forestalling questions he wasn't ready to hear, much less try to answer. It might have been easier if he'd been indifferent to her. Unfortunately, he was attracted not only to her body, but to her mind. Lust and like were a volatile combination.

On assignment in a war-ravaged country a few years ago he'd had to make his way through a minefield. What he was feeling now differed only in degree. Closing a door in his mind, he smiled across the table. "Why don't we order a selection of appetizers and then share a seafood platter?"

If there was a hidden analogy there, he was pretty sure it escaped her. Actually, there wasn't. At least, not intentionally.

"If we overdo it, we'll head for the beach and walk it off." He regretted the offer as soon as the words were spoken. *What the devil were you thinking about, Waters? A moonlight stroll on the beach with a beautiful woman?*

Well, hell—he could hardly rush her through dinner, then race back to Snowden, dump her out and hightail it back to his empty apartment in Chevy Chase.

She nodded, her smile just a little more guarded, a little less eager than it had been only moments ago. Which made him feel churlish. It was hardly her fault that something inside him that had been frozen for nearly seven years was beginning to thaw. Or that the thawing process was so painful.

They ate a variety of seafood, boiled, broiled and fried. They drank wine, probably a mistake, but the sound of Sarah's laughter as the meal progressed was enough to make up for any reservations he might have had. A long, leisurely walk on the beach with the wind blowing in his face should take care of any residual effects before they headed home. So what if he was rationalizing? As for the slight buzz he was feeling now, Sarah's laughter was more than enough to maintain that.

The tide was out, the beach flat and surprisingly uncrowded—perfect for walking. Arm in arm, carrying their shoes, they walked silently for the first few hundred feet, then paused to watch the moon emerging from the black waters of the Atlantic. Sarah told herself that someday she was going to show Kitty this same moon and the path it made, like a magic golden highway.

Holding hands, they talked very little, each content to absorb the beauty and peace of the moment. It was an oddly satisfying silence. Surprisingly comfortable. Reaching a place where erosion had narrowed the beach so that they would have had to pick their way past obstacles—parts of a boardwalk and the foundation of a cottage—Rocky paused, nodded back toward the way they had come. Without a word they turned, both smiling but silent, as if recognizing that as long as they didn't allow the real world to intrude, they were safe.

Then Sarah, still watching the rising moon, caught her foot on something half-buried in the sand and would have fallen if Rocky hadn't held on to her. Embarrassed, she allowed him to dust the sand off her foot and examine it for damage. "You think I'm a klutz, don't you? Well, I'm really not. Sometimes I just don't notice things when I'm thinking about something else."

"The old absentminded professor defense. Oh, yeah, I've heard that one before. So what lofty thoughts were you thinking that caused you to trip over a fully visible eight-by-eight timber?"

"If you really what to know, I was picturing a tiny yellow boat sailing off along a streak of yellow moonlight with a little yellow-haired girl at the helm and wondering what color the life preservers would be."

He stared at her for a full ten seconds. "Uh-huh. That's what I thought you were thinking."

The moon was bright enough that Rocky could see her expression clearly. She looked like a kid who'd been caught sampling the frosting with a finger. "Sarah? Is there something you're not telling me?"

"Of course there is. What do you want to hear first, that two of my teeth are crowns? That in college I made it a policy to read every banned book I could get my hands on? That I wish I'd had room tonight to try that lime-fig cake? Or that wine always makes me sleepy, and I'm afraid I'll snore on the way home?"

"Sarah, Sarah, Sarah..." As a klutz she was appealing. As a belligerent klutz, she was purely irresistible.

Blame it on the wine—blame it on the moonlight—blame it on the woman. Before sanity could set in Rocky gathered her to him, anchored his feet in the sand and lowered his face to hers.

She tasted of coffee. Smelled of sea, Sarah and Shalimar. It was a heady combination. "Oh, Sarah,

Sarah, what am I going to do about you?" Rocky whispered against fragrant wisps of windblown hair. He was embarrassingly aroused, and there was no way he could disguise the fact.

As one, they moved higher on the beach, to the dune line. Sea oats brushed past as he lowered her carefully onto the dry sand, still warm from the day's sun, then came down beside her.

"Put your head on my arm," he said. "You'll get your hair full of sand."

"I don't mind, but I do hate sandy sheets. Maybe I can wear a hat to bed tonight."

Stroking her side, his hand moved over her hips, along her waist, to her arm and then her breast. Rocky chuckled softly, picturing her lying nude in her bed, wearing that hideous straw hat she claimed was her gardening hat but never wore.

"Any woman who can make a man laugh and make him want to jump her bones at the same time is more valuable than, uh—rubies and pearls."

"Did you just make that up or did you read it in a book somewhere?"

"What do you think?" His lips traced a path from her ear to the hollow at the base of her throat. He shifted her so that she was lying on top of him—the least he could do, since he hadn't thought to bring a blanket. It had never occurred to him because this shouldn't be happening. Neither of them was ready for it. "Nowhere near ready," he murmured as he captured the sandy back of her head and lowered her mouth to his.

If he were any more ready, he wouldn't be able to move. Making out on the beach like a horny adolescent? Getting turned on by a zany, klutzy, sexy woman at his age?

Her breasts were small. She wasn't wearing a bra. Panties and a dress. Total nudity couldn't have been any more arousing. Her nipples peaked against his palms, sending a message to his groin.

Slowly he withdrew his hands from under her dress. Her skin was gritty—so was his. Hardly optimum conditions for what this was leading up to. Clasping her face in his hands, he brushed his lips back and forth over hers, savoring the drag of moist softness.

"I guess this wasn't too smart," he said.

"I guess it wasn't," she agreed.

He could hear the rueful smile in her voice. "It's been a while since I've gone for a moonlight walk on a beach. I forgot to bring a blanket."

"Just as well. I never go to bed on a first date," she said, trying unsuccessfully to make light of what had just happened. What was still happening. She rolled off his body and sat up. Heels dug in, knees sprawled apart, she proceeded to brush the sand from her hair.

By the time they reached the parking lot and he helped her in, brushed off her feet and slid her sandals on, they had both more or less regained their composure.

More or less.

You're forty-four years old, man. A little restraint might be in order.

"I thought I might head back home tomorrow," he said as they rolled back onto the bridge. "We've probably seen the last of the tabloid press, and the legitimate guys aren't going to bother you."

"I expect you're right," she said quietly, and Rocky told himself it was only his imagination that she sounded...

Stricken.

Eight

After a restless night, not entirely due to the grit on her pillow, Sarah opened her eyes and lay there, wondering if it was too late to salvage her dignity. Watching patterns of sunlight dance across the ripples in old floral wallpaper, filtered through the pines outside, she went over all that had happened—or so nearly happened—on the beach last night.

The man had lost his wife less than a year ago, for heaven's sake!

And what had she done? She'd shamelessly tried to seduce him, that's what! Going without a bra, dabbing perfume in strategic places so that body heat would make it rise around her. Drinking wine. Laughing.

Oh, Lord, she hoped she hadn't actually batted her eyelashes at him. Under the circumstances that would have been truly grotesque.

As for the perfume, it was probably rancid, considering it was several years old. Stan had hated it, claiming it was too old-fashioned. He'd given her a huge bottle of one of those aggressive new fragrances, which had gone to Goodwill along with what she had thought of as her work costumes. The neat little outfits that were neither too smart nor too dowdy for a politician's wife, all totally without personality.

"Sarah? You awake?"

Great. The day was half over, he was going to leave—the coward—and she was lying in bed, wallowing in regrets, embarrassment and a dozen other nonproductive emotions.

"Be down in a minute!" She jumped out of bed and scrambled through her closet for something flattering to put on. "Forget flattering, settle for decent," she muttered.

She settled for clam diggers, clogs and a camp shirt, which she buttoned up wrong and then had to do over again. No time for makeup—she splashed her face, gargled and made a pass at her hair with a brush, all without confronting the mirror.

This was the end. He was leaving. It was probably for the best, she thought, but it might take a few years—a few decades—to convince herself.

"Sarah, get a move on, will you? We've got company again."

Company? "Oh, shoot." Dropping the brush, she clattered down the hall, down the stairs and out onto the porch just as a familiar silver car, the kind that reeked status, pulled up in front of the house.

Clive Meadows. Why the devil couldn't they take no for an answer?

Rocky had chosen to stay inside this time, which was just as well. The last thing she needed was to have to explain him to another of her father's emissaries. For some obscure reason the senator had been pushing her toward Clive—or him toward her—since practically the day after Stan had died.

Her shoulders sagged, but she managed to hold on to a smile as the dapper, gray-haired man stepped out of the driver's seat. *Shake every hand, kiss every baby and smile, smile, smile, no matter that your feet are killing you and you're coming down with cramps.* She'd done the drill a thousand times. "Clive, how lovely to see you."

Lovely didn't quite describe what she was feeling at the moment. She knew for a fact that he was sixty-nine. Thanks to a personal trainer and an excellent tailor, he looked at least ten years younger.

Halfway up the front walk, the lawyer-turned-lobbyist stopped and gaped at her face. At her eye. "My God, Sarah, what on earth happened to you? R.C. said—but I never expected— How did it happen?"

"I ran into a door, and don't you dare say one word about what a klutz I am." Clive had seen her at her worst—stepping off the edge of a stage as she tried to escape the mob congregating around her father—getting her bracelet caught in her hair while trying to adjust her hat at a state funeral. The more exhausted she was, the more accident-prone she became.

If her smile now was a little too bright, at least it served to deflect his attention from her eye. The swelling was down, but the ghastly blend of yellow, green and lavender was still visible. "Are you on your way to the beach, or on your way back home?"

She had stayed at his beach house several times, occasionally with Stan, more often with the senator. Clive Meadows was an excellent host who frequently entertained the rich and influential. Which was why, Stan had once told her, his palatial beach house was a total tax write-off. Stan had been pressing her for years to go shopping with him for a beach place of their own, when they could barely afford the payments on their modest six-room house.

"I was on my way down when it occurred to me that you might enjoy a break from…" His expression when he glanced at the surrounding cornfields spoke volumes. As skilled as he was at lying, Sarah easily detected her father's meddling hand. "It's sweet of you to offer, Clive, but as you can see, I'm right in the middle of a serious attack of landscaping." She gestured toward the mass of grapevines, honeysuckle and pruned branches he was being forced to negotiate to reach the porch.

Reaching her side, he kissed her lightly as he'd been doing for years. "How are you, my dear? Aside from the obvious, I mean. We've been worried, your father and I."

"I can't imagine why. I told the senator I was perfectly well. I love it here, I always have."

"I can see you've been working too hard. You really should hire someone to do that, Sarah Mariah. You deserve a long, restful weekend at the cottage. On Monday or Tuesday we can drive up the Eastern Shore, stop in at St. Michaels for lunch and still arrive in plenty of time for your father's birthday celebration."

"No."

Ignoring her—he was almost as good at doing that as the senator was—Clive went on to say, "I met your great-aunt once. Lovely woman—lovely. But my dear, you can't hibernate forever. Now, what do you say to spending a quiet, relaxing few days soaking up sun— you can have the pool all to yourself, there's no one at the cottage but staff."

She crossed her arms over her chest. Dammit, why did he insist on treating her as if she were a rebellious teenager? Was this the way he'd treated his wives? She knew for a fact that the last one had just turned twenty when they met. No wonder none of his marriages had lasted much longer than it took the ink to dry on the prenuptial agreements.

And another thing—it had always irritated her that he insisted on referring to his beach house as "the cottage." Eight bedrooms and nine baths, including an outside shower and a full bath in the pool house, did *not* a cottage make! "You're too generous, Clive, but—"

Behind her the screen door opened and closed quietly. "What Sarah's trying to say, Meadows, is that she has a houseguest and she's far too conscientious a hostess to leave while I'm still here."

Not by so much as a raised eyebrow did the older man show his surprise. But then, he must have known all along. That was probably why he was here. R.C. had gone back and told her father that Sarah had a man staying with her, and the senator had called in the heavy artillery.

Stiff-lipped with anger and frustration, Sarah introduced the two men. Clive said, "Waters," and extended his hand. He laid on what Sarah had always thought of as his snake-oil smile. She might like him, but that particular smile was one of the things that kept her from ever taking him at his word.

"We've met," said Rocky.

The lawyer nodded genially. "I don't recall seeing you around town lately. Rumor has it you've retired."

Sarah watched as they sized each other up like a couple of strange dogs, each trying to establish dominance. Although in Rocky's case, with his six feet plus of prime masculinity, no effort was required.

"Oh, for heaven's sake, as long as you're here, Clive, you might as well come inside for coffee. I haven't even had breakfast yet."

Rocky obviously had. His dishes were neatly stacked in the sink. She watched as Clive took in every single sign of intimacy, from the dishes in the sink to the moccasins Rocky wore when he was working around the house, which shared a mat with her mud shoes beside the back door. His Braves cap hung on a hook beside the straw hat she wore for yard work when she happened to remember to put it on.

"I'll make a fresh pot," Rocky said just as if it were his kitchen and Clive was his guest instead of hers. He was doing it deliberately, and for the life of her, Sarah couldn't imagine why he should want to complicate matters any more than they already were.

"Don't bother. On second thought," the lawyer said, "I'd better not stay long enough for coffee." His narrowed eyes hard as agates despite his surface geniality, he added, "*This* time."

Stepping back toward the door, he smiled at Sarah, nodded at Rocky and touched the side of the old walnut wag-tail clock that had hung there between the door and the china cabinet for as long as Sarah could remember. "Nice piece. Not really valuable, but... rather charming."

In other words, Rocky interpreted, *There's nothing of value here, Waters, so buzz off.* Instead of the simple infrared detector he'd bought and installed at the foot of the lane, he should have bought a Doberman with a taste for Washington lobbyists.

Rocky stayed inside while Sarah saw her guest on his way. In the process of making a fresh pot of coffee, he just happened to stroll into the front hall as she was walking the jerk to his car. They lingered to talk for several minutes. Then Meadows kissed her again. She turned her head just in time so that the kiss slid harmlessly off her cheek, but Rocky, watching through the screen door, felt something snap in his hand. Swearing softly, he retrieved the plastic handle of the coffee measurer he'd been holding.

"Sounds like a nice vacation," he said with deceptive mildness when she came back inside. "Why didn't you take him up on it? A whole swimming pool all to yourself?"

"Oh, shut up!"

Grinning, he used a damp paper towel to clean up the few grounds that had scattered on the floor when the measuring spoon had broken. "Yes, ma'am."

She turned and glared at him. "Well, what would you do in my place? I've known the man practically all my life. He's my father's best friend, his lawyer and God knows what else."

"I don't recall seeing him much during the Senate hearings."

She shrugged. "He hasn't actually practiced in years. Stan said he directed the entire defense from behind the scenes."

"In that case, why didn't he do a better job of it?"

Her arms flew out in a gesture of helpless frustration. "How do I know? Why don't you ask him, if you're so curious?"

"He did what he had to do, Sarah," Rocky said gently. "Your father was guilty as hell, and we both know it. At least he didn't have to serve any prison time."

"Oh, I know, I know. I'm just feeling..." She hugged her arms around her and stared out the kitchen window at the flock of crows squabbling in the pines on the far side of her cornfield.

"Trapped?" Rocky supplied.

Sarah nodded. She rarely cried. For one thing it never helped. For another, she didn't cry any more gracefully than she did anything else. Her eyes turned red, her nose stopped up, and nothing short of a tourniquet around her neck could silence her wails.

When the first sob escaped she muttered, "Hellfire and damnation," but the words were punctuated by a shuddering hiccup. Rocky's arms closed around her, and she gave in and buried her face against his shirt. The dam burst then, and it all came spilling out—anger, fear on behalf of an innocent child whose whole life might be shadowed by Stan's sins if the connection was ever made.

And grief because of something she was only now beginning to understand—that here was a man she could have loved—one who might even have loved her, if only they'd met at a different time, under different circumstances. It was like discovering the end of the rainbow just as the lights went out.

The more she tried to stifle her tears—to shove the evil genie back into the bottle—the more impossible it became, until she gave up trying. Better to get it out of her system and move beyond it.

He was good at holding, good at comforting, offering empathy, not pity. Finally, after one last shuddering sob, she sniffed. Rocky shoved a handkerchief into her hand. She mopped, blew and managed to get control of her breathing, but she refused to lift her head from his shoulder. "I never, *ever* do this," she told him. "You obviously bring out the worst in me."

"Funny you should say that. Now me, I've got a totally different take on it. Sit down while I pour the coffee and make you some toast and I'll enlighten you."

Well, what could she do? He'd already seen her at her worst. Her rock-bottom worst. And she was starving. A morning person, she always ate a substantial breakfast.

While she got herself under control, he made *huevos rancheros*. She hadn't had them since her Mexican honeymoon. She'd hated Cancun, but loved the food. Now she gobbled up half her huge serving before she dared lift her face to look at him. He was seated across the table, nursing a cup of rich black coffee.

"It's great. Thank you. I—" She started to say, she'd thought he was leaving, but changed direction just in time. "I wish we could get real Mexican coffee here."

"You can. It just doesn't taste the same unless it's made with Mexican water."

Which brought on a smile, a sigh and another flood of useless emotion. "Sorry about the histrionics. I don't usually lose control that way."

"I know."

Oblivious of her naked face, her reddened eyes and her fading bruises, she gave him a searching look. "You do?"

"Sarah, I watched most of the coverage these past few years. Both times. It was brutal—even though it was largely deserved in both cases. You stood up under pressure magnificently. I was proud of you."

"You were?"

God, would you look at her, Rocky marveled. How could any woman look so beautiful with a week-old shiner, tearstained cheeks, pink eyes and a red-tipped nose? It had to be that sweet, vulnerable mouth—either that or the wistful, hopeful expression. Whatever it was, he was a sucker for it.

And that was a damned shame, because he hadn't figured on getting personally involved here. He'd done his Don Quixote thing. Now, if he had a grain of sense, he'd saddle up the Rover and ride off into the sunset. Get the hell out of Dodge. He could think of a number of clichés that all meant the same thing. Get out before he got into more trouble than he'd bargained for.

The driveway alarm went off again, and Sarah jumped. "Oh, no," she wailed.

He'd bought it without asking permission when he'd bought the hinges and had finished installing it just yesterday. He'd had in mind nosy reporters, not rabbits, deer and whatever other creatures, two- or four-legged, might be prowling the countryside. In such an isolated setting, a woman living alone needed more security. At the very least, she needed a warning.

"Probably just a deer. Wait here, I'll check it out," he said, sliding his chair back.

A moment later he was back. "Did your friend leave something behind? He's headed this way again."

"Clive? Why on earth would he come back?"

"Maybe he just doesn't like taking no for an answer."

This time they were both waiting on the front porch when the car pulled into the yard. Clive Meadows got out, shut the door and paused as if collecting himself to present his closing statement.

Rocky beat him to the punch. "Forget something, Meadows?"

"I believe I might have done just that. Sarah, I didn't tell you the whole truth before. I wasn't sure how you'd take it."

"Now, why am I not surprised?" Rocky muttered.

Sarah said nothing, but when his hand brushed against hers, she grabbed it and held on.

"It's about your father. The senator."

"I know who my father is," she said, not yielding an inch.

Meadows stopped at the bottom of the painted concrete steps, one tasseled loafer propped on the first step. "He's...not well, Sarah Mariah. I don't know how much he's told you, but your father suffers from a heart condition."

Sarah's hand tightened convulsively. She took a

deep breath and then, in a controlled voice, asked, "How long?"

"How long does he have? Or how long has he known?"

"Both. Everything! Why wasn't I told before now? Is he—is he hospitalized? Has he had a heart attack?"

When Meadows moved up another step, Rocky decided it was time to take over. The guy had just invited her to the beach for a cozy weekend. Would he have done that if her father's condition was critical? Something wasn't right here. "Give us the name of the senator's cardiologist. We'll take it from there."

The lawyer stared at him as if he'd just crawled up out of the primordial slime. "I don't believe this involves you, Waters."

"As Sarah's fiancé, anything that involves her happiness involves me. Now, you want to give me the doctor's name and the name of the hospital?"

"Her fiancé?" The older man looked from one to the other, his disbelief plain to see. "Since when?"

Rocky's smile was a wicked work of art. "Under the circumstances, we decided to keep things pretty low-key. I'm sure you understand."

Sarah hadn't said a word. Evidently she'd already depleted her emotional reserves. Thank God for that. If she fell apart on him now, it would be just the tool this jerk needed.

So he said softly, not caring whether or not the other man could hear, "Sarah, I'm pretty sure the situation is under control, considering Meadows just invited you to a private pool party."

Releasing his hand, Sarah moved to the edge of the porch. "Well? What about that, Clive? If the senator is in such dire straits, why didn't you offer to take me to him instead of down to the beach for a vacation?''

Way to go, honey. Put him on the defensive.

"Well, naturally I intended to explain once we were alone and could talk privately." The man was a master at subtle intimidation, Rocky thought with reluctant admiration. Evidently, it came with the territory.

But Sarah wasn't too shabby herself when it came to sending the opposition scurrying. After a few more attempts to persuade her to go with him, the lawyer stalked off, slammed into his dusty silver chariot and roared off down the potholed lane.

That's my girl, Rocky thought proudly. Whatever she needed to know about the senator's health, they would find out together.

Nine

Clogs were good for stomping, and Sarah was in a stomping mood. She stomped into the kitchen, yanked open the refrigerator door looking for canned milk. Finding the can empty, she slammed the door and stomped across to the pantry.

"Do you know how frustrating it is when a woman can't even believe her own father? Why is it," she demanded plaintively, "that all the men in my life are such world-class liars?"

Fresh can in hand, she jerked open a drawer and found an opener. Evaporated milk spilled on the counter when she popped it open. "Crooked, self-serving, conniving—"

"Present company excluded, I hope," Rocky said, testing her with a bit of gentle teasing.

It took some of the wind out of her sails. "Don't

push me too far, Waters, I'm not in the mood.'' She poured herself a fresh cup of coffee and cursed the cretin who had designed a coffeepot with a leaky, inefficient spout.

Sarah Mariah was on a roll. Silently, Rocky blotted the spilled milk and mopped up the rich brown puddle with a handful of paper towels. If the conversation needed a nudge, he'd nudge. Right now what she needed was to blow off steam.

She was worried but afraid to admit it. Perfectly understandable, Rocky reasoned. Whatever else he was, the senator was her father. He also reasoned that if the situation had been critical, Meadows would have told her straight out.

Instead he'd invited her to his beach house.

Obviously, the snake was up to something, and whatever it was, J. Abernathy was probably in it with him, up to their collective necks. Rocky had a suspicion of what was going on; what he didn't understand was why.

Unless the senator owed Meadows big time, which was a distinct possibility—and he was using Sarah Mariah as bargaining chip. Also a possibility, considering the old pirate's history.

Viewing the situation from Meadows's point of view, it was a bit harder to figure. If his past wives were anything to go by, then Sarah was hardly his type. Only child of a dedicated socialite and a crooked politician, her entire life had been constrained, first by her parents and then by that idiot she'd had the misfortune to marry. In some ways she was remarkably naive. The one thing that could be said of all of Meadows's wives was that they were far from naive.

The trouble, Rocky told himself, with trying to second-guess this particular situation was that one of the suspects was a lawyer and the other had spent more than half his life in politics. In both cases the thought patterns were so labyrinthine, so convoluted, that every word, deed or motive was suspect.

"I'll have to go, you know." Sarah continued to spoon sugar into her cup as she stared through the window at a wren that was busy exploring a section of newly exposed gutter.

"You could call."

"I could, but if I'm to have the slightest chance of finding out the truth, I'll have to see him face-to-face."

No need to ask who "him" was. The first time he'd ever met her, she'd had much the same look about her. Resigned, but far too vulnerable. Back then he'd tried to tease her out of it. This time teasing wasn't going to work. He ached to hold her. Ached to do far more than hold her, but she was still too fragile. For a man who had come here with only the most altruistic intentions—well, perhaps he might have toyed briefly with the idea of writing her story himself—he had already strayed too far off course. For both their sakes he needed to take a giant step back and regain his objectivity.

"When?" he asked, masking his concern.

She stared at her oversweetened coffee in disgust and poured it in the sink. "Today—no, tomorrow. I'll need to close up the house, stop the paper delivery, pack a few things—enough for two or three days, I guess. Lord only knows…" Her voice trailed off as she went off into what he'd taken to calling her minitrances.

He broke into her concentration. "I can close up the house for you, turn everything off and leave the key where you can find it when and if you come back."

"When, not if." There was a glittery look to her eyes that might be tears, but this time he didn't think so.

And then it dawned on him that the lady wasn't worried. What she was, was mad as hell. Rocky was amused. Amused, but no less concerned. "It's the Wye River place, right? You want company? It's not all that far out of my way."

"No, I..." She slapped her hand to her forehead, as if she'd just remembered the last straw. "Oh, Lord, Rocky, as bad as things are, why did you have to tell Clive we were engaged? Now I'm going to have to explain my way out of it, and the last thing I need is another complication."

Shrugging, he realized that he had no idea why the words had popped out of his mouth. He was not normally given to impulses—about one per decade was his usual rate. "I don't know, it just seemed like a good idea at the time. You'll have to admit, I'm probably safer than a Doberman."

She gave him a withering look. "Now, that I seriously doubt. By now Clive will already have been on the phone to my father. R.C. will have gained access to your F.B.I. file, checked out your voting record, your blood type, your bank balance, plus any outstanding traffic tickets."

"So? Is that a problem?" His life was an open

book. The few chapters not for public consumption, he had already ripped out and burned.

"Not for me—at least not after I explain that you were just—just—"

"Tilting at windmills?"

With a distracted sigh, she turned back to the window. In the clear morning light she looked both older and younger than he knew her to be. The shadows were back—those haunting, taunting shadows that he'd found so oddly intriguing the first time he'd ever met her.

Time to back off, he told himself. He'd done what he'd come to do; the next move was hers. "So what are you trying to say? That it's all over between us? You're giving me back my ring?"

If he'd hoped to erase that glittery look, he seemed to have succeeded. She swatted his arm with a handful of paper napkins. "What ring? The closest thing to a ring you ever gave me was offering to put phone jacks all over my house."

"That's me, Roland Waters, known on three continents as the world's biggest cheapskate."

"*Roland?*"

"You wanna make something of it?"

She bit her lip. The brittleness faded, but he wasn't fooled. She was still terribly fragile. So he said gently, "Hey, you can still use me if you think it'll help—or you can just go home, tell the truth and face the consequences. You're not your daddy's little girl any longer." Nor the wife of that jerk Sullivan.

"Which truth?"

Right. Which truth. He had a feeling it was far more than their phony engagement. "It's your call, Sarah.

If you don't want to face it right now, then don't. But, listen—you've got friends.''

She only looked at him, those large haunting eyes peeling layers off his heart like a pair of lasers. He wanted to hold her, but this was not the time. The lady was stronger than she gave herself credit for being, but to make that strength work for her, she had to trust it.

"Sarah, it might not always seem that way, but the world's a pretty terrific place—even Washington, in spite of what you read in the papers or hear on the nightly news. We both know what makes the headlines, but headlines aren't the whole story. Sometimes they're not even part of it. Honey, the world's mostly filled with decent people trying to live decent lives. Trying to create a little happiness for the people they love. You happened to get tangled up with a few of the exceptions, but that's just it—they're the exception, not the rule."

Spoken like a blind optimist. Which he wasn't, never had been—never would be. Odd, the way she had of making him act out of character.

She stared at him as if he'd lost his last marble. "Well. That was...inspiring. Is the sermon over?"

Rocky shrugged and tried not to look embarrassed. "Yeah, it's over. Now you know why I gave up writing."

"Pollyanna the journalist. Oh, my, you do have a problem." Sarah actually chuckled, and then, without thinking, she walked right up to where he stood massaging the muscles at the back of his neck and wrapped her arms around his waist. She knew precisely what her own problem was—make that plural.

She wasn't at all sure of his. So she just held him, sighing a little because despite her recent attempts at writing, she wasn't as good with words as he was, and anyway, it was going to take more than words to make things work out this time.

"Thanks for trying. It was a noble effort." And then, after several moments of utter stillness, she said, "I ran away, you know. I didn't know what else to do."

He nodded. At least she thought he nodded. He had a nice solid frame overlaid with a resilient layer of muscle that invited burrowing. And so she burrowed, pressing her face into that delicious hollow between chest and shoulder. "I didn't know how to fight back—or even who to fight. Running seemed the only logical choice. Is that what you did?" After your Julie died, she wanted to add, but couldn't quite find the courage.

The barriers were down. Rocky heard himself saying, "The first few years after the accident—once I finally accepted that Julie wasn't ever coming back—I took every assignment I could land. I'm not sure if it was running or hiding. Maybe both. But by the time I realized that the doctors were right—that she...that she wasn't aware—" He swallowed hard. "By that time I needed the money, too, so it wasn't only running away. It was—hell, I don't know."

"Staying busy helps. Wearing yourself out so you won't wake up at four in the morning and lie awake, wondering how much worse things could possibly get. Wondering why, just when you thought things were beginning to turn around, they..." She swallowed audibly. When she couldn't continue, he finished for her.

"They tanked. Got so much worse you actually toyed with the idea of surrendering. Four in the morning is a pretty vulnerable time for anyone. There's a physiological reason for it, only I can't think of what it is at the moment. I guess the practical solution is never to sleep alone. Then, if you wake up and see your whole life sliding downhill—"

"You'll have someone handy to apply the brakes. Did you ever think of writing a self-help column?"

He began to chuckle, causing sensations to race through her body that were indescribable, inappropriate and hardly helpful under the circumstances.

She disengaged and touched her hair, feeling as if she'd just been thoroughly kissed. Wishing she had. "For heaven's sake, I haven't even had breakfast and here it is past lunchtime."

"Hey, you've forgotten my *huevos rancheros* already? Lady, that's a low blow."

"Food doesn't count when you're stressed out."

He let her get away with it, knowing it was the quickest way out of a tricky situation. What he needed to do was make things easy for her and then step back and let her handle it. He had contacts in the medical world—hackers, if he couldn't get answers the legitimate way. She needed reassurance that the old coot wasn't about to pop off the mortal coil, needed to find out what Meadows was up to and set him straight once and for all. And then she needed some direction. Vegetating here in the country, while it might be pleasant, wasn't enough for an intelligent woman with a creative imagination.

But that was her call, not his. "You want to talk to your father and get his take on the situation?"

The look she gave him held a glimmer of the old Sarah Mariah—young, outnumbered but feisty as hell. "Now what makes you think he'd level with me? He never has before."

"I could find out for you how serious this heart thing is."

"You have access to confidential files?" She poked her head around the refrigerator door, then emerged with a jar of homemade preserves. "Watermelon rind. The last of Aunt Emma's stock. Well, do you?"

"Sure. I actually have a few legitimate sources, too, but if it will give you a thrill, we'll go underground first."

"Hand me the peanut butter. I guess it doesn't really matter, I'll have to go back, anyway. Lord, I dread it!"

Rocky handed her the jar from the cabinet, then took it when she was done with it. He got out a clean spoon, scooped out a big blob of extra crunchy and proceeded to eat it like a lollypop. "Will you stay?"

"With Father? Oh, Lord, no, I'd suffocate. But there's this birthday thing coming up, too. Whatever the situation is, I'll probably have to stay for that. He'd hardly be having a party, would he? I mean if he has a serious health problem?"

The rest of the day was spent getting ready to leave. Rocky hauled off the pile of vines and evergreen branches and dumped them into an irrigation ditch. By the time it could cause a problem with drainage, he'd be long gone. He fastened up a sagging gutter and cleaned out the pine straw, and while he was at it he swept off her roof. The thought of Sarah clambering around on the steep slopes was enough to cause him a few problems with his own heart.

How could a woman who moved with such regal grace, whose hand gestures might have been choreographed for butterflies—how the devil could she trip over her own feet? It wasn't her eyesight, he was pretty sure of that. Could the truth be as simple as she'd stated? That her mind was usually on other things instead of what she was supposed to be doing?

If she'd been an artistic type, he might buy it, but she was... Yeah, well—she was what she was. Sarah Mariah Jones Sullivan, daughter of a certified reprobate, widow of another one, and great-niece of Aunty Em. If he hadn't seen the name in the tax records, he might have thought she'd made it up—it was too much in keeping with their very first conversation.

Standing on the steep roof with a broom in his hand, Rocky surveyed the countryside. From that vantage point he could see seven buildings—houses, barns, sheds. Acres of woodlands, more acres of corn. A strip of blacktop and even, in the distance, a glimmer of water that was probably the Currituck Sound.

Cornfields and Aunty Em or not, this sure wasn't Kansas, but judging by the way she was attacking housecleaning, Sarah might have been leaving for Oz. Rugs were hung on the line. Sheets were laundered. Periodically she appeared on either the front or the back porch to shake out a rug or a dust mop.

There was something both satisfying and disturbing in the amount of work that got done before dark that day. For some people physical exertion was a means of escape—for others, a means of focusing the mind. In Sara's case, it might be a bit of both.

Rocky insisted on driving to the nearest barbecue place, a matter of several miles, and bringing back supper while Sara showered and packed her suitcase. He drove her car and filled the tank. Noticed it would need inspecting before the end of the month and made a mental note to remind her. The last thing she needed was another hassle.

He opened his laptop and caught up on his e-mail, deleting most of it without a second thought. Sarah wandered over, munching on a cold French fry, and watched. "I'm surprised you don't have one of these," he said. "Living so far off the beaten track, it's pretty handy to be able to check in now and then, read a variety of newspapers, see what's going on in the rest of the world."

"I'm sure it is."

"Sorry. Merely an observation, not meant to be taken personally."

"Bull."

"You want to try for an early start tomorrow?" They were skirting over some pretty thin ice. Neither of them mentioned the fact that she was about to beard the lion in his den. Or the fact that a man with all the scruples of a starving alley cat—with the help of his lawyer—was up to something that involved her.

Or the fact that once they parted, whether or not she returned to Snowden, there would be no reason for them to meet again.

"The sooner I leave, the sooner I'll be back," she said as if shoring up her resolve.

She was standing behind his left shoulder, frowning at the screen. His hands, too large for the small keyboard but agile from years of practice, rested on his thighs. "My offer stands," he said quietly.

"To go with me?" She shook her head and moved away, touching one polished surface after another, almost as if she were saying goodbye. "No, thanks. This is something I have to do by myself."

He nodded, knowing—sensing—she was waiting for him to argue. And dammit, he wanted to, but she was right. She needed to face down the enemy and walk away the victor—victress—whatever.

Sarah couldn't sleep. She was so tired she should have been able to lose consciousness instantly and sleep for a week, but her mind refused to shut down. It wasn't like that little computer of Rocky's—something, incidentally, that she was going to have to learn how to use if she was serious about writing. No matter how many times she hit the sleep switch, her mind wouldn't go blank. She continued to lie there, eyes open in the darkness, trying desperately to envision the next few days: "Hi, Father, you're looking well for a man who's supposed to be desperately ill."

He would say something gruff, turn away and pour himself a drink, whether or not he already had one. The senator wasn't a heavy drinker. Whisky, like his cigars—like his daughter—was a prop.

"I thought I'd drop by and wish you a happy birthday on my way to—"

He would see though it in a minute.

Rocky, dammit, I don't want to do this alone!

But she would, because she had to. Because until she dealt with the past, she couldn't begin to deal with the future. And the more she thought about it, the more determined she was that one way or another her future was going to include Kitty. Who else did she have? What were her chances of ever having a child of her own?

Rocky set his watch for six and settled down, knowing he wouldn't be able to sleep. He could do without for about twenty-eight hours before his judgment began to suffer. A few years ago he could have lasted at least forty. Fortunately, most of his other faculties were still intact. His libido, for instance.

His hearing was another. Sometime later he was just easing into the first stages of sleep when he heard a noise. A thud—something breaking...

Opening his eyes, he stared into the darkness, wondering if he'd dreamed it.

"Oh, damn, oh, damn, oh, damn, oh, blast!"

Adrenaline racing through his system, he was at her door within seconds. Waiting only for his eyes to adjust to the darkness, he called softly, "Sarah, are you all right?"

"No, dammit, I'm not all right! Go away!"

"Sorry—not an option."

"Then watch out for the broken glass, it's everywhere."

Ten

Without asking, Rocky switched on the overhead light. Sarah was sprawled on the floor beside the bed, her nightgown up about her hips, with one foot tangled in the bed linens. Near her outstretched hand were the remains of a broken glass.

"Don't laugh. Don't you dare say a word," she seethed. Reaching back, she tugged her nightgown down over her bare bottom.

Once his heart settled back in place and he assured himself that she wasn't seriously hurt, he said, "Don't move until I pick up the glass."

The scene told the story. She'd tossed off the covers, gone to the bathroom to get a glass of water, all without turning on a light, and tripped over the sheet on her way back to bed.

"I feel so...so stupid," she muttered.

"Yeah, it takes a really stupid woman to sprawl facedown when her foot gets tangled in a bedsheet." Kneeling beside her, he helped her turn onto her side, then scanned the length of visible flesh to be sure she wasn't bleeding anywhere.

"I'm all right—stop looking at me! At least I had sense enough to land on the rug."

"Nice planning. Next time aim for the mattress."

She whacked him on the shoulder as he lifted her from the floor and swung her over onto the bed. "Turn off that overhead light on your way out, will you?"

"Let me collect the glass first. You don't want to step on it when you get up in the morning." He was trying not to grin openly, knowing how defensive she could be when she was embarrassed. "The rug's wet—I'll roll it up and take it outside."

It was a white crocheted rug. Several slivers of glass sparkled on its nubby surface. Sarah, brushing off the soles of her feet, wondered if she could be genetically flawed. Her mother had never been clumsy. As for the senator, he'd always been surrounded by a coterie of aides who would have caught him if he even looked as if he was about to stumble.

Watching Rocky pick up broken glass, drop it in the wastebasket and then carefully roll up her bedside rug, her thoughts strayed from genetics to anatomy. Wearing only a pair of navy briefs, he reminded her of a Rodin sculpture. Gazing at the sweep of his back, the curve of his—

Yes, well...never mind.

Holding the carefully folded rug, he switched on the bedside lamp, put the rug outside in the hall, doused the overhead light and turned back toward her bed.

She followed his every move. There was no way she could help herself, he was such an alien presence in the room. He might even be the first man ever to set foot in the room that had once belonged to her maiden aunt.

Swallowing a sudden thickness in her throat, she lifted her eyes to his. And there it was again—that odd electricity, sharp as lightning in a summer squall, and just as hot.

Drawing her feet up before her, she wrapped her arms around her knees, creating a barrier that was no barrier at all when what she wanted so desperately was to break through every conceivable wall, including the wall of common sense.

"You still want a drink of water? I'll get another glass from the kitchen." The words were ordinary enough, but his voice sounded oddly strained.

"No, I want—"

He waited, his pale-gray eyes looking not at all cool in the light of a forty-watt bulb. Her gaze fell from his face to his chest and strayed down to the dark elastic band of his briefs.

She closed her eyes.

"Then I guess I'd better leave you to get some sleep," he said, and she shook her head.

"No, please—could you just—stay?"

He was visibly aroused, and obviously embarrassed about it. Sarah tried and failed to think of some graceful way to handle the explosive situation. In the world in which she'd grown up, plain speaking was a rarity. How did a lady gracefully tell a gentleman that she wanted him to take off his briefs, tear off her gown and make wild, passionate love to her without saying a word until neither of them had the strength to move?

"Sarah?"

"Please?" She opened her arms and reached up and quickly discovered that no words were needed.

The old mattress sagged under the added weight, toppling her against his side. She thought he might have said something under his breath, but by that time she couldn't have spoken if her life depended on it. Carefully he shifted her and resettled himself until they were lying side by side in the middle of the old-fashioned double bed. The sound of a shuddering indrawn breath broke the silence. His or hers—or both?

What are you waiting for? she wanted to cry. Just—do it! Pretend I'm someone you want—someone beautiful!

There was nothing in the least seductive about her nightgown. The most that could be said of it was that if her house caught on fire in the middle of the night and she had to run for her life, it wouldn't be terribly embarrassing.

What now? She'd made the first move; the next was up to him. If he wasn't going to do anything, then she might as well crawl under the covers and hide until he had the decency to leave.

The silence continued, loud as a ticking time bomb. *Coward! If you let him get away now, you'll regret it for the rest of your life!* Finally, eyes shut tight, jaw clenched, she said, "Would you—could we please make love?"

Moments later—it felt more like hours—Rocky said quietly, "Sarah, I'm not sure that's a good idea."

Then what are you doing in my bed? she wanted to ask. "Why not? Have you taken a vow of celibacy?"

You insensitive fool, his wife died less than a year ago!

The unspoken words hung there between them. She cringed, half expecting him to get up and walk away. She wouldn't blame him if he did. Finally he said, "No."

"I'm truly sorry, I had no right to ask. You can go now." Her eyes were still closed, as if by not seeing she could deny her part in the whole pathetic scene. "None of this is really happening, you know—you're only dreaming it. Tomorrow you'll wake up and we'll both get into our separate cars and leave. You'll probably drive south—maybe down to Oregon Inlet—you might even go fishing. Or maybe climb a lighthouse or something—there are lots of those around here. And after a while you'll wonder, what was that crazy dream I had a few nights ago all about, anyway? I'd better stop eating before I go to bed."

"Sarah?"

"You can never tell what brings on crazy dreams. Now me, I always dream really scary stuff when I eat pickles before bedtime. Pickled onions are the worst."

"Sarah?"

"I think it must be some crazy chemical reaction. Like batteries? You know, acid and—"

Rolling over onto his side, he took her face in his hands and kissed her.

Pity, she told herself. Oh, God, please not that!

But it didn't feel like pity. In fact it felt carnal from the first touch. In silent surrender, she wrapped her arms around his shoulders, her hands slipping on his sleek, warm flesh.

There were things she needed to say, but this was not the time. His hands moved down her throat to cup her shoulders and then they were on her breasts, his touch light as he gently cradled them in his palms. Against the heat of his palms, her nipples hardened almost painfully. Kiss me there, she pleaded silently, and as if he'd heard her wordless command, he moved lower.

Her gown was too much like a straitjacket. With his mouth tugging at her nipple, she reached down and grabbed a handful of the flimsy stuff, tugging it up as far as it would go. This was not the way it was supposed to work. In books, in movies, the heroine never got twisted up in her nightgown.

In books and movies, the heroine never had to beg. The hero would somehow manage to tear her gown down the front and it would fall from her shoulders, leaving him in silent awe of her newly revealed loveliness.

The trouble with reality was that nylon was tougher than duct tape and there was no graceful way to get naked without stopping the action.

Reality was when Rocky lifted her hips and eased the gown up a few more inches, and by twisting and wriggling she was able to work herself free. Reality was pulling the blasted thing over her head and having it catch under her chin.

Once freed, she reached toward his waist, but before she could do it for him, he removed his own briefs. Briefs were easier than full-length nightgowns. Feeling the satiny heat of him brush against her thigh, she nearly lost her nerve. You'd think she was a virgin, the way she was behaving, and she wasn't. She most certainly was not.

Even so, he was probably more experienced than she was. Her first affair had lasted only a matter of weeks until her lover had landed a job on the West Coast. She had always wondered if her father could have had a hand in his sudden departure. After that, there'd been no one until Stan.

But never before—not with her first lover, not even with Stan—had she felt such a fierce compulsion. Stan used to complain that her mind was never on what they were doing. But then, Stan had never been sensitive to her needs, her wishes, and after a while he'd been right.

This time she couldn't think of anything but her own need—the hot, heavy weight of her own desire. She was going to explode the instant he touched her, and his hand was inching closer, his palm on her belly, his fingertips brushing the slope of her mound.

Hurry, hurry, she wanted to cry—I need you now!

"Sarah—" His voice sounded as if he were choking on a bone. "I don't have anything to protect you. Do you happen to have—?"

She groaned audibly. "I don't care! Please?"

Fleetingly, she thought about the ways in which a single moment of pleasure could affect so many lives, but then he was moving even lower, kissing her where his hand had been, and then...

It took only a single touch—a single kiss. She shook with the explosive force of release—cried out as wave after wave of exquisite pleasure washed over her.

Gasping for breath, she clutched his shoulders and waited for the earth to settle down again.

And when it eventually did, she closed her eyes in despair.

As wonderful as it was, it wasn't enough. She'd wanted him inside her—wanted him to feel the same thunder, the same bone-melting fires. The heat that could fuse two individuals into a single entity.

He held her as if she were infinitely precious, and she wanted to cry. For him, not for herself. Or maybe a little bit for herself, too, because no other man had ever done this for her before. No other man ever could.

She loved him. There was no longer any room for doubt. She wouldn't say the words aloud, because to do so might imply an obligation, and that would ruin everything.

Not that she hadn't considered what it would be like to have sex with an agreeable partner. A nameless, faceless partner. She'd been told in all those sophisticated articles in women's magazines that good sex was a woman's right. She was free, unattached and certainly old enough to know her own mind. There was no reason not to enjoy herself sexually, as long as she used discretion. It was, if anything, a declaration of independence.

The one thing she had failed to take into consideration was that she might find herself deeply—head over heels, as the saying went—in love with the man.

So much for independence.

He made a trip to the bathroom, returned and slipped into bed again. Settling her against him, her back to his front this time, he wrapped his arm around her waist and whispered, "Go to sleep, Sarah—the alarm's set for six."

Certain she would never be able to sleep feeling so guilty and embarrassed, Sarah had closed her eyes. Hours later when she awoke, she was lying on her back. She stared up at the ceiling as incredibly detailed memories washed over her. It was like falling asleep and waking up in a brand-new world.

A sound from across the room broke the fragile process and she turned her head. "Rocky? What are you doing?"

He was seated at her desk, wearing yesterday's jeans and khaki shirt, his feet bare, a frown on his freshly shaven face. "You want to tell me about this?" He indicated the stack of manuscript and drawings.

Sarah closed her eyes again. It wasn't enough that she'd given him her body—now he wanted to claim her secrets? Her dreams?

"Dabbling," she said with a sigh, wishing there was some dignified way she could get out of bed and pretend last night had never happened. The story, she could deal with—there was nothing at all to tie it to Kitty.

The other—the unilateral sex—that was something else. She'd fallen apart in his hands and given him nothing at all in return.

"Would you mind?" she said, looking pointedly at the door. "I need to get showered and dressed if I'm going to get out of here anytime soon."

The trouble with morning light was that it was utterly merciless. Her hair was a mess, she had already discovered places where his beard had scraped her skin. She didn't want to think about how her face must look.

Her nightgown was folded neatly on a chair on the other side of the bedroom. Fine. Great! Then she'd wrap herself in the damned bedspread!

And trip on it? her inner voice jeered. Way to go, Sarah. You're a real class act.

Eleven

They might have been strangers for all the words spoken between them as they ate a hasty breakfast and cleaned up afterward. "Is one bag all you're taking?" he asked politely, checking the back door to be sure it was locked.

"That and my purse. I won't be gone long."

He gave her a searching look, but said nothing. How odd, she thought, that the event that had brought him here—the release of a book rehashing the scandals surrounding her late husband, seemed irrelevant now. There had been no more reporters since the first flurry.

"Ready?" He held the front door for her.

There were so many questions she wanted to ask about what had happened between them last night. With bitter amusement it occurred to her that she didn't even know how to frame the first question, even if she could have brought herself to voice it.

He'd been right to call a halt, of course—if that's what had happened. If Stan had been as responsible—or if he'd been a faithful husband in the first place, then she'd probably have still been living in Arlington. There would have been no Kitty. By now she might even have been pregnant with a child of her own.

"I topped off your tank yesterday," Rocky said as he put her overnighter in the back seat. "If you weren't so stubborn about getting a cell phone—"

"I know, I know." She shaded her eyes against the glare of the sky. "Look, I'm getting there, all right? I'm going to buy a computer and learn how to use it, and then maybe I'll try a cell phone, but don't rush me."

Actually, she had one. Stan had tried to show her how to use his home computer. He'd laughed when she hadn't been interested and told her to come out of the dark ages, that practically every kid in America was hooked up to the Internet. She was the only woman in Washington—possibly in the entire world—who didn't have e-mail. He'd tried to talk her into getting a cell phone and a pocket pager—he'd even mentioned some gadget she could carry in her car that could tell her where in the world she was at any given moment in time.

"I know where I am. That's what street maps are for," she'd told him. It had done no good to explain that she'd been far too accessible all her life. "There's such a thing as privacy, you know. I happen to value mine."

But Stan had loved gadgets—the more expensive, the better—almost as much as he'd loved the limelight. He'd insisted on giving her a phone that plugged into her car's cigarette lighter. The thing had never worked properly, and she'd never bothered to tell him or to find out why. It was somewhere in the trunk of her car, along with her tire-changing tools—which she *did* know how to use, if she had to.

Rocky looked angry and frustrated. She knew how he felt, having seen the same look on both Stan's face and her father's when she didn't instantly bow to their superior male knowledge.

"Look, I'll be all right, don't worry," she exclaimed. "Believe it or not, people were safely crossing continents before cell phones and global positioning gizmos were even invented." He was standing beside his car, which looked as though it had been driven a few thousand miles past its use-by date.

"Sure." He looked as if he'd like to say more. Instead, he climbed in under the wheel, closed the door and rolled down the window. "Stick with the writing, Sarah. Judging by the few pages I saw, you're good. And by the way, your left rear tire is wearing. You need to have your wheels balanced."

Sarah closed her eyes and prayed for patience. "Would you please give me credit for possessing a brain? I'll balance my own damned tires! That is, I'll—"

He was grinning. The righteous, meddlesome, wonderful, generous man was grinning!

"Oh, for gosh sakes," she muttered as she climbed into her car, tossing her purse on the passenger seat on top of her sunglasses, a candy bar and an envelope she couldn't recall seeing before. Probably an old shopping list.

She really should have called her father to let him

know she was on her way. If he was truly ill, she needed to know it. In that case she would stay with him until she could find someone—maybe a practical nurse—to live in. It would cost a fortune, and she didn't know if he still had insurance or not.

She would simply have to deal with the situation as she found it. If he wasn't really ill—if he was bluffing, something at which he was a master—then she might or might not stay for his birthday. It would depend on how much he gloated.

In either case, the sooner she saw him, the sooner she'd be able to find out the truth, satisfy her conscience and get back to Snowden.

Ever the dutiful daughter, she thought bitterly.

"Ever the doormat," she amended as she braked to avoid a suicidal squirrel.

When Rocky had asked her over breakfast about the drawings and manuscript on her desk, she'd told him it was a hobby—that she hadn't quite made up her mind whether to write children's stories or a survival guide. If he'd made the obvious remark—that anyone less qualified to write a survival handbook would be hard to find—she might have broken down and told him everything.

But he hadn't, and so she'd left it at that. After that, conversation had been practically nonexistent. They'd both been eager to leave. Besides which, she hadn't been able to look at him without thinking—without remembering—

And dammit, he'd known it!

Glancing in her rearview mirror, she swore again. If he thought for a single minute she was going to put up with being followed all the way to Maryland, he was in for a surprise. She might be technologically challenged, but she was a damned good driver.

She tried and failed to lose him on the 64 bypass around Norfolk. Once on the Eastern Shore, she took several detours, whipping suddenly off the highway onto narrow roads, passing farms and the few remaining fishing communities before looping back to the highway. By the time she stopped for a late lunch near Salisbury, he was nowhere in sight. Which should have made her feel triumphant.

Instead, she felt depressed.

Well, what did you expect? It's over, okay?

Not okay. Whatever had happened between them, it had ended with no real harm done on either side, she told herself. But she didn't have to like it.

Her crabcake sandwich suddenly lost its appeal. Finishing her iced tea, she dug out a tip, glanced through the plate glass window to be sure there was no slightly rusty, slightly battered, dark-green SUV among the half-dozen vehicles in the graveled parking lot.

Hearts don't actually break, she rationalized, it only felt that way. She had brought it on herself—this miserable, empty feeling—by falling in love with a stranger. A man she had known for little more than a week.

Plus twenty-odd years, technically, but that didn't count.

Back in her car she slung her purse on the other seat. The envelope slid off onto the floor. She leaned across and picked it up, felt something small and heavy, and curious, traced the shape with her fingers. A key?

Even more curious, she turned the envelope over. Someone had scribbled an address and phone number on the back. Now why in the world would anyone give her a key? What was she supposed to unlock?

There was no message, no note, only the phone number, and a street address in Chevy Chase.

"Damn you," she whispered. "If you think all you have to do is whistle and I'll come running—"

That very first day he had stood in the middle of her dusty, weed-grown lane and whistled. The piercing sound had slowed down the reporter—the first reporter—long enough for Rocky to catch up with him.

And she'd looked at him—at those icy eyes, that square, unshaven jaw, and something had happened to her. Whatever it was—hypnosis, airborne virus or a major tectonic-plate shift, it had obviously affected her brain, hormones, her judgment and totally destroyed any sense of self-preservation she might once have possessed.

The rambling rock-and-redwood house was large, but hardly palatial. The land itself was probably more valuable than the house, which had been built back in the seventies. A dozen or so acres, most of it in its natural state, on the banks of the Wye River. The shell driveway was edged with daylilies that had become naturalized over the years. Tall trees were just beginning to show a touch of fall color. It really was a lovely place, Sarah admitted as she drove slowly past the house and parked in front of the three-car garage. By all rights she should have been happy to live here. She'd been invited to do so after Stan had died, except that would have meant being constantly at odds with the senator, whose ideas concerning women and children had been set in concrete before she'd been born.

As a child, he'd used her for photo ops, but he'd never made the least attempt to get to know her. As a woman, he had chosen her associates, discreetly getting rid of a few of her closest friends, not that she'd realized at the time why they had suddenly cooled off or moved away or started seeing someone else. He had even engineered, she'd realized belatedly, her marriage to a promising young congressman.

Now that she was widowed, he would no doubt expect to oversee her social life, possibly even to the extent of marrying her off again to a suitable candidate. She had an awful feeling that this time that candidate might be Clive Meadows.

"When hell freezes over," she muttered as a weathered, middle-aged man came around the corner of the garage, rake in hand. Ollie had been with her father for years in one capacity or another. The senator was good to the handful of people he trusted.

"Hi, Ollie. How's Annamarie?" The handyman's daughter was in her third year at Annapolis.

"Hurt her shoulder playing soccer, Miss Sarah." He had called her Miss Sarah ever since he'd come to work for her father some twenty-five years ago. "She's doing real good, though. Smart as her mama was, God bless her."

"I know she is, Ollie. Will I be blocking anyone if I leave my car here for now?"

"Leave the keys in 'er, I'll shift 'er if I need to." Ollie came from a long line of Chesapeake Bay watermen. Cars, like boats, were of the feminine gender.

"The senator's out back on the patio with Mr. Meadows."

She was tempted to tell him to leave the engine running in case she needed to make a quick getaway. Instead, taking the flagstone path around the house, she told herself that the sooner she found out what was going on, the sooner she could cope with the problem and leave with a clear conscience.

Later, lying awake in the guest room she had used only a few times since her father had bought the property back in the eighties, she thought over the past few hours and tried to decide what it was all about—why she'd been summoned.

According to the senator he'd recently had a small scare, not that a man his age didn't expect such things. Simple angina, nothing to worry about...*this* time, he'd told her. She'd recognized the stoic martyr role. He'd gone on to tell her that he took pills for his blood pressure, which was a tad high. As for his cholesterol, he ate like a damned rabbit and took pills for that, as well. One bay of the three-car garage had been turned into a torture chamber where he was supposed to sweat out the rest of his days on a bunch of confounded machines.

"What do the damned medics expect from a man my age? Clive, get me my cigar."

"Father, you probably shouldn't—"

He silenced her with the same peremptory gesture he'd used whenever she'd tried to tell him something as a child. "I've cut down to two a day. Might as well die if I have to give up everything that makes life worth living." He cackled, and that, Sarah thought, was the most telling sign that he was pushing eighty. He could no longer manage the hearty laugh that had once been so much a part of his image—not without coughing.

She knew very well there was something more—something he wasn't telling her. J. Abernathy Jones had always been skilled at telling a partial truth and seamlessly blending it with lies. She'd do better trying to get the unvarnished truth out of that old willow stump down by the pier.

With Clive for companionship, plus R.C., Ollie and the woman who came in a few hours each day to do the cooking and minor housekeeping, her father really didn't need her. Any filial obligation she might have felt had ended when he'd let her go through the ordeal with Stan alone. Oh, he'd returned in time for the funeral, but that, she suspected, was more because it gave him an opportunity to play his favorite role before the photographers waiting outside the cemetery than out of any real concern for his daughter.

Exhausted, she finally fell into a deep sleep. Hours later she awoke when leaf-dappled sunlight fell across her face, feeling surprisingly refreshed. No wonder people often sought a change of scenery after a trauma. Distance really did help. Added perspective, at the very least. Hadn't she discovered as much when she'd cut all her ties and moved to Snowden?

Two days later she was no closer to discovering what it was that her father wanted from her. The three of them, she, Clive and the senator, had quietly celebrated his seventy-ninth birthday with a dinner of broiled fish with lime, baked potato with fat-free sour cream, a large salad with an olive oil dressing and an apple cake for dessert. J. Abernathy had complained bitterly as he scraped the last bite from his plate.

Sarah had to admit that he looked far better than he had the last time she'd seen him. Obviously, the new restricted regime agreed with him physically, even if it didn't do much for his state of mind.

"I'll be leaving tomorrow, Father." They had dined on a glass-topped table out on the back patio, with the hum of a distant outboard, a thousand tree frogs and the hypnotic sound of a bug zapper filling the silence.

"Surprised you stayed long's you did. I might be an old man, but you're not getting any younger, either, daughter."

"I'd noticed," she said dryly.

"It's still not too late." He cast a sly look at Clive, who was testing the flexibility of a new fly rod.

Reluctantly, Sarah took the bait, knowing that the sooner she put an end to whatever plans he might have up his sleeve, the sooner she could get away. "I'm afraid to ask...too late for what?"

"Legacy. Yes sir, a man my age, who's accomplished all I have, he needs himself a legacy. I'd like to think there'll be another generation coming along behind me to carry on."

Clive coughed discreetly. Sarah's mouth fell open.

His *legacy?* All he had *accomplished?*

The man had disgraced himself personally, lied under oath and endangered national security, for starters. His trial alone had cost the taxpayers millions, not including all the wasted hours involved. The press had been merciless and to her sorrow, Sarah knew he'd deserved every scathing headline.

"Is that what Stan was supposed to do—carry on your legacy?"

The senator dismissed the question with an expressive snort. "Sullivan was a lightweight. I thought the boy had possibilities, but turns out I was wrong." His shoulders slumped and he sighed. "I reckon I owe you an apology, daughter."

"That's not necessary. We were both—"

As if she hadn't spoken, the senator continued to speak. "If that baby of his had been a boy, we might've managed to salvage something."

Sarah caught her breath. *That baby of his?*

"Didn't think I knew about that, did you?" The old man's eyes took on a wicked gleam. "Not much goes on I don't know about, missy. It might pay you to remember that before you go shacking up with every Tom, Dick and Harry that comes along."

"Every Tom, Dick and...?" But of course he knew about Rocky. R.C would have told him, which was why and he'd sent Clive down to investigate. Dammit, couldn't she have a single thing for herself? "Father, please stay out of my private life. Believe it or not, I'm perfectly capable of choosing my own friends."

"Damned reporter. Nosy bunch of hyenas."

Not that he hadn't used them for his own ends over much of his public life, she thought with bitter amusement.

Clive, who'd been an unobtrusive bystander all this time, poured an ounce of brandy in a glass and placed it in the palsied hand. "One more won't hurt you, I guess. Want to try out that new fly rod tomorrow evening, just before dark?"

But Sarah wasn't about to be distracted. "Father, how did you know about—about Kitty?"

"How d'you think I knew? Damned leaches went to Clive when they couldn't get hold of me—it was right in the middle of all the mess. Told him if I didn't pay off they'd go public about Sullivan's brat. Said the girl was underage when he got her in trouble—said they could get DNA if they had to, but there'd been plenty of witnesses, more than enough to make the charges stick."

If a sigh could be said to express piety, his did. "Said to myself, more scandal's the last thing that little girl of mine needs, so I paid 'em off and told 'em if they knew what was good for 'em, they'd take the money and shut up."

Sarah felt sick.

Clive wandered over to the edge of the patio and stared out at the fireflies floating over the overgrown tangle of mock orange, spirea and wigelia. The senator drained his glass and traced the ring of moisture on the table with a thick forefinger.

"You knew about Kitty all along?" Her father frowned. Clive looked embarrassed. "Father, these people are no better than blackmailers. I've been paying them, too."

Her father nodded. It occurred to her then that he'd known all along about that, too. No wonder she suddenly felt as if a noose was tightening around her throat.

"Figured you'd be worried about the little nit. All that work you did with those poor kids. Good work, too," he added hastily, noticing her expression. "Admire you for it, always did. Noblesse oblige, and all that crap.''

Sarah stood, her jaw set in a way that would have served as a warning if he'd ever bothered to get to know her. "You don't even know the meaning of the word," she said grimly.

"Now, Sarah—"

"I want that child, Father. I'm not about to let her grow up with people who use her for blackmail, even if they are her own grandparents. They can't love her—they'll neglect her and possibly worse."

"Well now, that's what I thought you might say. Sit down, girl. Why don't we have another drink and talk about it, you, me and Clive, here? Did I mention they'd sent a picture of the br—the little girl?"

Later Sarah sat cross-legged on the bed and stared down at the snapshot of a child who had been fathered by a man she had once loved enough to marry. A man who might have given her a child of her own. In the picture Kitty was wearing a diaper and a pair of red tennis shoes. She should be out of diapers by now. Her hair was cottony white. There was dirt on her little face, and in one hand she held a doll with only one arm. Were those tear tracks down her cheeks?

Sarah's arms curved instinctively as if to embrace a small child and then fell back to her lap again. She was only a baby—babies cried over the least little thing. It didn't necessarily mean she was unhappy, or being mistreated.

But the Poughs—Kitty's own grandparents—had used that tiny innocent to line their pockets. According to Clive they had actually offered to sell her if the price was right. And of course Clive had known Sarah could never have come up with the money. He'd been the executor of her mother's will. He had handled Sarah's small trust fund and evidently poked his fingers into more of her financial affairs that he was legally entitled to do.

Sarah had pried the whole story from them. Neither man had wanted to talk about it at first, but she'd insisted. It was the first time she remembered ever winning in a tug-of-war with her father. She still wasn't certain which one of them had come out victorious, because the battle was still not over as far as Kitty was concerned.

Trust J. Abernathy Jones to come up with a convoluted scheme that would pay off his best friend for past favors, tie his daughter to him forever and, incidentally, salve his own conscience by making up for years of paternal neglect. Kitty was to have been the bait. Both men knew Sarah had been making monthly payments—they had known almost from the first. And knowing Sarah and the work she'd done, first as a senator's daughter, then as a congressman's wife, for underprivileged children, they had known precisely where to apply pressure.

She might even have agreed to stay on without the added inducement if her father's health had been precarious, but no way in hell would she ever have agreed to marry another of his handpicked candidates. Especially knowing they would stoop to using a child as bait.

Clive had recently undergone treatment for prostate cancer. He was in the wait-and-see stage now. He'd resigned from the lobbying firm and had recently suffered some severe financial reversals.

Oh, they'd worked out the perfect plan, Sarah told herself bitterly. Two old friends, once powerful, now sinking into obscurity together, sharing a house on which, incidentally, Clive had paid off the mortgage, back in the days when a friend in high places had come in handy.

Here, they were close enough to the political action to watch from the sidelines while they worked on their respective memoirs. Meanwhile, the dutiful daughter of one could look after them both.

What an enormous debt her father must owe the man. Evidently Clive knew where all the bodies were buried, so to speak. No longer able to attract, much less afford, younger wives, he faced spending his declining years either alone or with a cantankerous old widower.

Which was where Sarah came in. As her father had said, what else did she have to do, for God's sake? It wasn't as if she had a husband or a career. All she had to go back to was an empty, run-down house in the middle of a damned cornfield.

Knowing how Sarah had always hated being an only child, and how she'd spent almost her entire adult life working in some capacity with children—having heard all about a woman's biological clock—they had come up with the perfect plan.

No wonder Clive had come back for a second attempt at prying her loose after meeting Rocky. It had never occurred to either of them that there might be another man in her life. She wasn't beautiful, she wasn't wealthy, she'd been publicly humiliated. Except for her volunteer work, she'd never even been particularly outgoing. Socially she was barely adequate.

But then, their socializing days were largely over, so that hadn't been a consideration.

Neither man cared for children, although the senator had certainly kissed enough babies to get himself elected and reelected over and over, both to the House and then the Senate. But that was a sacrifice they were prepared to make.

Somewhere in another room, a clock struck eleven. Sitting cross-legged on her bed, Sarah continued to hold the photograph of the child she had pictured so differently. She'd given her Stan's face, his light brown hair. Whatever he'd been on the inside, the man had been physically flawless.

There was nothing at all familiar about that small, dirty face staring at the camera, and yet...

Kitty would be almost two years old. She shouldn't still be wearing diapers at that age. Someone could have washed her face before they took her picture, at the very least.

"Poor darling, you don't deserve any of this," Sarah whispered.

How many organizations had she helped raise money for that fed poor children worldwide? How many drives had she organized to help fund child health care and set up free walk-in clinics in poor neighborhoods? How many hours had she spent at children's hospitals, reading stories, listening to their shy confidences? Feeling their tiny hands creep into her own?

She had to do something about this child. Clive was

a lawyer, but if she asked for his help she'd end up caught in the clever trap they had devised.

Oh, they had known her weakness, all right. And under the gentlemanly patina, both men were equally without scruples when it came to getting what they wanted. And what they wanted now was a strong, healthy woman who would feel morally obligated to stay here and look after them in their declining years, regardless of any sacrifice it might entail on her part.

Sarah had learned last night that two cooks and three housekeepers had either quit or been fired. Annie had stayed on as long as she had for Sarah's sake, despite J. Abernathy's despotic ways. In a time of nearly full employment and high wages, it was a wonder Ollie and R.C. were still here. The senator must have promised to remember them in his will.

Clive had moved in during the course of his treatment. Which was only logical, as he was a part owner. The reason his beach house had been conveniently empty was that he'd put it up for sale, along with his town house on O Street.

Sarah gazed down at the snapshot again and felt the trap begin to close. It was far too easy to visualize a towheaded little girl running around the backyard, chasing butterflies, fishing from the pier, catching the school bus when she was a little older.

Once, briefly, she had dreamed about another child, the first of several, visiting a kinder, gentler grandfather....

It hadn't happened. Now it never would. Was it so very selfish of her to want this one child for herself? In the early months of her marriage, she'd had such dreams. Later, Stan had always said. After the next campaign, after the election. But even then things had begun to change between them. As a naive young bride, she'd been thrilled at the privilege of standing behind her statesman husband while he helped pass laws to right the nation's wrongs. As a wife, she had quickly learned to fill her daytime hours with volunteer work, attend the requisite social functions and lower her own expectations. After all, although he was her husband, he'd been sent to Washington to work for his constituents, for his country, not to play house with his bride.

How could she have been so naive, having grown up around politicians? Mariah Jones had quickly come to terms with her husband's demanding profession. She had become one of Washington's favorite hostesses and, as busy as she'd been, she had still found time to be a wonderful mother. "Get your head out of the clouds, child," Sarah could remember hearing her say more than once. "If you don't stop stargazing, one of these days you're going to walk into a tree and break your neck."

Instead, she'd broken her heart.

But hearts were resilient, and here was a child who needed someone to love her. That, Sarah told herself, she could do.

That she was *determined* to do.

Rising abruptly, she crossed to the dresser and felt inside her tote bag. It was still there—the envelope with the key. The more she thought about it, the more she was beginning to have bad feelings about Kitty's situation. If the Poughs had contacted her father, asking for money, too, then they didn't deserve this child.

She would deal with her father's health problems

later if she had to, but first she had to know the truth about Kitty's situation. If she was secure and happy where she was, then that would be that. Right or wrong, Sarah would go on sending money as long as she could afford it. Perhaps someday she might even find a way to be a part of the child's life. She could be to Kitty what Aunt Emma had been to her.

Aunt Sarah Mariah. She rather liked the sound of that—but first she had to discover the truth of the situation, and there was only one man she knew of who could help her do that.

Twelve

With the game being played out on television—eighth inning, score tied, two out, three on base for Atlanta, Rocky paced the floor, returning again and again to the window overlooking the street. Traffic was light. The view of the small parking area was blocked by the tops of two ginko trees and a weeping cherry. She could be out there right now, trying to make up her mind whether or not to come in, and he wouldn't know it. What if she made it all the way to his door, then lost her courage and fled?

He should never have allowed her to face that conniving old pirate alone. Whatever else he was, the man still was her father, and a woman like Sarah, with her queen-size sense of responsibility, would never be able to walk away if he managed to convince her that he needed her. She had stuck by his side throughout the hearings, her very presence giving mute testimony to the fact that he couldn't possibly be as wicked as he'd been portrayed, despite the damning evidence. A few years later she'd been thrown to the lions all over again.

But no more, dammit. He had allowed her to go in alone because it was something she had to do for herself if she ever hoped to be free of the man. After a year of living alone in Snowden, she'd still been afraid to answer the phone. He'd seen animals cower in their pens long after the gate was opened. Prisoners who huddled in their cell after years of confinement, unable to comprehend that they could simply walk out. Not answering her telephone wouldn't cut it. Sarah had to confront the man and then walk away unaided to be truly free. And she had to do it alone.

Rocky had halfway expected her the second night. Not the first, because knowing Sarah, she would give her father enough time to fully present his case. When she hadn't shown up, he'd called her number in Snowden and let it ring twelve times. That didn't necessarily mean she wasn't there. Sarah had a habit of not picking up. As far as she was concerned, the telephone was a one-way instrument, and that one way led out, not in.

Rocky shook his head in reluctant admiration. The lady might not look it, but in some ways she was as tough as that damned grapevine she'd been fighting all summer.

Sarah, Sarah, where the devil are you? One more day and I'm coming after you.

What was that old song about not having time to

play the waiting game? Sometimes it seemed as if he'd spent half his life playing the waiting game.

Suddenly Sarah couldn't wait a single moment longer. Arriving in the middle of the night meant she'd have a harder time finding the address, but if she waited until morning he might be gone. He might still be in North Carolina, for all she knew. Rescuing some other woman in distress. "Oh, stop it! It's going to be bad enough without imagining the worst!"

She had told her father at supper that she was leaving, knowing he'd assume she was going back to Snowden. Lying by omission. She hadn't lived with two politicians as long as she had without learning how the game was played. "I need to think it over, Father. I'll call in a day or so."

"We could fix up a room. One kid—how much trouble could she be? Get her some swings, slides—whatever you think she needs."

When had he ever concerned himself with what any child needed? "I'll call," she'd repeated. Then, for the first time in years, she had kissed him.

Back in her room she'd fretted herself sick, wondering if she had the right—if she even had the courage to ask for Rocky's help.

It wasn't just an excuse to see him again—at least, not entirely. He had resources—he would know how to go about handling something this delicate. The investigations, the personal negotiations, the legal aspects. Twice she picked up the phone, only to put it down again. If she called first, what could she say? *I want you to forget what happened between us and help me adopt a baby?* He'd think she had lost her mind.

It was nearly ten when she left. Her father had gone to bed early, and Clive was on the phone. Sarah felt no compunction at all in leaving without saying goodbye to him, although she couldn't help feeling a certain degree of admiration. His own career had risen and fallen along with that of his friend. Such loyalty, if that's what it was, was probably a rarity in their world of shifting alliances. She'd like to think they both deserved such loyalty.

Her car was still where she'd left it when she'd arrived. R.C. came by every morning. The housekeeper came for a few hours each afternoon. Other than that, no one but the mailman had been in or out. Driving slowly down the winding driveway, she had to admit it was a lovely place. Maybe someday she would come for a longer visit.

And bring Kitty?

One step at a time, she warned herself. And the next step would be a giant one.

Near the 301 exit, she stopped for gas, coffee and a bathroom. Pausing for a lull in the traffic, she toyed with the idea of turning south instead of continuing to the beltway. After her botched attempt to seduce him, Rocky was probably glad to have escaped with his virtue more or less intact.

On the other hand, he'd given her the key. Why would he have done that unless he expected her to use it?

Face it, Sarah. You've got the survival instincts of a lemming.

But dammit, she loved the man and she needed him, and whatever he thought of her—whether or not he could ever learn to love her back, she was pretty sure he would help her with Kitty because that was the kind of man he was. Decent, honorable, caring.

Against the eerie glow of the streetlights, the sky was pitch-black, adding further fuel to her doubts. It wasn't too late to turn back. She could be in Snowden by suppertime.

No, dammit, this was her decision and she would follow through, no matter what. If he wasn't there, she would let herself in, use his bathroom, maybe raid his refrigerator...he owed her that much...leave his key and maybe a note, thanking him for—

Well, whatever. He could interpret it any way he wished.

With the help of a detailed map, she finally located the street, then crept along until she found the right address. After parking illegally under a huge ginko tree, she sat for several minutes, going over in her mind what she would say if he happened to be there: Hi, I was in the neighborhood, and I thought I'd drop by.

Glancing at her watch, she wondered if she was crazy even to think about adopting a child, especially under the circumstances. She certainly didn't owe it to her husband.

What did she know about being a mother? Looking back, she realized now that quality time for her own mother had been a few minutes each morning to let her daughter know her day's schedule. "I'll be at the museum until one. You can reach me through the front office." Or, "I'll be at the fashion show until four— I'll try to bring you a scarf, or maybe one of those darling little berets."

Quality time for her father was whenever he was

slated to appear in public. His wife and daughter had been bit players, of slightly less importance than his speechwriter and his hairdresser. They represented living proof of what a worthy statesman J. Abernathy Jones really was. Defender of home, family and the American way of life.

"Bull," Sarah growled. Leaving her overnight case on the back seat—not a particularly smart thing to do, but she was too tired to be clever—she locked her car and headed toward the front entrance.

Tonight's game had gone to twelve innings. Rocky had slept through the final one. Fallen asleep in his chair. Then he'd got up and prowled in the kitchen, making a pot of coffee, scrambling the last two eggs in the carton. He was going to have to make a supply run soon, but he'd been afraid to go out, afraid of missing her.

He ate standing up, knowing he'd probably doze again if he got too comfortable. On the other hand, if he went to bed, he'd never be able to sleep.

Hell of a thing, not knowing. He should never have let her go without some sort of an understanding. And now one more night had passed. One more day of waiting and wondering. How long should he give her? Three days? A week?

Hell no. He'd give her until noon. If she'd decided to stay with her father, she could just damn well *un*decide. At least until he'd had a shot at changing her mind.

He had tried working on a column. Ideology, how it affected issues, and how it could be distorted for public consumption. About twelve hundred words in, he gave up.... Sarah, Sarah, don't waste what we could have together.

At first when the buzzer sounded, he couldn't think what it was. He glanced at the phone, scowled at his watch and when it hit him that it was the buzzer in the lobby, his first impulse was to go down and let her in personally. But if he was going to disgrace himself with a maudlin display of emotion, he'd as soon do it in the privacy of his own apartment.

What if it wasn't Sarah?

It was Sarah. He knew it in his bones. And if she thought for a single minute he was going to allow her to walk out of here without a commitment, she'd better think again.

He was waiting in the hallway when she reached the top of the stairs. Neither of them spoke, but it was all there. Whatever it was between them that had brought her here, that had made him so certain she would come.

There were shadows under her eyes. Her various cowlicks had defeated any attempt she might have made to groom her hair. And she was so damned beautiful he could have wept.

Rocky opened his arms, and she walked into them without a word. Long moments passed before she lifted her face from his shoulder. "I probably should have called first."

"No need to. If you hadn't showed up by noon I'd have come after you." Pulling her with him, he backed toward his door and closed it behind them.

"Where? Snowden or my father's house?"

"Hadn't made up my mind yet. I'd have followed

my instincts and found you, though, you can bet on it."

He was still holding her, swaying gently from side to side, his eyes closed to better absorb her essence. *She's here. She's actually here in my home, here in my arms.*

After so many anxious, sleepless hours, all he could think of was taking her to bed. If he did nothing more than hold her until she was rested, it would be enough.

The hell it would. At his age, mind over body should be no problem, but with Sarah, all bets were off.

"Are you uh—hungry?" he asked, easing her away before she realized what was happening to him. The last thing he wanted was to scare her off now.

"I had coffee. I would have had peanuts, too, but I spilled them in the car trying to open the pack."

His laughter broke the tension. "Why am I not surprised?"

He led her into his living room, noticing for the first time the lack of anything more than the basic furnishings. When it had become obvious that Julie would never be coming home again, he had moved from the town house they'd shared. Moved several times, in fact, as financial necessity dictated, paring his possessions down in the process. When it came to creature comforts, a man didn't need much more than the basics.

"You look bushed."

"I haven't been sleeping well," she admitted.

Nodding, he continued to embrace her with his eyes. She was actually here, within touching distance. "Would you like, uh—"

"I could use a bathroom," she said with that funny half smile he had come to look for. Come to love.

"Through here. Give me your car keys and I'll bring in your bag. Then we'll have supper—breakfast—whatever, while we talk."

She hesitated just a fraction too long.

"Sarah, you can prioritize any way you want to, but we're going to talk, we need to eat, and I have a feeling we could both use a few hours of sleep."

Lifting her hands, she raked her fingers through the layers of her thick brown hair. "If I could just splash some cold water on my face. Actually, all over would be better. I had to drive with the window open to stay awake, and I probably reek of exhaust fumes. There was a tanker ahead of me practically the whole way."

She didn't look grungy, she looked windblown. Exhausted. Irresistible. "Sure. Meanwhile, I'll see if I can scrounge up something to eat. Or I could send out."

"I'm not really hungry. Coffee would help, though, because the talking's going to take a while. There's something I want to ask, but first there's something I need to explain."

Rocky nodded. He had a feeling he was about to get to the heart of the matter. "Go shower while I put the pot on. Then we'll talk."

If he could keep his mind on what she was saying instead of what he'd really like to do. Suddenly he wasn't feeling quite so tired. Instincts grown dull from lack of use told him it wasn't about the Cudahy book. That had been launched a week ago, making a much smaller splash than the publisher had hoped, thanks to new offerings by a couple of perennial bestsellers.

"Give me your car keys, I'll get your bag while you wash up."

Some ten minutes later Sarah stepped out of the shower and wrapped herself in a lush, king-size bath towel. Whatever he might lack in decorative accessories, she thought with amusement, the man didn't stint on luxurious necessities.

Hearing movement just across the hall, she cracked the door and called out, "Rocky? Would you mind looking in my bag for my wrapper? It's the blue-flowered thing."

Clutching the towel more tightly around her, she tried to remember whether or not she had packed anything of an embarrassingly personal nature when she'd tossed everything into her overnighter. *He's seen you naked, you ninny! The sight of your underwear is hardly going to bring on cardiac arrest!*

When he rapped on the door, she opened it a few inches and reached for the cotton wrapper "What's that cliché?" she asked breathlessly. "'We've got to stop meeting like this'?"

"You mean, déjà vu all over again? I didn't know you were a baseball fan."

The sound of his husky murmur sent ripples along every nerve in her body. With his face mere inches away, Sarah struggled against a strange sense of lethargy. Heat pooled in the lower regions of her body, robbing her of the will to move—to think. "I...I—I'd better..." Tearing her eyes from his face, she stared down at the wisp of cotton in her hand. She meant to say, "I'd better put this on—make myself decent," but somehow the words wouldn't come.

Soap-scented steam drifted through the door, enclosing them both in a seductive cloud. Rocky reached for her hand. She dropped the duster he'd just handed her, clutched at the towel, and he said, "You don't need your robe, Sarah. We've got some unfinished business, remember?"

Wordlessly, she nodded, her gaze never leaving his face. His meaning was perfectly clear. This time there would be no halfway measures, no unilateral completion. This time they would make love in every sense of the word. Later they would have to talk, because she needed him for Kitty's sake.

But right now she needed him even more desperately for her own.

The bedroom was as uncluttered as the rest of the apartment. Bed, chest of drawers, chair. No pictures on the wall. No clothes tossed casually over a chair. The room reflected the man. Private. Self-contained. Understated. An easy man to love, but not an easy man to get to know.

Sarah perched on the bed, and he pressed her back against the pillow. Then slowly, deliberately, his eyes never leaving hers, he peeled her fingers from the damp towel she wore like a sarong and spread the ends apart. Feeling heat envelop her body, she hoped he would think she was still flushed from the hot shower.

His eyes never left hers, and Sarah wondered how she could ever have thought gray eyes were icy. Still wearing a rumpled white shirt open at the neck and a pair of khakis, he smelled of laundry soap and warm, clean male. She told herself that anyone who could bottle and sell the scent as an aphrodisiac would make a fortune.

"Wait. I have to tell you something first," she said,

suddenly feeling the urge to put all her cards on the table. She was sick of subterfuge.

His gaze moved slowly past the hollow at the base of her throat, lingered on her breasts, then on her navel before moving on. She wondered how merely looking, not even touching, could generate so much heat.

"I'm listening."

"Well. What it is—that is, I'm pretty sure I love you. I...I wasn't quite certain before."

She heard the sharp intake of his breath. "Mind telling me what decided you?"

"Now? Do I have to?" When he nodded, his features frozen in a stern mask, she looked away and whispered, "It just...came to me. And I wanted you to know before we—that is, I wanted you to know in case you wanted to back out."

With a softly muttered oath, he lowered himself across her body and began kissing her as if he were starved for the taste of her mouth.

Eventually Sarah's greedy hands found their way inside his shirt. When a finger brushed over his nipple, she felt him stiffen. Somehow, without breaking away from his mouth, she managed to free him of the shirt, and then they both went to work on his pants. Two pairs of hands fumbling desperately, driven by a desire so fierce it blocked out the rest of the world.

"Lady, you don't pull any punches, do you?" He groaned and closed his eyes.

Once she had freed him of his outer garments, Sarah gazed down over his splendid torso, and she said shakily, "I didn't mean to upset you." With one finger, she traced a path through the pelt of dark hair that embraced his male nipples, then led down to his waist and beyond.

The physical response was fierce and immediate. Breathing through his mouth in short, rapid gasps, he fought for control. "This is absurd in a man my age," he muttered.

Sarah—a shy, inhibited woman who had been called frigid more than once by her own husband, could only agree. "Me, too."

Who *was* this wanton creature? This teasing, taunting woman who actually laughed aloud as she pushed him over onto his back and sprawled across his body. Moving her hand slowly over his large body, she began a leisurely exploration of all the exquisite textures—the velvet and satin—the fur and hot steel.

"Whoa—hold on a minute, love," he whispered. Lifting her aside, he sat up and opened the drawer of his bedside table. Her eyes widened as she caught a glimpse of the contents. Catching her look, he said, "First stop I made after leaving my door key in your car, I stocked up. Is that blind faith, or what?"

"Oh, my. Maybe we should have talked first, after all," she whispered eagerly. "We might not have time—" And then she slapped a hand over her mouth.

Chuckling, Rocky said, "Later, I promise. First let's put out a few wildfires. Otherwise neither of us is going to be able to concentrate."

Moments later he lifted her hand to his lips and traced the fine lines across her palm with the tip of his tongue, savoring the sharp intake of her breath. Then, his gaze never leaving her face, he closed his mouth over the tip of one finger and suckled gently. By the time he was finished with the first five, she was lying on her back, clutching his thigh and whimpering.

By the time he finished saluting the last finger with a heated, moist caress, Rocky was close to the whimpering stage, himself, but he was determined that this time they would share the glory.

"Now? Please?" she whispered.

Seeing the feverish glitter in her eyes, knowing it was reflected in his own, he moved over her. How was it possible that a woman he had known less than a month—a month plus some twenty-odd years—could affect him so powerfully, in so many different ways?

They came together then, and his last glimmer of reason was eclipsed by a surge of white-hot heat.

Again they came together...and then again. Eventually they fell asleep in a sated tangle of limbs.

Rocky awoke to the sound of kitchen noises. Moments later, the events of the past few hours slipped neatly into place in his orderly mind, and he marveled that such a thing could happen twice in a man's lifetime.

It was more than sex, as mind-boggling as that had been. More than simple release. There had been no one in years who had meant anything to him other than momentary physical release. Even that had brought such feelings of guilt he'd finally accepted his celibate fate.

They'd probably been too young, he and Julie, but they'd loved as only the very young can love. Idealistically, with the future spread out before them, they had lain awake at night after making love, planning for the future—sharing dreams.

For months after the accident, his whole world had narrowed down to that one small room in a private hospital. He had watched her lying there day after day, week after week. Waiting for some sign. Gradually hope faded, replaced by anger at the senselessness of it all. And then slowly, even his anger had faded, replaced by a love that had deepened in ways he couldn't begin to comprehend. It would always be a part of him though—that love—tucked away in a safe place in his heart.

And now there was Sarah. His sweet, awkward Sarah with the earnest eyes and the funny half smile. Sarah, who had been the innocent victim of two men who should have loved her more.

Rocky was on his way to the bathroom when he heard the sound of breaking glass from the kitchen, followed by a soft, "Oh, damn, oh, damn, oh, damn."

Grinning, he stepped into the shower and turned on the water, full force. By the time he had shaved and dressed in jeans and his favorite black knit shirt, he was whistling. All of seven minutes had passed. Record time, and he hadn't even nicked his chin with the razor.

"I smell coffee," he said, pausing in the kitchen door. He managed to resist the urge to sweep her into his arms and carry her back to bed, but there was no way he could dislodge the smile on his face.

"I broke one of your plates. The green one. I'm sorry, but it was ugly, anyway. How can anyone make breakfast from bread, bottled tea, salsa and hot banana peppers?"

"What, you don't like fake pizza for breakfast?"

Over a makeshift breakfast, they talked. Sarah sprinkled sugar on her toast, Rocky spread his with salsa and peppers. Then she carefully placed her crust on her plate and faced him across the table. "All right," she declared, grimly earnest. "Here's what you have to know before you can help me—that is, advise me."

He let her run with it. Whatever secret she'd been guarding, she'd get it out in her own sweet time, in her own way. One thing he'd learned about Sarah—she was no pushover.

"You know about Stan—I mean, all that mess he was involved in. Some of it was illegal, most of it was just...messy. It all came out only because there were some celebrities involved, and somebody broke out a window and started throwing things out. Furniture. A neighbor reported it and a reporter heard about it on his car radio and...well, I guess you know all that. What you don't know—nobody does, because they don't publicize that kind of thing—is that at least one of the girls involved was underage."

He waited. In her own time, in her own way, she would get to the heart of the matter. He poured her another cup of coffee, sweetened it with one spoonful of sugar and added a splash of half-and-half.

"Well. The thing is, she had a baby. This girl, I mean. And she claimed it was Stan's."

"And you believed her?"

"Stan confessed. He told me he didn't realize how young she was, not that that makes it all right. The thing is, there's this child—hardly more than a baby—and her name is Kitty, and her mother doesn't want her, and her grandparents are getting money for her and—"

"Getting money from where? How? Sarah, don't

tell me you're being blackmailed." What possible difference could it make to her now, he wondered, if another of her late husband's sins came home to roost?

Small fists clenched on the table, she leaned forward. "They're her grandparents. They're old—living on social security in a trailer somewhere in Virginia Beach. The mother married and she's gone—I'm not even sure if they know where she is. But this much I do know—that baby deserves someone to love her, and anyone who demands money just to protect her from vicious gossip can't. Love her, I mean."

He waited. He had a feeling he knew where this was headed, but she needed to get it all out.

"They contacted my father, too, and he gave them money because he didn't think I needed to have all that mess come out again. And it would—especially with that awful woman's book. I can just imagine the headlines."

"Tabloids, maybe. No reputable newspaper would touch it."

"So? People read tabloids. I always read them while I'm waiting in line at the grocery store. Not that I believe them, but some people might, and Kitty doesn't deserves to grow up under the shadow of all that mess. Children can be cruel unless someone teaches them to be kind. Maybe it's part of the survival of the species thing, I don't know. I only know," she said with a sigh, "that a child needs to be loved for who she is, not used."

He didn't say a word. There was a wealth of understanding in those clear gray eyes of his, but she didn't dare trust too soon. She waited for him to tell her she was crazy—that it was none of her business.

That nothing could change what her husband had done.

Instead, he said quietly. "You want the child, am I reading you correctly?"

Sarah took a deep breath and closed her eyes. Then she nodded. "Yes, but there's more. You might as well hear it all."

So she told him about the plan her father and Clive Meadows had concocted between them to get her to move in and take over the reins so that neither of them would have to be bothered with petty domestic issues. "They don't have a clue—there's always been someone to do for them. Annie was with my parents since they were first married. R.C. said the last three housekeepers walked out, and the one they have now is a retired dietician who doesn't do floors, windows or much of anything but cook, send out the laundry and make the beds."

He could picture her managing her father's household like a feisty little general. But it wasn't going to happen. Not if he could prevent it.

"So now you see why I'm so determined to adopt that baby."

Setting his brain on fast forward, Rocky wondered if he had missed a vital clue. "Because you don't want to move in and take care of your father."

"Because Kitty needs me a lot more than my father does. And because I need her. And obviously they don't. The Poughs, I mean. And Kitty's mother. So why shouldn't she go to someone who will love her and take good care of her?"

"What if her mother decides she wants her back?"

Sarah frowned. "What if she doesn't?"

"Can you afford a child?"

"I can't afford not to try. She needs me."

It was as simple as that, Rocky told himself later, after he had agreed to help her explore the possibilities. Which would mean finding out the price, putting it in terms that could be done legally, locating the daughter and getting her to sign off.... It would take some tricky negotiating.

They both fell silent. Sarah picked up grains of sugar with her fingertip and thoughtfully licked them off. Rocky watched, wondering if he was crazy to be thinking of starting all over again at his age.

Well, hell...he'd never know without asking. "Sarah, you know about Julie. You know I'm currently unemployed. I have a few investments, a few royalties, but Julie's long illness maxed out my insurance and wiped out all our savings. What I'm trying to say is that I'm no bargain. Living alone for so long, I've picked up a few bad habits that I might be too old to change, but I'm willing to try."

"What are you trying to say?"

"This is not about Kitty, this is about us." Eyes shouldn't be that large, he thought. Nor that direct, that expressive. "A kid needs family—brothers and sisters. You didn't have any—I didn't have any. Julie came from a large family, but they're all on the West Coast and all a lot older. She used to call herself the afterthought."

He wasn't sure she was making the connection. Maybe he'd lost his skill with words, so he opted for plain talk. "You've got to know I love you. It's the only way I can explain a normally sensible guy behaving in such an irrational manner."

Seeing the look in her eyes, he had to wonder which she was questioning—the sensible part or the irrational part. "Like heading out on a rescue mission uninvited. Moving in with a woman I barely knew. Hanging shutters, for God's sake. You've had me tied up in so many knots, wondering if I was crazy to think—to hope—"

"Go back."

"Back?"

"Back to the beginning."

Mentally he backtracked through what he'd just said. "You mean the part where I said I love you?"

Beaming, she nodded. "Say it again."

So he did. And then she did, too. And hours later as they lay in bed, bare feet entwined, and discussed the possibilities, the words were spoken more than once in the silent language of lovers.

There were obstacles to be overcome—there would always be obstacles. But together they could deal with whatever the future brought. The healing time was over, the building time just begun.

Epilogue

"Hurry up, honey, Grandaddy will be here before you know it." Sarah waited while Kitty gathered up the toys she wanted to show her gruff, overindulgent grandfather. It was more than two small arms could carry, so Sarah took the big panda and the sock monkey.

"My book, Mommy, don't forget my book!"

"Don't you dare," Rocky warned, appearing in the doorway just as Sarah braced herself to squat and retrieve the book from the bottom shelf. Getting down, she had discovered, was no problem. It was getting up again, with her balance distorted by her seven-month pregnancy, that caused problems.

"I thought you were finishing up your column?"

"Proofing it. Figured I'd better see what my ladies were up to." He handed her the well-worn book and kissed the tip of her nose. It was Sarah's first published book, with the second one of the series almost finished. Kitty loved spelling out her own name in the dedication.

"I'm hardly breakable, you know," she said dryly to the husband who insisted on treating her as if she were made of spun glass.

He didn't have to say a word, all he had to do was raise his eyebrows.

"Oh, all right, but once Roland is born, I'm not going to let you coddle me this way."

"Right. After little Mariah is born, it's back to bungee jumping, motorcycle racing and skateboarding."

Laughing, Sarah swatted him on the arm as they followed Kitty to the front door. With his past, he would probably always be a bit overprotective. And after the constraints required of a politician's family, she was still exploring the parameters of her own independence. Secure in their love, they were both mature enough to work through any conflict.

"I see G'andaddy and Unca Clibe!" Kitty shouted. Wriggling free of Rocky's restraining hand, she raced outside, spilling toys down the front hallway. The screen door slammed shut behind her just as a car pulled up in front of the house.

On the front porch Rocky wrapped his arms around his wife's expanding waist and waited as two old reprobates he had learned to enjoy, if not to respect, braced themselves for Kitty's exuberant greeting.

"Remember," Sarah said softly, "no talking politics."

"I won't if you won't," Rocky said, his smile a wicked taunt. He loved sparring with her, and had even come to enjoy taking on her father and his crony. "Remarkable, isn't it, the way a couple of old guys who don't particularly like kids manage to spoil ours the way they do."

"They're just practicing up on Kitty. Wait'll they meet Roland."

"Mariah."

"Patience, love—we'll get around to using both names in due time."

With a private little smile meant solely for him, she murmured, "I'm game if you are." Then, with the smile she had honed for public consumption as the senator's daughter and the congressman's wife, she said, "Hello, Father—Clive. Come on inside, supper's almost ready."

* * * * *

NIGHT WIND'S WOMAN

by
Sheri WhiteFeather

SHERI WHITEFEATHER

lives in Southern California and enjoys ethnic dining, summer pow-wows and visiting art galleries and vintage clothing shops near the beach. Since her one true passion is writing, she is thrilled to be a part of the Silhouette Desire line. When she isn't writing, she often reads until the small hours of the morning.

Sheri also works as a leather artisan with her Native American husband. They have one son and a menagerie of pets, including a pampered English bulldog and four equally spoiled Bengal cats. She would love to hear from her readers. You may write to her at: PO Box 5130, Orange, California 92863-5130, USA.

This book is dedicated to those I've come to know through their involvement with big cats. Thanks to Lynn Culver for her extensive notes and videotape on cougar development; Mary Robbins, a fellow writer and animal lover; Dr. Scott Weldy, the best vet an exotic (or domestic) could ever have; Brian Werner, the director of Tiger Creek Wildlife Refuge; and finally to Jeanne Hall, a member of the Potawatomi tribe, who taught me the true meaning of mountain lion medicine. Her cougars, Jake, Yamari and Baby, inspired the fictitious Puma. Jeanne shared every aspect of her life with 'the boys.'

Without her, the unusual cougar events in this story wouldn't have been possible.

One

Kelly Baxter waited at her neighbor's door, miles of West Texas surrounding her. During the long, dusty ride, she had driven past cattle ranches and crooked wood fencing, abandoned trucks and fields of bluebonnets. And now she stood on the front porch of a large country house, sidestepping an arrangement of potted plants and sun-bleached cow skulls.

The Western charm hadn't eased her frazzled nerves. She had argued with her mother about making this trip. "You shouldn't be traveling alone," her mom had said, "and you shouldn't stay in some run-down, old cabin in the middle of nowhere, either. Not when you have a paternity suit to consider."

Kelly rested her hand on her protruding tummy. She had inherited the cabin from her grandpa and, at this particular time in her life, the middle of nowhere suited her just fine. But to appease her mom, she promised to stop by Dr. McKinley's, the neighbor Grandpa had considered a friend. She would introduce herself, then be on her way.

When the front door finally opened, she could only stare. The man on the other side wasn't Dr. McKinley. He was much too young and much too dark to fit Grandpa's description of the fifty-some-year-old veterinarian.

"I'm Kelly Baxter," she said hastily. "And you must be Shane Night Wind." The doctor's half-Comanche son, the man Grandpa had deemed "part wildcat."

"Kelly Baxter?"

He returned her stare with a deeply-fixed gaze, brown eyes shimmering with tiny flecks of gold. Those eyes scanned the length of her, settling momentarily on her protruding tummy.

She studied his posture: the long, rangy stillness, the muscles waiting to bunch. She took a step back. "Is Dr. McKinley here?" she asked, anxious to exchange the son for the father. Supposedly Tom McKinley had a friendly grin and Irish red hair. Shane's dark mane fell beyond his shoulders, and his lips bore not even the slightest trace of a smile.

"He's out on a ranch call. May I help you?"

"I just stopped by to introduce myself. I'm Butch's granddaughter. I'll be staying at the cabin for a few weeks. I'm on my way there now."

Recognition, then sorrow swept across his face. "Butch was a good man, Miz Baxter. I'm sorry you lost him."

"Thank you."

Her kind-spirited grandpa, an Ohio factory worker, had died ten months before. He had vacationed regularly at a rustic Texas cabin, the place where he had hoped to spend his retirement—a long-awaited dream that never came true. Lung cancer had claimed him instead.

Kelly took a deep breath. She missed him even more now. He would have understood her indecision concerning the baby, the uncertainty about embarking on a paternity suit. And he would have hugged her pain away, the ache that never left her heart.

Shane's gaze dropped to her stomach again. "Is someone meeting you at the cabin?"

"No, I'm..." She lifted her chin, unnerved by his presumption. "I came here on my own."

"You're alone?" He shook his head. "I'm sorry, Miz Baxter, but do you realize how far from town we are?"

Kelly fisted her hands, defiance surging into her weary bones. Her mother had said nearly the same thing. Grandpa's cabin was too far from civilization. It wasn't safe. She needed to stay home and face her situation. Running away wasn't going to help.

Shane stepped forward, and Kelly narrowed her eyes. If his next words sounded anything remotely similar to "this is no place for a pregnant woman," she just might have to deck him or, at least, give it her best shot. Her doctor had given her a clean bill of health, suggesting a routine appointment upon her return. The cabin was going to be her sanctuary, a quiet place to escape, if only for a few short weeks.

She squared her shoulders. "I should go." She had endured a long, turbulent plane ride and even longer, bumpier roads only to come face-to-face with disapproval from a complete stranger. She met with plenty of opposition at home, more than enough. Shane Night Wind she could do without.

"Wait." As she turned to leave, he reached for her arm, brushing her skin.

She met his gaze. The gold in his eyes had deepened.

"That cabin has been vacant for over a year."

Kelly swallowed. Decking him had been a ridiculous thought. This man in frayed blue jeans and scuffed leather boots towered over her by at least a foot. "I called ahead to the realty company Grandpa had used. They assured me the phone and utilities would be in working order."

Rather than respond, he slid his gaze over her body. He couldn't seem to take his eyes off her tummy, she noticed. And he had yet to smile. The combination made her more than uncomfortable. Maybe it was the "wildcat" in him, the dark windblown hair, the primitive sound of his voice, the slow drawl, the cautious way in which he moved, tilted his head. Then again, how dangerous could a man be who took in strays? Somewhere beyond her neighbor's fence was an exotic feline refuge—a rescue for abandoned and abused animals.

Carnivorous animals, she reminded herself. Big, restless cats who stalked their prey.

This time when Kelly turned to leave, he didn't stop her. "It's time for me to go," she said, anxious to escape. Kelly Baxter had come to Texas to be alone.

Three hours later Shane sat on the porch steps waiting for his dad. He had plenty to do, but couldn't bring himself to confront the paperwork that faced him. Ledgers, bills. He wasn't in the mood to find out what he already knew. Soon it would be time to plan another fund-raiser, the social functions he detested.

Yeah, right, a voice in his head said. It wasn't the impending fund-raiser that had him feeling so damn edgy. It was the woman. The *pregnant* woman. The one who'd darted off like a cottontail in the scope of a .22. He'd made her as uncomfortable as she'd made him.

As his father's dually rolled onto the graveled driveway, Shane breathed a sigh of relief. He had to get Kelly Baxter off his chest.

Tom exited his vehicle, his ruddy face alight with a smile. How different they were, Shane thought. Father and son. Men who had been strangers not more than five years before.

Tom stepped onto the porch and ruffled his son's hair. It was a gesture more fitting of the father of a six-year-old, but Shane let the affection pass without ducking his head. Tom probably used to do that to Danny, the half-brother Shane had never known.

He glanced up. Tom stood tall and broad, his shoulders blocking the sun. Shane had inherited his father's stature, but that was where the similarity ended.

"Butch Baxter's granddaughter stopped by today," he said finally.

Tom dropped onto the porch steps. "Really? Is she here to sell the cabin?"

"Maybe. I'm not sure. She plans on staying for a couple of weeks."

"Her name's Kelly, isn't it? Butch used to mention her quite a bit."

Shane squinted into the setting sun. Trust his dad to remember the name of a girl he had never met. Even though Butch only stayed in the cabin for a few months out of the year, Tom and the older man had become friends.

"She came out here by herself, Dad."

"Butch said she was independent. Besides, she's a grown woman."

"I suppose." Wheat-colored hair with a scatter of freckles just below the surface of her skin. She had looked more like a girl than a woman. Defiant one minute, vulnerable the next.

Tom turned his head. "What is it you're not telling me?"

"Nothing."

"Shane?" A scolding tone edged the other man's voice.

"She's pregnant." He clasped his hands together and held them away from his body. "Out-to-here pregnant."

"Oh, I see." Tom dragged a hand through his carrot-topped hair.

Shane knew his father didn't know what else to say. That part of Shane's life was supposed to be closed, the wound healed.

Suddenly he wanted to cry, paint his face and cut his skin. Mourn his loss the Comanche way, a loss that had become another man's gain. Five years had gone by, and now Kelly Baxter had brought every ounce of that old pain screeching back. The betrayal, the anger, the anxiety, the hope—the riot of emotions.

Why did she trigger reminders of the past? Was it the sadness he saw in her eyes? The loneliness?

Shane glanced at the fence that separated his home from the rescue. Deep down he knew. Something was desperately wrong in Kelly Baxter's life, the way it had been wrong in his.

"Why would a woman nearing childbirth want to stay in a cabin by herself?"

"I don't know." Tom looked directly into his son's eyes. "But maybe you better forget about her. Let her live her life and you live yours. You don't need to get tangled up in her affairs."

So Kelly had stirred all those old, painful memories. So what? Shane knew better than to get overly involved. "She's only going to be here for a few weeks. Come on, Dad, it's not like I'm going to get attached. I'm just concerned about a neighbor, that's all."

"You're right, I'm sorry. She's all by herself. I'm sure she could use a friend. Tell her I'd like to meet her."

Shane raised an eyebrow, and Tom smiled. "Don't pretend you weren't thinking about heading over to the cabin to see her. It's written all over your face, son."

He returned the smile and reached into his pocket for his truck keys. His father had come to know him well. The cabin was exactly where he intended to go.

When the small log dwelling came into view, he noticed the trees surrounding it had grown fuller, providing ample shade and pleasant greenery. But the rustic beauty didn't fool him. Even though the cabin contained indoor plumbing and a small but functional kitchen, it was, in Shane's opinion, as crude as cowboy carpentry could get. Too primitive for a pregnant Ohio waif. Her granddaddy had been made of stronger stuff.

Was she married? he wondered. The fact that she'd introduced herself as Kelly Baxter didn't mean she didn't have a husband. Some women kept their maiden names. He stood beside the truck, debating on whether to proceed. Another man's wife should be that other man's concern, not his.

Shane dug his heel into the dirt. If she had a husband, then the guy was a jerk for letting her run off alone like she had. A pregnant woman wouldn't take refuge in a remote Texas cabin over some frivolous marital tiff. Whatever plagued Kelly Baxter was serious.

He couldn't walk away. He just couldn't.

Rather than knock on the open door, he entered the cabin and turned toward the tiny kitchen. He could feel her there, knew she would be hovering over the sink, scrubbing the stained porcelain. He didn't stop to wonder how he knew; he wasn't the sort of man to analyze what some people referred to as a sixth sense. Shane Night Wind had accepted himself as the cougar he'd become.

Although the furniture was still draped with sheets, the cabin wore a layer of dust, cobwebs collecting in every corner. They clung to the beams, sticky against the wood. He hated that feeling, the sensation of being trapped in a web. He assumed she did, too. The kitchen corners had already been brushed clean, the clay-tiled floor swept.

Kelly stood at the sink, running water that was probably spitting rust. She had pinned her hair up, he noticed, clipped it with a metal barrette. Some of it had fallen loose, blond and flyaway. Her hair was nearly as long as his, but it appeared soft and light, almost feathery. From the back she didn't look pregnant. She had an urchin's body, small and frail, her wrinkled cotton dress giving the false illusion of being a size too big.

She turned, caught sight of him and gasped. "What are you doing here?" Water dripped from the sponge in her hand, running down her wrist.

He imagined her heart had lunged for her throat, and he cursed himself for invading her privacy, for not having the good sense to knock. She was afraid of him—the man and the cougar. Both sides of him made her uneasy.

"I'm sorry, I didn't mean to startle you. I just wanted to see if you were okay. If you needed any help getting settled."

She dropped the sponge into the sink and dried her hands on a paper towel. Exhaling an audible breath, she met his gaze. "I hadn't realized how dirty this place would be. I assumed the realtor would have taken care of it. When I called to complain, the receptionist apologized, but said they couldn't get someone out here for at least two days."

He motioned to the cleaning supplies littering the counter. "Looks like you came prepared anyway."

"Hardly. I went down to that little corner store and bought all this stuff."

Shane nodded. The One Stop was a two-pump gas station and minimart, overpriced and under stocked. Cities had those kind of places, too—convenience chains that got robbed in the middle of the night. Of course the One Stop had never been robbed, but then Barry Hunt told anyone who would listen that he kept a sawed-off shotgun beneath the counter.

"So you met Barry," he said.

She flashed an amused smile. "If you mean that nosy old codger with the wad of tobacco in his mouth, then yes, I met him. He's quite a character."

Shane returned her smile. Barry Hunt did poke his bulbous nose into everyone's business. He cussed like a sailor too long at sea, looked like a salty old miner and gossiped with the gusto of a matron at a church social. Everyone from here to the next county would soon know that a pregnant waif named Kelly Baxter was staying in her granddaddy's cabin. Shane dropped his smile, feeling suddenly protective of the urchin and her unborn child. Abused and abandoned creatures had become the focus of his life.

But not married women, he told himself a moment later.

"Does your husband know you're here, Miz Baxter?"

She flinched, his direct question catching her off guard. "No. I mean, I'm not—" She placed her hand on her stomach in what seemed like an unconscious and naturally maternal gesture. "I'm not married, but I have a mother and she knows I'm here."

The part about her mother sounded almost like a warning, as if Mom would call out the national guard if Kelly didn't make a nightly phone call.

She was still unsure of him, he realized, still wary. And no wonder. He hadn't been exactly neighborly on the porch. But opening the door and seeing her standing there had spun him back in time—to the most painful era of his life.

"I can help clean," he offered. "Maybe tackle the bathroom."

"Thank you, but that's not necessary."

"I used to live here," he said, gauging her reaction. Clearly Kelly Baxter couldn't fathom having him scrub her bathroom, the place where she would shower, comb her hair, smooth lotion on her skin. "I know this cabin pretty well."

She leaned against the sink. "Grandpa bought this place from some people by the name of Mendoza."

"Yeah, I know. I worked for the Mendozas. They offered me room and board in exchange for some repairs and construction work that needed done at the rescue. Of course they paid me a small wage, too." Shane paused, realizing he'd made himself sound like some sort of drifter. But explaining why he left a good paying job and nice suburban home in Oklahoma to live in a crude Texas cabin wasn't possible. It would mean mentioning Tami. And the baby.

Kelly stood watching him, so he continued, leaving deliberate gaps. "To make a long story short, Dad and I eventually took over the rescue from the Mendozas. We bought their house and most of their acreage, too. But we didn't really need the cabin and couldn't afford the extra land, so they sold it to your Grandpa instead."

"Grandpa was fascinated with the rescue," Kelly said, looking a tad more comfortable. "He liked the idea of having lions and tigers for neighbors."

"That was a relief to the Mendozas. They were worried about being able to sell the cabin. Most folks don't cotton to big cats the way your granddaddy did." Shane found himself wondering what Kelly thought about sleeping only a few miles away from the wild creatures that shared his life. The animals that had led him to his father, helped him overcome the pain of leaving a wife and child behind.

When their conversation faltered, he convinced Kelly to accept his offer to scour the bathroom. He couldn't imagine her leaning over the tub in her condition. She was all baby, he thought, a tiny girl with a huge tummy.

He walked into the bathroom and winced. A thin layer of dust had settled everywhere, not to mention a few active webs. Men weren't supposed to be afraid of spiders, but arachnophobia had surfaced during childhood. He'd rather enter a lion's den any day.

An hour later with dead spiders in his wake and sweat beading his brow, he returned to the kitchen to see if Kelly had a cold drink available. It appeared the cabin still didn't have a swamp cooler.

He found her sitting at the battered oak table, her face pale. "Are you okay?"

"Just a bit tired," she answered, her voice weary. "It's been a long day."

Too long for a woman carrying a child, he realized. Shane moved closer. "When's your baby due?"

She held a wet cloth against her neck. "Next month, around the twenty-eighth."

He wanted to reprimand her again, but couldn't get past her fragility. He had been through Tami's pregnancy, knew the toll the last trimester took on a woman's body. "You can't push yourself like this, Miz Baxter. You shouldn't be cleaning this old place."

"I hadn't intended to."

"I know." He sat across from her. "Why don't you stay with my dad and me until the realtor can get a cleaning crew out here? There's too much that needs done, and you can't sleep in all this dust."

"That's very kind of you, but maybe I should get a motel room instead."

"The nearest motel is in town and that's a good distance from here. Besides, it's a fleabag. Nobody but truckers bunk there." Truckers and drunken cowboys cheating on their women. This little waif didn't belong in that environment.

Apparently too tired to argue, she moved the cloth to her forehead and accepted his offer. "Grandpa said your dad was a nice man. I think Grandpa would have approved of me staying at your place. And truthfully, all these cobwebs are making me jumpy."

The cobwebs were making Shane jumpy, too, but he wasn't about to admit it. "Yeah, Butch and my dad were pretty good friends," he responded, wondering what her granddaddy had said about him. What had Butch Baxter told Kelly about the veterinarian's Comanche son? "I hope you don't mind eating breakfast for dinner. I think Dad plans on frying up some eggs and potatoes. It's his turn to cook."

"That sounds fine. Thank you. I don't know what I would have done without you."

"Just being neighborly." He resisted the urge to place his hand against her tummy, take comfort in the warmth. Even though the chemical smell of a household cleanser lingered on her hands, he still detected another scent. Watermelon. A gently milled soap or body lotion.

What would she do if he actually touched her?

Nothing, he decided. Most pregnant women became accustomed to forms of affection from strangers. Affection? The last thing he needed was to feel something for her. She was carrying another man's child. Just like Tami had been.

Shane cursed his memories. Tami hadn't liked her body then, but he had enjoyed the fullness, knowing a child grew there. He shifted his gaze. A child he had been denied.

"Come on, Miz Baxter, let's get going."

She rose, her skin still pale. "If we're going to be friends, then call me Kelly, please."

He nodded, wondering what the hell he was doing. The last woman who had claimed to be his friend had gashed his heart. And now this delicate-looking urchin with the flyaway hair and spray of golden freckles managed to show up at his door and reopen that wound.

Five years of living like a cougar had only reinforced one thing. The man in Shane still remembered what it felt like to hurt.

Kelly walked into Shane's home, deciding fatigue was her enemy. She had just agreed to spend two days with two men she barely knew. Barely knew? She hadn't even met Dr. McKinley yet.

"Come on, I'll introduce you to my dad," Shane said as though reading her mind.

Kelly followed her neighbor to a brightly lit kitchen. The stove was old but clean, the counters butcher-block style. The house boasted masculine charm, simple and stark with polished wood floors and heavy rattan furniture.

"Dad, I've got somebody with me."

Tom McKinley turned. He was as tall as Shane and possibly as muscular, but his features weren't as sharp as his son's, and his eyes weren't flecked with gold. They were pale blue, a complement to his sunburned skin and thick red hair. Tom had a nonthreatening appearance, whereas Shane had the kind of dark, dangerous looks that probably made women stop and stare. Kelly glanced away. Even she had stared a little.

"This is Kelly Baxter, Butch's granddaughter."

Upon hearing her name, she steadied her gaze and extended her hand to Dr. McKinley, realizing an introduction was being made.

The veterinarian shook her hand, then gave it a paternal pat. "You're as pretty as your granddaddy said."

"Thank you."

Shane explained her dilemma, and Dr. McKinley welcomed her to their home with a genuine smile. How warm their relationship was, she thought, how calm. Nothing like the recent disagreements that existed between herself and her mother. Those disagreements had brought her to Texas, that and the pain of a man's rejection.

The doctor went back to preparing supper, and Shane led her down the hallway, her luggage in tow. He offered Kelly a friendly smile—the polite, gallant host. An enigma, she thought, his renegade looks deceiving.

"You can sleep in here," he said as they entered a tidy little guest room.

The first thing Kelly noticed was the tall, metal cage. Inside of it was a spotted cat, surrounded by toys and snug in a padded box, its huge ears perked with curiosity.

Shane set her bags on the floor and moved toward the cage. "That's Zuni. I hope you don't mind sharing your space with her. She's more or less a houseguest, too." He knelt to slip a finger through the bars. The cat poked her paw back at him. "You know, come to think of it, I better move Zuni into my room. We're still bottle-feeding her. I doubt you'd appreciate being awakened every four hours."

"She's still a baby?" Zuni was already half the size of a full-grown domestic, fine-boned and adorable. "How old is she?"

"Five weeks."

Shane opened the cage and the kitten scampered out, rubbing and purring between his legs. "She's a serval. A medium-size cat from Africa." He reached for a toy and shook it in front of Zuni. The kitten batted it immediately. "But this little girl was born in captivity. She's never been to Africa."

"Is she a rescue?" Kelly wanted to snag Zuni and cuddle, but wasn't sure if it would be the proper thing to do.

He shook his head. "Kittens and cubs rarely need rescuing. Everyone adores baby animals. It's when they get big that they become a problem. Zuni belongs to a friend of mine, and he's prepared for the handful she's going to become. I'm only baby-sitting while he's on vacation."

Shane looked up from the kitten and smiled. Kelly assumed she had a sappy look on her face, the expression of an expectant mother eager to nuzzle someone else's toddler. Shane appeared amused. "Do you want to hold her?"

He didn't need to ask twice. Kelly extended her arms and waited for the transfer. The kitten had soft, fluffy fur and long, spindly legs. Her little nose was pointed, her eyes round and dark. It was thrilling, Kelly thought, to stroke an exotic creature, listen to the low rumble of its purr.

"Do you think you could teach me to feed her? I'm willing to get up every four hours. It's something I'm going to have to get used to anyway."

"Are you sure?" he asked.

She brought the kitten closer. "Positive"

Ten minutes later Kelly had been instructed on how to mix the formula and warm the bottle. She stood beside Shane in the kitchen while his father peeled a batch of potatoes.

Shane handed Kelly the bottle. "We're a little off schedule, but I'm sure Zuni won't mind."

She glanced at Tom McKinley. He sent her a smile, then looked over at his son. He was proud of Shane, she thought. Father and son treated each other with respect. Did they ever argue? she wondered. Kelly and her mother used to get along well, too. But the paternity suit issue had caused a rift between them.

Shane and Kelly returned to the guest room where the kitten had been left to roam. The moment Zuni spotted the bottle, she sat at Kelly's feet and made a noise that sounded as if it had come from a bird, an odd little chirping.

"That's the most common way servals communicate," Shane explained. "Not all cats roar or meow."

They settled on the edge of the bed, Zuni climbing onto Kelly's lap, anxious and jittery for her meal. Shane leaned in close, and Kelly swallowed. Suddenly his presence seemed too intimate. The bedroom door was closed, the lamp turned low.

"Feed her as though she's nursing from her mother," he said quietly. "Keep her on her tummy and guide her head. Cats aren't like human babies. You shouldn't cradle them while they're eating. They can get milk in their lungs."

Kelly listened to his instruction and watched Zuni latch onto the nipple. The kitten's ears drew back as she suckled, her round eyes slitting languorously.

Shane slipped his arm around Kelly and readjusted the bottle. "You need to give her something to knead. See how she's trying to find a place for her paws? Let her use your hand."

Kelly nodded. Did Shane realize how close he was? That his breath stirred against her cheek?

The sound of Zuni's suckling intensified the quiet. Shane kept his arm draped across her shoulder, his gaze focused on the kitten. She had the sudden urge to lean into him, absorb his kindness. She had dreamed of moments like this. The players were wrong, but the feeling was right. The tender stillness. The human warmth.

Zuni released the nipple, gazed up at Kelly, then latched onto the rubber again and began to chew.

Shane wiggled the bottle. "No, no, little one. This isn't playtime."

He lifted his arm from Kelly's shoulder. She felt an immediate loss. The spell had been broken, reality creeping back in. Shane wasn't Jason. He wasn't the father of her child, the man who should be treating her with kindness.

After turning the light up, Shane took the bottle and charted the amount the kitten had consumed. He appeared to be a nice person, but then Jason had fooled her into believing he was nice, too. Unlike Shane, her baby's father wasn't long and lean, nor did he wear frayed denims and scuffed leather boots. Jason Collier had neatly styled hair, his features classically handsome, his medium build well-suited to collegiate-type sportswear. He had been her romantic fixation since high school, the popular boy most folks in her hometown seemed to like.

"Zuni needs to be burped."

"What?" She blinked away her thoughts, then glanced down at the squirming kitten. "How—"

"Just lift her onto your shoulder and pat."

"Like a baby?"

Shane nodded and returned to Kelly's side. She raised the kitten. "I can't believe I'm burping a cat."

"I can't believe she hasn't tried to nip you." He placed his fingers over Kelly's and urged her to continue the gentle tapping. "Servals tend to be nippy. Mostly it's just play-biting but, regardless, it can hurt." He stroked the kitten's head. "Disciplining this little girl isn't going to be easy."

When Zuni erupted in a loud burp Kelly looked at Shane, and they both laughed.

"I guess she told you."

"Yeah. I guess she did." He grinned, then smoothed a strand of Kelly's hair, removing it from Zuni's curious reach.

That tender sensation came back, the unspoken compatibility. Kelly released a slow steadying breath and pushed away the feeling. In two weeks she would return to Ohio to face an important decision in her life. A decision that didn't include Shane Night Wind.

Two

Shane hadn't slept well. He had tossed and turned, wondering about Kelly Baxter. The same thought still plagued him: Why had she come to Texas to spend two weeks in her granddaddy's cabin a month before her baby was due? That made no sense.

They had shared dinner last night with his father, but the conversation hadn't led to any clues. Her personal life hadn't been broached.

Strange how Shane wanted to be near her, yet her presence stirred such raw emotion within him—painful reminders of the past. The turbulent years between Shane and his father. The bitterness in Shane's childhood. The wife and baby he had been forced to leave behind. The wife and son Tom had lost.

Kelly Baxter had brought a battered suitcase of ghosts with her—haunting memories Shane had struggled to overcome.

He poured a cup of freshly brewed coffee. It wasn't Kelly's fault, the emotions swirling around inside him. She hadn't come to Texas to torment him. She had come out of her own torment.

Maybe, just maybe, he thought, he was meant to help her. Maybe the Creator had placed her in his path for a reason. It was possible his own pain had resurfaced as a reminder of what it felt like to be needy and alone—the way Kelly appeared to be.

Shane sipped his coffee, suddenly sensing Kelly's impending presence. He could feel another person approaching and knew it wasn't his dad. Tom had left for work already.

She appeared in the kitchen entryway, sleepy-eyed, her flyaway locks spilling over her shoulders. She wore a modest nightgown that flowed to her ankles. Pretty and pregnant, he thought, wrapped in pink.

"Oh, hi." She smiled a little shyly. "I didn't know anyone would be up at this hour."

"We start our day early around here." Watermelon still lingered on her skin, the same scent he had noticed the day before. Shane moved a little closer. Watermelon was significant in his life, the treat his favorite cougar salivated for. He moistened his lips as a masculine urge took hold. Suddenly he imagined nuzzling her neck, burying his face in her hair.

"I came to get Zuni a bottle," she said.

"Huh? Oh, yeah. There's one in the fridge." Guiltily, he rejected his coffee, thinking caffeine was probably the last thing he needed, especially since his heartbeat had quickened.

So he had romantic urges. So what? He wasn't having full-on sexual fantasies about a pregnant woman, just odd little flutters, feelings that leaned more toward tenderness. The kind of touches that led to cuddling. Kissing.

Kelly turned to warm the bottle, and Shane gave himself a mental lashing. Romantic urges. She was carrying another man's child. Hadn't he learned his lesson from Tami? Been down that painful road before?

Damn. Was it Kelly's pregnancy that drew him in—the overwhelming reminder of a child he still missed? Or was it actually her? The feminine defiance and girlish vulnerability? A combination he found difficult to resist.

It didn't matter, Shane decided. He wasn't about to lose the peace he'd made with himself, not now, not after all he'd been through. If the problem in Kelly's life centered around her baby's father, then he'd find out why. And if it was too serious of a problem to fix, he'd encourage Kelly to move forward, find a new direction to take, focus on her baby, maybe even consider a new career. Start over the way he had.

"Do you want to take a tour of the rescue later?" he asked.

"You don't have to entertain me, Shane. I've taken enough of your time already."

"I'd really like you to see it." And he wanted to get to the bottom of her pain, the reason she'd left home. "It's really incredible. We've spent a lot of time and money building natural habitats, and we even have a picnic area for the tourists."

"Would I be going through the tour with other people?"

"No, just me. We only give scheduled tours on the first Saturday of every month. We just don't have the staff available to offer them more frequently. Besides, the cats deserve their privacy." He tilted his head. "I would never put you in any danger, Kelly. The rescue is safe." And free of the toxoplasmosis that could harm an unborn child. Having a veterinarian in the family kept the strong cats healthy and the ones who required constant medical care well tended. Tom was available day or night, a dedicated doctor who had been treating exotics for years. "Please say yes."

"Okay." She tested the temperature of the formula. "I'd like to see the animals Grandpa found so fascinating."

"Good. We can pack a lunch. Spend some time in the shade." And talk, he hoped. Once he helped Kelly sort out her problems, he could go back to his own life. The solitude he had come to rely on.

Hours later Kelly walked beside Shane, thoroughly enjoying the outdoors. Jungle Hill Rescue was a sight to behold. Spring greenery flourished beneath a vast Texas sky, and wide dirt paths led to large caged compounds.

"Most of our residents are cougars," he said. "But we have other cats, too." He guided her toward a grassy compound where a tiger peered down at the world from a tree house, its sleek body stretched across the bark. "We don't pick and choose our animals. We take them in with the intention to keep them, regardless of their health or disposition. We're not a temporary shelter." He turned to gaze up at the tiger. "Once they arrive, this is their permanent home. Their last stop."

Kelly studied Shane's profile. The inflection in his voice spoke of sadness, as if he understood the feeling of being homeless, of needing a caring place to live. "So they've been abused?" she asked.

"Not all of them." He shifted the backpack that contained their lunch. "Some are more or less orphaned. Think about it, if a primary caregiver dies, who is going to take in their three-hundred-pound cat? It's a misconception that all of the animals in rescues have been abused or purposely abandoned. There are some responsible private owners out there. We've acquired our exotics from all sorts of situations. Unfortunately, though, some of those situations were deplorable."

"I can't imagine having a big cat for a pet."

He turned to look at her, his brown eyes glinting gold. "That's because they're not pets. It's not the same as owning a dog or a domestic cat."

Kelly understood what he meant. The people who purchased exotics and expected them to behave like domestics were the ones who ultimately ended up abusing or abandoning their animals, realizing the nature of the beast much too late.

"You really love them."

He smiled. "Yeah, I do. I feel like I belong to them somehow."

Because he was one of them, Kelly thought, as his hair blew around his shoulders. Long, lean, golden-eyed Shane. Part Comanche, part Irish, part wildcat.

"Tell me about the tiger," she said, deciding she liked her

host. Kelly didn't have many male friends, especially men who wore their hair longer than her own. It was difficult not to find him fascinating.

"That's Sammy." Shane observed the big cat as though pleased by its royal disposition, its ability to accept their presence without swishing its tail or batting an eye. Although they stood a good distance from the spacious habitat, the tiger watched them through a regal gaze—a prince looking down on the peasants. "He came from a tiger mill. Tigers breed easily in captivity, and the demand for white tigers has created a problem. The only known white tiger gene came from a male in India that was bred to his daughter, so the lines aren't pure."

Shane sighed, the sound rough and masculine. "Sammy's an orange tiger who carries the white gene, the product of a breeder trying to capitalize on producing white tigers. When a white tiger is bred to an orange one, the litter is often mixed. So you see, Sammy's immune system isn't what it should be. Besides the gene he carries, we think he was a result from even more inbreeding. An irresponsible mill who mated relatives."

"That's sad."

"Yes, it is. And Sammy's not the only discarded tiger out there. I know of rescues that are filled with them." Shane moved his gaze over Kelly's body. "Are you doing all right? Do you want to sit down for a while?"

Startled by his quick change of subject, she smoothed her windblown hair, feeling suddenly fat and unattractive. It bothered her that his gaze always managed to stray to her protruding belly. She had the sensation that her pregnancy made him uncomfortable, that he found her added weight an unwelcome distraction. "Why? Do I look tired?"

He swallowed, his Adam's apple bobbing. "No. It's just that once I start talking about the cats, I lose track of time. And you're…you know…"

Pregnant, she added silently, wondering why he had trouble saying the word. Maybe it was the bachelor in him, the single, childless male. Jason had trouble with the word, too. And the image. The father of her baby didn't want to be a father.

"Why don't we have lunch and finish the tour afterward?" he suggested.

"Okay." In truth, she was actually ready for a break. Swollen feet and backaches came more regularly these days, the baby in her womb growing rapidly.

The picnic area was located just outside the rescue. Wooden benches provided rough-hewn seating and ancient oaks offered shelter from the dusty winds. She found the parklike setting appealing, especially since beyond the chain-link fence were endless miles of uncultivated land. Shane's property sat on a small hillside, overlooking the plains. The wide-open space gave her a sense of freedom.

"What's that building?" she asked, referring to a large tiki-type hut.

"It's going to be our gift shop. We just haven't had the chance to stock it yet. We plan on having some T-shirts made. Coffee cups, too. You know, things that promote the rescue. We survive on donations and membership support."

She took in her surroundings once again. "I really like it here."

He smiled and unpacked their food. "Yeah, me, too."

They had chosen to make a simple lunch: turkey sandwiches, cheese-flavored crackers, apples and bottled water. Everything in Duarte seemed simple to Kelly, at least all that she had seen so far. She hadn't been to town yet, but remembered that Grandpa had described it as a secluded corner of Texas, as old-fashioned as a blue-chip stamp, a place where time stood still.

Kelly reached for her water. Time was just what she needed. Time to be alone, to think and make decisions. Being far from home helped, knowing that she didn't have to argue with her mother or obsess about Jason's return from his business travels—a trip she believed he had scheduled to avoid her.

"So what's your hometown like?" Shane asked.

She glanced down at her sandwich. Strange how he always

managed to tap into her thoughts. "It's a nice place. A small suburban town where most of us know each other." Kelly had been born in Tannery, Ohio, attended school there, sold Girl Scout cookies, landed her first and only job, buried Grandpa in the hilltop cemetery. It was home, yet she didn't want to be there. Not now.

"So you're a grocery checker, right?" he asked.

Kelly nodded. She had told him what she did for a living the previous evening over supper. "The pay is pretty good, and I've got excellent health benefits."

He studied his apple, then buffed it against his shirt. "Yeah, but it's not right for you."

She wasn't sure if she should take offense. No one had ever questioned her job before. "I like talking to the customers, seeing the people I grew up around."

He met her gaze, the polished apple gleaming in his hand. "Yeah, but there's more to you than that. There's something you have a passion for. I can feel it, even see it in your eyes."

A shiver worked its way up her spine. Being held within his stare was unnerving. Soul-piercing, she decided, like being stalked by a mountain lion. And she did have a passion. Nothing glamorous, just a quiet hobby. She liked to draw. Just for herself, pictures of plants and animals—her mother's garden, a neighbor's puppy, things that made her feel good. But even so, she wasn't foolhardy enough to believe her drawings would please anyone but herself.

"I'm fine with my job," she said, even though she wasn't. Nothing was fine in her life. Nothing. Rather than look forward to becoming a grandmother, Kelly's mother had turned the welfare of Kelly's child into a lawsuit. And Jason? His bitter feelings hurt most of all. One minute he insisted the baby wasn't his, and the next he accused Kelly of getting pregnant on purpose.

Shane continued to stare into her eyes, his voice gentle. "If you feel like talking about it, I want you to know I'm here. I'm a good listener."

Kelly tore at the crust on her sandwich. "Am I that obvious?"

"You're all alone in Texas a month before your baby is due. That in itself says something."

Suddenly she wanted to cry. She needed a friend, someone who wasn't close to her situation. But could she tell Shane about Jason? About how much his rejection hurt? Or how inadequate she had been as a lover?

"I'm happy about the baby," she said. A little scared about being a single parent, but grateful that God had given her a child. "I appreciate your concern. But I'm going to be fine." She couldn't imagine talking to Shane about Jason. Especially about all the awful things Jason had said to her. The personal, humiliating things.

Shane wondered what to do now. Kelly looked like a lost little girl, an urchin trying to act brave. "How old are you?" he asked.

"Twenty-four."

He took a deep breath. The same age he had been when Tami had become pregnant. "I'm thirty," he told her for lack of something better to say.

"Oh." She glanced down at her food.

Great, he thought, awkward conversation. His brilliant plan to help her wasn't working. Should he share something private, something from his past? Would that encourage her to open up?

Shane bit into the apple. He couldn't tell her about Tami. That was too personal. Admitting that his wife had found him lacking as a husband wasn't something he cared to admit. Tami wouldn't have slept with another man if Shane had satisfied her.

Pushing Tami out of his mind, he decided to test the waters, determine if Kelly's pain was centered around her baby's father. He knew firsthand about reluctant fathers. "I just got acquainted with my dad five years ago."

"Really?" She scooted forward.

"Yeah." He wondered how to tell this story without making Tom seem like the bad guy. Making fathers look bad wasn't the idea, especially if the guy who had made Kelly pregnant was shirking his responsibility. Although the fear of fatherhood hit some men harder than others, Shane believed most guys eventually came around.

"My parents had this sort of casual affair, I guess," he began. "They met in Oklahoma. My dad was from Texas, but he was in school at the time, attending the veterinary college in Stillwater." Shane could see that he'd captured Kelly's attention, so he continued. "Anyway, they ended up sleeping together, and my mom got pregnant."

This, he decided, was where the story got complicated. "But my mom didn't tell Tom about me. And she refused to tell my grandma where Tom could be found. She was afraid Grandma would try to force them into getting married."

"Your mother sounds like an independent woman."

"Yeah. She doesn't believe in loveless marriages, people getting together for the sake of a baby. Of course my traditional grandma saw things differently."

Kelly watched him through interested eyes. "So what happened?"

"By the time Grandma tracked down my dad, I was almost a year old. And Tom...well...he was married to someone else by then." Shane knew it was odd for a son to refer to his father by his given name, but Tom had been a stranger long before Shane had ever called him Dad. "Not only that, but Tom's wife was pregnant. He was about to become a father for the second time."

"Oh, my." Kelly's jaw dropped a little. "It sounds like a soap opera."

"Yeah." He didn't watch daytime TV, but he'd heard how angst-ridden those shows were. "Tom told his wife, and they both agreed that he should take financial responsibility for me. So he sent my mom child support, even though he promised his wife he would never bring me into their lives in any other way."

"And your dad was okay with that?" she asked, uncertainty in her tone.

Apparently Kelly was thinking about the father of her own child. A man Shane had come to wonder about. Had he loved Kelly or had he used her? Had it been a serious relationship or a one-night stand? A hundred scenarios, he realized, were possible. And if Kelly didn't confide in him, he'd probably lay awake that night counting off each and every one.

He discarded his half-eaten apple and answered her question. "Tom felt guilty as hell, but he loved his wife and figured it was the only way to save his marriage."

"What about your mom?"

"She appreciated the child support, especially since she hadn't intended to tell Tom about me in the first place. My grandma was upset, though. Of course there wasn't much she could do about it." Nothing but argue with Shane's mother and insist that Tom had shamed his firstborn by excluding the boy from his life. Shane had been seven years old when he'd first stumbled upon one of those arguments, an innocent second-grader when he'd learned that he had a half brother. A white child his white daddy was raising. Shane's innocence had quickly shattered. He had hated Tom then, hated him with every fiber of his being—a burning that had grown with each passing year.

"You seem close to your dad now," Kelly observed. "He appears to care very deeply about you."

"Tom came to see me when I was eighteen," Shane admitted, "but I told him to go to hell. I didn't want to have anything to do with him." Shame welled in his throat. Shame for hating so deeply, for not recognizing Tom's grief. "His wife and son had just been killed in a plane crash. Emotionally he was a mess."

And Shane's kindhearted, free-spirited mother had reached out to Tom, offering friendship and compassion, something Shane wasn't capable of doing at the time. "I just wanted him to go away. I didn't want to be his instant son, a replacement for the one he had raised—fair-haired, fair-skinned Danny—the boy he had really loved.''

Kelly flinched, and Shane realized his voice had taken on the hurt from his youth. "I spent over half my life comparing myself to Danny. Wondering why Tom wanted him over me. I was bitter and rebellious, but I swear, Kelly, I've come a long way since then. I don't blame my dad anymore." And he found himself mourning Danny, the brother he had never known.

"I believe you." Her smile was faint but sincere. "It couldn't have been easy."

"No, it wasn't. But neither was Tom losing his wife and son. Regardless, I avoided my dad for the next seven years. I didn't see him again until I was twenty-five."

"Five years ago," she remarked, pushing her flyaway hair out of her eyes.

"Yeah, five years ago." Right after he had left Evan behind, the baby he couldn't keep, the child who wasn't really his.

"What made you decide to get to know your dad then?" she asked.

"Just some stuff going on in my own life." A paternity test he didn't want to take, a divorce he had tried to stop. Sheer and utter hell. "It's over now."

It had been, he realized, until Kelly Baxter had showed up at his door. Pregnant, lost little Kelly. He looked across the table at her. The wind had made a beautiful mess of her hair, and the sun peeking through the trees highlighted the scatter of freckles dusting her nose. "Do you want to finish the tour?"

"Yes."

Her voice was as quiet as his, and he decided she wasn't going to open up, not even after what he'd just told her. But then, he'd only revealed half of his story. The other half involved his wife and child, the family he had struggled to keep.

Although Kelly and Shane agreed to finish the tour, neither made a move to leave the bench. They sat silent for a time, picking at the remainder of their food, each absorbed in their own thoughts. Kelly's strayed to Jason. The story about Shane's parents had triggered an emotional response inside her. Shane's mother hadn't been in love with Tom, but Kelly still had feelings for the father of her child. And now she believed that Jason had only dated her because he enjoyed being admired. Her long-running affection for him was no secret. She had been attracted to Jason since she was a sophomore at Tannery High, and he seemed to thrive on female attention.

And yes, she still had the deep and painful hope that he would take responsibility for his child. Not with money, but with love. She wanted her baby to know its father. If she refused to file the paternity suit her mother was pushing for, would Jason feel less threatened? Less pressured? Would he return from his so-called extended business trip to discuss the welfare of their child?

"Are you ready?" Shane asked.

"Oh, yes. Of course." She discarded her trash in a nearby can. She didn't want to dwell on heartache, especially this afternoon. Shane offered what appeared to be genuine friendship, and she hadn't spent quality time with a friend in ages. Everyone back home was too caught up in the gossip surrounding her and Jason. Would there be a lawsuit? Was she after Jason's money? Had she gotten pregnant on purpose? After all, he was a wealthy young heir and she was just an average middle-class girl.

Kelly placed her hands on her tummy and found herself rewarded with a hearty kick. Comforted by the tiny foot, she smiled. She still had two weeks before she returned to the turmoil surrounding her life. Today she would clear her mind and enjoy the beauty of Texas.

Fifteen minutes later Kelly and Shane stood about four feet from an enclosure that incorporated water, a variety of vegetation and a rocky terrain—a natural habitat. Or as natural as a confined area could be, Shane explained.

The resident was a cougar, an alert, tawny-colored cat. They had looked in on several cougars, but this one, Kelly decided, was different from the rest.

"I wish I could get closer," she said.

Shane unhooked the rope barrier. "With this boy, you can."

As Kelly moved forward, she felt an odd pull toward the animal, a strange affection. Maybe it was the way the big cat moved, the interest he appeared to show. He moved toward the wire fence, then stopped as though anxious for human interaction. Kelly noticed all of the habitats had secondary enclosures attached, a safety precaution, she supposed—a lockdown while the primary pens were being tended.

"Oh." She brought her hand to her heart. The cougar's striking face displayed only one eye.

"Hey, Puma." Shane greeted the cat and received a friendly-sounding *"yaooow"* in return.

Kelly smiled. She assumed the enthusiastic call meant "What's up?" or "How's it going?" in cougar talk. And when Shane mimicked the sound to near perfection, she found herself even more intrigued. A conversation was definitely taking place. But rather than ask what was being said, she posed a more generic question.

"Puma is another word for cougar, isn't it?"

He nodded. "They're considered the cat of many names. Panther, painter, catamount, mountain lion, night screamer, just to name a few."

A small wind kicked up a cloud of dust. "Night screamer?"

"The early explorers used to tell stories about the unearthly screams that came from the mountains." He smiled at Puma. The cat remained at the fence, watching the humans curiously. "Cougars are vocal animals. Besides caterwaul, they hiss and growl. And make mewling sounds. But they don't roar. That's why their babies are referred to as kittens instead of cubs. They're not considered a member of the *Panthera* species, the big cats that have the ability to roar."

"What happened to Puma's eye?"

"It ruptured from something similar to glaucoma. A result

of poor nutrition. He was bottle-fed as a kitten, but the formula was lacking.''

''He's still gorgeous.'' Kelly wanted to sketch the tawny cat, draw the muscular formation of his body, shape of his face, curve of his ears, the exotic flare of his nostrils. She wanted to capture the essence of his nature. What would he feel like? she wondered. ''Do cougars purr?''

Shane's voice took on a slow drawl—a husky, almost lazy quality. ''Yeah, and if you get much closer to the compound, Puma's going to be rumbling up a storm. Salivating, too.''

She took a step back. ''He likes women?''

Shane lowered his head, bringing his mouth close to her ear. His breath was warm, she noticed, as it stirred against her hair.

''Watermelon, Kelly. Puma likes watermelon. Drools all over it before he eats it.''

''Oh.'' A shiver shot up her spine. She had applied her scented body mist liberally that morning, and from the way Shane breathed it in, she assumed he enjoyed watermelon, too.

As he moved back, she decided Shane and Puma seemed like one and the same—two primal creatures. Striking and exotic.

Kelly chewed her bottom lip. Now she wondered if Shane could purr. She studied his profile and noticed the wind seemed to favor his hair. The sun, too. The glossy strands shone with faint auburn highlights. Maybe he could mimic a cougar's rumbling purr. But since her heartbeat had accelerated to a furious pounding, she decided she was better off not knowing.

Three

The cabin had begun to feel like a home. Or a home away from home, Kelly thought. The cleaning crew had done a wonderful job. The rooms reflected pure Western charm. She loved the rough-hewn detail: the beamed ceilings, the stone mantel over the fireplace, the cedar chest filled with Texas trinkets. Since the cabin was so different from her suburban dwelling, she enjoyed the therapy it provided. An old place that felt new—the perfect getaway.

A part of Kelly never wanted to return to Ohio. Of course her home state wasn't the problem. She was still hiding from the decisions that awaited her there. Four days had passed since she'd arrived in Texas, and she wasn't any closer to settling her life.

She sat at the battered dining table, stealing light from a small window. The spring weather had turned gloomy, but that hadn't stopped Kelly from pursuing her current subject. Puma, the one-eyed cougar. She had been sketching pictures of him every morning since she had moved into the cabin.

She couldn't explain her affection for Puma, couldn't quite understand it. Being in the cabin made her feel closer to the tawny-colored cat, something that didn't make much sense.

Drawing from memory wasn't easy for Kelly, in fact she had never done it before. Yet Puma's image filled her mind, even the smallest detail.

A loud knock sounded. Kelly jumped to her feet. She had a pretty good idea who her visitor was. Shane stopped by daily, her gentlemanly neighbor with the slow drawl and worn leather boots. She closed her sketchbook and covered it with a magazine she had found in the cedar chest, then went to open the door.

"Hey, Kelly." A straw cowboy hat shielded his eyes. But not enough, she noticed, to conceal the amber sparkle in them.

A flutter of attraction had her slipping into that flash of gold. The baby kicked just then. A scolding. A reminder that pregnant women shouldn't flirt.

She glanced away. "Come in."

He removed his hat upon entering the cabin, leaving his hair the way it fell. Shane didn't appear to fuss over his appearance. Jason was always groomed to perfection which had her constantly wishing she was prettier and that her body had more curves. Pregnancy fullness didn't count.

Shane set his hat on an end table and placed a plastic animal carrier on the floor. "Zuni wanted to see you."

"She did?" Kelly watched the serval kitten scamper out of the carrier. "Will you pick her up for me? I don't think I can."

"Sure." He lifted Zuni before she darted off. "Guess you're having a little trouble touching your toes these days, huh?"

She appreciated his easy response. It was certainly better than the uncomfortable glances he usually gave her tummy. "Are you kidding?" She motioned to the barrel chair that faced the fireplace. "I can hardly sit without getting stuck."

He eyed the offending chair, then smiled. "It does looks a mite deep. Maybe you better avoid it from here on in."

She returned his casual smile. "So how's my little Zuni?"

He adjusted the kitten with pride. "She learned how to kiss."

"Really?"

"Yep. We've been working on it for days." He moved closer. "Zuni, give Kelly a kissums."

Kissums. Delighted, she leaned forward as Zuni poked her nose out. The kiss resulted in a quick nudge. Kelly squealed and met Shane's gaze over the serval's massive ears. They grinned at each other, smiled happily until the moment turned strangely quiet. They stood inches apart, Shane's arm brushing Kelly's stomach.

The kitten leaped onto the sofa. Kelly wasn't sure what to do or say. Shane didn't move his arm, nor did he step back. Zuni explored the cabin while they faced each other, their gazes locked.

Kelly's mouth went dry. She moistened her lips. Suddenly she wanted to kiss him—gently, with the kind of tenderness she longed to receive from Jason. She didn't want a sexual kiss. She craved comfort, a sensation that would take the hurt away.

A rustling noise caught her attention, but it was Shane who turned away first, breaking their haunting stare. Zuni sat on the dining table, amusing herself with the magazine Kelly had placed over her sketchbook, tearing and crumbling pages.

Shane started toward the kitten before Kelly had the chance. "No, Zuni," he corrected in a stern voice.

Avoiding his reprimand, the serval jumped off the table, sending the magazine and Kelly's sketchbook tumbling to the floor. Shane reached down to right the papers. Kelly stood nearby. Her sketchbook had fallen open, displaying a drawing of Puma.

Embarrassment washed over her. She rarely shared her hobby with anyone. "I was just messing around," she said hastily, wishing she could move fast enough to snatch the booklet off the floor. She had never felt so exposed—naked while being fully clothed.

Shane lifted the drawing to study it. "It's Puma." A breathtaking image of the cougar that had given Shane his heart back, the animal that had lived in his dreams since childhood.

"This is really good." Unnerving, too. The picture could have been him, not in looks but in spirit. Shane had spent years with Puma—pain-cleansing years. He placed the sketchbook on the table. "May I?" he asked Kelly, curious to see her other drawings.

She nodded, then shifted her feet, visibly uncomfortable. "It's just a hobby."

Mesmerized by her hobby, he paged through the booklet, starting with the first sheet. She favored flowers, he noticed, and tall trees—weeping willows draped in beauty and sadness. Another page depicted a puppy, a cute little mutt, the next a row of tomato plants. She had even captured the moisture beading the fruit, making the tomatoes seem red and succulent. He could see rich, vibrant color where there was none.

"Do you paint?" he asked.

"Not really, no."

But she did, he decided. She painted in her mind. He came back to Puma's image. There were four sketches in all, each depicting a different mood. He especially liked the close-up, the one that filled the page, Puma's head lowered in a primal pose. The missing eye didn't detract from the animal's striking appearance. If anything, it added an air of mystery.

Why Puma? Why did she feel compelled to draw his cat? The one that had changed his life? "You spent a lot of time on these pictures." And plenty of passion. He could see it in every line, every dark, primitive shadow. She had breathed life into Puma's sketches. Shane could feel the cougar's sleek fur, even hear the loud hum of his purr. She had captured everything.

Kelly released an audible breath. "I draw almost every morning. I don't drink coffee and I don't jog. So when I wake up early, I take out my sketchbook."

He wanted to ask if he could keep his favorite picture, but

noticed the rendering wasn't quite finished. Apparently he had interrupted her work.

"I feel sort of attached to Puma," she said, her voice shy. "I just keep seeing him in my mind. Every detail."

Images, he realized, that she'd put on paper. "He used to live here."

She cocked her head. "Excuse me?"

"The cougar. Slept here, ate here. Tore up the place a bit." He tried to keep his tone light, even though this whole experience had left him shaken. Kelly Baxter had felt Puma's spirit. Now Shane knew, without a doubt, that he was meant to help her. He scrubbed his hand across his jaw. How could he make a difference in her life in less than two weeks? Kelly still hadn't told him what troubled her.

"A cougar actually lived here?" She leaned forward. "How? I mean why?"

"I was trying to prove something to myself, I guess. And to my dad. I was having some trouble warming up to Tom then. About the only thing we had in common was our interest in big cats."

Kelly sat at the table and looked up at him. "So your dad introduced you to the Mendozas, the people who owned the rescue?"

"Yeah. Tom was their vet. But he didn't get paid. He volunteered his time. Most rescues can't afford to pay a vet, especially since so many of their animals are in poor health when they first arrive. It made me sort of mad that he was so damn noble, but deep down, I respected him for it, too."

Shane seated himself across from Kelly. "Regardless, I was still hurt that my dad had raised his white son instead of me." And Shane was devastated that his Comanche wife had cheated on him with a white man—a wealthy, young lawyer— a man who had claimed the child Shane had loved. *Paternity* and *test* were two words he never wanted to hear paired up again. "I only came to Texas because my mom suggested it. She thought it was time for me to make peace with my dad. And myself."

Kelly scooted her chair forward, just enough, Shane noticed, to keep her tummy from bumping the table. He had the feeling she had come to Texas to make peace with herself, too. She looked pretty today, her hair spilling out of a messy ponytail, her face void of makeup. He admired her fresh, clean glow. The aura of motherhood.

"How did you get interested in big cats?" she asked. "It's not a very common interest. Not to the degree of living with one."

He had to smile. Puma hadn't been the easiest roommate. "When I was a boy, I started having dreams about cougars. My grandma called it mountain lion medicine. She was pretty deep into the old ways. Comanches are supposed to know the difference between a regular dream and a revelation, and she said I wasn't having ordinary dreams. She convinced me that mine were special. They were my *puha* or power. And that meant they would guide me someday."

"And they did," Kelly commented. "You run a rescue now. That's pretty special."

"Thanks." He resisted the urge to cup her cheek, touched by the awe in her voice. "The mountain lion in my dreams was different than most. He only had one eye."

Her stunned gaze met his. "Oh, my God, Shane."

"Yeah, well, it wasn't as mystical as my Grandma made it sound. I thought so at first, certain that I had found this magical animal, but in actuality, Puma was just a cougar. Sure, he represented a vision, but he was still a dangerous animal. Everyone, including my dad, thought I was insane to bring him into the cabin with me. Of course no amount of reasoning was going to stop me."

"Where did Puma come from? Who had him before you?"

He sighed. "You mean who caused his eye to rupture? That's a story in itself." He could see that Kelly wanted to hear it, so he decided it was time to check on Zuni. It wouldn't do to talk about one animal while another got into trouble. He'd learned firsthand that exotics didn't behave like domestics, no matter how cute and fluffy they were.

"Just looking for Zuni," he told Kelly while he circled the room. He caught sight of the kitten and smiled. The serval wasn't interested in making mischief. She slept peacefully on a braided area rug.

Shane settled back into his seat. "The Mendozas got a call from this terminally ill man named Alex who was looking for a home for his cougar," he began. "So my dad and I went to Alex's house to check out his story. I was working actively at the rescue by this time, learning everything I could about the cats." But he had yet to heal. Tami and the baby still occupied his thoughts, and mental pictures of that family-stealing lawyer had kept the hurt and resentment alive. "Anyway, Alex's story checked out, even if he was a bit eccentric."

Shane explained that Alex had purchased Puma from an auction with the intention to raise the kitten for a while, then release him into the wild. "This can't be done, not in this manner. Once a cat imprints with people, they can't be expected to behave like an exotic who has lived in the wild. They become a danger to themselves and humans as well."

"Why?" she asked.

"They tend to venture too close to civilization, and that can lead to disaster. The animal usually ends up taking a bullet or hurting someone."

"I never thought about that."

"Most people don't. So basically that's how Puma came to me. Alex had bottle-fed him, but wasn't given proper feeding instructions, so Puma suffered from it and lost his eye. After that, Alex spared no expense to take care of the cat. He learned everything he could and realized he couldn't set Puma free. But when Puma was about four months old, Alex's disease progressed, so he started searching for someone to adopt his one-eyed cougar."

"You," Kelly said.

"Yeah, me. And I agreed to all of Alex's crazy demands. I mean, he was dying, and I had been dreaming about a one-eyed mountain lion all of my life. We were both a little mixed up. I promised him that I wouldn't cage Puma, at least not until I could afford to build the cougar a natural habitat. The rescue wasn't set up the way it is now. The compounds weren't very extravagant, and he wanted the best for his cat. He had been babying the hell out of Puma, guilty about what he'd done."

"So you inherited a spoiled cougar."

"Yeah, but Puma was still young then, and I fooled myself into believing that living with him was going to be fairly easy. I was still a little too caught up in those dreams."

"I'll bet you were in for a rude awakening."

"Yeah." He grinned. "But I was too stubborn to admit it. I didn't want my dad having the last word—the 'I told you so.' I kept Puma in the cabin with me for over two years. Eventually he even shared my bed, although I wouldn't recommend it. There's nothing worse than waking up with a hundred-and-eighty-pound cat who wets the bed."

Kelly burst into laughter. "You're crazy, Shane."

"No, sweetheart," he teased, striking an austere pose. "I've got mountain lion medicine."

Her expression turned suddenly serious. "You really do. And so does this cabin." She looked around, her voice respectful. "That's why I feel so close to Puma. In a way, he still lives here."

Shane only nodded. He wished Puma had all the answers, that the cougar could tell him how to heal Kelly Baxter's heart. Ten days, he thought with an inward grimace. He had ten days to change the course of her life. He closed his eyes. Somehow that just didn't seem possible. Mountain lion medicine or not.

Rain fell from the sky the following day, muddying the ground. Parking in front of the One Stop, Kelly dashed inside the mini mart. White-haired, bearded Barry Hunt sat behind the counter.

"Afta'noon." He greeted her, speaking around his usual wad of tobacco.

Did he ever spit that stuff out? she wondered. And if he did, did it trickle onto his beard? Kelly tried not to wrinkle her nose. "Do you think you could give me directions into town?"

He shifted his behind. He wore bib-overalls, looking like a cross between a dirt-poor farmer and a grizzly old miner who'd just struck gold—in his mouth. Despite the tobacco, he grinned, displaying a shiny metal tooth. "Suppose I could. You here for some sandwich fixings?"

"Not today." Kelly had a craving for some real food—her favorite treat—cantaloupe and vanilla ice cream. Chicken sounded good, too, seasoned with curry and served with a side of steamed rice. "I thought I'd shop in town."

He grunted and poked a finger out. "Yer belly's gettin' bigger."

Gee, the man was so tactful. "Babies grow," she said, picking up a package of powdered doughnuts. She knew Barry wouldn't let her go until she bought something. "How about those directions?"

She took out a pen and a scrap of paper from her pocketbook and scribbled furiously while Barry supplied her with country instructions, things like "turn right at the Newton's place, then travel on yonder to the Harris Farm, and if you see Mrs. Harris, ask her when she's gonna bring me another jar of that elderberry jam her Aunt Millie made."

Kelly did her best to pry streets names and clearer descriptions out of Barry, paid for the doughnuts and rushed back to her utility vehicle, dodging puddles in her quest.

The windshield wipers swept across the glass. The weatherman had claimed the rain would be short-lived, although another storm would soon follow. Spring was unpredictable, Kelly thought. Clear one day, wet the next.

She angled the utility vehicle onto another narrow stretch and realized she had taken a wrong turn somewhere. The road ahead ended at a fallen tree, one that had probably blocked this path for years.

She backed the vehicle up and cursed Barry's directions. She hadn't found the Newton's blue house or the ranch that belonged to the Harris family. In fact she hadn't seen anything remotely resembling civilization.

Kelly attempted a different route, but failed. She ended up on another dirt road, one that appeared to lead to nowhere. The highway to Duarte wasn't anywhere in sight. Texas didn't look quite so appealing covered in mud. Wild grass and brush littered the ground, making landmarks nearly impossible. One acre of earth seemed as lonely as the next, the scattered hills no help at all.

Kelly tore into the doughnuts. Don't cry, she told herself, even though her eyes had begun to burn. Don't turn into a hysterical female. She drove and drove, in circles probably, spilling powdered sugar and blinking away tears.

When a familiar hilltop came into view, she squinted through the windshield. Home. Or close enough. She wiped her watery eyes. She recognized Shane and Dr. McKinley's house. The potted plants and cow skulls had never looked so inviting.

She knocked on the door. All she needed was some good solid directions. And some groceries from the supermarket, wherever that was.

Dr. McKinley answered. "Well, hello, Kelly. Come on in."

Rainwater had curled his hair, she noticed, and dampened his clothes. He padded through the house in white socks, but as they entered the kitchen, she spotted a pair of muddied boots by the back door.

"I made some rounds today," he told her. "Checked up on one of Shane's cats, too. A tiger named Sammy."

Kelly nodded. She remembered Shane had said that Sammy had a poor immune system. "I just stopped by for some directions into town."

"Oh, sure." He placed a teapot on the stove. "How about some hot chocolate first? You look a little teary-eyed, hon. Is everything okay?"

"I got lost," she admitted, realizing she had a lot more to cry about than that. She had spoken to her mother last night and learned that Jason still hadn't returned from his trip. Of course her mother had started in about the paternity suit again, spewing insults about Jason and his family. "I drove around for over an hour."

"Then some hot chocolate will help." Tom reached into the cabinet. "Little marshmallows, too."

Kelly smiled and removed her jacket. Dr. McKinley had an easy way about him. It was hard to believe that he had agreed to raise one son and not the other. But then she supposed saving his marriage had been his priority at the time. Her smile fell. She wondered if Jason would marry someday. And have other children. Sons and daughters he would welcome into his life.

They sat at the table and sipped their drinks, rain slashing against the kitchen window.

"Shane's cats don't like me much," Tom said. "They see me coming and they run into their lockdowns."

She tilted her head. "Why?"

"Because they know I'm the guy with the dart gun. Being a vet doesn't make you popular, at least not with your patients."

The image of a four-hundred-pound tiger hiding from Dr. McKinley had Kelly smiling again.

The back door blew open just then, bringing in a gust of cool air and Shane Night Wind with it. Rain dripped from the brim of his hat, and a tan duster trailed to his knees.

"Oh, this is nice, Dad," he said, winking at Kelly. "You're sitting at the table with a pretty girl, and I'm soaked to the bone."

"I was out there, too," Tom reminded his son good-naturedly. "And so was Kelly. She got lost going into town."

"It's true, I never made it," Kelly admitted as Shane wiped his boots on an indoor mat. "I drove around in circles until I ended up here. I came to the door to get directions."

"And I plied her with chocolate," Tom added, raising his cup.

"Well, you're a fine pair." Shane strode over to Kelly and

draped his coat over a rattan chair. "I'll give you a ride into town. You shouldn't be driving in this weather."

The man had an overly protective nature, she decided. But she liked him. A lot. "I'm from Ohio. It snows there."

"Yeah, well, this is Duarte, Texas. And it's been known to flood here. Storms are rare, but they do happen." He tipped his hat, spilling droplets of water onto the glass tabletop. "Besides, I can give you the grand tour."

The grand tour, Kelly learned an hour later, existed of a post office, a diner with a jukebox selection at every table, a cowboy bar called the Two Step and a run-down motel known as Duarte Flats. The market sat between a Laundromat and a pharmacy that sold cherry colas and root beer floats. The entire town faced the highway, a paved road that led to other small Texas establishments in other small Texas towns. Of course there was plenty of empty land in between.

"We've got one physician in town," Shane said, as they entered the market. "His practice is up the road. He's got a little clinic in front of his house. It's not much, but Doc Lanigan is a good old guy."

"I thought the expression was good ol' boy."

He grinned. "Yeah, that, too."

The old-fashioned market differed from the superstore where Kelly worked. There were only three check stands and no scanners. Her hometown seemed like a major metropolis compared to Duarte. Fast-food chains didn't exist in this tiny West Texas town, and she ventured to guess the privately owned market didn't offer union benefits, either.

Shane pushed the cart, and Kelly loaded it. They stood in front of the spice rack, looking for powdered curry. "Don't see any," he said.

She supposed Indonesian dishes weren't a favorite in Duarte. "How about tarragon?"

He scanned the shelf. "Nope."

She settled on a bottle of imported teriyaki sauce. As they continued up and down the aisles, her stomach jumped and jittered, making her wonder if the baby suffered from a case of hiccups. Kelly placed a calming hand over the commotion, feeling suddenly sad. She wanted to share moments like this with the father of her child. She had never planned on being a single parent.

She looked over at Shane. What would he do if he impregnated a woman he didn't love? Would he marry her? Become the husband and father Jason wasn't willing to be?

Shane turned toward her. "Steak, right?"

"What?" She realized they stood at the meat counter, the butcher waiting for her to make a selection. "No, chicken."

"This is beef country," Shane countered. "The steaks here are so fresh they practically moo."

That thought didn't hold appeal. "Chicken breasts," she told the butcher. "Fillets." She ordered enough for two hearty portions and then chose halibut for another home-cooked meal. Aside from her frantic, teary-eyed doughnut bout and an occasion bowl of ice cream, her baby had gotten used to low cholesterol foods.

"Puma likes chicken," Shane said as they moved on. "Except he takes his feathers and all."

Kelly winced. "Remind me not to invite him to dinner." She studied her neighbor's teasing smile. He was so easy to talk to, so easy to consider a friend. "What about you?"

He steered the cart toward the produce section. "I prefer my fowl without the feathers."

She laughed and bumped his arm. "I was inviting you to have dinner with me tonight."

"Oh." He grinned. "Okay. Sure."

An elderly woman walked by and smiled, but not with the kind of smile that said she knew Shane. Kelly realized the lady had mistaken them for an expectant couple—happily married and awaiting the birth of their first child. Loneliness stabbed her chest like Juliet's dagger.

She lifted a cantaloupe. Should she tell Shane about Jason? Ask for his opinion about the paternity suit? Turning the melon, she examined it without really seeing. She was leaving in nine days. She wouldn't have access to Shane's friendship forever, and she had come to Texas to make an important decision. Kelly took a deep, nervous breath. Shane had offered to listen once before.

But still…

She set the melon down and picked up another. Maybe she should warn him to be prepared for a serious dinner conversation that night.

"Are you very good at giving advice?" she asked.

"About what?" He glanced down at her hand, then back up, his amused gaze meeting hers. "Cantaloupe?" He made a show of sniffing the air. "Truthfully, I'm more of a watermelon guy myself."

Her pulse tripped. "I was thinking more along the lines of what I should do about my life."

His expression turned serious, the amber sparkle in his eyes softening to a pale glow. "I don't know if I'm much good at handing out advice, but I'll be here if you need me."

"Thank you." Kelly placed a cantaloupe in the basket, trying to appear unaffected by the gentle sound of his voice. The kindness he offered.

I'll be here if you need me.

Jason Collier, not Shane Night Wind, should have whispered those words.

She had heard that unborn babies choose their parents, that their tiny spirits decide who will give them life. Kelly cradled her tummy, comforting her womb. If her child wanted Jason for a father, then maybe, just maybe, Shane could help her find a way to make that happen.

Four

Shane walked into Kelly's cabin, dripping rain. He handed her a bouquet of mixed flowers. "For the table," he said.

The flowers were wet, she noticed, glistening with beads of water. "Thank you. Did you pick them?"

"Yeah." He reached into his coat pocket and removed a small bundle of what looked like dried herbs. "I brought some sage along, too."

She studied the offering. A fragrant aroma rose from it. "Do you want me to season the chicken with it?" she asked, feeling a bit perplexed. The chicken breasts were already in the oven, baking in a marinade of teriyaki sauce, rings of canned pineapples on top.

A smile spread across his face, softening his features. "This is for smudging. I thought it would be good for the baby."

Kelly glanced down at her tummy, then back up at her dinner guest. "Smudging?"

He stepped farther into the room. "You've never burned sage?"

Dumbfounded and still holding the flowers, she shook her head. Why would burning a dried herb be good for her baby?

Shane removed his duster and placed it on the barrel chair. His rain-dampened hair had been plaited into two long braids. Aside from pictures of Indians in history books, she had never seen a man with his hair braided. It suited him, she decided, complemented his striking features and masculine clothes.

"Your granddaddy used to smudge," he said, nodding to the cedar chest. "Isn't there a small clay pot in there? And some loose feathers?"

"I think so." There were all sorts of interesting items in the chest, Texas trinkets she assumed her grandpa had collected.

She knelt to open the trunk. Shane lowered himself to his knees beside her. He found the articles he was looking for, and she came across a mason jar for the flowers. He clasped her hand to help her up. Kelly could have sworn she'd gained at least five pounds this week.

They walked to the dining table, and she placed the bouquet between two tall, white candles. She had already set the table with Grandpa's chipped stoneware.

"Smudging is a purifying ceremony," Shane explained. "Sage, cedar or sweetgrass can be used. It rids the environment of negative energy." He lit the bundle, then fanned it with a feather.

Kelly watched as he circled the cabin and directed the smoke, cleansing each area. When he returned to the table, he lifted his gaze to hers. "I can smudge you if you'd like."

Curious, she whispered a shy "okay" and tried to picture her grandpa doing this.

Shane positioned himself in front of her, then backed up slowly, searching, he said, for the energy field that surrounded her, an aura he hoped to feel.

What would he find? she wondered nervously. Her tattered emotions? The loneliness that followed her each day?

Kelly kept her eyes trained on him, and as he came closer and fanned the fragrant smoke, she began to relax. The experience had become almost mystical. His hazy form looked like that of an ancient warrior, a vision drifting through the fog.

Shane Night Wind intrigued her. Even his name stirred an engaging image—this man who rescued cougars, picked wildflowers in the rain, braided his hair.

They stared at each other through the sage-scented haze. "Thank you," she said. "For thinking of the baby."

He set the clay pot on the table. "You're welcome."

She wanted to take his hand and place it against her tummy. The baby was moving gently—a tiny angel fluttering its wings—cleansed and whole, awaiting the world.

"I should check on dinner," she said when the moment turned much too quiet. She couldn't possibly reach for his hand. What would he think?

They ate fifteen minutes later, seated across from each other at the scarred table, rain slashing against a small window. The sage had burned out, but the candles were lit, white wax melting, golden flames dancing.

Her nervousness returned. She had no idea how to start the conversation they both knew was supposed to take place.

Shane looked up from his plate. The ice in his glass crackled. Kelly could hear everything, including the pounding of her own heart.

"It's okay," he said. "We can talk about what's bothering you after dinner."

She startled, a forkful of food frozen in her hand. "Can you read minds? You always seem to know what I'm thinking."

The flickering candlelight illuminated his features, hollowing his cheekbones even more. "Sometimes I feel things, other people's emotions, I guess." He lifted his glass and smiled. "But I'm not psychic. I'm just observant, that's all."

Fascinated, she leaned forward. "What about earlier? Did I really have an energy field around me?"

"I think everyone does, but I can't always feel them." He caught her gaze and held it. "But with you I did."

His admission made her heart pound a little faster. "I've never met anyone like you before."

His lips tilted into another small smile. "Nor I you."

They fell silent then, a stillness that intensified the rain—a companionable quiet, Kelly thought, indoor warmth amid a spring storm. She studied him while they ate—the angular shape of his face, gold in his eyes, the mannerisms that seemed so naturally cat-like.

"Have you always worn your hair long?" she asked finally.

Shane nodded. "I was taught that a Comanche man should take pride in his hair." He set his fork down and picked up his water. "They were a bit obsessive in the old days, though. Sometimes they would attach horsehair to their own to make it longer. Or they would beg locks off a mourning woman."

"Comanche women cut their hair when someone died?"

"Sometimes the men did, too. But not as often as the women."

Kelly's mind drifted to her grandpa. Ten months had passed, but she still mourned him. She glanced at the clay pot, wondering if Shane had taught the older man the practice of smudging. Grandpa's Texas vacations seemed almost secretive now. Magical, too.

"Will you light the sage again?" she asked. She liked the earthy aroma, the calming effect of the scented smoke.

He smiled. "Sure."

While the dried herb smoldered, they cleared the table, then sat in the main room sampling Kelly's favorite dessert—cantaloupe and vanilla ice cream. Shane reclined in a leather chair, and she claimed the sofa. The rain hadn't let up; it crashed against the windows in crystalline sheets.

"My mother and I haven't been getting along lately," she said, knowing her statement wouldn't seem out of the blue to Shane. If he was sensing her emotions, then he would understand the direction she was taking.

He set his half-eaten dessert aside. "Because of the baby?"

"Because of the baby's father," Kelly admitted hastily. "She wants me to force him into taking a paternity test."

She waited for Shane to respond, but he just sat there, staring at her. She glanced down at her ice cream, wishing he would say something. Anything. Talking about this proved difficult enough, but now his strained silence managed to clog her throat.

Paternity test. Those familiar words banged against Shane's chest like a row of brass knuckles. Already he could feel welts forming on his heart, recalling bruises from his past.

He steadied his gaze and tried to focus on Kelly. She needed a friend, someone to talk to. Reliving the pain from his marriage wasn't going to do either one of them any good.

"Who is your baby's father?" he asked. And why was her mother rallying for a paternity test?

Kelly's breath hitched. "His name is Jason Collier. But he never paid much attention to me, except for a smile or two when we were in high school…."

Her words drifted, and Shane decided she was recalling the teenage smiles this Jason character had given her. "So he wasn't your high school sweetheart?"

"Heavens, no. He was one of the most popular boys at Tannery High. He dated cheerleaders and girls from prestigious families."

Shane didn't like the inflection in Kelly's voice, the tone that said she didn't think she measured up to Jason's standards. As an image of himself and Tami came to mind, he pushed it away. There had been a time when he had questioned his self-worth, too.

Kelly toyed with her ice cream. "I was shocked when Jason asked me out last summer. Of course he knew I was attracted to him, but I never expected him to act on it."

"So you dated him?"

"For two weeks before we—" She glanced away quickly.

"Slept together?" Shane provided, wondering why the admission made Kelly uncomfortable. She was twenty-four years old. Having a lover was natural.

"It was my first time," she offered suddenly.

Surprised, he leaned forward. When a glimmer of shame drifted across her face, he frowned. Virginity hadn't dawned on him. "That's okay. Everybody has to have a first time."

She placed her dessert on the coffee table. The ice cream had begun to melt, pooling inside the cantaloupe half. "It wasn't okay," she whispered. "I mean... I wasn't very good at it." She sighed and raised her voice to a more audible level. "I don't know, maybe it was nerves. Jason was going out of town for a month, and that seemed like such a long time to be without him. I was a little desperate, I suppose, not quite myself."

A knot formed in Shane's stomach. "He pressured you?"

She shook her head. "No. I was inexperienced, but I thought lovemaking would bring us closer, that when he returned he would be anxious to resume our relationship."

"And he wasn't?"

"He was angry when he found out I was pregnant."

Her eyes misted. Shane noticed they had changed colors, the deep hazel washing to a pale brown. She looked hollow, he thought, and sad, so very sad. What kind of jerk was this Jason, anyway?

"Are you in love with him?" he asked.

Those faded eyes shifted focus, away from his questioning stare. He wanted her to say no. For some unfounded reason, he didn't want her to be in love.

Shane righted his posture. Not loving a jerk would be easier on her, he told himself. The churning in his stomach wasn't jealousy, it was concern.

"I don't know, maybe," she said finally. "I think about him a lot, and thinking about him makes me ache." She twisted the napkin on her lap, then tore at it, spilling tiny pieces onto her dress. "He's very charming, or he was before I got pregnant. Jason's handsome and friendly. Both men and women like him. He was popular in high school because he was nice to people."

Shane got an image of a young entrepreneur—clean-cut,

well-spoken, well educated—just like the lawyer who had turned Tami's head.

The churning in his gut intensified. "I suppose he's rich."

Kelly practically jumped to her feet. The shredded napkin flew to the floor, the tiny pieces scattering. "I can't believe you said that."

She tore out of the room, Shane staring after her. He waited a beat before he followed her.

She had retreated to the kitchen, her back to the open doorway. He couldn't see her face, but it didn't take a genius to know she was crying. Not loud enough to hear, he realized. Soft tears spilled from her eyes, the kind that ached. Tears he had somehow caused.

"Kelly?" He moved closer and reached for her hair, but before making contact, he dropped his hand. "I'm sorry. I didn't mean to upset you."

She turned slowly, her watery eyes meeting his. "You think I'm after Jason's money."

"No, I don't." She was so fragile, he thought. Her dress flowed to her ankles, a pale floral print draping elegantly over the fullness she carried. "I think you're too sweet for something like that."

She swiped at her tears as though suddenly embarrassed by them. "Jason thinks I'm after his money. When he first found out about the baby, he said it wasn't his. And then later, he accused me of getting pregnant on purpose. I'm not sure what he believes now."

Shane wanted to tell her that Jason Collier was an idiot and she should just forget about him, but he knew that advice stemmed from the clench in his gut—the reminder of his own past. Kelly cared about her baby's father, maybe even loved him. "Jason is probably just nervous. Fatherhood scares some guys."

"So you think he'll come around?" she asked, her voice still a little broken.

Shane nodded. "Yeah, I do."

"You're not just saying that to make me feel better?"

He wanted to touch her, run his fingers through her hair, graze her cheek. Consoling gestures, he told himself. He understood pain.

"I'm speaking from experience, Kelly. I told you about how guilty my dad had been over me." And Tami's lawyer factored into his opinion, too. Reluctant fathers often redeemed themselves, accepting financial and emotional responsibility for their children. After all, Kelly hadn't described Jason as a monster. A bit of a jerk, but plenty of guys overreacted to unexpected pregnancies. Not all of them turned out to be deadbeat dads.

Kelly dried the rest of her tears. "Tom didn't question your paternity, did he?"

"No." He gave in to his urge and reached for her hand, held it lightly in his. "At least not that I was told. But it's tough for a guy to know if a child is really his. Sometimes women lie. Or sometimes they just don't know for sure. Multiple lovers aren't that uncommon."

Kelly squared her shoulders, but didn't release his hand. "Jason is the only man I've been with. I didn't lie, and I'm not interested in his money. I want him to care about this baby."

"I understand." It was difficult not to raise their joined hands to his lips and brush his mouth over her knuckles, kiss the hurt away. "Come on, let's go sit down."

He led her to the front room and sat beside her on the couch. She took back her hand and placed it against her stomach. Comforting the baby, he thought.

Shane fixed his gaze on her tummy and pictured the tiny life residing there, nesting snugly amid the feminine warmth. "Babies suck their thumbs in the womb," he said before he could think to stop himself.

Kelly gave him a startled glance. "How do you know that?"

Because he had watched Evan's ultrasound video with an expectant father's pride, marveling at the wonder of life. He shrugged, hating himself for the lie. "Read it somewhere, I guess."

"Me, too," she commented. "I've read every baby book imaginable. I even brought some of them with me."

He swallowed, envying what Jason had. "You're going to be a terrific mom."

"Thank you." The break in her voice hadn't quite mended. "That means a lot to me."

The rain had stopped. Stillness engulfed the cabin. He inhaled the scent from the smoldering sage. "I think you should consider a court-ordered paternity test. Jason probably won't come around until he knows for sure that the baby is his."

"But I don't want to sue him," she countered. "It's not money I'm after, it's love and acceptance I want. Dragging Jason into court won't give my baby emotional security. And it won't make things any easier on me, either. I hate that there are people in my hometown who believe that I got pregnant on purpose."

"Why does Jason think that?"

"He..." She exhaled a heavy breath. "When he discovered that he was out of condoms, he asked me if I was 'safe.' I thought he meant from disease, but that was his way of asking if I was on the Pill. I told him yes because I misunderstood." A rosy hue flooded her cheeks. "I thought he would...you know...before he..."

"I understand what you mean," Shane supplied since she was stumbling over the words. She had expected Jason to withdraw before he climaxed.

"I know that isn't a proper birth control method," she said, her tone not quite as shy as before. "And I probably sound like some sort of imbecile for not insisting that Jason use a condom. But in spite of our misunderstanding, we're both still responsible for this baby."

Shane agreed wholeheartedly, but apparently the father in question didn't. "You're not an imbecile."

Kelly brushed a lock of hair from her eye. "At least it

happened in the dark. That made it a little easier to hide my nervousness. I don't think he knew it was my first time.''

Shane tilted his head to study her, deciding Jason hadn't treated her the way a lover should. The guy must have been too caught up in his own pleasure to give Kelly the care she deserved. Shane wouldn't have made love to her in the dark. He would have left a low light burning. And he would have catered to her needs, touched and kissed and—

"Shane?"

He blinked. Twice, maybe three times. He couldn't be sure. "Yeah?"

"So you really think I should consider a court-ordered paternity test?"

As guilt clawed its way into his mind, Shane ducked his head. He was supposed to be giving Kelly advice, not envisioning himself in bed with her, making a baby who belonged to someone else. "I'm not saying to sue Jason, just file a petition for the tests that will prove he fathered your child. He can't ignore you once he knows the truth."

"I hope he returns to Ohio before I have the baby. Not much can get accomplished until he comes back."

"Where is he?" Shane asked, upset that Jason was avoiding her to such a degree. Somebody needed to pound some sense into the guy and, at the moment, Shane wished it could be him.

"I don't know. On a business trip somewhere. His family owns a string of restaurants. He travels often, but I doubt he's ever been gone this long before."

Shane glanced down at Kelly's hands. She wore no jewelry, no bracelets or rings. No shining 14 karat gold bands or diamond promises.

If Jason had reacted more honorably, would Kelly have accepted a marriage proposal from him? Of course she would have, he decided. Kelly might be independent, but she wasn't like Shane's mother—a woman who didn't believe in marriage for the sake of a child.

Shane loved his mom, but her free-spirited ways hadn't

rubbed off on him. He valued commitment, especially for those raising children. Jason should have offered to marry Kelly. Maybe he still would. After the baby was born, the paternity test could change everything. Shane assumed Jason came from one of those rich, traditional, tight-knit families, which meant Kelly's baby would have society grandparents—the kind who found illegitimacy unacceptable. Surely they would encourage a wedding once they knew the truth.

Now why didn't that thought give him comfort?

"Eventually he might ask you to marry him," Shane said, forcing himself to accept the idea. Kelly deserved a marriage proposal, and she was already half in love with Jason.

She met his gaze with a disbelieving look. "Somehow I doubt that."

"It's possible. His family might encourage him to consider it."

She sighed. "That's what I had hoped for in the beginning. And then I started wishing for smaller things. Concerned phone calls, a ride to the doctor's office. Just the slightest indication that he cared."

"Don't worry. Your baby will have a father. I'm certain of it."

She smiled. "Is that one of your official nonpsychic feelings?"

"Yep." He grinned back at her, then stood and rolled his shoulders. "I should get going. It's late."

She came to her feet a little awkwardly, the way pregnant women sometimes did, clutching furniture for support. Shane noticed she appeared to be carrying the baby a tad lower. He searched his memories for the old wives' tale that accompanied that position. Girls were high in front, boys carried low through the hips. Or was it the other way around?

"Thank you," she said. "I really needed someone to talk to."

"No problem."

She walked him to the door. He turned to say goodbye and as he did, she leaned forward.

The hug was automatic. Gentle and right. She put her head on his shoulder and closed her eyes. He stroked her hair and felt her breath stir against his neck.

"I'm glad you're my friend," she whispered.

He swallowed around the lump in his throat. "Me, too. Promise that when you go back to Ohio, you'll keep in touch?"

She lifted her head. "I'll call every week."

"Good." He drew her closer and held tight. On this rain-soaked Texas night Kelly Baxter was right where she belonged. In the willing arms of a friend.

Five

Although the prediction of another storm brewed, the rain had stopped, giving way to a pale-blue sky and thriving greenery. Kelly sat on a log stump near the side of Puma's containment, watching the cougar with an appreciative eye and an emotional heart. Concentrating on the cat soothed her tremulous spirit. At the cabin, she had spent the morning detailing her drawings, pulling strength from the creative force. For the first time in her life, her artwork came alive, giving her a deeper sense of self-worth.

Normally she thought of herself as average, but today she felt special. Today she absorbed the elements—the rain-soaked ground, the leaves glistening on the trees, the breeze blowing by. The one-eyed cougar. The half-Comanche man.

Yes, they were part of her, too. Puma was her inspiration and Shane her friend. On this windy afternoon, Kelly wasn't a simple girl from Ohio. Complexity pumped through her veins, giving her the power to face Jason as an equal.

She had already called her attorney about the paternity tests.

Jason was her baby's father, and if it took DNA samples to prove it to him, then so be it.

Kelly smoothed her breeze-ravaged hair. Did she love Jason Collier? She honestly didn't know. Time, she decided, would tell, especially now that she had discovered a slice of inner peace. When she returned to Ohio, she would hold her head high—explore herself and her feelings.

Don't worry. Your baby will have a father. I'm certain of it.

Those words, Shane's words, soothed her like a balm. Loving Jason or hurting from his criticism wasn't the issue. Encouraging him to take an active part in his child's life was key. Kelly's father had died many years before, but thanks to her grandpa she hadn't been forced to survive without paternal love. And if she could find a way to make it happen, her baby would know paternal love, too. Once the child was born and the tests proven, how could Jason ignore the truth?

He couldn't. Shane had said that as well.

The sound of footsteps caught her attention. A smile lit her face before she turned. She knew who it was.

"Hi." Shane returned her smile, his unbound hair lifting like dark, auburn-tipped wings. "My dad told me you were out here."

"I wanted to visit with Puma. I hope you don't mind."

"Of course not. I would have rather been here than cooped up in my office. The toughest part about running a rescue is organizing fund-raisers. I'm not very social, so planning these things are a nuisance."

She glanced over at Puma. The cat, peering through a crop of vegetation, observed them through that lone eye. "A necessary one, right?" Jungle Hill had plenty of feline mouths to feed.

"Yep. A necessary nuisance. It costs about $200 a month to feed each animal," he offered, supplying an answer to the question she had yet to pose.

He shifted his stance, sporting his usual attire—a soft cotton shirt tucked into the waistband of faded jeans. Shane often wore Western hats and boots, but he didn't resemble a crisp, Texas cowboy. His gait was more fluid, that of man who had lived his life among big cats, becoming one in the process. How else could he have shared the cabin with Puma? The cougar must have thought Shane was another mountain lion.

Kelly smiled and patted her belly. Puma probably thought she was a walking watermelon.

"I like this weather," he said, stretching his arms. "If feels good to be outside."

"Yes, is does."

Kelly scooted over, leaving him a portion of the stump. He sat beside her, aware of her silent invitation. Another small wind kicked up, blowing Kelly's hair across her cheek.

"It's like wheat growing wild," he said.

She knew he meant her hair. A compliment, she decided, unpretentious poetry in Shane's quiet drawl. Strange, but a few moments ago, she had been thinking metaphorically about *his* hair.

They fascinated each other, she realized. Mutual admiration. Male and female friends.

He leaned against her shoulder. "Why do you look so different today? So free?"

"Because I know everything is going to be all right," Kelly answered. "I called my attorney this morning. I decided to follow through on the paternity test."

"Good. I'm glad."

He caught a strand of her hair and held it. Suddenly their faces were only inches apart, close enough to inhale the same gust of air—and quite possibly the flavor of each other with it. Kelly could almost taste the peppermint candy in Shane's mouth.

"What about your mom?" he asked.

"What about her?" She tried not to focus on his lips, but he kept darting his tongue over them.

"Did you talk to her? Tell her what you decided?"

"Yes." Because Kelly wanted to kiss him, she froze. A pregnant woman shouldn't want a man who wasn't responsible for her condition. She studied the shape of his lips, the moisture his tongue had made. Why hadn't her baby kicked? Wasn't it time for a scolding?

Shane blinked. His eyes looked glazed, the flecks of gold a metallic sunburst. "What were we talking about?"

Using his sturdy shoulder for support, Kelly rose to her feet, wishing the baby would give her a healthy jab of reality. Since when did she look into a man's eyes and see the sun? "My mom, I think."

"Oh, yeah." He pulled a hand through his hair, settling the metaphoric wings. "Is she okay with your decision?"

"She would prefer I file a lawsuit. Make Jason pay, so to speak. But you know how I feel about that." Yes, he knew. Shane, her dear friend with the moist, sexy lips understood better than anyone. Forcing Jason into child support and court-ordered custody visits didn't work for her. "I'm glad we're so open with each other," she added, looking directly at Shane. "I don't know what I would do without you."

"You'd do just fine."

He turned his head, and for an instant Kelly wondered if he concealed his expression. Through the mass of hair that blew around his face, she thought she detected a frown—an uneasy slant to those sensuous lips.

The following day Shane invited Kelly to go for a drive with him. He had to. It was time to open up, become the kind of friend she assumed he already was—the kind who didn't keep secrets.

I'm glad we're so open with each other.

Her words chipped at his conscience like an imaginary pickax, making the headache he'd suffered through the night quite real.

Kelly pulled the seat belt across her body. She got prettier each day—a beauty that bloomed from the inside out. The type, in Shane's opinion, that mattered most.

He turned the key and gunned the engine. "It's supposed

to start raining again tomorrow. Figured we should take advantage of the dry spell while we have the chance."

"I packed some sandwiches." She motioned to a plastic grocery bag she had brought along.

"That's fine." He wasn't the least bit hungry. His stomach was already full—with anxiety. A cheating wife served as an appetite suppressant, even five years after the fact.

They drove in silence. He chose scenic roads for Kelly's benefit, passing cattle ranches and horse farms. She peered out the window, clearly enthralled with the grazing animals. When she *oohed* and *aahed* over a herd of mares with their foals, he couldn't help but smile.

"Sweet," he said, reaching over to touch her hair. She wore it loose, one side clipped away from her face with a butterfly-shaped barrette. How appropriate, he thought, studying the colorful ornament. Delicate, elusive Kelly. She would be gone in less than a week.

"I know. Aren't they adorable?" she responded as he drove forward, her gaze still fixed on the horses.

He withdrew his hand. She hadn't realized that his "sweet" had been meant for her.

The next ten miles led to narrower dirt roads, distant hills and scattered brush. Kelly shifted beside him. "It's hard to believe it's going to rain again. It's so peaceful now. Barely even a breeze."

He pulled the four-wheel-drive off the road and parked near a gnarled old tree. "The calm before the storm, as they say."

Shane studied his hands while Kelly turned his way. Suddenly the truck seemed stuffy. He could barely breathe.

"Do you want to sit outside for a while?" he asked "I can pad the tailgate with a blanket."

"Okay."

She brought the lunch sack, and he folded the blanket. When she handed him a small bottle of mountain springwater, he accepted it gratefully. Not only was his breath clogged, but his mouth had gone dry.

He twisted the cap and raised the plastic to his lips, then

guzzled the cool liquid. Afterward, he helped Kelly onto the cushioned tailgate.

Silent, they sat side by side. She looked his way, but rather than turn, he stared straight ahead. He hated talking about the past, thinking about it. Reliving it through words and painful memories.

Kelly touched his shoulder. "What's wrong, Shane? You're not acting like yourself. You seem a little uneasy. I noticed it yesterday, too."

Not himself. It struck him an odd thing for her to say, even if it was true. They had known each other for such a short time, yet she had determined his mood. "Maybe this is just one side of me you've never seen," he responded in a tight voice.

She removed her hand from his shoulder. "Are you mad at me? Did I do something to upset you?"

"No, of course not." Feeling like a first-rate heel, he met her wounded gaze. "What's on my mind happened years ago." He brushed her cheek with the back of his hand, offering a physical apology. "But it's something I should have told you about before now. I haven't always been a bachelor. I was married once, and I had a child, too."

Stunned by Shane's words, Kelly looked into his eyes and noticed the absence of gold. They were dark, as lonely as the impending storm.

He'd spoken in past tense. Why would someone talk about their family in past tense? "Dear, God," she whispered. "You lost them."

"Yes, but not in the way you think." He pulled a hand through his hair. "They didn't die. It wasn't like that. It was a different kind of loss."

One he still struggled to overcome, she realized. "Do you want to talk about it?"

"No." He gave her a sad smile. "But I'm going to, anyway. I owe you this, Kelly. As a friend you have the right to know."

Suddenly his despair seemed connected to her somehow. The thought made her uneasy, but she kept the discomfort to herself. Shane seemed anxiety-ridden enough for both of them. "I'm listening."

"I met Tami in high school. Like you and Jason."

Kelly toyed with her water bottle. The parallel had already begun. "What's she like?"

"Different than me. She comes from more of everything—money, education, ambition. Her family is successful and sort of…uppity, I guess."

Like Jason's family. Kelly nodded. "I understand."

"They didn't like me much," Shane admitted. "But I pursued her anyway. And I think she was attracted to me at first because it was exciting to defy her family. I was a novelty, I suppose. The illegitimate mixed-blood who'd been raised by a free-spirited mother and an overly traditional grandmother."

"What does Tami look like?" she asked. It was a woman's question, but she couldn't help it. Was Tami Comanche or white? Tall or petite? Lean or curvaceous? What sort of girl had Shane Night Wind fallen in love with?

"I haven't seen her in years, but I suppose she looks much the same. Willowy. Long black hair, long legs, dark eyes."

Willowy. Jealousy nipped like a snapping turtle. Even the word in itself was beautiful. "She's Comanche, then?" The descendent of an Indian princess, no doubt.

"Yeah. I wouldn't have thought to date outside of my race at that time. I still hated my dad and everything I believed the white world represented." He looked down at his hands, then back up, his eyes still a distant shade of brown. "Tami was the love of my life, my best friend. The person I wanted to spend forever with."

"Did she feel that way about you, Shane?"

He shrugged, but not indifferently. The gesture hunched his shoulders, pulling him toward the center of his pain. "I thought she did, but after we got married, I guess the novelty wore off. She went to college, then got a job as a paralegal in this fancy law office, and I was just a high school graduate doing construction work. A disappointment."

Kelly wanted to console him, draw his head to her breast

and encourage him to forget. But there was more to be said, she realized, much more.

She gentled her tone, keeping her voice quiet. "Tell me the rest."

"Three years after we were married, Tami found out she was pregnant. I thought it was the best thing that could have happened to us. I was so sure the baby would make us a true family."

When Shane took Kelly's hand, she knew his pain had come full circle. His grip was shaky, almost desperate. This was how she fit into his past. Something had gone wrong while his wife was pregnant. "This is the difficult part, isn't it?"

"The beginning of it, yeah." He expelled a rough breath. "We went on with our lives, preparing for the baby—discussing names, decorating the nursery. But toward the end of her pregnancy, Tami broke down and told me the baby might not be mine. She'd had an affair with this out-of-town attorney. Some hotshot white guy, and she didn't know which one of us was the father."

Kelly kept his hand in hers. How could Tami have been with someone else when she had Shane? How could she have destroyed a beautiful young man? Saddled him with despair?

"I can't even describe how I felt," Shane went on. "When I wasn't envisioning Tami in bed with her lover, I was fighting the notion that the baby in her womb might be his." He tightened his fingers around Kelly's. "It wasn't right. I'd been a part of everything—the morning sickness, the doctor visits, the ultrasound." He glanced down at Kelly's tummy. "I felt the baby move for the first time. And I bought all those soft, fluffy toys and assembled the crib. I was the father, not him."

A soul-piercing image came to Kelly's mind. Shane alone in the newly decorated nursery, an animated mobile turning above an empty crib. His head in his hands, his heart hovering over the infant's bed. "You forgave Tami, didn't you?"

"I had to," he answered. "Her affair was over, and we were bringing a child into the world."

He was so honorable, she thought. A valiant husband, a dedicated father.

Shane met her gaze, looking as though he'd just read her mind. "It wasn't easy, not any of it. We spent the next few months in counseling trying to repair the damage. I told Tami that she had to think of the baby as mine. I made her promise that she would never ask me to take a paternity test to determine otherwise, and that she would never contact the other man for any reason."

Kelly remained quiet, giving her companion time to rein his emotions. She could see them in his eyes—those alluring, cat-like eyes.

"We had a boy," he said finally. "Evan Tyler. The perfect little *ona.*"

She tilted her head. *"Ona?"*

"Baby," he clarified. "The perfect little Comanche. God, I loved him. I used to go into his room and just stare at him for hours. Watch his chest rise and fall, listen to him breathe. He had Tami's eyes, dark and kind of almond shaped, and he had my—" Shane paused, his voice turning distant and sad. "I thought he had my hair, the color and the texture, but…"

He released Kelly's hand and clenched his fist, a tightness that matched his voice. "When Evan was six months old, Tami heard from her old lover. He was opening a practice in our hometown and wanted to see her again."

"She went to him, didn't she?"

"Yes."

"What about Evan?"

"The baby turned out to be his."

A small breeze, the first stirring of wind, rustled leaves on a nearby tree. The branches reached out like arms, drooping, clawing their way to the earth. To Kelly, the image seemed fitting. Someone had stolen what belonged to Shane, torn and clawed and ripped at his heart.

"You took a paternity test?" she asked quietly.

"Yes," he answered again.

He had taken it, but not without defiance, she realized. He

had struggled to keep his son. And probably his wife, too. "Are they together now?"

He nodded. "Tami divorced me and married him." He gazed up at the tree, at its haunting branches. "I lost everything. Even visitation rights. I haven't seen Evan in over five years. They told me I had no place in his life."

Kelly closed her eyes. Battling a successful attorney for custody of a child who wasn't biologically his must have been a nightmarish ordeal. "I'm sorry," she whispered. "So sorry."

"I am, too."

As another small breeze brushed by, she felt him watching her. She opened her eyes and saw a glint of gold in his. Just a glint.

Unable to stop herself, she touched his face—the strong, smooth jaw, the high ridge of his cheekbones, the lashes that framed those exotic eyes. When she slid her fingers into his hair, he moved even closer, just a heartbeat away.

His lips touched hers, lightly, ever so lightly. She wanted to taste him, give and take comfort, wrap herself in his warmth. She followed the length of his hair, encouraging the strands to flow through her fingers.

She opened her mouth under his and felt herself slipping, drifting on a wave. The tips of their tongues met, a solace they both needed.

He pulled back to look at her, and when their eyes connected, he smiled.\

"Motherhood is beautiful," he said, his voice a husky whisper. "You're beautiful."

A response didn't seem necessary, not now, not while he lowered his head to nuzzle her neck. He could have been a cat—a strong, sensual creature—sleek and lean with a hint of auburn running through his hair and flecks of gold shining in his eyes. He was beautiful, too. This man who had lost the child he'd loved.

Kelly brought his hand to her tummy and felt the baby stir in welcome. Before she went home, she wanted to share her child with him, if only for a few brief moments.

Shane lifted his head. "I'm going to miss you."

"I know. Me, too."

She placed her hands on his shoulders, and while he splayed his fingers over her stomach, she renewed their kiss. A kiss caught between friendship and sensuality—an emotion neither would allow themselves to analyze. She would be gone soon, and then it wouldn't matter.

Three days later Shane accepted a steaming mug of tea from Kelly. She didn't drink coffee, but she kept plenty of decaffeinated tea on hand, he noticed.

Averting his gaze, Kelly sipped from her mug. "Have a seat, Shane."

He backed into the barrel chair, feeling like a nuisance. Since the storm had blown in, he stopped by the cabin daily, mooching tea and dripping water all over her hardwood floors.

"Are you sure you don't want to stay with my dad and me?" he asked. "I hate the idea of you being out here all by yourself in this weather. The roads are a mess. They never really got the chance to dry out from last time."

"Thank you, but I'll be fine," she responded. "I don't plan on going anywhere. I have plenty of reading material, and the fridge is stocked."

Shane shifted his feet. He wished he had access to Zuni to use as a bribe, but the serval kitten had gone home to her rightful owner. He couldn't very well claim that Zuni needed her, so he tried another tactic. "Is your heater working okay?"

She sat on the edge of the sofa, wearing one of her floral maternity dresses. This one bore a hint of lace. "Yes. The propane tank is full. The realtor took care of it, remember?"

"Oh, yeah." They still hadn't made eye contact, at least not for an extended period of time. It was that kiss, he decided, that had them both feeling so damn awkward. He turned toward the window. The shutters were open, exposing the rain. Pellets hit the glass like hail. "It's really coming down hard."

She followed the line of his sight. "Hasn't let up for days."

Shane nodded. It had been days since he'd touched her lips,

too. Three long, lonely days. He wondered what she would do if he initiated another kiss. One, moist flavorful taste.

He tried to catch Kelly's gaze, but noticed she appeared absorbed with the rain. Maybe kissing again wasn't such a good idea. Their friendship seemed to be suffering because of it. They had confided in each other, revealed their deepest pain, and now they couldn't get past the weather.

"What sort of stuff do you have to read?" he asked, hoping to resume a semblance of comfort between them. He didn't want to leave just yet. He wanted to be near her a while longer. She was going home on Friday, leaving his tiny corner of the world.

Kelly set her tea on a nearby table and picked up a paperback. "Suspense."

Shane felt like an idiot. If the novel had been any more obvious, he would have been the one reading it.

"I have those baby-care books, too," she added.

As he recalled the fullness of her tummy beneath his hands, his heartbeat skipped. "How is the little *ona?*"

A smile drifted across her face. "Fine. Restless, actually."

"Really?" He wanted permission to touch her again, encouragement like she'd given him on the day they'd kissed. He wanted to feel the baby move, feel it greet him with a hearty kick.

But she didn't offer, so he didn't ask. He sat in the barrel chair, still wearing his coat, his tea losing warmth, their gazes never quite meeting.

A clock could have ticked between them—one of those tall, antique timepieces that reminded people how quiet their home was. Or how uncomfortable their guest was making them.

Shane gave in to his urge to stare, study her carefully in the silence. Suddenly concerned, he scooted to the edge of his chair. Pale shadows worried her eyes, a lavender hue that made her appear frailer than usual. Even her freckles had faded a little, her cheeks lacking their usual glow. "Are you feeling all right?"

She tucked a loose stand of hair behind her ear. Most of it

had been secured with a metal clip, but a few flyaway pieces rebelled from the confinement. "Truthfully, I am a bit tired."

He knew he'd overstayed his welcome. Kelly needed her rest. He supposed the pregnancy took its toll, not to mention her personal concerns. Jason still hadn't returned to Ohio. No response had been made regarding her request for a paternity test. But court procedures didn't happen overnight, and there was still time. A test couldn't be conducted until the baby was born.

He rose to his feet. "I better get going. Promise you'll rest, okay?"

"I will." The proper hostess, she relieved him of the lukewarm tea and set the sturdy mug beside hers. "Let me walk you out."

She opened the door, and together they stepped onto the porch. A powerful wind blew the driving rain toward them, just close enough to feel the damp chill.

Her driveway was already packed with mud, the landscape pooling with water. "Another day like this and the roads might flood," he said in a last-ditch attempt to convince her to come home with him.

"I don't plan on traveling," she responded. "Besides I'm from Ohio, remember? I'm used to all sorts of weather. I'll be fine." She brushed his shoulder. "You worry too much."

"I suppose." He brought his hand to her cheek. "I'll call you tomorrow."

Her eyelids fluttered, a reaction, he thought, to his touch. A reminder of their kiss and how good it had felt. They stood a little awkwardly then. He wanted to hug her, but drew back instead.

"Go inside before you catch cold," he told her.

"Okay." She nodded and turned. "Bye, Shane."

"Bye." He stood watching her, wishing her fragility didn't make him ache. Despite her brave front, Kelly looked lost. A delicate young woman in need of protection.

Six

Kelly closed the door behind her. She was beyond tired. Exhaustion weighted her weary bones. She headed for the bedroom and opened the dresser, searching for a nightgown. She would shower, then sleep off her fatigue.

Facing Shane these past few days hadn't been easy. Whenever she saw him, she wanted to snuggle in his arms. Absorb his strength. Kiss him again. And it was wrong, she thought, to want those things. Wrong to prey on Shane's emotions. Two weeks in Texas hadn't given her the right to need him. Not when she carried Jason's child.

"I'm sorry, Shane," she said aloud, "for confusing your life. For making you think about Evan. For making you miss him all over again."

Regardless of the storm, she couldn't possibly stay at his house. Shane had given her enough of himself. And what had she given him?

She turned on the shower. Problems. She had given Shane her problems.

Kelly let the warm water sluice over her. Friday was three days away. She would be home in three days. And when would Jason be home? When would he return to face her? Soon, she hoped. Because once Jason acknowledged her concerns, kissing Shane would be a distant memory. He would be her long-distance friend. A phone call instead of flesh and blood, his masculine beauty unattainable.

Kelly glanced at her reflection in the foggy mirror. A lonely woman stared back at her. God help her. She missed him already.

Turning away from the mirror, she dried hastily, then slipped on her nightgown. Next she entered the dimly lit bedroom and climbed under the covers, sleep taking hold.

Hours later she awakened to use the bathroom. On her way back to bed, she squinted at the clock. 2:00 a.m. The rain hadn't let up; she could hear it pounding against the cabin.

Hugging herself, she glanced out the window. Tree branches loomed, the howling winds forcing them against the glass. Just the stuff horror movies were made of, she thought with a sudden chill. A girl alone in an isolated cabin, ghastly shapes forming outside her window.

Bounding off the bed, Kelly latched the shutters. She knew better than to let her imagination run amok. But even so, going back to sleep seemed out of the question. Maybe she should draw for a while, create new images in her mind. She could sketch another likeness of Puma, maybe—

Kelly gasped. A cramp clenched her stomach, sending her entire body into a tight ball.

Wide-eyed, she looked up at the window. A girl alone in an isolated cabin...

The shutters remained closed. There were no ghastly shapes haunting the glass, only pain, a terrible pain.

The baby.

No! She shook her head as the cramp subsided. Fear. Indigestion. Anything but the baby. It was too soon.

Climbing back into bed, she glanced at the phone on the nightstand. Without a second thought, she lifted the receiver.

Shane would be there in an instant. He would know what to do, he always—

Kelly's pounding heart lurched.

Silence.

No dial tone greeted her. The phone line was dead.

She tried again. Then again, punching buttons, tapping the receiver, willing it to work. She released a choppy breath, unshed tears burning the back of her eyes. Not a spark. Not the slightest sign of life.

She should have gone with him. She should have listened to Shane. With a shaky hand, Kelly placed the phone back on its cradle. She could go now. She could drive to his house.

Another day like this and the roads might flood.

Shane's words flew into her head like a warning. A pregnant woman alone on a washed-out road? Could she take that chance? Her rental vehicle wasn't a four-wheel-drive. What if it got stuck in the mud? Then where would she be?

Kelly remained in bed, rocking herself for comfort, the torrid sound of the rain an eerie companion. Once daylight surfaced, she would feel better. One severe cramp meant nothing in the scheme of things. A false labor pain. She gazed around the cabin, her eyes settling momentarily on the inactive phone. Her baby wasn't ready to come into the world. Not now. Not on the heels of a storm.

But as a burst of lightning flashed through the slats on the shutters, Kelly closed her eyes and prayed. Morning was a long way off.

Shane adjusted the hood on a yellow slicker, protecting his face from the downpour. His volunteers knew better than to show up at the rescue this morning, especially since he had refused their services during the last hard rain. He only had two volunteers, one, a biology major, interested in wildlife research; the other, a cat enthusiast, hoping to work as a trainer someday. Neither had gone beyond the stage of cleaning cages, but both proved themselves invaluable. But not today. On this turbulent morning, Shane would take full responsibility for the animals. The young men who volunteered their time didn't deserve to be caught up in this weather, fighting hazardous roads.

As he strode across familiar pathways, his rubber boots sank into the mud, making each step thick and cumbersome. Thank goodness the rescue sat on a hill, keeping the habitats free from water damage. The cats would take shelter if they so desired, surviving on instinct. Food, of course, was another matter. Meals had to be provided, come rain or shine.

A crack of thunder ripped through the heavens, giving Shane a start. He blew a windy breath. How in God's name was Kelly going to get to the airport on Friday? If the storm continued as predicted, the roads would be washed out by then, a gully of nothing but water. Didn't she realize how primitive Duarte was? Damn it. Shane grabbed the front of his jacket as a strong gust threatened to pull it open. Why hadn't he insisted that she stay with him?

Well, he sure as hell would today. He'd call her as soon as his work was done. And he'd demand a postponement of her trip, too. He wouldn't allow her to leave until the storm passed. This weather wasn't safe.

Shane sighed. At least it wasn't a twister, one of those run-for-the-storm-cellar tornadoes Mother Earth raged upon Texas. As long as Kelly remained indoors, she would be fine. She was probably curled up in bed with a book, sipping that berry tea she liked so well, refreshed from a much-needed sleep.

The tears burning Kelly's eyes threatened to fall. She had been willing herself not to cry, insisting her labor was false, that the intermittent pains throughout the night didn't mean the baby was coming. But now she knew different. Her water had broken.

The front of her nightgown bore a large stain, the fabric damp and clingy. She twisted the hem and held tight. How soon before the next pain arrived? How far apart had they been?

She didn't know. God help her, but she honestly didn't

know. Nor could she count how many times she had tried the phone.

Kelly lifted the receiver yet again. The silence was deafening. As she returned it to its cradle, the tears she'd struggled to contain made their way down her cheeks.

Feeling like a child who had lost her way, Kelly cried. A silent, dazed, lonesome cry. Daylight hadn't eased her fear. The shutters were open, yet gloom enveloped the cabin, rain pounding the roof like a thousand angry fists.

Her baby was coming, and she was alone, trapped in a vicious storm.

Where was Shane? Yesterday he'd said that he would call. Surely he would check on her once he discovered her phone line was dead.

How many hours would pass before he attempted to call? She clutched the damp section on her nightgown. Two? Three? By then, it might be too late.

Too late.

The thought nearly knocked the wind out of her. Catching her breath through small, shaky gasps, she studied her surroundings. An antique armoire stood in lieu of a closet, a rough-hewn dresser displayed a wrought-iron candelabra and a scarred wooden nightstand held a useless telephone. This room, this rustic old room, would be the place in which her child would enter the world. Cry its first cry. Focus its tiny eyes on its mother.

Kelly sniffed, then dabbed at her runny nose, her plan suddenly clear. No more tears. It was time to get a hold of herself and start behaving like a mother. Her baby needed her strong and whole.

Making her way to the dresser, she removed her soiled nightgown and panties. Opting for a sleeveless cotton gown, she slipped it over her head and secured the ribbon at the bodice. Aside from her trembling hands, the task proved relatively easy.

The damp sheets were another matter. She struggled with the corners of the mattress, fearing another pain would immobilize her. Unable to secure the clean linen properly into place, she tucked it haphazardly, grateful she had come this far, her rebellious limbs shaky and weak.

At least her baby would be born on fresh sheets, she told herself, using the headboard for support. As she eased herself onto the bed, she caressed the posts, wondering if she would grip them later, if the cool, dark wood would be her salvation.

Don't get melodramatic. Stay strong. Be prepared.

Forcing herself to stand once again, she gathered clean towels and stacked them on the nightstand. Beside the towels, she placed a small pair of scissors and an antiseptic in which to sterilize them. She didn't know much about delivering a child, but she knew this much—she wasn't about to gnaw her way through the umbilical cord.

The image made her laugh—a laughter she prayed her baby could feel. She didn't want the child to absorb her fear, the overwhelming panic rising in her throat.

Would she need a basin of water? Damp washcloths? A makeshift…

Kelly's questions went unanswered. The severity of her next pain pitched her forward. She collapsed onto the bed, knowing the onset of hard labor had begun.

Soaked to the bone, his boots sloshed with mud, Shane entered his house through the back door. He stood in the cluttered service porch that led to the kitchen and removed his rain slicker and boots. Normally he just wiped his feet on the kitchen mat, but then his legs weren't usually knee-deep in mud. Scanning the clothes rack for dry garments, he blessed his dad for having the good sense to do their laundry that morning. He checked his watch and frowned. Morning? It was almost noon. He'd been outside for hours.

Shrugging out of water-logged Levi's, he washed up in a utility sink, drying his face and hands on a nearby towel. After donning clean jeans and a denim shirt, he headed for the kitchen, hoping his dad had a strong pot of midday coffee brewing.

Tom was in the kitchen, but the smell of roasting beans wasn't wafting through the air.

"What's going on?" Shane asked.

His dad stood at the counter, inserting batteries into a heavy-duty flashlight. An arsenal of portable lights littered the table, including several kerosene lanterns.

"The power has been going on and off. I figure it's just a matter of time before it's gone for good," Tom said, emphasizing his statement by motioning to the microwave clock where bright red zeros flashed across the display panel.

Shane raked his hands through his rain-dampened hair. The day had gone from bad to worse, and it was barely noon. "I better call Kelly."

The older man tested the flashlight, shining the beacon across the room. "I don't understand why she didn't come home with you yesterday."

"Tell me about it. I guess I should have insisted." He reached for the phone. "But you know how stubborn women can—" The disconnected line rammed him like a hard punch to the gut. He gulped the air that whooshed out.

Something was wrong. Terribly wrong. Why hadn't he sensed it before now?

"Dad," he said, his voice catching on the lump in his throat. "Will you come with me to Kelly's place? I think she's going to need us."

The kitchen light flickered, then went out altogether, but neither man paid it any mind. "Why? What happened? Didn't she answer?"

"The phone's dead."

Tom's ruddy features relaxed. "That's no reason to panic, Shane."

"But I've got this awful feeling." A feeling he couldn't shake, a sudden ache in the pit of his stomach. "Besides, Kelly didn't seem well yesterday. She was overly tired. And she looked so pale."

Further explanation wasn't necessary. Tom accepted his son's response, and together they worked side by side, hastily gathering emergency supplies. The power appeared to be off for good, and the possibility that Kelly was ill plagued them both. Once they reached the cabin, they would probably remain there, at least for the night.

"Get some blankets," Tom said, as he headed outside to load Shane's truck.

Shane tore off down the hall. Thank God for his father's organizational skills. It was Tom who kept hurricane supplies in the cellar—bottled water, non-perishable foods and over-the-counter medicine that would come in handy in case Kelly was sick. There were probably blankets in the cellar, too, but Shane raided the linen closet instead. He was too damn nervous to think straight.

He tossed the blankets into the extra cab of the truck, then glanced at his watch. They had packed within a matter of minutes.

The road conditions were bad, but not as troublesome as Shane had feared. The tires spun through a sludge of mud at the bottom of the hill, but the four-wheeler made it through without incident. A smaller vehicle might not have fared so well. He exhaled an anxious breath, grateful the Ford hadn't let him down.

Shane turned onto the narrow road that led to the cabin, then exchanged a nervous glance with his father. Debris floated in pools of water, tree branches and leaves that had fallen by the wayside. He maneuvered the truck toward their final destination, his heart pounding faster than the rain.

The cabin looked more isolated than usual, a tiny wooden structure surrounded by vast amounts of foliage and a weather-beaten porch. Shane prayed Kelly was safe and warm inside, that the knot in his gut wasn't what it seemed.

He thumped his fist against the door, hoping to be heard above the storm. His father stood beside him, tall and quiet. Shane knew Tom took his premonitions seriously, which, at the moment, wasn't a comforting thought. Shane wanted to be wrong this time.

"Damn it, why isn't she answering?" He pounded again, then yelled through the door. "Kelly! It's me! Shane!"

When she didn't appear, he turned to his dad. "What should we do?"

Just as Tom began to form an answer, the door opened. Shane could see the change of expression on his father's face. He turned back and caught sight of Kelly.

Sweat bathed her skin, and her wheat-colored hair hung in limp strands. Pale, he thought. Deathly pale. As he opened his arms, she stumbled into them and burrowed against his chest.

"The baby's coming," she said, her voice barely audible. "Soon."

"It's okay, sweetheart, we're here now." Shane lifted her off the ground, then realized he had just violated an ancient taboo—Comanche men, other than medicine men, were not permitted to be present during childbirth, let alone participate in labor.

A balloon of panic burst in his chest, but he continued to hold her, praying silently for forgiveness.

He entered the cabin, Tom on his heels. Whether his father had heard Kelly's words or understood by instinct, Shane couldn't be sure. Either way, Tom seemed to know exactly what was happening.

The older man took charge. As Shane settled Kelly onto the bed, Tom held her hand and asked about her labor, his tone gentle and soothing. She answered in a quiet, shaky voice, tears glazing her eyes. Tears of relief, tears of discomfort. Shane thought her expression mirrored conflicting emotions.

"I deliver babies all the time," Tom told her. "You're going to be fine."

Shane knew the babies the veterinarian delivered were gangly foals and spotted calves, but that didn't seem to matter. Tom McKinley was a doctor just the same—a medicine man.

While Tom scrubbed his hands, Shane sat beside Kelly, confused and fearful. He reached out to stroke her hair, then drew back. He couldn't continue to touch her. Not now.

Grandma had instilled the old ways into him, and she had

been so strong in her convictions, Shane had respected her wishes by keeping his distance during Evan's birth. Rather than remain by Tami's side, he had behaved like a nineteenth-century father, waiting quietly for the announcement.

Tom returned from the bathroom and gave Shane a verbal list of articles to gather. He did as his father bade and noticed some of the items were already on the dresser. His heart clenched. Sweet little Kelly had been preparing to deliver her own child. God help him, but how could he walk away now? How could he explain that he had no right to be there?

Thirty minutes might have passed. Or possibly an hour. Shane had no idea, although he assumed his dad knew. Tom appeared to be timing the contractions, cramping pains that rammed through Kelly with the force of a Mack truck. Each time they hit, she pitched forward and bit back a scream, her lips straining from the pressure.

Protect her. Please, keep her safe.

His hands clasped tightly in his lap, Shane prayed once again—prayed that his now deceased grandmother was mistaken, that his masculine presence wouldn't harm Kelly or her baby.

Tom remained at the foot of the bed. He had draped Kelly's lower half with a sheet, for modesty's sake, Shane assumed. The sheet tented around her drawn knees.

"It's not time to push," Tom told her. "Not just yet."

Kelly gazed up at Shane when the pain subsided. He still sat beside her, silent and nervous, clutching a portion of the sheet to keep himself from touching her. He struggled between the old ways and the new—never quite knowing where he fit in. He wanted to touch her, wanted to give her a part of himself, yet he had been taught...

She touched him instead, her shaky hand connecting with his.

"Hold me," she whispered. "Please."

Unable to deny her plea, he reached forward. She felt as fragile and frightened as she looked. Her lips were parched, her skin bathed in sweat, her heartbeat erratic. It pounded against her rib cage—hard and fast, just like his own. He stroked her matted hair, offering strength and comfort. It felt right, he thought, to take her in his arms—to keep her there.

When Kelly's next contraction hit, Tom ordered her to push, and she did so willingly. Shane supported her shoulders, holding her as close as humanly possible. Over and over she pushed, clinging to him as though he provided a lifeline.

Grandma had been wrong. Kelly needed him. He couldn't possibly harm her. Nor could he endanger her child.

On the wings of Shane's revelation came a strong infant cry. His breath hitched until Tom's proud voice seized the moment.

"It's a girl," the doctor said, placing the tiny babe against her mother. "And she's perfect."

The next hour was the most incredible sixty minutes of Shane's life. Not only had he participated in Kelly's labor, but he had helped his father prepare the baby for her introduction into the world. With Tom's instruction, Shane had bathed the golden-haired infant, then brought her back to Kelly swaddled in a downsized blanket.

As he lowered the baby into Kelly's arms, their eyes met—just long enough to make his breath catch. As he stepped back, Kelly unwrapped her daughter, then inspected tiny fingers and toes, counting each one, cooing as she did.

Shane smiled. He had done that, too. He had examined every tiny appendage while marveling at the baby's perfection.

Tom sat beside Kelly as Shane stood back, absorbing the moment.

"Thank you," Kelly said to the doctor, "for everything." She looked weary, yet beautiful, an elated new mother, tired eyes shining.

The older man touched the newborn's cheek. "Have you thought of a name?"

Kelly nodded. "Brianna Lynn."

"Brianna Lynn." Tom tested the sound on his tongue, his Texas twang taking on a lilting brogue, something Shane had never heard his father do. "'Tis a fine Irish name for a wee Irish lass. Your grandpa would be proud."

Kelly smiled and looked down at baby Brianna. "I think so, too." She stroked the top of the child's head with gentle hands. A mother's hands, naturally soothing. "Clever diapers."

Tom turned toward Shane, his voice beaming of Texas once again. "My son's idea."

Shane shrugged a little boyishly. He had cut an even stack of squares out of the softest quilt he could find. Baby Brianna wore an Aztec print on her little bottom, fastened with safety pins he'd retrieved from a sewing kit.

"Thank you," Kelly said, and he knew she meant for more than just the diapers.

He met her gaze, his voice husky with emotion. "You're welcome."

Tom excused himself to prepare the sofa bed in the front room, giving Shane and Kelly time alone. Neither spoke until the older man closed the door behind him.

"Will you stay here with us?" Kelly asked Shane, shyness creeping into her voice.

Us. She wanted him to sleep next to her and the baby. He wanted that, too. Very much. "Are you sure?"

She nodded, and he stepped forward. "I could find something to make a night cradle out of. It's an old Comanche practice, placing the baby in a cradle between its—" he couldn't very well say parents; he wasn't Brianna's father "—beside its mother."

"That's a good idea," she said, cuddling her daughter. "I'll dress her in one of my T-shirts to keep her warm."

"I'll be back soon." Shane toured the cabin and found a large, sturdy gift basket the realtor had sent Kelly as an apology for the house cleaning delay. He emptied the current contents and removed the handle. Next he padded the basket with the remainder of the diaper quilt, tucking the fabric all around.

Tom reclined in the sofa bed, reading an old magazine. It was still daylight, but the power was off, making the cabin dim. "I left a couple of flashlights on the dresser," he said. "And a kerosene lamp for later."

"Thanks, Dad." Shane held up the makeshift cradle. "It's for Brianna."

"She's beautiful, isn't she?"

Shane smiled, recalling the child's soft baby skin and cap of smooth golden-colored hair. "That she is."

He returned to the bedroom to find Kelly waiting anxiously for him, Brianna asleep in her arms. She didn't want to be alone, he realized. She wanted his company, a friend with whom to share the joy.

He placed the basket-cradle beside her, and she lowered Brianna into it. The child stirred, but didn't waken. "I was worried that she was born too early, but your dad said she's fine. Those last few weeks didn't matter."

Shane climbed into bed, settling himself on the other side of the baby. "As soon as the phone lines are restored, we need to call your mom." He tucked the blanket around Brianna when she kicked at it, loosening its hold.

Kelly didn't mention Jason, for which Shane was grateful. Jason would claim Brianna soon enough. He would see the child, and he would want her. Kelly would have a father for her baby—the rightful father.

As an exhausted Kelly closed her eyes, Shane listened for the rush of rain, but the only sound he heard was the soft, even breaths of a newborn.

A smile caught his lips. "Hey, little *ona*," he whispered, stroking her tiny back. "You sent the storm away." And brought a ray of sunshine into Shane's lonely heart.

He glanced at Kelly. Bordering on sleep, her eyelids fluttered. She was sunshine, too. Pretty Kelly with her scatter of golden freckles and pale yellow hair. He would miss them both—mother and daughter. The perfect family that wasn't his.

Hours later Shane remained awake, cloaked in the dark, the weather outside quiet. He heard Kelly lifting her daughter from the basket. Brianna hadn't cried, but she hadn't nursed yet, either. Shane knew why Kelly reached for the baby.

I shouldn't be here, he thought.

Kelly whispered to little Brianna, something soft and sweet.

Shane closed his eyes. If Kelly needed him would she ask for help?

Help? He swallowed nervously. Why would she need him? Mothers had been nursing their children since the beginning of time. It was instinctual, wasn't it? Shane frowned. He couldn't be sure, especially since Evan had been a bottle-fed baby.

Although Shane's eyes remained tightly closed, he knew Kelly had untied the ribbon on her nightgown, sliding the fabric off her shoulders to bare her breasts.

He tried not to picture her, but couldn't help the image that surfaced in his mind. God help him, but he wanted to remove that makeshift cradle and slide next to her, become a part of something he had no right to share.

A suckling sound filled the room, and he smiled. Brianna nursed eagerly, a healthy, happy baby.

If he offered to stay with Kelly would she let him? Would she welcome his company? He could cook for her while she recovered, tidy the cabin, help take care of the baby. He knew childbirth took its toll on a woman's body. She deserved to rest. And deep down, he wanted to be there for as long as possible. Shane wanted to lie in bed night after night and listen to Kelly nurse her infant daughter.

Seven

At 5:00 p.m. Kelly stood in the kitchen, preparing a cup of tea. The storm had passed, Brianna was seven days old, and Shane had stayed at the cabin. It seemed natural to have him there, eat the meals he cooked, say goodbye each morning when he left for the rescue, relax in the evening together, tend to Brianna.

She stirred a small amount of sugar into her cup. Even sleeping in the same bed with him felt natural. She was, after all, recovering from childbirth, so what harm could come of it? Her nipples ached from nursing Brianna, not from thinking about Shane.

Didn't they?

Kelly pushed away her last thought and the tingle that came with it. Shane was her friend, and their compatible routine was about to end, only he didn't know it yet.

She glanced at the kitchen clock. 5:05. He would be back soon.

He entered the cabin a long time later, longer than she had anticipated.

Edgy from the wait, she snapped at him the moment he crossed the threshold. "Where have you been?"

He closed the door behind him, but rather than respond in the same harsh tone, his voice was patient, a little wounded. "I had some things to do. What's wrong? Has Sunshine been fussy today?"

Wonderful. Now she felt like an ogre. Since Shane was convinced that Brianna's arrival had chased away the rain, he had nicknamed the baby Sunshine. "No. She's been just fine." Her daughter had napped most of the day, a perfect little angel, still asleep in her makeshift cradle. "My mom called."

"Oh." He sat on the sofa. "Did you have an argument?"

"Sort of." Rolling her shoulders, Kelly joined him on the couch. "Mom wasn't too happy when I told her I planned on spending the rest of my maternity leave in Texas. She doesn't understand why I decided to stay here for the next two months."

But Kelly had her reasons. Good reasons. Jason hadn't returned to Ohio yet, so why should she? Besides, being in Texas made her feel closer to Grandpa.

And to Shane, she added hastily, her pulse tripping a little. Shane Night Wind lived in Texas, and at the moment, he lived with her. "Since I won't be going home anytime soon, my mom is coming here instead. She wants to see Brianna."

"That's understandable." He cast his eyes to the floor, studying it as though it held great importance. "I guess she'll be staying with you, huh?"

Kelly nodded. "She'll be here on Tuesday."

"That's only three days away," he remarked, still studying the braided area rug in front of him.

Kelly glanced at her roommate, and he pushed his hands through his hair. In profile, the thick dark mass concealed one eye. It made him look more like Puma—rangy and dangerous. Stunning.

Were they playing house? she wondered. Pretending they had a right to live together, even temporarily?

"Maybe this is better for you," she said.

He lifted his head. "What do you mean?"

She met his gaze and delved into the subject that had plagued her since the storm. "Brianna must remind you of Evan."

He didn't respond right away. Instead he took a deep, audible breath. Kelly heard it catch before he released it.

"Of course she does," he said finally. "But that doesn't mean I can't separate the two. You're my friend, Kelly. I like being here with you and Brianna."

"And we like having you here." Okay, so they weren't playing house. They were friends, a man and a woman who just happened to sleep comfortably in the same bed, her baby daughter snug between them.

Right. As Kelly smoothed her dress, she became even more aware of her tender nipples. What about those awkward moments? The sensual heat that thickened the air?

Like now, she thought. They sat quietly, their breaths shallow, their gazes locked. Shane's hair had fallen forward again, and her bra chafed the fullness of her breasts.

Suddenly she wanted to kiss him—lean forward and press her mouth against his. But she had no business lusting after Shane. She had just given birth to Jason's child. Besides, kissing would only complicate their friendship, especially while they slept under the same roof.

"So where did you go earlier?" she asked, forcing herself to sound normal.

"Shopping." He smiled, his lips tilting like a half-moon. "Wanna see what I bought?"

"Sure." Did he know how devastating that crescent smile was? How boyishly bright and heart-stopping?

He headed out the door, then returned carrying a big, flat box and several plastic bags. After dumping the bags on the barrel chair, he pointed to the box. "It's one of those portable cribs. You know, the playpen type. Brianna certainly can't sleep in that basket for the next two months. She'll be rolling over before you know it."

The joy in his eyes warmed the mother in her. She stood to examine his gift. "Thank you, Shane. It's perfect." The picture on the box depicted its contents, but his excitement made the gesture even more special. His generosity knew no bounds. He had already supplied a car seat—an item they had used when he'd driven her and Brianna to the doctor three days before.

"I bought more of those little drawstring nightgowns, too," he said, reaching into one of the bags to retrieve the pink and yellow clothes. "Oh, and check this out." He lifted another cloth item. "It's an *ona* carrier."

Kelly smiled. She liked the way he spiced his sentences with the Comanche dialect. *Ona* in his unusual drawl was a word she had come to know well.

He adjusted the straps, then slipped them over the front of his shoulders. The corduroy pouch rested against his chest. "I think Brianna's going to like this. Little ones love to be hauled around."

The baby carrier didn't detract from his masculinity. If anything, it added an air of paternal appeal. But then Shane Night Wind knew all about fatherhood. For six months, a child named Evan had been his son.

"I bought two of these," he said. "One for each of us. That way we won't have to keep readjusting the straps." He met her gaze and lifted another pouch. "This is yours. I thought a tan color would look pretty with your hair."

And his was deep blue, she realized, a shade that complemented the faded denims he always wore. "Thank you."

The forbidden urge to kiss him returned. Kelly swallowed. They had kissed once, over a week ago, yet she could still taste him. He had an unmistakable flavor—exotic, like the blend of his heritage.

Brianna's piercing wail broke the silence. Kelly turned, Shane on her heels. They entered the bedroom at the same time. She lifted her daughter and held her close. Sweet, perfect Brianna. Texas sunshine.

"Is she wet?" he asked.

Kelly nodded, and Shane reached for a disposable diaper. Kelly almost missed the cloth diapers he'd made. Disposable were more practical, of course, and more absorbent, yet wrapping her daughter in homemade diapers seemed fitting somehow.

Brianna fussed while Kelly changed her, the baby's tiny faced puckered with discontent.

"She must be hungry," Shane commented, lifting the child from the bed.

They had fallen into such an easy routine, Kelly thought, tending to Brianna together.

No, not quite together, she amended quickly. Brianna's feedings didn't involve Shane, at least not consciously.

As he placed the baby in her arms, their eyes met.

A lingering stare. Gentle. Intense. Almost sexual.

If she unbuttoned the front of her dress, would he stay? Would he watch the baby nurse?

Kelly's breath hitched. Did he listen at night when she lifted Brianna to her breast? He never stirred during those moments, never said a word. The room, of course, was dark, but the child suckled noisily, greedy for her meal.

"I better go," he said when Brianna fussed even louder.

Kelly only nodded. She couldn't possibly ask him to stay, no matter how much she wanted him to.

Kelly sat in Shane's living room, studying her mother. Why did her mom seem different now that they were away from home? Was it Brianna? Much to Kelly's surprise her mom doted on the baby the way a proud new grandmother should. Not that Linda Baxter wasn't a good person. It was just that she seemed so calm and pretty, not stiff and angry the way she had been before Kelly left for Texas.

Tom leaned forward to coo at Brianna, who lay in a blanket bundle on Linda's lap. Tom and Shane had invited Kelly and her mom for dinner, and now the foursome relaxed in the living room, socializing companionably.

Well, sort of companionably. Kelly hadn't said much and neither had Shane. Their parents had done most of the talking. And smiling.

Kelly cocked her head. Just how many times had Tom and Linda smiled at each other? Good heavens, were they flirting? Her mom and Shane's dad?

Maybe it was her imagination. Her mother wasn't the flirtatious type, nor Tom the man-about-town sort of guy.

But they did look good together. Linda with her petite frame and blond bobbed hair, Tom with his Irish complexion and muscular physique. They were both attractive, yet conservative in their own way.

Tom reached for Brianna, and as Linda handed the baby to him, their eyes met. Kelly glanced down at the floor. How many times had that very same look passed between herself and Shane? This was embarrassing, she thought. Mortifying.

The room hummed, time ceasing in the way it did when two people made the air turn thick. Good grief. Tom and her mother were stealing oxygen—sucking it right up.

While Shane shifted beside her, Kelly studied her shoes. Not that her simple tan flats deserved special attention, she just didn't know where to focus her gaze.

"How about some coffee or tea or something?" Shane said, rising from the rattan sofa, clearly anxious to duck out of the room.

"Coffee for me," Tom responded. "How about you, Linda?"

"Tea sounds nice."

Before someone could ask Kelly for her preference, she hopped up. "I'll give Shane a hand."

She followed him into the kitchen, and he opened the cabinet and removed a large can. While he measured coffee grounds, she set about to make tea. They approached the sink at the same time, but he stopped and motioned her forward. Silent, Kelly filled a small pot and set it on the stove.

Great, she thought. Here they were, friends who had slept in the same bed, yet they couldn't think of a thing to say. She sifted through tea bags, trying to look busy while he placed the coffeepot under the faucet. When he turned abruptly, he bumped her arm. Both jumped from the unexpected contact.

"Sorry," he mumbled, his voice raspy.

"That's okay." More than okay, she decided, as her heartbeat tripped and fell. She missed those accidental touches. The cabin wasn't the same without Shane. It didn't look the same, feel the same. It didn't even smell the same, even though she knew Shane avoided cologne because of its effect on the cats. His scent boasted of nature—soap and water, air, rain, sunshine. Texas elements.

He leaned against the counter, looking rugged and handsome, his clothes sturdy ranch wear. His hair, combed away from his face, hung down his back in a thick, dark ponytail. She had the wicked urge to release it, let it flow into her hands. Would it feel like a waterfall? Cool and luxurious slipping through her fingers?

Kelly glanced at the coffeemaker. The liquid dripped slowly. Shane, too, focused on the coffeepot, his gaze intense. Were they overly aware of their parents' attraction because their own proved difficult?

"So how are you getting along with your mom?" he asked suddenly.

Kelly breathed a sigh of relief. Words, any words, made the moment more bearable. "Pretty good, actually. Of course it's only been three days."

"She's not hassling you about suing Jason?"

"No, but I'm sure she will eventually. Right now she seems preoccupied with being a grandmother."

He smiled. "That's a good thing."

"Yes, it is."

Shane missed Brianna. Kelly could see it in the uneasy tilt of his lips—the soft, sad smile edged with paternal need. Her child had found a place in his heart. He wanted to move back into the cabin and share his nights with the baby he called Sunshine. The baby who reminded him of Evan.

He turned and shrugged. Was he shaking off his emotions? she wondered. The ones attached to his sleeve?

"The water's boiling," he said.

"Oh." She turned off the burner, her movements jittery.

They prepared a tray, adding store-bought cookies, a small pitcher of cream, cinnamon sticks and a bowl of sugar cubes. It looked festive, warmly domestic in a way that made Kelly ache.

He lifted the tray. "Ready?"

She nodded. They hadn't mentioned their parents, yet both took a slow, steadying breath, working up the courage to reenter the living room and face the sensual vibrations there. Guilt, Kelly decided. Guilt over their own forbidden desire—a new mother and a man who had lost a child, using lust to combat loneliness.

Shane placed the tray on the glass-topped coffee table, and Kelly noticed Brianna lay in her portable crib, sleeping soundly.

Tom handed Linda a cup of tea. She thanked him and directed a question to Shane. As they engaged in small talk about the rescue, Kelly stole a glance at her mom.

Linda sported a beige blouse and brown trousers. She favored natural colors, subtle hues that suited her simplicity. She wore no jewelry, not even the wedding band Kelly's dad had placed on her finger a lifetime ago. As long as Kelly could remember, her mom had been widowed. Although she never dated, she didn't talk about her late husband, either. She spent her days as a single mother—hardworking, slightly nagging—a woman who understood the hardship of raising a child alone.

Kelly frowned into her tea. Would that be Brianna's description of her twenty-four years from now?

Just as the conversation lulled, a loud knock sounded at the door.

"I'll get it." Shane hopped out of his chair, leaving Kelly alone on the sofa, mulling over her last thought. Funny how she had never really analyzed her mother's life before, never sympathized with her plight or wondered if she was happy.

When Shane returned, everyone looked his way. Beside him stood the most stunning woman Kelly had ever seen. Dressed in a colorful ensemble of dyed cottons and silk scarves, jet-black hair cloaked her shoulders. As she tilted her head, purple stones winked at her ears, enhancing the rest of her sparkling jewelry. Her eyes were as dark and exotic as a moonless night, her lips boasting burgundy. She was neither young nor old—a slim, mystical muse suspended in time.

The lady smiled at Shane, and at that dawning moment Kelly knew the enchanting gypsy was his mother.

"Grace." Tom left his chair and came forward to hug her. "What a surprise."

Fascinated, Kelly wanted to keep staring, but realized her curiosity might be interpreted as rude. *It's not polite to stare.* How many times had her mom drilled that expression into her head?

Oh, goodness. Her mom. She turned to see Linda with a frozen smile on her face, sinking a little into her chair. Kelly's heart constricted. Clearly Linda felt bland and boring next to a woman as brazen and beautiful as Grace Night Wind.

They would endure the introduction, then make a polite but hasty exit. For once in her life, Kelly wanted to protect her mom. If Shane's willowy ex had just walked through the door, she, too, would be eager to escape.

Morning dawned a bright spring day, light spilling through the window, birds chirping in the distance. Kelly relished the moment, the beauty she'd found in Texas. Friendship and peace. The birth of her daughter.

"Who was on the phone?" Linda asked as she entered the bedroom, her hair damp from a shower. "I heard it ring before I turned on the water."

Kelly finished diapering Brianna and cradled the child in her arms. Brianna smelled of talcum powder and lotion—a clean, sweet baby scent. She stroked her daughter's head and released a nervous breath, hoping her news wouldn't provoke an argument.

"Marvin called, Mom."

"Your lawyer? What did he say?"

"Jason agreed to take a paternity test. We won't have to force him into it."

Linda struck her fist in the air, a quick, triumphant motion. "Thank goodness. He's back in Ohio, then?"

Kelly shook her head. "Not yet. But he plans on returning in two weeks."

The older woman sat on the edge of the bed. "Good. That means you can go home with me. I'll call the airlines and book you on my flight." She tightened her robe when it slipped open. "We should probably get an extra ticket for Brianna. We can put her in the car seat between us. If we don't get an extra ticket, we'd have to hold her through the entire flight."

Apparently her mother had already checked with the airlines about traveling with an infant. It irked Kelly that decisions were being made for her. "I don't want to go home that soon." She wasn't ready to leave Texas or the peace it offered. "I'm staying until I have to go back to work."

"I can't believe this." Openly frustrated, Linda pulled a hand through her hair. "That's nearly two months away. You're going to wait that long for the paternity test? You can't exactly sue Jason for child support if you drag your feet on the test, Kelly."

"I'm not dragging my feet. I spoke with Marvin about this." And the attorney had been understanding and patient, treating Kelly in a professional, respectful manner. "Jason can have his blood drawn in Ohio, and I can take Brianna to a lab here in Texas. There are ways to do this long distance." She didn't want to rush home just because Jason would be there. She wanted to enjoy her maternity leave, not fret about what he was doing and who he was doing it with. "Once the test results are in, I'll wait for Jason to contact me." She would give him time to accept the fact that Brianna was his, time to shake off the fear of fatherhood. "I'm not suing him for child support."

"This is insane." Linda raised her voice, then lowered it when the baby let out an irritated squawk. "Do you know how hard it is to support a child on one income? Brianna deserves more. Her father is rich. Why shouldn't he pay?"

Kelly placed the baby in the portable crib, tucking a blanket around her. What Brianna needed was love and tenderness. Jason's money wouldn't give her that. "Mom," she said, lifting her gaze to study Linda's pained expression. "This isn't really about Brianna, is it? It's about you and me, and the things you think I missed out on. The things you couldn't buy."

The older woman blinked, her eyes turning watery. "When you were younger I wanted to give you pretty dresses and fancy dolls, all the finery a little girl should have. And then when you were older, I wanted to send you to college."

Saddened by the catch in her mother's voice, she sat down beside her. "I never mentioned college. I never even considered it."

Linda sniffed. "That's because you knew we couldn't afford it."

Kelly tilted her head. "That's not true. It's because I had no idea what I wanted to do with my life. What would I have majored in? I'm not the brainy type."

"You could have majored in art," Linda said, stunning her speechless.

Art? Her mother thought her drawings were that good? Good enough to plan a career around? Parents didn't encourage their kids to study something as risky as art, did they?

She glanced down at Brianna, at the tuft of blond hair and tiny fingers curled around the blanket. Sweet, perfect Brianna. If her daughter were gifted in music or theater, would she support those gifts? Kelly's eyes misted. Of course she would.

She lifted her gaze. "Thanks, Mom."

Linda met her misty stare. "For what?"

"For loving me."

They both cried after that, cried softly in each other's arms, woman to woman. Kelly closed her eyes and took comfort in the feeling. "I'm going to stay in Texas for just a while longer. I can't explain it, Mom. It's just something I need to do."

Linda stroked her hair. "Then I'll try to understand. Do you forgive me for nagging you all these months?"

"Yes."

The shrill ring of the telephone pulled them apart. Linda, closer to the nightstand, grabbed the receiver before the sound woke Brianna.

"Hello?"

Kelly watched her mom and realized the person on the other end of the line was Tom. Her mother sat a little straighter, spoke a little softer.

"I...um...suppose we could," she said. "Of course, we'd like the chance to get to know her, too. All right, then. We'll be there at two." She paused and said goodbye.

"What's going on?" Kelly asked.

"That was Tom." Linda twisted her hands in her lap. "I accepted an invitation for us. I hope you don't mind."

"We're going to Tom's house?"

She gave a tight little nod. "For lunch. Shane's mother wants to get to know us. She was disappointed that we didn't stay longer last night."

Kelly pasted a smile on her face, hoping to appear more relaxed than she felt. Was Grace Night Wind curious about her or her mother? Or both?

"Lunch sounds fine." But what in the world were they going to wear? All Kelly had were maternity clothes—big, clumsy dresses. "After Brianna wakes up, do you want to check out the emporium in town? Maybe buy a new blouse or something?"

"Why not?" Linda gazed around the room. "We're in Texas. One of those fancy Western shirts might be a nice change of pace."

Kelly's smile turned real. It felt good to have her mom nearby. Really good.

Eight

Shane sat at the table with Kelly, Tom and Linda, waiting for his mom to serve lunch. She insisted on handling the meal herself, refusing the help that had been offered.

"Did I mention my boyfriend is a musician?" she asked, directing the question to no one in particular.

Shane shifted in his chair. "Yeah, a flute player, right?" His mom had brought her boyfriend into the conversation at least three times, and Shane was getting a wee bit tired of hearing about David Midthunder.

"Boy, is he handsome," she went on. "Young, too."

Wonderful. Couldn't she find a man her own age? Someone with crow's feet and graying temples? Shane didn't like the idea of his mom dating a guy young enough to be his brother.

Grace placed a mixed-green salad in the center of the table, then studied the seating arrangement. "Whose chair is this?" she asked, indicating the empty seat between Tom and Linda.

"Yours, Mom," Shane answered. She did happen to be the only person standing. Why was she acting so weird? Or weirder, he should say. His mom had always gone her own slightly eccentric way. She didn't walk to the beat of a different drummer. She was the drummer. Or was it bongos she played when he was kid?

Grace squinted. "Linda should sit here," she said, placing her hands on the back of the empty chair. "That way Tom and I can both get to know her."

Linda turned toward Grace. "That's fine. I don't mind moving." She scooted onto the empty chair and placed her hands in her lap. Beside her, Tom picked up his water and took a huge gulp.

Shane glanced at Kelly. She sat staring into her empty salad bowl, a smile quirking one corner of her lips.

Shane raised an eyebrow. Lord have mercy. His own discomfort about his mother's boyfriend had blinded him from the obvious. Grace was playing matchmaker, pushing Tom and Linda together, letting the other woman know that Tom was no longer her type. These days Grace Night Wind had a young musician to tease her fancy.

Satisfied with the current seating arrangement, Grace went back to the stove, her bracelets clanking. Within minutes, she served meatballs in a sour cream sauce with fettuccini noodles, stuffed bell peppers on the side. Her cooking methods were as eclectic as her wardrobe, but Shane appreciated the variety. Her creative meals beat the simple stuff he and his dad normally prepared.

Grace took her seat and said a blessing, thanking the plants and animals, the living, growing things that had made their lunch possible. An old-fashioned Comanche custom, Shane realized, that his modern-day mother hadn't outgrown.

"Tell us about the upcoming fund-raiser," she said, looking across the table at him.

He shrugged. "What's there to tell? We're having one of those big ol' Texas barbecues like we always do."

Grace snorted. "Can't you spice it up somehow?"

Shane frowned. "What do you mean? With like a chili cook-off or something?"

She rolled her eyes. "Spicy, Shane. Artsy, exciting. Different."

"What about an art auction?" Linda said. "There must be wildlife artists who would love to have their work showcased at the rescue."

As Grace clasped her hands together, sterling bangles chimed a merry tune. "Now you're talking. That's a wonderful idea. Isn't it, Tom?" she coaxed, encouraging him to praise Linda's suggestion.

"Yes, it is." He smiled at Kelly's mother, then asked. "Do you know much about art?"

"No, but my daughter does."

All eyes turned to Kelly, and she froze, a fork midway to her mouth. "I...don't," she stammered nervously. "Not really."

"Yes, you do," Shane protested gently, admiring her appearance. A peach-colored blouse highlighted her complexion while a cloth belt cinched her already trim waist. Her hair, fastened high upon her head in a deliberately messy ponytail, made him yearn to touch the loose tendrils framing her face. "You're a terrific artist. The sketches you did of Puma are outstanding. So good, in fact, that I'd like to reproduce them on T-shirts and coffee cups for the rescue. We've got to get the gift shop stocked before the fund-raiser."

Kelly met his gaze. "I'm honored, Shane. Those drawings mean a lot to me. Puma's very special."

And so are you, he wanted to say.

Suddenly the conversation buzzed around them, with Grace putting Kelly in charge of the art auction and herself as head of a jewelry sale that would accompany it. "I'm a jewelry designer," she told Kelly. "That's my expertise."

In one afternoon, the fund-raiser had gone from a West Texas barbecue to a West Texas festival, a blend of color and brilliance, the participants eager to bring it to life.

Shane noticed Linda and his mom sat with their heads together, Linda admiring Grace's emerald necklace, an unlikely friendship dawning.

When Brianna's cry echoed from the guest bedroom, Kelly excused herself from the table and removed a baby bottle from the refrigerator.

Shane studied her through confused eyes. He knew Brianna was being breast-fed. He had lain awake that first week, listening to Kelly nurse her daughter. Night after night, he had immersed himself in the sweet, suckling sound, wishing he could watch.

"Did you wean Brianna already?" he asked, blinking away the fantasy. Thoughts such as his didn't belong in a crowded, noisy kitchen.

"I'm only giving her an occasional bottle," Kelly answered. "Dr. Lanigan said it would be okay. It's easier in public-type places, and by the time I go back to work, she'll be used to the bottle."

So she breast-fed when she was alone with the baby and bottle-fed around other people. It made sense, he supposed. Of course he wasn't an expert on the subject since Evan had been bottle-fed from the start, something his traditional grandmother and career-minded wife used to argue about.

Kelly left the room to tend to her daughter, and Shane scrubbed his hand across his jaw. What kind of man would ask a new mother about her nursing practices? He glanced down at his plate, his appetite suddenly gone. The kind who missed being a father. Missed it in the worst way.

Four days later Kelly stood in front of the beveled glass. The antique mirror reflected her anxious image.

"You look pretty," her mother said from behind her. "You've got your figure back."

Kelly smoothed her dress. It was new, her second purchase from the Western emporium in town. She had even charged a pair of inexpensive cowboy boots to match. When in Rome...she thought, studying herself critically. "How could I have gotten my figure back when I never had one to begin with?"

Linda smiled. "Well, you've got one now, sweetie. Hips and breasts, too."

But not nearly as much as the bombshells Jason normally dated, Kelly noticed. Of course, Jason wasn't taking her to dinner, Shane was. Kelly tilted her head. What kind of women did Shane like? She frowned as the appropriate word popped into her head. Willowy. Long, lean, lithe. Nothing like herself, she supposed.

But then Shane's preference in women shouldn't matter. This wasn't a date, not in the romantic sense of the word. He just thought she deserved a night out. Kelly turned away from the mirror. As much as she appreciated the gesture, leaving Brianna alone for the first time made her jittery.

"If Brianna cries, Mom, promise me you'll pick her up, even if she isn't hungry. I don't believe in letting babies cry themselves to sleep."

Linda laughed. "I wouldn't dream of letting that baby cry. I'm a grandma now, remember? Besides, she'll get plenty of attention from Grace and Tom, too. I asked them to stop by for some dessert. They've been entertaining us almost every night, so I thought it was time to return the favor."

"That's fine," Kelly said. She had seen the way Shane's mom and dad tripped over themselves to get to Brianna. The more doting grandparents the baby had, the better.

Shane arrived before his parents. Linda answered the door and invited him in. Kelly stood back a little awkwardly. Suddenly this felt like a date, especially since Shane wore something other than denim. His pants and shirt were black, separated by one of those fancy Western belts garnished with silver. His hair, combed back into a ponytail, left the angles of his face unframed, displaying raw-boned masculinity and flashing amber eyes.

Linda excused herself and went into the kitchen to check the pie she was baking. Kelly and Shane stood staring at each other. The smell of the warm pastry filled the air, giving the rustic cabin another layer of charm.

"This is for Brianna," he said.

Kelly stepped forward and took the gift bag from his outstretched hand. She removed the toy and squealed with delight. A stuffed cougar. Now Brianna had her very own wildcat. "This is adorable. Thank you so much."

The gold in his eyes deepened. "Sure. Where is Sunshine? She's not asleep, is she?"

"No. She's just sort of cooing in her crib, making those little bubbling noises. Come on." She invited him to the bedroom, where he leaned over Brianna's portable bed.

"She's such a happy baby," he said, his husky voice wistful.

"Yes, she is." Kelly placed the toy cougar beside her daughter, realizing how much Shane missed Evan. It wasn't fair, she thought, that he had been denied visitation rights.

They left the cabin ten minutes later, both in a quiet mood. The drive into town was peaceful, Kelly thought, and the steak house where they now sat filled with Texas magic. The tables were split-log booths, the walls covered with animal skins and Western relics. It was neither fancy nor plain. An establishment that belonged right where it had been built—in the lonestar state, on the edge of a tiny town.

The owner's daughter, who also served as their waitress, took their order with a friendly "How y'all doin' tonight?"

When the young woman departed, Shane asked Kelly about the art show.

Being on a fund-raising committee both scared and thrilled her. She had never been involved in anything quite so cultural before. "I've been calling galleries that specialize in wildlife art, and most of them seem eager to get involved." Which made her proud as a peacock. "Of course they understand a portion of the proceeds will go to the rescue, but I assured them the exposure would be well worth it." Shane had a wealthy following, animal activists who appreciated the natural habitats Jungle Hill provided. "I've been in touch with some local artists, too. Nobody famous, just the up-and-coming." But she found it exciting nonetheless.

"You've done all that in four days?" He lifted his water and toasted her. "I knew you deserved this dinner."

"Thank you." Laughing, she clanked her glass against his.

Their salads arrived, so they adjusted their napkins and picked up their forks, still smiling at each other.

"My mom invited your parents over tonight," Kelly told him.

"Yeah, I know." He studied his lettuce for a moment. "But I have a feeling my mom won't make it. She started complaining about a headache before I left."

"Oh." Kelly frowned. "I'm sorry she isn't feeling well."

Shane raised an eyebrow, a wicked slash above his candlelit eyes. "That's okay. I think she's faking it."

The reason behind Grace's feigned headache made Kelly fidget. "She's giving Tom and my mom an opportunity to be alone."

"Yep."

She wondered if Tom was going to kiss her widowed mother. Good heavens. A middle-aged couple kissing while they baby-sat. "It's a little embarrassing," she found herself saying. "They're our parents."

"No kidding. And what about my mom? Miss matchmaker herself."

Grace's bulldozing had them both grinning, then laughing like foolhardy kids. They looked away to curb their adolescent fit, but only ended up laughing harder when they stole a quick glance at each other's silly, tight-lipped expression, knowing it mirrored their own.

By the time dinner arrived, they quit giggling and enjoyed their food, the steaks and company just right.

An hour later Shane paid the bill. "Do you want to go for a walk?" he asked, glancing at his watch. "It's still early." And he wasn't ready to let Kelly go yet. He couldn't remember the last time he'd spent an evening out with a beautiful woman.

She smiled. "A walk sounds nice."

He offered his arm, and when she moved closer, he could

smell the fragrance that seemed uniquely hers. The scent of watermelon and woman—a fresh, thirst-quenching combination.

As they exited the restaurant and stepped onto a crooked sidewalk, a thousand stars winked from the sky. The simple town of Duarte looked prettier with Kelly nearby, the paved highway and street-front businesses giving way to nature. Flowers bloomed and leaves rustled while streetlights and a fairy-tale moon competed for brilliance.

"It's so old-fashioned here," she said. "Like a Western movie town. Or maybe the real thing." She leaned against him. "I almost feel like I've been zapped back in time."

He understood. He felt it, too, touches of the Old West, especially on the corner where they stood, in front of the expansive feed store that served the community.

She pointed to the emporium across the street. "I bought my dress there."

"You look pretty," he responded, turning to study her. "So pretty."

Her voice quavered. "I wasn't fishing for a compliment."

"I know." He touched her hair. She wore it loose, spilling over her shoulders and down her arms. The night loved her hair. A gentle breeze blew it around her face, each long, silky strand bathed in moonlight. She could have been a painting, he thought. An artist's conception of nocturnal beauty.

They glided toward the shadows, both knowing what came next. He lowered his head, and she parted her lips. The kiss was tender, a little shy. A test, he thought, each wondering how far the other was willing to go.

Shane moved closer and deepened the kiss, slipping his tongue past her teeth. He wanted to go as far as she would let him. He wanted to sip from her mouth, then devour it.

Their tongues danced. A mating ritual, he thought, as his body hardened in response. She tasted like the night, like moonbeams and moist flowers. Shane caught her hips and pulled her tight against him. He wanted more than just a taste. He wanted to feed, fuel the fantasy that she had become.

She made a breathy sound, and he felt her fingers skim his face, her breasts press his chest. He imagined them full and creamy, the tips pink and aroused.

They continued to kiss, their mouths fusing then coming apart, over and over. Tender nibbles, little bites, deep tongue thrusts.

Finally they drew apart and stared at each other. A sexual stare in the dark. A vibration.

He brought his hand to her dress and brushed lightly over her breasts. "Do they hurt?" he whispered. Did they ache for his touch, his tongue?

She nodded, and he nuzzled her neck. "I hurt, too," he said, his groin throbbing.

They stayed like that for a long while, in each other's arms, aching for relief.

"Ice cream," he finally managed to say against her hair. "We should get some ice cream." Something cold, something to douse the fire.

"Strawberry," she answered, disengaging herself from his arms.

Shane knew they weren't going to talk about the kiss. And apologizing for it or claiming it shouldn't have happened would be as good as a lie. They both took what they wanted. Not as much as they wanted, but enough to make their blood swim.

"The pharmacy is open until nine. They have a soda fountain." He guided her from the shadows and into the light. Like jewel thieves, he thought, after a heart-pounding heist.

They walked side by side, but didn't touch. No hand holding. No linked arms. Touching proved dangerous. The night held too many shadows, too many secluded spots to slip into. Too many out-of-the-way places to kiss.

The pharmacy was bright, but not overly crowded. They sat in one of the red vinyl booths and looked across the table at each other. Her lips were still moist, he noticed, and slightly swollen from where his teeth had staked their claim. Windblown and passionately kissed, she made his blood swim all over again.

"Is strawberry your favorite?" he asked.

She eyed the napkin dispenser. "Vanilla, too. But I'm in a strawberry mood tonight."

Yeah, vanilla was too plain, he thought. Not enough kick to compete with misbehaving hormones. "I'm thinking a chocolate malt. I like that malted flavor." And it was just strong enough to confuse his palate, especially since the taste of flowers and moonbeams still lingered on his tongue.

The soda fountain waitress took their order and departed in crepe-soled shoes, her ruffled pink skirt and white blouse a standard uniform of years gone by. Shane knew her name, had spoken to her often, yet this time he felt almost surreal. "This end of town is more like the fifties than the Old West, don't you think?"

Kelly nodded and reached for a napkin. "Duarte's an unusual place. I can see why my grandpa loved it. He was sort of caught up in the early days. You know, with those old-man suspenders of his."

Shane grinned. "Yeah, Butch was an interesting guy. Ohio and Texas all rolled into one." Kind of like his granddaughter. Kelly wore a Western dress and boots, but Ohio was still there, in her eyes, in the scatter of freckles across her nose.

Darlene, the pink-and-white waitress, brought their milk shakes, then went about her job, wiping down the front counter.

Shane watched Kelly pick up her straw, remove the paper and slip the straw into place. But before she took a drink, she dipped her finger into the whipped cream topping. Smiling, she tasted it.

There was nothing deliberate in her movements. Nothing purposely sensual. They were almost girlish, innocent in a way that had him swallowing back an aroused groan. The fact that she could seduce him without intent was nearly more than he could bear.

He sampled his own drink, but the malt wasn't potent enough. Nothing compared to the taste of a woman. A sweet, vibrant woman named Kelly.

He frowned as another thought crossed his mind. It hadn't taken his mother's matchmaking to bring him and Kelly together. They had done that all on their own. Of course Grace wasn't trying to set them up. She wouldn't dream of pairing Shane with a woman who had ties to another man. His mother had been there during the fallout of his marriage. She had seen his pain firsthand. A pain he sure as hell hoped he wasn't in danger of repeating.

A week later Kelly stood beside Grace on the porch, both women watching the scene before them. Tom loaded his truck with Linda's luggage, and Kelly's mom clucked over Brianna, saying goodbye to her grandchild as though she would never see her again.

"Everyone looks so sad," Grace said.

"Leaving is always hard." Kelly glanced at Shane's mother. "I'm glad everyone was here, though. You know, together."

"Me, too." The other woman sighed. "Tom's going to miss Linda. He needs someone in his life."

"They live so far away." Kelly watched her mother turn Brianna over to Shane. He tucked the baby into the cloth carrier he wore, her tiny body snug against his chest. I live so far away from Shane, too, she thought. None of us are meant to be together. "My mother never dates. Tom's the first man who has sparked her interest since my dad, I suppose."

"Yes, she told me. Your mother and I talked about a lot of things. Our hopes, our dreams. Being single mothers from the same generation is something we both understand."

"I'm a single mother, too," Kelly said, feeling her eyes mist. Shane stood beside the truck, rocking his body, lulling Brianna to sleep. Watching him with her daughter made her heart throb. In less than two months, they would say goodbye. Shane would no longer be a part of her everyday life.

"Yes," Grace responded finally. "You are a single mother. But you're not widowed like your mom." She turned to face Kelly. "You're unmarried like me."

Kelly gazed into the other's woman's dark eyes and caught her own reflection. Or at least she thought she did. The familiar image disappeared as quickly as it had surfaced. Grace

Night Wind looked like a gypsy, her jet-black hair blowing in the Texas breeze, sunlight glinting off her jewelry. Could she see the future? Tell fortunes? "Shane said you weren't interested in marrying Tom."

"I wasn't. And that's because I knew I wasn't in love with him." She took Kelly's hand and held it lightly in hers. "Having no man is better than marrying the wrong one. Remember that, okay? Being a single mother isn't such a bad thing."

"It's lonely, though."

"But you shouldn't marry for loneliness. Or for the sake of a child. You should marry for love."

Because the conversation was making her maudlin, Kelly forced a smile. "Since Prince Charming hasn't appeared at my door on bended knee, there's a good chance that I'll be single for quite some time."

"Maybe," Grace said. "And maybe not. The future is impossible to predict. But in the meantime, Kelly, be happy. Live each second as if it's your last."

Wise words from a Comanche gypsy, Kelly thought. A woman who relied on instinct rather than a crystal ball. A beautiful gypsy who had raised a beautiful son.

They stood quietly for a moment, then turned toward the porch steps where they descended together. Linda came forward to hug them both, then accepted Tom's help into the truck. He had offered to drive her to the airport, a man keeping his own emotions in check.

Shane waved as Tom backed up the truck and turned onto the dirt road. Walking over to where Kelly and Grace stood, he slipped between them.

"I'm leaving tomorrow," Grace said. "But I'll be back before the fund-raiser."

Shane nodded, and Kelly looked his way. Brianna's tiny head was barely visible, her golden hair peeking out from the blue cloth. When Kelly's turn came to go home, she would miss Shane Night Wind. Miss him terribly.

Nine

On the following Sunday, Shane, Kelly and Brianna relaxed at the cabin. Brianna lay in her portable bed, a teddy-bear mobile spinning above her. Although still too young to focus on the toy, her reflexes churned like well-oiled machinery. Arms and legs moved, hands waved, feet kicked. Pride swelled in Shane's chest as he watched her.

Kelly sipped a tall glass of sun tea and sent him a contented smile. They were both pretending their friendship would go on like this forever, he supposed.

"Shane?"

"Hmm?"

"Was Tami your first lover?"

His pulse made a quick, unexpected leap. The question could have fallen from the ceiling and he wouldn't have been more surprised. "Does it matter?"

She stirred her tea, clanking the spoon against the glass. "It does to me."

Okay, take a deep breath, he told himself. Friends were

allowed to discuss old lovers. "Yeah, it happened when we were in high school."

Kelly moved closer, and he knew that meant another question would follow. Her eyes locked onto his, keen with interest. "Was it Tami's first time, too?"

"Yeah."

"Was it good? You know, for both of you?"

He shrugged, uncertain of how to answer. "I guess, I mean it was a long time ago. It's a bit tough to remember." Kelly frowned, and he knew he'd said the wrong thing. She wanted honesty, he realized, the candid truth. "Sure, we both enjoyed it. I know I did. I was young and in love. And it seemed as though Tami was, too."

She blew an errant lock away from her eye. "It wasn't like that for me."

"I know." He wanted to grab hold of her flyaway hair, feel it flutter around his fingers. "Did it hurt, Kelly? Did Jason hurt you?" Shane recalled working through Tami's initial discomfort. A woman's virginity, he'd been taught, was a gift, something a man should treasure. Even an eager teenage boy.

"Not really, no. There was a little pain, but that wasn't really the problem. It was just so, I don't know, different than I'd imagined. Our fantasies don't always live up to reality, I guess."

"I suppose not." He stared across the room, depression just a heartbeat away. "You know what was awful for me?" Without giving her time to speculate, he told her, his past surfacing like a dark cloud. "Knowing that my wife felt the need to turn to someone else. Not just emotionally, but sexually. It made me feel so damn inadequate, like maybe I hadn't been satisfying her all along."

She reached for his hand, urged him to look at her. "A woman would have to be crazy to give you up."

The gentleness, the sincerity in her voice had him aching to lay his head against her breast, take comfort in the warmth. "Thank you."

They didn't speak after that. They sat quietly on the sofa

while Brianna cooed and kicked, lost in her own little teddy-bear world.

"Shane?" she said finally.

"Yeah?"

"What do you think is sexy? You know, in a woman?"

Wheat-colored hair, he wanted to say. Freckles and kisses that taste like moonbeams. He shrugged. "I don't know, all kinds of stuff, I guess."

She left the couch and stood beside Brianna's crib. "Do you know what I think is sexy?" she asked, winding the mobile.

Enchanted by her smile, he leaned forward. "No, what?"

"A man who likes children."

"Yeah?" He felt a grin tug at his lips. "Then I'll cast my vote for motherhood."

She shot him a suspicious look. "You're just saying that."

"No. No, I'm not. I'm attracted to everything about it." The changes it left on a woman's body. Rounder hips, fuller breasts, a tummy that pouched just a little. "It makes a woman seem more real. Gentler. Sexy in a subtle way."

Brianna's mobile played a lullaby, a soft, sweet sound that had Shane looking from the baby to her mother. "I didn't get a lot of sleep the week Brianna was born," he said. "I was awake when you fed her. I kept my eyes closed, but I could hear." The rustle of Kelly's nightgown, her soft murmur to the child, the baby's hungry suckling.

Kelly's breath rushed out, and he glanced down at his hands, suddenly shamed. "I'm sorry, I had no right to intrude. Those should have been private moments between you and Brianna." Moments that, through his own loneliness, he had longed to be a part of.

She came to him and knelt at his feet. "I invited you, remember? I wanted you there."

He looked up and into the face of an angel. "Will you kiss me?"

She smiled and touched her finger to his lips. "Handsome Shane."

"Beautiful Kelly."

"Beautiful Kelly."

She climbed onto his lap, and their mouths met, soft and warm and slow. He let her take the lead, let her touch and explore, bathe his bottom lip with her tongue and then sigh into his mouth. The taste of her poured over him like wine, and he felt it seeping into his pores, drugging him.

She rocked her hips. Unconsciously, he thought. A feminine reflex to the masculine hardness beneath her. Her movements were experimental—a curious caress, a timid touch, the scrape of teeth, flutter of an eyelash.

Her first time in charge, he thought, deciding to keep his hands still. He wouldn't push her, wouldn't ask for more. Physically she wasn't ready, the birth of her child still too recent. Emotionally, he couldn't be sure. In her eyes he saw strength, yet vulnerability glittered there, too.

Rather than touch her, he whispered in her ear. She wouldn't understand his words because they spilled from his lips in the Comanche dialect, but his intent was clear. If she wanted him, he would wait.

As Brianna's cry tore through the air, Shane and Kelly startled, then stopped to listen. Their eyes met in understanding. They had come to know Brianna's moods, and the little *ona* craved attention.

"She's only going to get louder," Kelly said.

He touched her cheek. "I know."

Kelly answered her daughter's call, and Shane came to his feet, slightly dazed. The sexual charge had vanished, yet an underlying feeling remained. Tenderness. Human warmth. A bond he couldn't help but feel.

She went about to change Brianna, powder and diaper, then poke the baby's belly with a finger. No longer angry, Brianna gurgled—a sound of pleasure that made Shane smile. For now, Kelly and her daughter belonged to him. And he wasn't about to spoil this moment by dwelling on their upcoming appointment. Next Monday was still six days away.

On Monday afternoon, Shane sat in the waiting area of the hospital lab, hating everything about it. The sea of unfriendly, tired faces, the sterilized smell permeating the halls. But most of all, he hated the feeling, the memories that lingered too close to his heart.

Brianna had been fussy during the drive, and it had been a long, anxiety-ridden trip, one he couldn't let Kelly make on her own. But in spite of that, Shane figured Kelly preferred going to a big, impersonal city hospital. No one would wonder about her there, no one would care that a paternity test was being conducted.

Both Brianna and Kelly were to have blood drawn. Shane understood the process of DNA analysis, and a child's mother as well as the alleged father played a part in it.

Damn Jason Collier anyway. Kelly didn't deserve this.

And neither do I, he thought, recalling another hospital lab, another woman and another baby.

Shane tugged a hand through his hair. "Do you want a cup of tea or something?" he asked Kelly. She sat next to him, holding her daughter.

"No, thank you," she answered, her smile a tad too brave.

He cursed Jason once again, then caught sight of Brianna's tiny face. Her eyes, at half-mast, bore long, luxurious lashes. And her nose—a round, little button, was edged in pink, a remnant from her crying jag. She resembled Kelly, yet she didn't. Shane suspected the cleft in Brianna's chin had come from Jason, and probably the color of her eyes, too.

He touched Brianna's hair. The soft, golden curls slipped through his fingers. He couldn't hold on to the silky locks no matter how hard he tried.

What would it feel like to see yourself in a child? he wondered. To know you helped create a life? Sure, he'd looked for himself in Evan, but what he'd found had been a lie. A manifestation of hope.

"Kelly and Brianna Baxter," a female voice said.

Shane turned. A young woman, a hospital employee, wearing a pastel smock and stark white pants, called the familiar names.

The moment Kelly stood and adjusted Brianna in her arms, the child protested with an agonizing wail, alerting everyone in the room. Kelly cooed and rocked, sending the uniformed woman a nervous smile.

She knows, Shane thought. Brianna knows. He came to his feet, but Kelly halted his plan. "That's all right. We'll go alone," she said.

Feeling useless, he watched her approach the other woman. They disappeared behind a heavy wood door, the barrier muffling Brianna's heart-wrenching cry.

The tired faces in the waiting room went back to their out-of-date magazines. One old man closed his eyes and attempted to nap in his chair.

Since Shane was already standing, he walked around the corner to the nearest vending machine. Reaching into his pocket, he removed several quarters and inserted them into the slot. He chose coffee, even though he knew the strong, bitter brew would burn his stomach.

As the dark liquid dripped into a plastic cup, he heard movement behind him, then the sound of coins jingling in someone's hand. Shane removed his coffee and turned. The man behind him nodded, his face somber.

He returned the nod, then went back to the waiting room. The chair he'd deserted was being occupied by someone new, an elderly lady with bluish-gray hair, so he picked a seat closer to the heavy wood door, intent on being nearby when Kelly and Brianna emerged.

Sipping coffee and clock watching, he waited. And waited.

Had Kelly shooed him away for his own good? Or would it have made her uncomfortable to enter the lab with a man when the paternity of her child appeared to be in question? Maybe the technicians in a city lab weren't any different from those who worked in a small town. Curiosity was human nature.

Damn you, Jason. Damn you all to hell.

When Kelly exited the lab, Brianna whimpered in her arms.

"Hey, little Sunshine." Shane kissed the baby's forehead, his heart heavy.

"She was scared," Kelly said.

"I know." Evan had cried that day, too. "Let's get out of here."

They buckled Brianna into her car seat and headed back to Duarte, the highway a long, lonely road. The child drifted off to sleep, and Shane sighed.

"If you're hungry I can stop at a drive-through," he told Kelly.

"Thanks, but I'm fine."

She stared straight ahead, a bundle of nerves. Hardly fine, he thought. "Are they going to mail you the results?" He knew the procedure, but asked anyway. Not talking about it would only worsen the tension.

"Yes. Once a comparison is made, Jason and I will both receive a copy."

Both. The unity of the word made the coffee in his stomach turn sour. How could Jason ignore Kelly and Brianna once he knew the truth?

"How long did they say it would take?"

"Two to three weeks. It would be quicker if we all would have gone to the same lab, but I prefer it this way. I can keep busy until Jason contacts me."

Rather than curse Brianna's father once again, Shane berated himself. Jason claiming his daughter would be a good thing, yet the idea had Shane gripping the steering wheel in jealousy and despair.

He had lost Tami and Evan and soon he would lose Kelly and Brianna, too. It was only a matter of time before Jason Collier acknowledged what was rightfully his.

In the weeks that passed, spring gave way to summer, bringing drier winds, floral aromas and warmer temperatures. But inside the cabin, Kelly's mind wasn't on the weather. The paternity test results weren't in yet, so she had yet to hear from Jason. Of course on this balmy evening, Jason wasn't occupying her thoughts, either. Shane was.

She fluffed the pillows on the sofa bed. Was it too obvious? Would he know the minute he walked through the door? She glanced over at Brianna. The child lay in a cradle swing, the tick-tock motion her latest form of therapy. The swing, of course, had come from Shane. Another generous gift that would eventually be shipped to Ohio.

Kelly turned back to the bed. She didn't want to think about going home, not now. Not while she planned a seduction.

The knock on the door nearly sent her flying out of her skin. Oh, God, was she ready? Could she really do this?

"Come in," she called out, sparing the bed one last nervous glance.

Shane entered the cabin with a smile on his face, his blue jeans fitting just right. His shirt snapped in front, the buckle on his belt fairly simple. Tonight, his clothes seemed important. And so did hers. She had chosen a cotton dress from the emporium, a cool summer print.

Suddenly he frowned at the bed. Kelly twisted her hands together.

"Have you been sleeping out here? Are you sick?" he asked.

She found her voice, grateful it wasn't as erratic as her pulse. "No. I made it up for us. I figured we could relax and watch the movie."

"Sure, that sounds good," he responded casually. "Sunshine likes her swing, huh?"

"She loves it." Kelly made her way over to her daughter. "It's about time for a bottle, though."

Shane's eyes brightened. "Can I feed her?"

Kelly smiled. "Sure."

Within minutes, the milk was warmed and Shane had Brianna settled in his arms. He sat in the chair near the fireplace, looking far too paternal. Kelly's chest constricted as she watched him. He adored her daughter, and her daughter adored him. Brianna responded to the sound of his voice, the strength of his hands. He represented the father figure in her young life, the man she expected to see.

"Sunshine's starting to doze," he said.

"She didn't nap today, so she'll probably sleep through the night." The baby's unconscious part in the seduction, Kelly decided, her nerves flaring once again.

Shane came to his feet, and Kelly took a deep breath. Seduction? That word sounded much too sultry to apply to her. Too experienced. Too worldly. Too everything, she thought, smoothing her simple cotton dress. Women who seduced wore miniskirts, push-up bras and stiletto heels.

"I'll put Sunshine to bed," he said, shifting the groggy baby.

"Thank you." Kelly kissed her daughter's forehead, then locked gazes with Shane. His eyes glittered in the pale amber light. Did he know how badly she wanted him? Could he tell?

She looked away first. "I'll fix us a snack."

As the popcorn came to life in the microwave, she poured two tall glasses of soda. After the movie, she would ask him to stay the night, share the sofa bed with her while Brianna, asleep in the other room, dreamed of teddy bears and fluffy toy cougars.

I can do this, she told herself. She needed to. Imagining Shane's breath against her cheek had become an obsession. His hands on her breasts, his tongue in her mouth, his...

"Kelly?"

She turned and spilled the soda; it splashed onto the counter in a bubbly pool, the plastic liter bottle bouncing.

"Oh, my goodness." She grabbed a towel, her hands shaky.

"Let me help." He dampened a wad of paper towels and went after the liquid that dripped onto the floor. "Are you okay?" he asked, looking up at her with those metallic eyes. "You seem kind of jumpy tonight."

I'm a basket case, she wanted to say. A woman who didn't have the slightest idea how to offer herself to the man she wanted. "I'm fine. You just startled me, that's all."

Once the spill was properly cleaned, she removed the popcorn and dumped it into a big bowl. "Are you ready for the movie?" She had rented a film Shane suggested, but doubted her scattered brain would be able to concentrate on a science fiction thriller. Two hours seemed like forever at this point, a galaxy light-years away.

He reached into the bowl. "Ready and willing."

A double entendre? Not likely, she thought. He appeared more interested in another mouthful of popcorn than in romance.

He placed their sodas on an end table, removed his boots and climbed into bed. For a moment she just stared. His skin looked dark and rich next to the crisp white sheets, his unbound hair silky against the pillow.

"Shane?"

He looked up and smiled. "Yeah?"

She stood in front of the television, holding the remote control, the VCR power light a small red dot behind her. She couldn't wait for the next galaxy, she had to do this now.

Her breath whooshed out. "I had an appointment with Dr. Lanigan today."

He leaned forward, concern creasing his brow. "Something's wrong, isn't it? That's why you're so edgy."

"Nothing's wrong." She studied the buttons on the remote. "He said that I...that it was fine for me to—" she lifted her gaze and plowed straight into his "—resume sexual activity."

Silence. The absence of sound. Nothing but the pounding of her heart.

Inside the cabin, the air grew thick, warm and heady, like a muggy Southern night. She didn't break eye contact and neither did he. They remained six feet apart, staring at each other.

Kelly locked her knees to keep them from buckling. Suddenly he moved. A jungle cat in his prime, eyes flashing, muscles bunching, crawling to the edge of the bed.

He stopped when he reached her. She stood, motionless, unsure of what to do. What to say. How to breathe. The air in her lungs was trapped.

He placed his hands on her waist. They looked dark against the fabric of her dress, big and slightly scarred. And his hair...that satin-draped hair fell across his shoulders like a waterfall, the low-burning lamp intensifying the subtle auburn streaks. Fire she could touch.

"Are you sure this is what you want?" he asked.

Her fantasy knelt before her on the bed, and she couldn't breathe. Couldn't talk.

Dizzy, she thought, so dizzy.

"Kelly?" he pressed gently, his gaze never wavering. "Please, I need to hear you say it."

"Yes," she managed finally, the air in her lungs spilling out.

He swallowed, a soundless motion that drew her attention to his throat and the copper flesh just below it. She knew his chest was free of hair, a smooth mass of muscle and sinew. How would it feel to lay her hand upon it? Cover his heart with her palm? Feel the strong, rapid beat?

"What about protection?" he asked, swallowing again.

She tipped forward a little. "I bought what we need." More than they needed. Boxes of condoms, ribbed, lubricated—the choice was his.

"Will you undress for me?" he asked. "Will you let me see you?"

With a quiet nod, Kelly reached for the buttons on her dress and felt herself tremble. Tonight she would deny him nothing. The front of the garment fell open, exposing her bra, a glimpse of her belly. When she slipped the dress from her shoulders and let it pool at her feet, he smiled.

She stood before him in her bra and panties, simple undergarments she had chosen with him in mind—white with a flutter of lace. She was no longer a virgin, but with him she felt pure. Chaste of heart, a young mother he admired.

Moonlight shone through the windows, slashing across the bed in a beam of light. It illuminated Shane in a heavenly glow, melding with an amber hue. He removed his shirt, and when he did, the light bathed his skin. He could have been a sculpture set in bronze, she thought, real yet not. A work of art. Too beautiful to be human.

But he was, she realized. Alive and breathing just for her, his chest heaving from the air that filled his lungs. Hoping to please him, she reached for the clasp on her bra and unhooked it.

Her breasts filled his vision, and he lifted his hands to touch. Lightly, she thought, ever so lightly. He skimmed her nipples with the tips of his fingers, then leaned forward to taste her with his tongue.

A shiver tingled at the base of her spine, and she knew this was what fantasies were made of. The tip of a man's tongue, the scent of his skin, the fever shining in his eyes. Shane Night Wind. She could have dreamed him. A waking dream. A midnight secret.

Her nipples peaked against his mouth. He was careful, she thought, gentle with the part of her that nourished a child. He laved tenderly, kissing as he licked, a rumbling building in his chest.

A masculine purr.

She gripped his shoulders as dizziness swept over her. He purred. Like a cat, only louder. The deep, strong rumble of a mountain lion.

He slipped his hand into her panties. "I want to do this for you," he said, his mouth damp against her nipple. "I want to make it happen."

Kelly shifted her legs. He didn't remove her panties. Instead he kept his hand inside of them, like a naughty teenage boy, his fingers a slow steady rhythm.

She let the sensations guide her—the wave rocking her body, the moonlight kissing Shane's skin, his callused fingers.

She breathed his name and stroked his hair. He lowered his head to her belly, teasing and licking. Lingering.

And then he removed her panties, tugged them over her hips, the wisp of cotton and lace soon forgotten. With masculine fascination, he combed through her curls. She grasped his shoulders and widened her stance, her hips bucking. He put his mouth against her—that hot, sexy mouth.

She bucked again, then looked down at him. He steadied her hips and kissed between her legs. Kissed that sensitive nub while his fingers delved deep inside.

The climax ripped through her hard and fast. Color blurred her vision. Gold, copper, red. His eyes, his skin, the fire in his hair.

Her heart slammed against her ribs, pounding so loud, it thudded in her ears. A vibration. A sound. Sheer, blinding pleasure. She absorbed every flicker of light, every movement. Every flame that doused her skin, every shudder that sizzled through her system, then left her weak and mindless.

Was she on the bed? She gazed around the room, but couldn't see through the haze fogging her eyes. She reached out and connected with flesh. Hard, muscular flesh.

With a dazed smile, she blinked him into focus. Shane. Alluring Shane. The man who had made it happen.

Ten

Her freckles looked like fairy dust, he thought, golden lights sprinkled across an upturned nose. Her hair fell across the pillow like a tangle of wheat, and creamy breasts swelled and peaked into rosy crests.

He skimmed her tummy and smiled. It was trim, yet slightly pouched. The declaration of motherhood pleased him. As did her dazed expression.

"You're still wearing your jeans," she said.

Shane nodded. Being clothed while she was naked felt strangely erotic, as if he held her magic in the palm of his hand. If she had wings, she wouldn't fly away. At least not tonight. Tonight she would stay beside him, bathed in the afterglow of an orgasm.

"Kelly?"

"Hmm?"

"Where's the protection?"

She smiled a little shyly. "Under the bed. There's…um…a few choices."

He smiled back at her and reached beneath the sofa. Locating the condom boxes, he opened one and secured a foil packet. He didn't have a preference, but her careful selection had him grinning like a randy schoolboy. "You can take my jeans off now."

In response, she worked free his buckle and tossed the belt over the side of the bed. His zipper came next. He bulged beneath it, anxious for her touch.

She didn't disappoint. She reached into his boxers and stroked him, rubbed her thumb over the tip. Losing himself in the sensation, he kissed her. A long, slow, agonizing kiss.

She seduced him, this enchanting woman, this elusive butterfly with her imaginary wings and warm, gentle hands. She had taken the power back, the magic, and he was caught in her spell. He needed to be naked. Needed to feel his aching flesh against hers.

"Take them off," he growled, pressing his lips to her ear. She smelled like summer, fresh-cut watermelon and flowers that grew wild. Damn if he couldn't taste her.

As she tugged at his jeans and the boxers beneath them, their mouths came together in animalistic fury. Flesh against flesh, they rubbed and kissed, their teeth scraping, tongues diving. He wanted to devour all of her, every curve, every feminine swell. Their legs tangled around the sheets as they rolled over the bed, hungry for each other.

He tore open the foil packet, then braced himself above her. Lifting her hips, he sank into her, his penetration deep. She closed around him—warm and wet, all woman, creamy and sweet.

So good, he thought. So damn good.

When he felt himself teetering for control, he pulled back to look at her, stroke her cheek, count her freckles. Slow down, his mind said. Don't go too fast. Don't let this end too soon.

Sheathed inside of her, he didn't move. He stayed where he was, poised above her, gazing into her face. And then time stood still, trapping his soul in shadow and light.

How could he miss her when they breathed the same air?

How could he long for her when their bodies were already joined?

As though answering his questions, she smiled, the tenderness in her eyes a sudden balm. She brought her hands to his chest and caressed him, sculpting his form. Intrigued and aroused, he watched her. She skimmed his belly, then slid her fingers into the nest of hair that surrounded his sex. He refused to blink, refused to lose sight of her. She touched him where they mated, fascinated by the closeness, he thought. The unity.

Now was all that mattered, he realized. This moment.

Shane rocked his hips, intent on loving her, giving them both the pleasure they craved. Her kissed her. Everywhere. Her face, her neck, those luscious pink-tipped breasts. She moved with him, danced his erotic dance, ran her fingers through his hair.

The pressure built, that wonderful high that came with human arousal. They rode the wave together, and when he felt himself falling, slipping into that climactic abyss, he clasped her hands and held tight.

Their mouths met, and on her lips he could taste the ocean, the depth of his need, the warm, woozy liquid surging through his veins. He kissed her hard, then flung back his head, gripping her hands, pulling her with him.

He heard her call his name, a siren's call, a seduction. He answered with his body, with heat and hunger—a lethal, maddening orgasm that pushed him deeper. Deeper into the sea. Deeper into pleasure. Deeper into the woman beneath him and the emotion he saw in her eyes.

Spent, he collapsed in her arms, his mind quiet, his body almost boneless. Turning his head, he breathed against her hair, inhaling the floral scent. Flowers, he thought, wild, tangled vines.

"I wish we had forever," she said.

Shane sighed. Wishes were daydreams, a long way from reality. He shifted onto the bed, releasing her from his weight. Forever, they both knew, wasn't possible. "What made you plan this?"

She flexed her body, expanding imaginary wings. "Because I wanted you, and because something your mother said made sense."

"My mother?" Curious, he raised an eyebrow. "Now what could that be?"

Kelly turned and smiled, smoothed the hair that fell across his forehead. "She said to live each second as if it was my last."

"I see." That made sense, he supposed. And seconds weren't forever, but rather fleeting moments of time. His new lover would be gone by the end of the month. "I'm glad you planned it." Rolling back on top of her, he kissed the tip of her nose. "And I think we have enough protection to last a while."

She wiggled her nose. "I didn't want to get the wrong kind. I've never bought condoms before."

"I know." And that pleased him, he realized. "Do you want to take a shower with me?"

She chewed her bottom lip, looking far too innocent for her own good. "Right now?"

"Yes, ma'am," he answered, anxious to see her slick and wet and hungry all over again.

Kissing through the steam, they washed each other, warm water pelting their skin. He explored every inch of her, then let her choose the protection. While she rolled the ribbed latex over him, he waited—hard and hot and greedy. Pulling her close, he took her mouth. She wrapped her legs around his waist, and he thrust into her, deep and full.

When they were depleted and panting in each other's arms, they dried lazily and stumbled back to bed. She put on her panties and bra, so he slipped into boxers and ignited the remote. The VCR tape lit up the television screen with flickering images. She snuggled in the crook of his arm, and while he watched the movie, she fought heavy eyelids, then finally succumbed to sleep.

Beautiful sleep, he thought, touching her cheek. Beautiful Kelly.

An hour later, Shane dozed while the movie played, falling and waking endlessly. Hearing a strange noise, he squinted at the TV, then realized Brianna cried in the other room.

Blinking and rubbing his face, he went to the kitchen and opened the refrigerator door. Groggy, he searched for a bottle, but found none. Waiting a minute to his clear his head, he entered the bedroom and lifted Brianna. Uncertain of what else to do, he carried the baby, snug in a blanket and whimpering for a midnight meal, to her mother. Kelly had expected Brianna to sleep throughout the night, but apparently the baby had other ideas.

Kelly woke instinctively and reached for her daughter, clearly accustomed to the slumber-deprived routine. Shane turned, but her words stopped him.

"Stay with me," she said. "With us."

While she nursed the baby, he sat beside her, a sheet draped across their hips. Brianna rooted at Kelly's nipple, and Shane watched with a sense of belonging. On this moonlit night, they felt like a family, and he knew without a doubt, that for as long as he lived, he would never forget this moment, this woman or this child. Kelly and Brianna would be a part of him forever, even when the Texas sun still shone and they were gone.

The following morning Kelly made herself a cup of tea while Shane and Brianna slept. She carried the steaming brew into the front room and stood quietly to study them. After her meal last night, Brianna had fussed for attention, so Shane and Kelly had kept her in bed with them. And now in the light of day, Brianna snoozed against Shane's broad chest, her padded bottom in the air. Even in sleep, he handled the child gently. One long, muscular arm held her lightly, keeping her tiny body in place.

Kelly sipped her tea and glanced back at the envelope that had arrived in the mail. Somehow she had known it would come today, so she had dressed and walked to the street-front box, breathing the fragrant air, telling herself it shouldn't matter. But it did, of course. If she received the results, then Jason must have, too—discovering, without a doubt, that Brianna was his.

When would he call? When would he make a decision about his daughter? She set her tea on the end table where last night's uneaten popcorn remained. How could she be so confused? So emotionally careless? Wanting Jason to claim Brianna, yet losing her heart to Shane. Little by little she was falling in love, and she had no idea what to do about it.

Shane stirred. Opening his eyes, he looked down at Brianna and smiled. Kelly watched as he lifted the sleeping child and placed her in a snug corner of the sofa bed. Brianna scooted forward on her own, butting her head against a pillow.

Shane met Kelly's gaze, and they shared a smile, the kind adults reserved for puppies, kittens and babies.

"How are you doing?" he asked, his night-tousled mane falling over one eye. That happened often, she noticed, his one-eyed likeness to Puma.

"Fine." She toyed with a button on her blouse. Did he remember purring last night? Probably not. The sound had seemed instinctual—unconscious eroticism. The reminder sent a tingle up her spine. He had purred in the shower, too. Warm water, scented soap and Shane's deep, sexy rumble. "Would you like some breakfast?"

"Sure. Do you happen to have any coffee?"

"I still have some from last time you stayed here." Condoms and coffee. Shane essentials. "I'll start a pot."

"Great. I'll put Sunshine in her own bed."

Kelly nodded appreciatively. "Thank you."

"She's really wiped out," he commented as he lifted the child.

"I guess she should be. She was up most of the night." Kelly glanced at the envelope she'd placed on the TV stand, hoping Shane wouldn't notice it. Brianna's biological father seemed like an awkward subject to broach on their first morning after.

When he left the room with Brianna in tow, Kelly grabbed

the envelope and stuck it in her purse. By the time he returned, she had a pot of coffee brewing. He came up behind her and kissed her neck. She leaned into him as he held her, fear coiling in the pit of her stomach. How could she leave? Survive without him?

Kelly took a deep breath. Did she have a choice? She had a life in Ohio, a job, a home with her mother. Shane wasn't making promises. She was the one who had invited him to her bed, not the other way around.

Suddenly his touch hurt. The kind of pain that came with loss. A deep, dark lonely ache. "I should get breakfast going."

She slipped away from him and went about cracking eggs and frying slices of ham. Shane poured himself a cup of coffee, and although she didn't turn around, she knew he stirred two teaspoons of sugar into it, followed by a dash of milk. She had no idea how Jason prepared his morning coffee or if he drank a second cup by midday.

They sat at the scarred dining table, she fully clothed, Shane in frayed jeans and little else.

He poured ketchup over his eggs, and Kelly imagined them like this for the next twenty years, sleeping together every night, sharing breakfast each morning. He would look much the same, she decided. Perhaps a bit more mature, a touch of gray in his hair and tiny lines around his eyes, additions that often made men more attractive.

"Kelly?"

She blinked and cut into her ham. "Yes?"

"What are you thinking about?"

The ham nearly slid off her plate. "Nothing, really." *Just you and me and a lifetime together.*

He studied her for a long, drawn-out moment, and she worried he could see the truth in her eyes, the love, the hope, the fantasy of forever. Avoiding his gaze, Kelly lifted her fork and brought it to her lips.

"Why didn't you tell me the test results came in?" he asked just as she swallowed a bite of honey-baked ham that suddenly lost its appeal.

He had seen the envelope, she realized, and had been waiting for her to confide in him. "Does it matter? We both know what it says."

Shane pushed away his plate. "Yeah, but now Jason knows, too."

Had he lost his appetite? She stole a glance at his breakfast and felt the weight of her heart, a treasure sinking to the bottom of the sea. His food was nearly gone.

"You're going to hear from him, Kelly. It won't be long." Shane pushed at his plate again. "That's what you want, right? For him to take an interest in Brianna?"

The question wasn't fair. Of course she still hoped Jason would contact her about Brianna; he was the baby's father. But on the other hand, she had fallen in love with Shane. Fallen hard. "I want what's best for my daughter," she said, answering the only way she knew how. "Brianna will always come first."

The days that followed were hectic. Preparations for the fund-raiser were in full swing, with Shane's mother arriving to help. But Shane decided a break was in order, so he asked his mom to baby-sit Brianna while he whisked Kelly away for a few enchanted hours. The sun shone in a vast blue sky, a perfect afternoon for what he had in mind.

Kelly slanted him a sideways glance, looking like a bright-eyed little girl. She sat beside him in the truck, her hair in twin ponytails, a familiar butterfly barrette restraining bangs that had long since grown out.

He turned onto a narrow path, the four-wheel-drive handling the rough terrain. They rode up a small hill, the only access to their final destination. He had instructed Kelly to dress comfortably—jeans and safe, sensible shoes.

He maneuvered the vehicle in between some dense foliage and parked. "We have to walk from here."

He strapped on a backpack and led her up the hill. "This isn't walking, Shane," she said. "This is hiking."

He chuckled. "Yeah, but it's worth it. Besides, it's not far."

Once they reached the appropriate spot, he pointed to the valley below. "That's where we're going, Kelly. You can't get there by car."

"Oh, my." She stood beside him, clearly awed.

Shane smiled. The rainy season had done just what he'd expected: nourished the ground so wildflowers grew as far as the eye could see. In another area, trees huddled together, providing a natural haven for squirrels and nesting birds. "Let's go."

He started down first, then reached up to help her. The grade wasn't as steep as it appeared, but Kelly handled the descent carefully—mindful, he noticed, of the scattered brush and loose stones. When they reached the bottom, they stepped onto a carpet of flowers.

"This is so beautiful," she said, a light breeze fluttering the hair that escaped her barrette. "Heaven on earth."

Shane nodded. "I used to come here a lot." He took her hand and guided her toward the copse of trees. "But I've never brought anyone with me before." He needed to tell her that, he realized. Needed her to know how special she was to him.

As they walked across the field, he breathed the fragrant air and tried not to dwell on Kelly's impending departure. He would enjoy this day with her, this quiet, beautiful day. "Sometimes I picture my ancestors here," he said. "You know, when the Comanche used to roam this land on horseback."

"Before they lost it," she said.

"Yeah." He supposed the spirit of his ancestors tied him to West Texas, restoring in him what they had fought so valiantly to keep. Pride. Honor. Hope.

Hope? He shook his head. He would lose Kelly as surely as the Comanche had lost Texas. No amount of hope would change that. Destiny had sealed his fate. Her child belonged to another man, and his experience with Tami had taught him a painful lesson—biological bonds weren't meant to be broken. His only recourse was to step back when the time came.

And it would come. Jason Collier would contact Kelly. Of that, Shane felt certain.

They reached the copse of trees and ducked inside. The leafy branches provided shade, but slats of sunlight peeked through, creating a small, magical forest. Clusters of flowers spotted the ground, their colorful blooms growing toward the light.

Shane opened his backpack and unrolled a large, beach towel. Kelly sat cross-legged on one end and he on the other, a carefully selected lunch between them. He knew how much she enjoyed picnics, and today he wanted to please her.

"The chicken came from the deli in town," he said, as he began unwrapping aluminum foil and opening small, plastic containers. "But I did the rest." Simple things he knew she appreciated. Cheese squares and whole wheat crackers, raw vegetables and ranch dressing, chilled grapes and watermelon. The watermelon balls, he supposed, were for himself. Tasting the ripe melon was like kissing her, running his tongue along her flesh.

She loaded her plate. "It looks wonderful. Thank you." Glancing up through the trees, she sighed. "I can imagine your ancestors here, too. Even feel them, like spirits in the wind."

Such poetic words, he thought, such beautiful sentiment. "Do you know who Quanhah Parker was?"

Kelly titled her head. "The name sounds familiar."

"He was the last free war chief of the Comanche." Shane reached for his soda. "He was my idol when I was a kid. He was part white, and for me it helped to know that a famous chief was a mixed blood. Especially at a time in history when half-breeds were looked down upon."

Kelly scooted a little closer, picking at her food delicately. "Who were his parents?"

"You mean which one was white?" He opened the cola and took a swig. "It was his mom. Her name was Cynthia Ann Parker, and she was captured by the Comanche when she was a child. But she wasn't mistreated. Instead she was adopted into the tribe."

"So when she was older she married one of their chiefs?"

Shane nodded. "Yeah, his name was Wanderer. Supposedly they were really close. Madly in love as some folks prefer to tell it. Of course like all great love stories, theirs ended tragically."

Kelly glanced up at the trees again. Searching for spirits, he supposed. Lonely lovers drifting through the sky. "What happened to them?" she asked.

"Cynthia was separated from Wanderer and their sons when she and their baby daughter were captured by the Army and returned to her white family. But by this time, Cynthia didn't fit into the white world anymore. People either pitied her or thought she was odd."

"Did she ever see Wanderer or her sons again?"

"No. They searched, but never found her. Wanderer lost hope and died from an infectious wound. The younger son died, too. Only Quanhah lived to tell the story."

Kelly's eyes turned watery. "What happened to Cynthia and her daughter?"

"The baby took ill and died, and after that Cynthia didn't last long. Some reports say she died of a broken heart. Others claim she starved herself to death." Shane dropped his shoulders. "Either way, Quanhah was left to carry on alone and fight for what he believed in."

"Your childhood idol," she said, blinking back tears.

"Yeah." He set his plate aside. "I'm sorry, Kelly, I didn't mean to make you cry."

She rubbed her eyes. "I'm fine. Just oversensitive, I guess." She reached for her plate, encouraging him to do the same. "We should be enjoying our lunch."

They ate in silence. Neither, it seemed, sure of what to say. Shane drank his cola and tasted the chicken while she sipped water and nibbled on crackers and celery sticks.

A butterfly winged by. Shane turned his head and watched it light upon a nearby flower. "It looks like your hair barrette," he told her.

She touched the ornament, then dropped her hand self-consciously. "When I was a child I used to sit in my mom's garden and study them. The symmetry of their wings, the way they flutter. They're beautiful, don't you think?"

"Yeah." Like her, he thought. Delicate and beautiful. "You still look sad, Kelly."

"I do?" She brushed cracker crumbs from her lap. "Honestly, I'm fine."

She wasn't, he decided, and neither was he. They were missing each other. Sharing the sunshine and missing each other. It made no sense.

He moved their plates out of the way and reached for her. She sank into arms and made a sniffling sound.

"Don't cry," he said.

She buried her head against his shoulder. "I'm not."

But she was, and it made him ache inside. "I need you," he whispered, knowing she needed him, too. Their time together neared its end, and on this bright summer day, he wanted to make memories. Thoughts and images. Sensations.

He reached for the buttons on her blouse. She sat back on her heels, then stilled his hands, opening the blouse herself. Shane watched her, his body growing hard in response.

Instead of removing her bra, she released the cups. It was a nursing bra, making access to her breasts a simple, erotic task.

Reaching out, she brought his head forward, inviting his touch. Accepting her offer, he licked her nipples, tasting and teasing. She made a soft sound of pleasure and held him there.

"Shane." Kelly caressed his cheek, her voice breathy. Aroused.

When he looked up and saw her watching, her eyes glowing with promise, he raised his head and kissed her. Kissed until they melted together like wax, their bodies warmed by the sun, their hearts beating in unison.

She undressed, stripped away the barrier of her clothes while he undid her hair, releasing the ponytails. Only the butterfly remained, the delicate ornament.

She could have been a forest nymph, he thought. A beautiful

creature with pale skin and tangled hair, fairy dust dancing around her.

She unbuttoned his jeans and freed him, then lowered her mouth.

To experiment. Learn how to please a man.

Drive him mad with desire.

When he was dizzy, glassy eyed and desperate, she reached into his pocket and removed the condom he always carried, the protection that would keep them safe.

Slipping it on, she kissed him, openmouthed and carnal, her tongue diving down his throat. He met her ravenous onslaught with the same voracious need, then pulled her onto his lap.

Smiling, she impaled herself, taking him deep, stroking his length. Shane caught his breath. She rode him, slow and rhythmic, the motion a smooth, liquid current.

The world around them stilled. There was nothing but the pounding of their hearts, the hunger in their bodies, the taste of each other on their tongues.

She quivered, and their eyes met. He could see her losing control, rocking deeper, wanting more. He raised his hips and thrust into her, increasing the tempo, challenging her stroke for stroke.

She met his maddening pace, her hair a wild mass around her shoulders. It cascaded over her face and across her breasts, tangling like vines.

Together they tripped and stumbled, wildflowers sweetening the air, the world tilting on its axis. She grabbed hold of the earth, and while they shuddered through a mind-shattering orgasm, she spilled a handful of dandelions into the air.

They fluttered around Shane like feathers from an angel, guiding him to Heaven in one slow, sliding motion.

Gloriously spent, he closed his eyes and let the feeling sweep him away.

Eleven

While Brianna napped in a guest room at Shane's house, Kelly sat across from Grace at the kitchen table, guacamole and chips between them, virgin strawberry margaritas on the side. They had been working diligently on the fund-raiser, comparing ideas, notes and final decisions.

Kelly scooped a chip into the chili-seasoned avocado dip and savored the flavor. Mexican food was a rare treat. As was her involvement in the fund-raiser.

Grace sipped her frothy drink. "Isn't it great not having the men underfoot? Girl time is important."

Kelly enjoyed having Shane underfoot, but appreciated Grace's sentiment just the same. Girl time meant guilt-free snacks and easy conversation. "I wish my mom could have gotten time off to help with the fund-raiser. Her boss is so stingy."

Grace tucked her hair behind her ears, unmasking a striking set of earrings, silver that offset her bronze complexion and onyx that matched her eyes. "Linda's not just your mom. She's your best friend, isn't she?"

Kelly nodded. She didn't need to stop to think about her answer. Linda Baxter was the constant in her life, the woman she could rely on. "But we don't always see everything eye to eye. She's a little more opinionated than most female friends would be, but I guess that's the mother-daughter relationship coming into play."

"That it is." Grace stirred her drink and smiled. "My mother had the tendency to poke her nose into my affairs, too."

Kelly bit into another chip. She recalled how conservative Shane had said his grandmother was, and since Grace was anything but conservative, the disagreements that must have existed between them wasn't hard to fathom.

"My mother called me a hippie, but I thought of myself as New Age. She didn't understand my lifestyle, but in spite of that we were still friends. We lived together for over forty-five years. We shared everything, including Shane. He's the man he is today because we both raised him."

"He's a wonderful man." The man Kelly could picture forever with. The man her heart had given itself to. "But he seems a little more traditional than New Age, though."

Grace laughed. "Yes, well, my mother, God rest her soul, certainly left her socially-proper mark on my son. But then again, Shane has a daring side, too. A dance-naked-in-the-woods, bring-a-mountain-lion-home sort of attitude that most people wouldn't understand."

"Yes," Kelly agreed, hoping her cheeks didn't look as hot as they suddenly felt. She knew all about being naked in the woods with Shane—making love while the trees surrounded them like an enchanted forest.

Grace stood, a red dress flowing to her ankles. "Why don't we go to my room. There's something I'd like to show you."

Kelly followed Shane's mother down the hall and into the bedroom where the other woman often stayed. Although the furnishings were stark and masculine like the rest of the house,

Grace's presence shone through. A colorful scarf was draped over a straight-back chair, and a tangle of jewelry glittered on a practical oak dresser.

She opened the closet and removed an article of clothing. "It's a perfect blend of New Age and traditional. Don't you think?"

Awed, Kelly studied the deerskin vest. A floral pattern of seed beads decorated the leather, lending traditional Indian appeal, whereas buttons made of semiprecious stones added modern flair. "It's incredible."

"I thought so, too. Try it on, Kelly. I bought it for you."

"Oh, my." She reached for the vest and held it against her. "I've never owned anything like this before."

"Well, then it's time you did."

Grace dug through a case of carefully packed necklaces while Kelly removed her blouse and slipped on the vest. Studying herself in the mirror, she smiled. The leather clung to her like a second skin, the buttery feel cool and sensual.

Grace came up behind her. "Look at you." Slipping a choker around Kelly's neck, she fastened it and stepped back.

Kelly touched the delicate necklace. It was stunning in its simplicity—deerskin with a single beaded flower.

The other woman fluffed Kelly's hair, sending it flying wildly about her shoulders. "You're a very beautiful girl."

"Thank you. This makes me feel beautiful."

"Wear it at the fund-raiser," Grace said. "An artist like yourself should make a statement."

Months ago Kelly wouldn't have thought of herself as an artist, but these days she did. Shane had driven into the city to pick up the gift-shop items that bore her drawings of Puma. Later this afternoon she would see her work exhibited on T-shirts, coffee cups and a commemorative poster.

"Thank you so much, Grace."

"You're welcome, honey."

Kelly hugged Shane's mother, wishing she could reveal her heart. But how could she tell Grace Night Wind that she had fallen in love with Shane when she was still gathering the emotional courage to tell the man himself?

Kelly worked beside Shane in the gift shop, stocking shelves and setting up displays. He munched on red licorice while he unpacked a box of stuffed animals, and she eyed the strawberry-flavored candy with disciplined longing. The chips and guacamole had been enough junk for one day. As a nursing mother, Kelly thought it only fair to eat a mild, well-balanced diet, and candy and chili-spiced foods didn't fall under that category.

Focusing on the stuffed toys instead, she grinned. She had convinced Shane to purchase them for the gift shop, and now that she saw their sweet, fluffy faces lined upon a shelf, she knew her instincts had been correct. What parent could resist them? Brianna adored the cougar Shane had given her; she curled up beside it every night. Maybe Brianna needed a toy tiger, too. And a leopard with a pink bow. A girl leopard, Kelly thought.

Shane looked up and caught her planning her daughter's zoo instead of pinning T-shirts on a corkboard display wall. Of course she had already stared at the shirts with a sappy expression, marveling at her drawings, imagining them being worn by strangers.

"Sorry. I'm being kind of lazy," she said.

"No, you're not. You've been working nonstop for weeks. It's okay to get a little dreamy eyed."

Dreamy eyed. If he only knew about her daydreams, the fantasies of love and commitment that involved him. "Those toys are awfully cute."

"Yeah. We should get Sunshine one of each."

Kelly's heart bumped against her chest. His *we* almost sounded like a commitment. How would he react if she told him how she felt about him?

Maybe she should do it right now. Spill her soul. Let it pour out.

She chewed her lip. Then again, maybe she should wait

until after the fund-raiser. A few days after, when the stress levels associated with it lessened.

"I wonder if Sunshine will get attached to a special blanket," Shane said, musing out loud. "Puma has one. Heck, he's still crazy about it."

Kelly blinked, then stared for a moment, assessing his odd comment. Not about her daughter, of course. Children often acquired a fondness for a particular blanket or toy. But cougars? "Puma has a security blanket?"

"Sort of, yeah. It's an old saddle pad he fell in love with at his original home. And when he came to live with me, it came with him."

"What exactly does he do with it?" she asked, trying to picture a hundred-and-eighty pound cat dragging a security blanket behind him.

"When he first moved into the cabin with me, it helped keep him calm. He would sit on it and tread, then nurse and purr like crazy. He'd pretty much stay wherever his sucky was placed."

Kelly grinned. "His *sucky?*"

Shane shrugged, then laughed a little. "I had to call it something. Besides, he made this sort of chewy-sucky noise when he nursed on it. The name seemed to fit."

The more she heard about Puma, the more she adored him. "And how does he react to his sucky now that he's older and living outdoors?"

"Covets it mostly. He keeps it hidden in his lockdown." Shane flashed a telling smile and leaned forward. "But when I wash it for him, sometimes I notice the corners are spit-soaked, like he still sucks on it once in a while."

Kelly studied her lover's expression, the emotion she saw in his eyes, the same glittering pride that often shone for Brianna. "The relationship you have with him is amazing. The way you talk about him, he seems almost human."

"But he's not," Shane responded, his voice serious. "We lived together successfully because Puma decided I was another cougar. A tall one who walked funny, I suppose. But a cat just the same." He picked up one of the stuffed animals and stroked it. "Most exotics either mark you as predator or prey. There's nothing in between. You're either one of them or you're not."

And Shane Night Wind was definitely one of them, she thought. "Did he ever bite you?"

"In the beginning, yeah. I was pretty much covered with bruises, but eventually he learned roughhousing wasn't acceptable. I suppose he thought I was a grump most of the time—this ugly cougar who never wanted to play." Shane met Kelly's gaze, then smiled. "He didn't give up easily, though. He was always trying to figure out ways to sneak in a bite."

"How?" she asked, thoroughly charmed. If Shane was an ugly cougar, then a beautiful one didn't exist.

"Sometimes when I was standing near him, he would yawn really big. Kind of nonchalant. You know, like it wouldn't be his fault if my arm just happened to fall into his mouth."

Kelly couldn't help the spurt of laughter that erupted from her chest. Shane joined her in the merriment, and when their laughter faded, they stared at each other.

A stare that intensified the longing in her heart.

"We should get back to work," he said.

"Can't we take a short break instead? Maybe visit with Puma?" Suddenly Kelly needed to be near the cougar, the animal that shared its medicine with Shane. "I'd go by myself, but I know you have strict rules about guests roaming the grounds unescorted." Although she had been permitted out there a few times by herself, on those occasions, she had studied Puma from an artistic standpoint. Today was spiritual. She wanted the cougar to see her and Shane together. Wanted Puma to know that they were lovers.

Kelly pushed her hair away from her face. Was that possible? Would Puma sense a change in her relationship with Shane? Or was it wishful thinking on her part? A romantic notion that a wildcat would know the difference?

"Sure," Shane said. "We can take a break."

As they headed toward the compound, she slipped her fingers through his, giving in to the urge to keep him close. To her, even the simple act of holding hands strengthened their bond. It made them seem more like a couple. Two people who belonged together.

What would he say when she told him that she loved him? Kelly glanced at his profile, that gorgeous angular face. Maybe he already knew. Shane had learned long ago how to read other people's emotions, tap into their energy field. He claimed he wasn't psychic, but he was gifted just the same.

Kelly relaxed her grip. If he already knew, then there was no reason to worry, to cling too hard. Desperate women did desperate things, making doormats of themselves. Hadn't she done that with Jason? Let him abuse her affection? Well, she sure as hell wouldn't let him hurt Brianna. Jason Collier was going to treat his daughter with kindness and respect.

When they reached Puma's habitat, Kelly stood back while Shane greeted the cougar through the metal fence. Shane would help her deal with Jason, wouldn't he?

Of course he would, she decided with a slow, steady breath. A man like Shane would never abandon the needs of a child. Or the woman who loved him.

She looked up to see Puma staring at her with that lone eye, his tawny frame crisscrossed by the security fence. She stepped forward and stood next to Shane, her concentration focused on the cat.

"I wish I could touch him," she said softly.

"I can't let you," Shane responded just as quietly.

"I'm aware of that." But a part of her couldn't help but wonder if she would be considered friend or foe. Prey or predator.

Puma moved closer to the edge of his enclosure as he let out a loud *"oooow,"* and Kelly realized he had just said hello. Friend. It was the same greeting he had given Shane only moments ago. Excitement bubbled in her chest.

"Hi," she said in return. "I'm Kelly. I'm the one who looked like I had a watermelon in my tummy. Only it was actually a baby. I named her Brianna."

Clearly amused, Shane shot her a sideways glance. She smiled and looked back at Puma. The cat made a similar noise, only this one quieter, more personal.

An odd feeling came over Kelly. She couldn't enter Puma's cage and she couldn't touch him, yet he seemed to be asking why she had come.

To tell you that I'm in love with Shane, her mind answered.

Puma assessed her with his eye, that one golden beam of light. Kelly shifted her feet. This was silly, she thought, expecting a cougar to carry on a telepathic conversation. She turned toward Shane, and as she did, Puma made another noise. Stunned, she turned back.

This time the cat's throaty call sounded remarkably like a long, drawn-out "I *knoooww*."

The fund-raiser was in full swing, the smell of a deep-pit barbecue drifting through the air. The picnic area of the rescue bustled with activity as volunteers filled the serving table with side dishes and salad fixings. A party tent housed the art show and a large exhibitors' booth displayed cases of hand-crafted jewelry. The other temporary booths provided carnival-type games, offering family fun and novelty prizes. While a local band played country cover tunes, adults and kids alike strolled in and out of the gift shop, their Texas attire blending into the festive atmosphere.

Shane couldn't have asked for a better turnout. Friends and neighbors lent their support as did the corporate sponsors and wealthy animal activists whose generosity helped make the rescue a thriving facility.

Shane adjusted Brianna in her carrier. She rode like a backward kangaroo, her face resting against his chest, tufts of hair peeking out from the pouch. He had offered to baby-sit since Kelly manned the art show and he roamed the grounds, free to socialize, playing the role of the proper host, no matter how foreign it still felt to him.

He scooped his arm around Brianna, balancing her in the carrier as one of his sponsors approached. Nelson Pickles stood a good foot shorter than Shane with thinning yellow hair and wire-rimmed glasses. Shane figured the quiet millionaire had been considered a nerd in his youth, thus his preference to animals over people.

"Hello, Shane," Nelson said in his nasal twang, extending his hand. "It's good to see you."

He shook the other man's hand. "You, too. I hope you're enjoying yourself." Their conversations were usually sparse as neither forced the other to engage in party talk. Shane knew the drill. Nelson would stop by the fund-raiser, say hello, then send a sizeable donation the following week. Asking for money made Shane uneasy and he suspected Nelson understood his discomfort, even respected it. Their relationship might be unusual, but at least there was no pretense.

"What do you have there?" Nelson asked, indicating the blue pouch.

Shane removed the little girl from the carrier and adjusted her red-and-white gingham dress. Smiling, he said, "This is Brianna Lynn."

Nelson studied the child curiously. "A human baby."

Apparently Nelson had been hoping for a clinging monkey or a frisky cub. Shane supposed that was where he and the other man differed. Babies, no matter what their species or gender, pleased him. He delighted in having a daughter as much as he had enjoyed having a son.

As soon as the weight of his last thought hit him, he agonized over the blunder, blinking back his pain. Brianna wasn't his daughter any more than Evan had been permitted to be his son.

"I bought a painting," Nelson said.

"You did?" Still struggling with his emotions, Shane placed Brianna against his shoulder so she could peer over it. She gurgled and grabbed hold of his hair, signaling her approval. She smelled soft, like lotion and powder—a gentle creature tucked in cotton, ribbon and lace. "I'm glad to hear it. This is the first time we've gotten the local galleries involved, so your patronage is certainly appreciated."

"It's an interesting piece. Wildlife art has always been my favorite." The other man straightened his bolo tie and excused himself before their conversation faltered. "I think I'll go sample some of that barbecue, then be on my way."

"Be sure to say hello to my dad. I know he'd like to see you."

"Will do." The millionaire gave Brianna's shoe a quick pat and disappeared into the crowd.

Shane shifted the baby, cradling her in his arms. She looked up at him and stared—that funny, perplexed gaze babies seemed to have down to a science. Her little eyebrows furrowed, and he grinned. "I guess you haven't quite figured me out yet, huh? Me or my friends."

She studied his grin, kicked her feet, then smiled back at him, telling him she had figured him out just fine, even if the jury was still out on his friend.

"Hey there!"

Shane took a deep breath, preparing for twenty-questions as Brianna's head bobbed in the direction of the greeting. Barry Hunt, the bulbous-nosed owner of the One Stop Gas Station and Mini Mart lumbered toward them, a gossip-induced gleam in his eye. Another offbeat friend, he thought, wondering what Brianna would think of this one.

"She's a cute little bug, ain't she?" Barry flashed his gold tooth. "'Course it's obvious she ain't yers. You with that dark skin and all, and her being pink-faced and blond."

Great. Shane tried not to scowl. Just what he needed, another reminder that Brianna wasn't his. "I never claimed she was."

"True, but everybody in town knows yer dating her mother."

If everybody knew, it was because Barry had told them. Shane ran his fingers through Brianna's hair, the silky wisps of golden curls. Then again, he had taken Kelly out to dinner, kissed her in public, driven her to Dr. Lanigan's office. And in a small town like Duarte people were bound to notice. "Kelly's a good friend."

"How come the baby's father's ain't in the picture? He dead or something?"

"No, he's just a fool." Lying to Barry wouldn't do any good and neither would avoiding his questions. Being evasive would only encourage the old codger to gossip even more.

"Well, it's nice of you steppin' in like you have." Barry's white hair and full beard made him look a little like Santa Claus at a Texas hoedown. "I was raised in a boy's home. My mommy and daddy were both fools."

Which meant, Shane assumed, that the old guy had been unwanted and unloved. Growing up tough and ornery might have been Barry's only defense. Faulting him for it now didn't seem fair. "Kelly's going home next week. I didn't step in forever."

"Maybe you ought to," the old man said before he spotted Martha Higgins looking his way. "There's a lady waiting on me, son. I'll catch up with you later."

With a bounce in his stride, Barry made his way over to the widow Higgins, leaving Shane staring after him. *Maybe you ought to.* As if it was just that damn simple.

Shane glanced down at Brianna and felt his heart tug. She stared up at him with those bright blue eyes. The baby who had chased away the storm. "You have a daddy, Sunshine," he whispered. "And it's only fair to give him a chance. I gave Tom a chance and he turned out to be a fine father."

As Shane headed for the art show tent, he acknowledged his guests, clusters of people eating and drinking, their lives seeming carefree. At the moment, Shane's was anything but. Playing the proper host wasn't easy when losing Kelly and Brianna occupied his thoughts. But asking Kelly to become a permanent part of his life would be like signing his own emotional death warrant. Sooner or later Jason would enter the picture, and Shane would be pushed by the wayside.

He carried Brianna into the tent and scanned the art-show arena for Kelly. Spotting her in the thick of things, he brought Brianna next to his face and nuzzled her cheek, inhaling her sweet baby scent. "There's your mommy." Looking like she was right where she belonged, in butter-soft deerskin and feminine jewels, surrounded by painters, gallery owners and patrons of the arts. Kelly had taken to the fund-raiser like a mermaid to the sea, fitting in eloquently with the money crowd. It wouldn't be long before Jason Collier saw this side of her, too. In no time, the Ohio heir would realize her potential as a social companion. A beautiful, young society wife. The mother of his child.

Shane kissed Brianna's cheek, the pain almost too much to bear. As he approached Kelly, the baby made a happy crowing sound and flapped her arms, excited to see Mommy.

"Hi." She greeted them both with a radiant expression, reaching for her daughter. Brianna bobbed her head and bumped Kelly's nose, making Kelly laugh and kiss her—a sweet smacking kiss right on the lips. The little girl blew bubbles and gurgled, then smiled that chubby baby smile, the one that dimpled her chin even more.

Shane knew that in another month Brianna's smile would turn to a broad grin, then soon after that, laughter. Her sensory and motor skills would continue to develop, but he wouldn't be there to see any of it. Brianna Lynn would grow up without him.

A lump formed in the back of Shane's throat. Brianna was only two months old. She wouldn't remember Texas or the man who wished he was her father. The man who had no claim upon her.

"When are you scheduled for a break?" he asked Kelly, knowing she and his mom had secured a throng of university art students to help out.

"Soon." She bounced the baby, her eyes filled with excitement. "I'm having so much fun, Shane. We've sold so many paintings, and the Wild Winds Gallery even offered me a job if I ever needed one."

"That's great," he said, forcing the air from his lungs. She wouldn't need a job in Texas. Jason lived in Ohio, and he could afford to buy Kelly her own gallery if she wanted one. Tomorrow, Shane thought. Tomorrow or the day after Jason would call. He could almost hear the telephone ringing in his mind, hear Kelly answering it—a premonition he couldn't stop, couldn't interfere with no matter how much he wanted to.

When Kelly's relief arrived, Shane led her outside and toward the food. He had spent most of the afternoon chatting with his sponsors and now he intended to have lunch with Kelly, covet her while he still could.

They filled their plates, then found an empty table, taking turns holding Brianna while they ate. The baby appeared to enjoy the festivities, the breath of color, music and art.

"Your mother's boyfriend is nice," Kelly commented while bouncing her daughter on her lap. "Don't you think?"

"Yeah." Shane had to admit his mom's younger beau seemed like a decent guy. A lively match who fit right into Grace's unorthodox world.

Kelly reached for her drink and sipped, keeping Brianna snug against her. "Your dad's been awfully quiet, though. Sort of alone in a crowd."

"I noticed that, too." And he understood it well. Tom missed Linda and being around hordes of people made that loss even harder. His father had developed deep feelings for Kelly's mother, even if their time together had been short. It took a lonely man to recognize another, Shane thought. A man who knew when the right girl wasn't meant to be. "Dad doesn't get into these fund-raisers all that much. Neither one of us is the party type. We do this because we have to." Shane took another bite of his meat and pushed away the melancholy that threatened to ruin the moment. "But you're having a good time, aren't you, Kelly?"

She nodded and smiled, her hazel eyes bright, her hair glistening in the sun. "The weather's perfect, the food's wonderful and there are people walking around wearing T-shirts with my drawings on them. That makes me feel special."

You are special, he thought, aching to touch her. "What about the music? Do you like the music?"

"It's terrific." She tilted her head toward the country notes, a Western ballad drifting through the air. "Very Texas."

"Then dance with me," he said. "You and Brianna." Shane wanted to hold both of them—mother and child.

She met his gaze, her smile tagging his heart. "We'd love to."

They walked to the grassy area where other couples danced. With the baby between them, they swayed to the music. Lulled by the motion, Brianna closed her eyes and slept against her mother's shoulder. Shane moved a little closer to Kelly, then bent to nuzzle her hair. She smelled like watermelon, the fresh, cool scent he had come to expect. The scent that made him hungry.

Needy. Aware of his body and what it wanted.

"Can I visit you tonight?" he asked.

She turned her head until their lips brushed. "Yes," she said, the word a whisper against his mouth.

"No matter how late it is?" he pressed.

This time her response came in the form of a kiss, warm and full of promise.

Shane slipped into the taste, the flavor he craved. The night would be theirs. Moonbeams, wildflowers and lovemaking until dawn. And when it ended he would ask Kelly for nothing more.

He would keep her and Brianna locked safely in his heart, and when Jason Collier called, he would send them home to the other man. Back to Ohio, where they belonged.

Twelve

Kelly had been excused from cleanup duty because Brianna required a long, quiet sleep, exhausted from her lively day. So she had come back to the cabin, bathed and nursed her daughter, then put Brianna to bed in the front room, nuzzled beside the toy cougar.

Kelly stretched and smiled. Her cougar hadn't arrived yet. He was probably still breaking down booths and packing carnival supplies.

Fighting heavy eyelids, she sat on the edge of the bed and reached for a book. She had agreed to "no matter how late," and she intended to keep that promise by staying awake. Tonight she needed Shane as much as he appeared to need her.

Need was a good word, she thought. A sexy word.

Forcing herself to read, she scanned the pages, but couldn't make sense of them. Her mind was elsewhere. She was naked beneath her nightgown, and the silky fabric felt erotic against her skin. Like the flutter of Shane's hair when he kissed her.

Giving up on the book, she placed it back on the nightstand.

Instead she would close her eyes and think about Shane, imagine his mouth and his hands, that long muscular body.

She fanned her hair around the pillow. Fantasizing about him wasn't wrong. He was the man she loved. The man who touched her in secret places and made her moist and warm inside.

Ready.

She shot up like an arrow and looked across the room, catching her reflection in the mirror. She was ready now, her hair mussed, her eyes glassy, her nipples protruding against a filmy gown. And the heat, she thought. The heat between her legs. The fire fantasizing about Shane had ignited. Yes, she was ready.

Lowering herself to the bed once again, she let his image fill her mind. Those gold-flecked eyes, that dark, auburn-streaked hair. The muscles that shaped his body, the tight torso, narrow hips. Full, aroused sex.

Soon, she told herself. He would be there soon.

Turning down the three-way light, Kelly remained in bed, washed in a pale glow, thinking about her lover. And as she pictured him leaning over her, his hands lifting her nightgown, she slept.

And then dreamed.

Her dream felt so real, so alive. He smelled like the night air, like Texas at midnight, the elements clinging to his skin— the grass that grew wild on the plains, the flowers that dotted canyons, the jagged rocks that formed the hillsides.

Warmth radiated from her apparition. A breath upon her cheek, an erotic whisper.

"Kelly."

Upon hearing her name, she fluttered her eyes, caught between wake and sleep. "I'm dreaming."

"No, sweetheart, it's me."

Me, her mind said. Him. She knew who fueled her subconscious, her fantasy. "But I dreamed you. I'm dreaming now."

"No," the voice said, his tone deeper, less of a whisper. "I'm real."

She felt her hand being lifted, placed upon a solid object. Groggy, she moved her fingers, then laid her palm flat. A man's chest, warm and smooth. A heartbeat, strong and steady.

"Shane?" She opened her eyes and forced her vision to focus.

His hair fell over his shoulders in a thick curtain, and his shirt was open, his jeans unfastened. The light sent shadows across his face, hollowing the ridges beneath his cheekbones even more so. His lips looked full, a slight smile tugging at the corners.

Sexy, she thought.

"I fell asleep," she managed to say. "I tried to stay awake, but I couldn't."

"That's okay. I still have a key." He stroked her cheek, his fingertips a slow, hypnotic movement. "It's late. After two."

She wanted those fingers everywhere. All over, stimulating her. "You smell good. Like the outdoors."

"All I could think about was getting my work done so I could see you." He lowered himself onto the bed, placing his body next to hers. "I need you, Kelly."

Need. Yes, she liked the word. The feeling. Awake and aware now, she trapped his gaze. "I fantasized about you, Shane. I imagined you touching me."

He made a throaty sound, a raw primal noise. Skimming her shoulders, he asked "Did I touch you here?" When she swallowed and nodded, he slipped his hands down the front of her gown and cupped her breasts, rubbing his thumbs over the tips. "And here?"

Her nipples peaked, hard and aching. "Yes."

The game continued. He removed her nightgown and let the air flow over her skin. "Did I put my mouth on you?"

Kelly kept her eyes open, wanting to watch her own seduction, her fantasy come to life. "Yes."

He kissed her nipples, then teased them with his tongue, licking until they were moist and pink. Trailing kisses down her body, he stopped at her quivering navel. Slipping work-roughed hands beneath her, he lifted her hips.

"And did I touch you here, Kelly?"

"Yes."

"With my tongue?"

She gasped through an aroused breath. "Yes."

He lowered his head and licked her, teased with his fingers and his mouth. It excited her to admit that she had fantasized about him. It made her feel wanton and free, a woman comfortable with her own sexuality. A woman who wanted more.

She delved into his hair and pressed herself against him, rocking her hips, knowing a climax was near.

"Shane," she said his name as the first shudder slammed through her. It pulled her under and into a current of sensation. Fresh blinding heat.

The rest became an edgy blur—a haze of color and passion, moans and labored breaths. He didn't stop until she clawed his shirt and tugged, ripping the fabric as she pulled him up.

She wanted him naked, hot and hard and taking her to the next level. She reached for his jeans and saw that he was as desperate as she. The gold in his eyes shone like shards of amber glass, jagged and dangerous. She yanked the denim down his hips, felt the silk of his erection spring against her belly. She grabbed hold and stroked, greedy for masculine flesh.

They tumbled into each other's arms, kissing and nipping, never getting quite enough. He grabbled for the protection she kept in the nightstand, knocking the drawer off its hinges as he fisted the foil.

He tore the package, cursing and fumbling, kissing her while he sheathed himself with the condom.

"Look at me," he said, his voice a husky pant. "Know it's me."

She met his gaze and caught her breath. Yes, it was him. Her dream, her reality. Kelly clung to him as he drove himself into her, praying the depth she saw in his eyes was love.

Focusing on that prayer, she let herself believe it was true. For Kelly, living without Shane Night Wind didn't seem possible. Slowly and very surely, he had become her world.

* * *

The morning sun spilled light across the bed, cloaking Kelly in warmth. Shane lay beside her, six foot plus of gorgeous, rumpled male. She reached out to touch his hair, brush it from his face.

His lashes fluttered before he opened his eyes and squinted at her. "Please say it isn't time to get up yet."

She scooted closer. Since she had already risen to feed Brianna, she wore a nightgown and panties. Shane, on the other hand, was still naked. "How about almost time?"

When he stretched, the sheet fell just below his navel, exposing a shadow of hair. "Does that mean it's almost time for breakfast, too?"

Kelly's gaze strayed to the masculine sight. She could see through the outline of the sheet that he was hard. A condition, she supposed, that happened to most men first thing in the morning, whether they had female companionship or not. "Breakfast could be arranged." She wanted to touch him, slide her hand beneath the covers. But it wasn't necessarily sex she was after. She longed for familiarity. The feeling that he belonged to her, that she could touch him anytime, day or night. She wanted to wake beside him every morning, watch his muscles bunch and flex, hear his husky voice.

"We can make breakfast together," he said. "You don't have to wait on me."

Together sounded perfect. "Okay."

He rubbed his eyes and braced himself against the headboard "I don't know how you function without caffeine."

She berated herself for not starting a pot of coffee. Shane drank coffee every morning, and if they were going to have a life together, then she needed to provide a sense of familiarity for him. Small, simple luxuries he could appreciate.

Kelly sighed. She wasn't fooling herself that their situation wasn't complicated or they didn't have a lot to discuss. Technically she still lived in Ohio. And then of course there was Jason. But as far as she was concerned, Jason was an obstacle they could overcome. Times had changed. People these days were married and divorced, had children with other partners. The family from the fifties didn't exist anymore and neither did living by those old-fashioned standards.

Kelly studied Shane's morning-after appearance. Did he love her? He must. He wasn't the sort of man to use a woman—make love to her, then toss her aside. This wasn't an affair. It was more. Much more. What they shared came from the heart.

"I guess you didn't get much sleep," she said finally, recalling his comment about caffeine.

He grinned at her, his smile lopsided, his hair tousled, the sheet still draped low on his hips. Morning-after suited him. "I'm not complaining."

"I didn't think you were." A tingle, warm yet edgy, shot up her spine. Why couldn't she tell him that she loved him? Say it easily rather than fret about how to broach the subject?

Because he still seemed like a dream, she thought. Too good, too beautiful to be true. Her cougar. Her Comanche knight. An apparition her subconscious had conjured.

She rubbed her fingers over his chin just to be certain he was real. The whiskers were only slightly abrasive, but they chaffed her skin just the same. Kelly's nerves settled. The contact felt good. Right.

He caught her hand and kissed each finger. Pleased with his reaction, she smiled. They belonged together. Now and always. "Are you ready to tackle breakfast?"

"Aren't you going to feed Sunshine first?"

"I already did. She was up about an hour ago."

"Oh."

Disappointment dulled the gold in his eyes, and she knew he wanted to watch her nurse the baby, sit beside her and listen to Brianna's sweet little suckling sounds. But there would be other nursings, even other children, she decided. Shane would want more babies, wouldn't he?

He leaned over the bed and grabbed his jeans and boxers from the floor. "Can I use your shower after breakfast?"

"Of course." As Kelly watched him dress, she swallowed,

her mouth suddenly dry. He was still a little hard, not enough to hamper the fastening of his jeans, but enough to make her want him. Maybe she would join him in the shower later, let the water sluice over them while she wrapped her legs around him. Tight, she decided. Tight around him.

Once they entered the kitchen, he made a beeline for the coffeemaker, and she chastised herself for having forgotten again. "How about an omelet?" she asked.

"That's fine. I'll be right back."

He left the coffee perking while she removed eggs, milk and cheese from the refrigerator. When he returned, he kissed her—a warm, spicy kiss flavored with cinnamon mouthwash.

"Hey, that's my brand," she said, laughing when he nipped her ear.

"I forgot my toothbrush. I guess I'm not much good at sneaking into a woman's house in the middle of the night."

Yes, she thought. She could get used to this. Dream-induced sex and domestic compatibility. She glowed from both.

Halfway through breakfast the phone rang. Kelly dashed into the bedroom to answer it before the noise woke Brianna. The baby still slept in the front room, but the sound carried.

"Hello?"

"Hi, Kelly. It's Tom. Is Shane there?"

"Sure. Just a minute." She went back into the dining area and called Shane to the phone. "It's your dad."

While she stood nearby, he took the receiver. "What's up?" Glancing at the alarm clock, he cursed. "I'm sorry. I didn't realize it was so late. I'll be right there."

He hung up and dragged his hand through his hair. "I was supposed to help my dad load the U-haul. We've got to get the tables and chairs back."

"I understand." And she remembered the party-rental place had been overbooked this weekend, making pick up and delivery impossible. "Did your mother and her boyfriend leave already?"

"Yeah, they took off last night. My mom has another jewelry show coming up."

He shoved on his socks and boots, then located his wrinkled shirt on the floor. Kelly noticed it was torn. "I'm sorry," she said, recalling how she had practically ripped it from his body.

He grinned, then shrugged. "That's okay. It's old anyway." He gave her a quick peck on the cheek. "I better go."

She followed him to the front door. He rushed out, breakfast and the impending shower forgotten. Kelly looked down at Brianna, who stirred in her sleep. When the phone screamed again, she went sailing back into bedroom, wishing the cabin had come equipped with a cordless telephone. Apparently Shane's dad was in an impatient mood.

"Tom," she said the moment she picked up the receiver. "Don't worry, he's already on his way."

"What? Who's Tom?" a masculine voice asked.

Kelly's heart slammed against her ribs. She knew immediately who the person on the other end of the line was. "Jason?"

"Hello, Kelly. Your mother gave me this number. She said you're in Texas."

"That's right." He sounded so calm, so civilized, yet her voice vibrated. "Did you receive the results of the paternity test?"

"That's why I'm calling. I'd like to arrange a meeting with you. When are you returning to Ohio?"

"Next week."

"Will you contact me when you get back?"

"Yes, of course." Why couldn't she catch her breath?

"We'll go to lunch. Just the two of us."

And Brianna, she thought. "That's fine, Jason."

"All right. I'll see you soon."

He said goodbye and hung up, his cool, aristocratic demeanor clogging her lungs with confusion. She was sleeping with one man, yet had a two-month-old baby with another. Suddenly her situation seemed immoral. Dirty.

She sat on the edge of the bed and struggled to breathe. She needed to see Shane. Needed him to hold her, tell her that he loved her, soothe her fears, confirm that their relationship was based on more than sex.

Love wasn't immoral, she told herself as she forced air from her lungs. And Shane loved her, just as she loved him. They just hadn't spoken the words yet.

Clinging to that thought, she headed back to the kitchen to clean up the breakfast dishes. Shane would give her advice about Jason, and he would understand if Jason wanted to become a part of Brianna's life. He would think it was the right thing for the other man to do.

Just as Kelly turned on the faucet and filled the sink, Brianna woke with an angry wail. Kelly dried her hands, then answered her daughter's call. Lifting the baby, she rocked gently, quieting the child instantly. It would be hours before Shane returned. Hours before she could tell him about Jason's call.

"We'll just have to keep busy," she told Brianna, who stared at her with eyes the color of Jason's, and a smile so sudden, so tender, it reminded her of Shane. Some traits, Kelly decided, had nothing to do with genetics. Nothing at all.

At dusk Kelly arrived at Shane's house. She parked her rental car and removed Brianna from the baby seat. Shane sat on the porch waiting for her. She had called ahead and asked if they could see each other. He looked tired, she thought, but then he had worked a long day—loading party supplies, driving into the city, then returning to Duarte to resume his chores at the rescue.

Kelly carried Brianna up the porch steps, and Shane stood to greet her. His hair, loose and damp, fell past his shoulders. Apparently he had found the time to shower after all. He smelled faintly of soap, water and a simple, masculine shampoo.

He reached for Brianna, and the baby waved her arms, anxious to be held by him. His dark skin intensified the child's fair coloring; her hair seemed blonder, her eyes bluer.

Kelly sat in one of the weathered chairs and watched Shane do the same.

"What's going on?" he asked, although he sounded like he already knew.

Something in his voice, she thought, a tightness, a pain. A guarded emotion she couldn't quite fathom. A tone that frightened her suddenly, made her think of dark and lonely places.

"I heard from Jason today," she said, shaking off the feeling of doom. Shane cared about her, loved her. He would make everything all right. "Jason called right after you left this morning."

He let out a quick, audible breath. "I've been expecting this. And I've thought a lot about it." He combed his fingers through Brianna's hair with a touch that seemed distant, almost detached. Afraid to feel. "What did he say to you?"

"He asked me to call him when I get back to Ohio." Something was wrong, terribly wrong. Shane was supposed to be her best friend, her lover, her confidant, yet their conversation was strained. "He received the test results and now he wants to have lunch."

"That's good," he responded, his Texas drawl only vaguely familiar. "You should go back early. There's no point in waiting until next week."

A ball of pain exploded in her chest. No point? "What are you saying?" she asked, even though she knew. Dear God, she knew.

"It's over for us, Kelly. What we had isn't important now." He trapped her gaze, his eyes brown instead of gold. "It's time for both of us to move on. Brianna belongs with Jason, and so do you."

Kelly fought back the threat of tears. She didn't love Jason. It was Shane she wanted—the man who just sliced her heart in two. Did he know she was bleeding inside? Or didn't he care?

"Jason didn't even ask about the baby. Not even her name."

Shane rocked Brianna in a slow, mechanical motion—a

movement so unlike him. "He already knows her name. It was on the test results, wasn't it? And that's why he called. To make things right."

She looked up at the sky. The setting sun still shone, blending into a sea of color—red, gold, mauve and a bright stream of blue. It was beautiful, but she hated it. Suddenly she hated Texas, and she wanted to hate Shane, too. He had used her, and now she felt cheap and immoral. Sick inside. She should snatch her baby and run, but Brianna cooed in his arms, fisting a strand of his hair. Brianna couldn't let him go, and neither, God help her, could Kelly. She still loved him.

"Kelly?"

She turned. "Yes?"

"If Jason asks you to marry him, promise me you'll consider it. Brianna deserves to have her birth legitimized."

She went numb, stiff and cold. Her only defense, she thought, to keep herself from breaking down into racking sobs, from shaking until she collapsed. "Please don't presume what's best for my daughter."

He glanced down at the child in his arms. "I'm sorry. I just want both of you to be happy. To have the things you deserve."

Things, she thought, inanimate objects Jason's money could buy. "How noble of you," she said, her words tasting as bitter as they sounded. "To let us go so easily."

"That's unfair." His features twisted, but he kept his tone level. "This isn't easy for me, Kelly. I—" His voice cracked, and her heart jumped.

Say you love me. Please, Shane. Say you love me.

"It just isn't easy," he continued, maintaining control of his voice again. "But we both knew it would end. Neither one of us talked about forever. Jason was always there, like a ghost between us. He's your destiny, not me. He's Brianna's father."

"And what were you, Shane? What have you been all this time?"

"A friend," he answered simply. "Just a friend."

No, she thought. He meant more to her that than that. She loved him, wanted him to be a part of her life—her lover, husband, a stepfather to Brianna. She had wanted it all. The suddenly impossible dream.

What had become of the man who had made passionate love to her last night? Used her mouthwash this morning? Nibbled on her ear? Now all of it seemed like a lie, every last tender moment.

As she studied Shane's face, the determined line of his jaw and slant of his cheekbones, the truth became painfully clear. He could disregard her and Brianna so easily because they had only been a substitute for Tami and Evan, the woman and child he truly loved.

She reached for her daughter. "I have to go."

As she turned and walked toward her car, she kept her head held high. Shane stood behind her, but she didn't look back to see his expression. Pride was her companion, pride and a baby girl who had begun to cry.

Shane hadn't seen Kelly or Brianna for two days, and now they were leaving.

He paced the living room floor, checking his watch for the hundredth time. Kelly must be packing, preparing for her flight. Shane forced out a breath. Unable to stand the anxiety-ridden solitude a moment longer, he grabbed his keys from the coffee table and tore off out the door.

The drive to the cabin didn't take long, but by the time he arrived, his hands were clammy and his mouth dry. He parked beneath a tree and exited his truck. Her front door was open, just as it had been the first time he'd stopped by the cabin, the day she'd stood in the kitchen, eight-months pregnant, scrubbing the sink.

Shane approached the threshold, preparing to knock. As close as they had become, he realized he hadn't told her everything about himself. He hadn't admitted that he was afraid of spiders or that he...

His next thought grabbed his heart and squeezed it, leaving

a hollow ache. Loved her. He hadn't told her that he loved her.

He lifted his hand and rapped on the door, each knock pounding in time with his pulse.

"Just a minute!" she called out.

Silent, he waited, wondering why he had come. He couldn't ask her to stay. He wasn't the right man; he wasn't her baby's father.

Kelly walked toward the door and when she spotted him, she stopped, clearly startled. "I was expecting Tom."

"Sorry, it's just me." He didn't enter the cabin, and she didn't invite him in. "It's still a little early for my dad to come by, isn't it? He's still at work."

"I wasn't sure what his schedule was like."

Shane knew his father planned on being there to say goodbye. Tom was still welcome, even if his son wasn't. "I'm sure he'll be here before you leave."

"I'm still packing," she said, smoothing her dress in what seemed like a self-conscious gesture.

He liked the way she looked, her hair long and flyaway, her floral-print dress familiar. He wondered if she would still wear it once she got back to Ohio. It had a slight Western flair as it had come from the emporium in town.

How long would it take for the hurt to go away? he wondered. To be able to live in Texas and not think about her? Feel her presence in every flower that grew wild, every cloud that floated across the sky?

Shane looked down at his boots and noticed how scuffed they were. Jason probably wore nice clothes, designer fashions, sports coats and loafer-type shoes.

How could he have encouraged Kelly to marry her old lover? How could he have just given her to the other man?

Because of Brianna, he told himself. Because the baby was Jason's child, and that tied him to Kelly. It made them family. Shane had only been a pretend daddy to Brianna, a temporary lover to Kelly. He had no right to want them, to long to keep them.

"Is Sunshine awake?" he asked.

She nodded. "Yes."

"Would it be all right if I came in to see her?" He felt like a beggar in his scuffed boots and torn, ragged heart. A man on the edge of society looking in, a man who kept losing the women and children he loved.

Avoiding his gaze, Kelly stepped back and allowed him to enter. "Brianna's in the bedroom."

She led the way to the room Shane would never forget, the room that housed the bed where Brianna was born, the same bed Shane and Kelly had shared three nights before. He had known then that it was over, yet he hadn't been able to stop himself from touching her, from making love to her one last time.

The cabin would forever harbor ghosts, he thought. His, Puma's, Kelly's, Brianna's. And Butch's, too. Kelly's grandpa had spent his vacations there, an Ohio factory-worker who delighted in everything cowboy. What would Butch have thought about Shane and Kelly's love affair?

Maybe the old man knew. Maybe Kelly had talked to him about it in her prayers. Maybe she had told her grandpa that Shane Night Wind had chipped a piece of her heart.

He took a deep breath, defending his decision to let Kelly go. Her heart would mend, and her affection for him would fade. Jason had been her first love, the man she really wanted, the one she had cared about for years.

Taking another deep breath, Shane scanned his surroundings, then forced a smile. Brianna lay in her portable crib, kicking her feet, the toy cougar beside her.

He leaned over the padded rail. "Hey, little Sunshine."

The baby waved her arms, but he didn't pick her up. He couldn't bear asking for permission to hold Kelly's daughter.

"Your dad said he would ship the crib for me," she said as she folded clothes into a leather suitcase. "The swing, too."

"That's good." Shane noticed the tan-colored baby carrier he had bought for Kelly lay on the bed. He still had the blue one. He had placed it in his dresser as a keepsake, he supposed. A sentimental item that would remind him of Brianna.

Shane looked over at Kelly, and their eyes met in one of those long, painful, awkward stares. He swallowed, and she bit down on her bottom lip, both of them visibly shaken.

"I'm sorry," he said, his voice as parched as his throat. "I never meant to hurt you."

"Don't...please," she responded, her eyes turning watery, her hands unsteady. "Don't try to explain it away. I don't think I can handle it." She fidgeted with the suitcase, zipping it shut. "I have to get Brianna ready."

"I'll go wait on the porch." He couldn't leave, yet he couldn't stay inside with her, either. "I'll let you know when my dad gets here."

Tom arrived an hour later, and soon the three adults gathered in the front room, Kelly holding her daughter. Shane lingered back, uncomfortable and uncertain of what to do. Would Kelly let him hug her, kiss her one last time?

"I'm going to miss this little girl," Tom said as he reached for Brianna.

Kelly's eyes misted. "She's going to miss you, too."

Brianna peered over Tom's shoulder at Shane, and he smiled at the baby, the ache in his chest growing. Brianna looked like a bright yellow flower, a golden-haired buttercup dressed in summer ruffles, her tiny feet encased in shiny white shoes.

"Thank you for everything," Kelly said to Tom, her eyes clouding even more. "I don't know what I would have done without you. You brought my daughter into the world."

"Promise you'll keep in touch. That you'll send pictures and letters," the older man responded, his voice thick with emotion.

"I will. I promise."

Tom kissed Brianna's cheek, then handed the baby to Shane. While Kelly and his dad embraced, Shane held Brianna, inhaling her powdery scent.

When the hug ended, no one spoke until Tom took charge,

offering to load Kelly's luggage into her rental car. Within minutes Shane and Kelly were alone, Brianna still snug in his arms.

"Take care of yourself," he said, wishing he didn't have to let them go. He wanted to keep the mother and the child, pretend they belonged to him.

"You, too."

She took her daughter back and struggled to keep her tears from falling. Shane gazed into her watery eyes, knowing she wouldn't welcome his touch. A hug would only make her leaving that much harder.

"I better go." She turned away and headed out the door, her breath hitching as she lost the battle and began to cry.

Shane remained inside the rustic old cabin, whispering that he loved her, even though he knew she was too far away to hear.

Thirteen

Unable to face his father, Shane left the cabin alone and retreated to the rescue.

Looking up at the sky, he squinted. The sun rose high and bright—a yellow ball of warmth that left him cold and achy inside. Sunlight would forever remind him of Brianna, yet he knew nightfall would bring no solace. He would lie awake and think about Kelly, recall the taste of her lips, the feel of her touch.

Shutting out the world, Shane closed his eyes, avoiding the flowers that dared to bloom, their brilliance mocking his mood. God help him, he thought. He needed to see Puma, draw strength from the cougar's medicine.

Shane walked along the dirt path. With the volunteers gone for the day, and the animals resting in the shade, a hush lingered over the rescue. Even the air barely moved, the leaves on the trees still.

When he reached Puma's habitat, he stopped at the fence

and called out in the cougar's language. He waited for a greeting, and when he received none, he tried again.

Puma finally answered in a full-throated *"yaooow,"* and Shane responded in the same strong tone. The conversation continued until Shane knew an invitation had been granted. He entered the cougar's habitat and started toward the animal. Puma lounged in his favorite spot, and when Shane neared, the cat stood.

The magnificence of the mountain lion never ceased to amaze him. The danger and the beauty. He knew the drill. Thrived on the thrill. *Never turn your back on a cougar. Use eye contact cautiously. Read its body language. If it challenges you, look away. Don't roughhouse with a big cat; it can kill you in play.*

Shane leaned down and scratched Puma's chin, and the cougar purred in response. The affection felt good, a temporary balm.

"Maybe I could sleep here tonight," he said to the cat, although he knew better than to invade Puma's territory. Too much time had passed since they'd lived together, and reliving those early days wasn't possible. Puma had grown and changed, and so had Shane.

The cougar lowered himself into a resting position, so Shane continued to talk, knowing his friend was listening. "Kelly sketched some incredible pictures of you, and we used them on T-shirts and coffee cups. You're our mascot now. A symbolic figure for the rescue," he explained. "A good luck charm."

Puma rumbled like a motorboat and rubbed his face against Shane's leg. He scratched the animal's chin again. "I'm glad you're pleased." He sighed and caught his breath. "I'm going to miss her, Puma. So much."

The cougar nudged him and started to talk. A series of tiny chirps. A message, Shane thought. A message he couldn't comprehend.

"I wish I could understand you. But I can't. Not today." And maybe not ever. When Shane had let Kelly and Brianna go, a part of him died—coiled and burned, then drifted into dust.

He remained in Puma's habitat, touching the dirt, the leaves, the rocks that made up the animal's home. Nothing penetrated him, nothing gave him strength. The land inside the fence wasn't his. It belonged to Puma, and as much as Shane liked to think they shared the same spirit, they were still two separate entities. Mountain lions were loners. They didn't fall in love, didn't mate for life. After a mating took place, a male assumed no further role. The female accepted full responsibility for the young.

Yet Shane, who thought of himself as part mountain lion, had fallen in love with Kelly, wanted to help raise her daughter.

Suddenly Puma's message became disturbingly clear. This time Shane couldn't rely on the cougar to mend his damaged heart. He would have to draw strength from his own medicine—the human soul that made him a man.

During the week that followed, Shane decided he didn't like being a man. He didn't like the loneliness, the ache that followed him each day. He wanted to go back to being a cougar, but Puma wouldn't let him. And Shane knew why. Hiding inside himself would be cheating. He couldn't go on pretending to be a loner when deep down he craved companionship. A family. The woman and child he had lost.

As Shane came through the front door, he could smell dinner, a homey aroma of pork chops and mashed potatoes.

"Hi, Dad." He knew the food was supposed to enhance his appetite, make him feel better, but it only reminded him that two lonely men would be sharing the meal.

Tom turned away from the stove. "I have some news."

"Yeah?" Shane noticed the table hadn't been set. He opened the top cabinet and removed two dishes. "What's that?"

"Kelly called."

The dishes nearly slipped from his grasp. He had been waiting to hear about her, wondering, living in agony, barely surviving. "What did she say?" he asked, hoping he could handle the blow—the news that Kelly and Jason had been working through their differences. Sending her back to Jason had been torture enough, but picturing them together made him ill. Kelly with her butterfly wings and fairy-dust freckles and Jason with a face Shane couldn't bring himself to conjure.

"She met with Jason," Tom said. "But it didn't go well. Jason didn't even look at Brianna. He isn't the least bit interested in being that baby's father."

"What?" Shane's head reeled with sadness, confusion, a rush of guilt-ridden relief. "I don't understand."

"Jason asked Kelly to lunch so he could present her with a document outlining a financial settlement. He's willing to pay for 'his mistake' as he put it, but that's as far as he'll go." Tom leaned against the counter. "I got the impression from Kelly that Jason was acting on the advice of some high-profile attorney, offering a settlement so he didn't get slapped with a paternity suit."

The sadness in Shane's chest grew deeper. An ache for Brianna. Could the baby feel her father's rejection? "Kelly doesn't want the money. She never did. All she ever wanted was for Jason to care about his daughter."

When Shane's statement drifted too close to home, they both fell silent. Tom pulled a hand through his hair, and Shane studied his dad. Suddenly he saw reflections of himself, features he had never noticed before, little things—the arch of their eyebrows, length of their fingers, shape of their nails. Similarities that reminded him of the physical traits Brianna must have inherited from Jason.

"Shane?"

Realizing he still clutched their dinner plates, he set them on the table, his hands as unsteady as his heartbeat. "Yeah?"

"I know why you let Kelly go, why you encouraged her to give Jason a chance."

"That doesn't matter—"

"Yes, it does," Tom interrupted, his voice edged with

shame. "It's because you didn't want Brianna to feel the pain of being shut out of her father's life. You didn't want her to suffer the way you had."

The tightness in his chest intensified. The ball of emotional confusion. "This isn't your fault, Dad. I've forgiven you for the past. We've both worked through that."

Tom's eyes turned a paler shade of blue. "But it still affects your life. Your decisions." He paused and let out a breath, the pork chops sizzling on the stove beside him. "Kelly loves you, son. Loves you with everything she's got."

Shane's unsteady heartbeat quickened. "Did she say that?"

Tom shook his head. "No, but she didn't have to."

No, but she didn't have to. Hours later Shane sat on the edge of his bed and picked up the phone, his father's words echoing in his mind. Dialing the number the information operator had given him, he waited for the other party to answer.

When a man came on the line, Shane squared his shoulders, knowing his first encounter with Jason Collier had just begun.

Two days later Kelly sat across from her mother at their dining-room table, toying with her breakfast. She appreciated her mom's effort, the perfectly round stack of golden pancakes, but she didn't have much of an appetite. The single daisy on the table was a thoughtful touch, too, but it only reminded her of Shane and the wildflowers he'd picked in the rain. She missed him desperately, and the reminder hurt.

"Eat up, sweetie, or you'll be late."

Kelly sighed. She had never been late for work a day in her life. "All right." She cut into her pancakes and took a small bite, wondering if the ache deep inside her would ever go away.

Most people had weekends off, but Kelly worked them now. Evenings, too. It was the only schedule that fit into her current lifestyle. Neither she nor her mom could bear to have a stranger watch Brianna, so Kelly worked the opposite hours of her mother, leaving Linda free to baby-sit.

"I'm proud of you," Linda said. "You did the right thing with Jason."

She met her mother's gaze. "Thank you, that means a lot to me." Telling Jason to go to hell had been easy. She didn't want his "I'll-pay-for-my-mistake" money. She would provide for Brianna on her own. She would love and nourish her child. They wouldn't be rich, but they wouldn't be poor, either. Kelly would work extra hours to make holidays and birthdays special. And her mom would always be there, helping out. Like today. Fixing breakfast, baby-sitting Brianna and offering to drive Kelly to work since her own car was in the shop.

Linda lifted her tea. "I'm sorry he hurt you."

Kelly adjusted her napkin. "What I felt for Jason was just an infatuation. It's Brianna I'm worried about. She deserves better."

"Sweetie, I was talking about Shane."

Kelly caught her breath. How many years would pass before she stopped wondering where he was or what he was doing? "I'm okay, Mom. I'll survive." Because she had to. Because she had a baby to raise. A precious little girl with Kelly's fair skin, Jason's clear blue eyes and Shane Night Wind's heartwarming smile.

Shane entered the restaurant and took in his surroundings. He had never been to a country club before, but he thought the place was appealing in an austere, refined kind of way. He also knew that he didn't fit in, not with his rugged denim clothes and Western boots. But then he had agreed to meet Jason Collier on the other man's turf.

As the hostess led him to the back of the restaurant, he noticed several big picture windows overlooked acres of green. Golf. A sport Shane knew nothing about. He was definitely out of his element. A tall, broad-shouldered Comanche wearing plaid and putting after some little ball didn't quite cut it.

When the hostess directed him to his table, Shane came face-to-face with his opponent. Jason met his gaze, then stood and extended his hand. Proper, Shane thought. And wary. They were both wary.

He sat across from the other man and noticed the color of his eyes. Bright blue, like Brianna's.

"So you're from Texas," Jason said, his manners slipping as soon as the hostess was out of earshot. "The big, strong cowboy-type."

"Sorry," Shane corrected, the mockery setting him on edge. "I'm more the big, strong Indian-type. Comanche. We're a warring tribe."

Jason leaned back casually, but Shane knew he hadn't missed the warning. Suddenly, scalping the other man seemed like a damn good idea. Jason's light brown hair was styled with a bit too much mousse for Shane's tastes.

"Hmm." Jason studied his manicured hands, then looked up. "Now I'm not so sure you're on the level. Maybe Kelly sent you to kick my butt. Or up the ante."

"Kelly doesn't know I'm here. And your money has nothing to do with why I came."

The waitress interrupted with two tall glasses of water, a slice of lemon floating in each. Jason flashed a charming smile and ordered lunch, and when the waitress sent Jason an admiring look in return, Shane figured that practiced smile had fooled Kelly, too. She was too sweet, too trusting.

Shane declined to order, and the smitten waitress departed.

"Okay, so you're on the level," Jason said, resuming their conversation.

"That's right. I want to adopt your daughter. And marry Kelly, if she'll have me."

"Fine." Jason reached into his pocket, removed a business card and handed it to Shane. "That's my attorney's number. You can work out the details with him. He'll be more than glad to accommodate you."

Stunned, Shane stared at the card. That was it? "Don't you even want to know anything about me? Aren't you curious about what I do for a living? If I go to church? Pay my taxes?

Don't you care about what kind of husband or father I'll make?"

The other man raised an eyebrow. "Not particularly, no. If you want Kelly, you can have her. The kid, too."

A muscle twitched in Shane's cheek. He could feel it ticking like a bomb. Telling himself to relax, he took a deep breath. "Look, you're only twenty-four years old. Someday when you're older, you might wonder about your daughter. I'll understand if you want to keep in touch, if—"

"I'm twenty-five. And kids don't interest me."

Cocky bastard, Shane thought, wishing he saw just a flicker of emotion in those icy blue eyes. Brianna deserved more. Much more. "Then just listen, okay? I'll be the best parent I can be, but I won't lie to Brianna about who her biological father is. For the rest of your life, you need to remember that there's a little girl out there who carries your genes, and someday she might come looking for you." Leaning across the table, he drilled the other man with his gaze. "And if she ever does, you sure as hell better be good to her."

With that said, he pushed away his chair and stood. As he made his way to the door, the waitress passed him with Jason Collier's lunch. Shane nodded to the girl, then pocketed the attorney's card without looking back.

Tired and glad her workday was about to end, Kelly stood in the check stand, ringing groceries for a familiar customer. She knew most of the people who shopped at the market, and they, of course, knew her. Not personally, but enough to chat and smile. Unfortunately chatting and smiling took energy, and today hers was nearly sapped.

Glancing up to ask the last customer in line to pull the gate, an adrenaline rush hit her like a fist. Her knees threatened to give way, and the cereal box in her hand stumbled over the scanner, missing its mark.

A tall, dark-skinned man holding a blond, pink-cheeked baby waited at the end of the line.

Shane and Brianna.

She didn't have to look twice. He stood quietly, his shirtsleeves shoved to his elbows, Brianna snug against his body, the side of her face peeking out of the cloth carrier.

He made eye contact, then smiled. Kelly wasn't sure if he had the right to smile at her, but her knees reacted again, buckling a little. Rather than meet that masculine smile, she pulled the cereal box across the scanner and reached for the last few items. Her current customer dug through an oversize purse and presented a small stack of coupons. She took them, hands shaking, heart bumping.

Why was he here? How could he rip her emotions to shreds, then walk into her place of employment a week later looking gorgeous and fit?

Kelly focused on her job. Drawing strength from the adrenaline pouring through her system, she made it through the next order, then found her voice and politely asked Shane to pull the gate. He latched it behind him, his gaze searching hers.

"I stopped by your house, and your mom told me you needed a ride home," he said when they stood face-to-face.

He flew in from Texas to drive her home? "My car's in the shop," she answered, unsure of what to do with her quaking hands.

Reacting to Kelly's voice, Brianna turned her head. Shane lifted the child from the carrier and held her up. "There's your mommy, Sunshine."

A smile brightened the baby's face, and Kelly's heart melted. She reached out to touch her daughter's cheek, and as she did, the proximity of Shane's body shifted the building, tilting her world. The one she had been living in without him.

"Why are you here?" she asked.

"To talk. Can we go someplace more private?"

He cradled Brianna, his hands gentle against the baby. They looked good together, she thought. The tall, powerful man and the bright-eyed little girl. Brianna seemed happy to be with him, content in his arms, blowing bubbles and gurgling.

"I can't leave just yet," Kelly answered finally. "I still have to run a tape on my till."

"Okay. We'll wait over there."

He nodded toward the gumball machines and smiled. A shyer smile this time, one that said he was a little unsure of himself, possibly nervous about their talk. His sudden vulnerability eased her quaking hands, and she began to cash-out her drawer on steadier ground.

Fifteen minutes later they headed out to Shane's rental car and strapped Brianna into the baby seat. Kelly sat beside Shane and faced the window, unsure of her emotions. Hurt, anger, anxiety, hope...she didn't know which one took precedence.

"I noticed a park on the way over," he said. "Can we go there? It's not as hot as it was earlier."

"That's fine." The muggy day had turned pleasant, the stifling heat dissolving into a soft breeze. "When did you get here?"

"This morning."

They drove in silence the rest of the way. An awkward kind of quiet, Kelly thought. When they reached the park, she expelled a sigh of relief. She needed air. Lots of it.

They claimed a shady spot beneath a tree. Shane removed a baby blanket from the diaper bag, spread it on a soft bed of grass and placed Brianna on it. She took to the outdoors immediately and closed her eyes, her tiny fingers curling.

Shane sat directly on the lawn and drew his knees up, his jeans a fluid line of blue against long, muscular legs. Kelly lowered herself to the ground, suddenly wishing she wore something prettier. Her work shirt wasn't the most flattering garment.

"I'm sorry," he said. "So sorry I hurt you."

Her emotions struggled to sort themselves out. She wanted to touch him, make sure he was real. "I can't believe you're here."

He released a heavy breath. "I saw Jason this afternoon."

Stunned, she sat staring at him. "What? Why?"

"To talk to him about Brianna. And you." Shane met her gaze, his eyes sending off sparks of gold. "I didn't like him,

Kelly. I wanted to kick his teeth in, but another side of me said 'This is the man who fathered Brianna and he deserves a chance to redeem himself.'"

The park and everything in it blurred. Tears, an oceanful, rushed her eyes. "And did he?"

"No." Shane shook his head and cast a gentle glance at the baby. "But I told him not to forget that he had a daughter, that she might seek him out someday." He fisted a handful of grass. "And if that happens, and Jason doesn't treat her right... I swear, I'll kill him."

The conviction in his voice had her catching her breath. "Did you tell him that, too?"

The corners of his lips tilted. "More or less. I figured he had it coming."

She wanted to kiss that smile—that warm, sexy mouth. "Thank you." He had come a long way to champion for a child. "You really are a friend."

He moved closer. "I hope I'm more than that."

Her heart pounded against her breast. "You said you weren't."

"I was wrong." He released the torn grass, and it fluttered back to the ground. "I'm the guy who loves you. Who wants to marry you and adopt your daughter."

A knot formed in Kelly's throat. The tears fogging her vision fell, and the woman inside her battled for control. No matter how long she had waited to hear those words, she couldn't accept his proposal. Not when she knew who Shane really wanted. She couldn't bear to be a substitute for Tami, nor could she allow Brianna to live in Evan's shadow.

"I don't think it's that simple," she said, hating the part of her that couldn't cheat, couldn't accept only half his love.

Shane glanced up at the tree, his pulse a quick, jittery ache. He could feel his heart teetering on a live wire. One push, one off balance step, one devastating answer and it would fall. Crash to the earth and die.

He brought his gaze to Kelly's, questioning hers. "You don't want me?"

She closed her eyes, then opened them, her fairy-dust freckles swimming in tears. He wanted to take her in his arms, hold what he had lost. But instead he looked over at Brianna, at her perfectly formed hands, the tiny body heaving with each sleeping breath. Her hair could have been a halo, he thought, a shimmer of golden light.

"I want you," Kelly said. "But I wish I didn't."

"Why?" He prayed he wouldn't lose his strength, wouldn't emasculate himself with tears a Comanche man wasn't supposed to cry. Kelly had a right to shed her emotions that way, but he didn't. "Please tell me why."

"Because I need to be your future, all of it, not just half."

Confused, he searched his mind to absorb her meaning. The sixth-sense he so often relied on had abandoned him. She talked in riddles, and his heart hurt. He wanted to marry her, love her for the rest of his days. Wasn't that the future? "I don't understand."

She rubbed at her face, pushing away tears. "I don't want to be a substitute for Tami."

"So that's it." Shane bit back a smile. He saw jealousy in her eyes, and God forgive him, he found pleasure in it. He had meant to clear the air about Tami, but Kelly's reaction to his proposal had jumbled his thoughts. "I called Tami before I came here. We talked for a long time. I told her about you and Brianna."

She gulped a breath, and Shane let himself smile. She looked like a teary-eyed waif. A sprite little butterfly. A beautiful urchin with wings. How could she doubt that he loved her?

"You talked to your ex-wife about me?"

"I had to. I needed the past to be over." And he needed to know that Evan was happy and well. "What Tami and I had was youth. There was no maturity in our love. It's different with you." He lifted her chin, refusing to lose her, to let her flutter those delicate wings and disappear. "What I feel for you is real. I'm not a boy anymore. I understand my heart."

And he wanted to give it to her, have her tuck it away for all time.

Kelly blinked. Happily stunned, he hoped. She leaned into him, a dizzy sort of glow on her face. "If you love me, why did you send me away?"

He inhaled the clean, summer fragrance she wore, the mist of watermelon that bathed her skin. "I sent you away because I thought I had no claim on your daughter. I thought I didn't deserve her because my blood doesn't run in her veins." He took Kelly's hands and held them. "And I was afraid Jason would lure you away, that your tie to him was stronger than what you felt for me."

"You were wrong. It's you I love." Her head found his shoulder, her body curling into his. "And now my daughter belongs to you, too."

Should he let himself cry? God only knew he wanted to. He stroked Kelly's hair and watched the baby sleep. His woman. His child. Magic and sunshine. "I kept battling with myself over Brianna. I wanted her to be mine. There were so many moments I forgot she wasn't."

Kelly pulled back to look at him, touch his cheek with a gentle hand. "You haven't mentioned Evan, Shane. Did you talk to Tami about visiting him?"

"No." There would always be a part of him that missed the little boy, but he knew Evan didn't need him. "Evan has a father. A good one from what Tami says. Too much time has passed. Me coming into his life would only confuse him. It wouldn't be fair."

"Maybe you could visit them as a family, see for yourself that Evan's happy. Maybe all of us could go. You, me and Brianna."

"Maybe." This woman, he thought, this delicate butterfly had spread her wings right before his eyes. He could see color all around her. Wildflowers and moonbeams. Beauty and love.

He brought his mouth to hers and felt a liquid response, her lips parting sensuously under his. Kelly Baxter was meant to be his wife. Of that, Shane Night Wind was certain.

* * *

Later that night Kelly reclined next to Shane on her bed. They were dressed for sleep, but both remained wide-awake.

"So this was your room when you were little?" he asked.

She nodded. "I've redecorated since then." But she knew it was still feminine. Grown-up frill, she supposed. The canopy over the bed draped a smooth beige fabric, the pillows down, their covers satin.

On a whitewashed dresser, she kept a collection of painted figurines. Mythical creatures—dragons and wizards, mermaids and unicorns. Shane seemed especially interested in the winged fairies. He had traced their tiny bodies with his finger, mumbling that he "should have known." Kelly didn't understand what he'd meant, but his fascination pleased her.

"We'll take this furniture with us," he said. "All of it. This can be our bedroom."

She tried to imagine her frill mixed with Shane's masculine decor—the dark rattan and solid oak cabinetry. It seemed right somehow—a blend of who they were.

She turned toward him, suddenly worried. "How can I leave my mom behind? She'll be so lonely here."

He shifted onto his side. "She can sell this place and come with us."

"And where exactly is she supposed to live?"

A mischievous grin tilted his lips. "With my dad."

Kelly bumped his shoulder and laughed. "Your dad and my mom. Granted, they're attracted to each other, but we can't expect them to live together right off the bat. They're too conservative for that."

"She can rent a room from him. That's proper enough. And she can find a job in her field. Maybe a bookkeeping position at this feline rescue I just happen to know."

She laughed again, delighted with the idea. "You've got this all figured out, don't you?"

"You bet I do. Our parents can keep the house, and we'll add on to the cabin. I can do the work myself. Besides, it's more us. An enchanted place with a rickety porch and flowers peeking through the cracks. Smoke drifting from the chimney, sage and candles burning.''

The picture he painted made her think of her figurines—fairies dancing in the moonlight, wizards conjuring potions, a unicorn darting through a maze of trees. A magical cabin in West Texas. Who would have guessed.

"I love you," she said.

"I love you, too." He kissed her then, a kiss vibrating with need. A sudden gust of hunger.

She felt his muscles beneath her hands, the bunch, the flex, the unspoken language that had her lusting for more. She roamed his chest, then caught the waistband of his shorts while he lowered the straps on her nightgown and tasted a bare shoulder.

She thought she heard music, Comanche drums mixed with lilting harps and flutes—their music, their magic. Wizards and warriors and tiny ladies with wings.

He was power, she thought, and passion—a man with fire in his hair and copper melting over his skin. In his touch she felt strength and beauty, a hard male body eager for hers.

Their clothes came away easily and drifted to the floor. She slid her hand over his belly, then lower to stroke and caress, to watch his eyes shimmer, to listen to the sound of arousal purr from his chest.

They kissed, over and over, absorbing the moment, the sensations only they could create. It was glorious to be naked with him, to rub and tease, anticipate what erotic treasures came next. A fluid hand, a moist tongue, a muscular leg tangled with hers. She felt everything—every subtle movement, every pore that opened, every nerve that jumped, every sigh she breathed into his mouth.

He slipped into her without protection, arched his back and rocked her body with slow, sexy strokes. She met his dizzy rhythm, the feel of his flesh smooth and silky inside her own. They moved at a languid, dreamy pace—a gentle mating.

The music rushed back, filling her ears with splendor, her mind with flowers and feathers, warbonnets and faraway places only he could take her. He tongued her nipple and smiled. She held his head to her breast and watched him suckle, draw the peak into a moist, hungry mouth. Gripping his shoulders she raised her hips, desire swirling—its sensual voice calling her name. Teasing and begging.

"Tell me," he whispered. "Tell me what you want."

"You," was all she could say. "More of you."

He thrust deeper and gave her all that he was—his heart spilling love, his seed pouring warmth and promise into her womb. And at that moment, that incredible climactic moment when they were steeped in pleasure, liquid flames dancing between them, she knew they had become one.

Epilogue

At two-and-a-half, Brianna Night Wind chattered excessively and smiled even more. Today she wore a pale lavender dress with puffy sleeves, ribbons, bows and heart-shaped buttons. A white lace petticoat peeked out from the hem, and ruffled socks flared at her ankles. Her shoes weren't scuffed—not yet, Shane thought, as she wiggled through his second attempt to straighten the barrette in her hair.

"Me bring Cougie to the church, Daddy."

"Of course you will." The barrette slipped again, and he grinned. Cougie was the toy cougar that had become her security blanket, the battered stuffed animal that followed her everywhere. She slept with Cougie at night, fed him breakfast in the morning, told him secrets and insisted he could purr. Brianna had her own form of mountain lion medicine, he thought. Her own brand of beauty and charm. She was, in his opinion, the most perfect child on earth—an angel with bright blue eyes and a generous heart. She prayed for everyone, people she knew and those she didn't.

"Where's Mommy?" she asked, shuffling her anxious feet.
"She's getting ready, too."
"Are you ready, Daddy?"
"Just about, " he answered, still struggling with the barrette as Brianna's soft curls rebelled.

Shane wore a black tuxedo and stiff white shirt, but his jacket hung over a chair, and his feet were bare. Within the hour Tom McKinley and Linda Baxter would be married in a quaint little church just outside of town. Family members would each have a special role in the ceremony, including Shane's gypsy mother and her current lover.

"Mommy!" Brianna squealed as Kelly entered the nursery.

Shane lifted his gaze, his pulse suddenly tripping. A waterfall of flowers crowned her head in a spray of petals, and her dress, a shimmer of lavender silk, draped luxuriously over a swollen tummy. Kelly Night Wind was eight months pregnant, and a more beautiful woman didn't exist. She glowed like magic, a vision of maternal elegance.

He reached for Brianna and brought the child to her mother. They huddled together as a family, in the circle of each other's arms, secure and content.

Brianna patted Kelly's tummy and grinned. "Hello, baby," she said, happily greeting her unborn sibling.

As Shane and Kelly exchanged a proud smile, he searched his wife's gaze. In her eyes he saw the world they had created—their private haven of happiness—the corner of Texas where wildflowers bloomed and fairies fluttered their wings. The place where exotic cats lolled in the shade, and men and women fell hopelessly in love.

On this sunny afternoon they would celebrate a new marriage, the new life in Kelly's womb and a little girl who chased away storms. For today, Shane knew, would lead the way to forever.

* * * * *

SILHOUETTE DESIRE

AVAILABLE FROM 16TH AUGUST 2002

TAMING HER MAN

THE TAMING OF JACKSON CADE BJ James
Men of Belle Terre
Haley Garrett knew she wanted Jackson Cade from the moment she saw him. But despite their searing attraction Jackson fought and resisted her. Could Haley penetrate his heart's defences?

COWBOY FOR KEEPS Kristi Gold
Dana Landry was mesmerised by Will Baker but his eyes showed he was one hundred per cent male...and zero per cent husband! Dana longed for the fairytale—but how to get Will to agree?

SURPRISE BABY

SINCLAIR'S SURPRISE BABY Barbara McCauley
Secrets!
Amnesia meant Lucian Sinclair couldn't remember his passionate night with Raina Sarbanes. But one look into the eyes of Raina's baby daughter and Lucian realised this child was *his*.

HIS BABY SURPRISE Kathie DeNosky
After just one sweet night with Lexi Hatfield, Dr Tyler Braden discovered that Lexi was pregnant! Ty didn't want a wife...or a son, so why was he fantasising about a lifetime of loving?

HIS BRIDE AT LAST

THE BRIDAL ARRANGEMENT Cindy Gerard
A marriage-of-convenience to naïve virgin Ellie Shiloh meant that Lee Savage could claim his ranch. Lee wouldn't admit to needing his bride but was his promise really made out of duty...or love?

A COWBOY, A BRIDE & A WEDDING VOW
Shirley Rogers
Jake McCall and Catherine St John had been lovers. Time had hardened Catie's heart to Jake but, once he knew he had a son, he vowed to keep the boy, and to have Catie—in his bed and as his bride!

AVAILABLE FROM 16TH AUGUST 2002

SILHOUETTE®

Sensation™

Passionate, dramatic, thrilling romances

HARD TO RESIST Kylie Brant
HEART OF A HERO Marie Ferrarella
A HUSBAND BY ANY OTHER NAME Cheryl St John
BORN TO PROTECT Virginia Kantra
THIS PERFECT STRANGER Barbara Ankrum
CASSIDY AND THE PRINCESS Patricia Potter

Special Edition™

Vivid, satisfying romances full of family, life and love

THAT'S OUR BABY! Pamela Browning
DATELINE MATRIMONY Gina Wilkins
THE MARRIAGE AGREEMENT Christine Rimmer
THE McCAFFERTYS: MATT Lisa Jackson
DAUGHTER ON HIS DOORSTEP Janis Reams Hudson
BELOVED BACHELOR DAD Crystal Green

Superromance™

Enjoy the drama, explore the emotions, experience the relationship

SHELTERED IN HIS ARMS Tara Taylor Quinn
THE LISTENER Kay David
THAT SUMMER THING Pamela Bauer
HER SISTER'S BABY Janice Kay Johnson

Intrigue™

Danger, deception and suspense

NIGHT AND DAY Anne Stuart and Gayle Wilson
HIDDEN HEARTS Susan Kearney
LICENSED TO MARRY Charlotte Douglas
THE MAN BEHIND THE BADGE Vickie Taylor

THE STANISLASKI
Sisters
NORA ROBERTS

From the bestselling author of the Stanislaski Brothers, Nora Roberts brings you the spirited, sexy Stanislaksi Sisters.

Bestselling author of Night Tales

Available from 19th July 2002

*Available at most branches of WH Smith,
Tesco, Martins, Borders, Eason, Sainsbury's
and most good paperback bookshops.*

Diana Palmer

WEDDINGS IN WHITE

A fabulous collection of three irresistible wedding stories

On sale 20th September 2002

Available at most branches of WH Smith, Tesco, Martins, Borders, Eason, Sainsbury's and most good paperback bookshops.

THE COLTONS

FAMILY PRIVILEGE POWER

Look out for our fabulous brand new limited continuity series
THE COLTONS,
where the secrets of California's most glamorous and talked about dynasty are revealed!

Available from 16th August

On Sale

16th August 2002
Beloved Wolf *by Kasey Michaels*

20th September 2002
The Virgin Mistress *by Linda Turner*

I Married a Sheikh *by Sharon De Vita*

18th October 2002
The Doctor Delivers *by Judy Christenberry*

From Boss to Bridegroom *by Victoria Pade*

15th November 2002
Passion's Law *by Ruth Langan*

The Housekeeper's Daughter *by Laurie Paige*

20th December 2002
Taking on Twins *by Carolyn Zane*

Wed to the Witness *by Karen Hughes*

17th January 2003
The Trophy Wife *by Sandra Steffen*

Pregnant in Prosperino *by Carla Cassidy*

21st February 2003
The Hopechest Bride *by Kasey Michaels*

SHERRYL WOODS

about that man

It was going to be a long, hot summer...

On sale 18th October 2002

Available at most branches of WH Smith, Tesco, Martins, Borders, Eason, Sainsbury's and most good paperback bookshops.

SILHOUETTE® SENSATION™
proudly presents

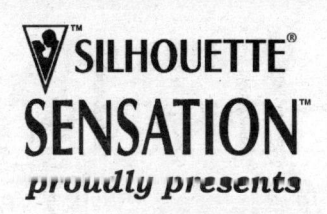

a sensually addictive trilogy, only from Kylie Brant

Charmed and Dangerous

With their quick wits and killer smiles, these men are irresistible.

HARD TO HANDLE
August 2002

HARD TO RESIST
September 2002

HARD TO TAME
October 2002

SILHOUETTE® SENSATION™

brings more...much more from

Suzanne Brockmann

TALL, DARK AND DANGEROUS

These men are who you call to get you out of a tight spot—or into one!

TAYLOR'S TEMPTATION
August 2002

WILD, WILD WES
March 2003

SILHOUETTE® INTRIGUE™

proudly presents

a brand-new trilogy from
REBECCA YORK

Mine to Keep
is a new branch of her

43 Light Street
mini-series.

THE MAN FROM TEXAS
August 2002

NEVER ALONE
October 2002

LASSITER'S LAW
December 2002

SILHOUETTE® INTRIGUE™

wants to play

HIDE and SEEK

with bestselling author

Susan Kearney

For years a deadly secret kept a family apart, but now it's out... Suddenly, Jake, Alexandra and Melinda have to hide from mortal danger and seek passionate love along the way!

THE HIDDEN YEARS
August 2002

HIDDEN HEARTS
September 2002

LOVERS IN HIDING
October 2002

SPECIAL EDITION

SENSATION

DESIRE 2 IN 1

SUPERROMANCE

INTRIGUE

REVEALING OUR FANTASTIC NEW LOOK SILHOUETTE...

FROM
18TH OCTOBER 2002

SILHOUETTE®

1102/SILNEW/SH38

FREE!

1 Book
and a surprise gift!

We would like to take this opportunity to thank you for reading this Silhouette® book by offering you the chance to take another specially selected title from the Desire™ series absolutely FREE! We're also making this offer to introduce you to the benefits of the Reader Service™—

- ★ FREE home delivery
- ★ FREE gifts and competitions
- ★ FREE monthly Newsletter
- ★ Books available before they're in the shops
- ★ Exclusive Reader Service discount offer

Accepting this FREE book and gift places you under no obligation to buy; you may cancel at any time, even after receiving your free shipment. Simply complete your details below and return the entire page to the address below. ***You don't even need a stamp!***

YES! Please send me 1 free Desire book and a surprise gift. I understand that unless you hear from me, I will receive 2 superb new titles every month for just £4.99 each, postage and packing free. I am under no obligation to purchase any books and may cancel my subscription at any time. The free books and gift will be mine to keep in any case.

D2ZEB

Ms/Mrs/Miss/Mr ....Initials ....

BLOCK CAPITALS PLEASE

Surname ....

Address ....

....

....Postcode ....

Send this whole page to:
UK: The Reader Service, FREEPOST CN81, Croydon, CR9 3WZ
EIRE: The Reader Service, PO Box 4546, Kilcock, County Kildare (stamp required)

Offer not valid to current Reader Service subscribers to this series. We reserve the right to refuse an application and applicants must be aged 18 years or over. Only one application per household. Terms and prices subject to change without notice. Offer expires 29th November 2002. As a result of this application, you may receive offers from other carefully selected companies. If you would prefer not to share in this opportunity please write to The Data Manager at the address above.

Silhouette® is a registered trademark used under licence.
Desire™ is being used as a trademark.